3 DETECTIVES:

FEMMES AUDACIEUSES

3 DETECTIVES:
FEMMES AUDACIEUSES

Stories by
Samuel Merwin
Charles Somerville
Hulbert Footner

COACHWHIP PUBLICATIONS
Greenville, Ohio

3 Detectives: Femmes Audacieuses
© 2019 Coachwhip Publications

Lady Can Do published 1929
    Samuel Merwin (1874-1936)
Alice Royce, Girl Detective stories published 1912-1913.
    Charles Somerville (1873-1931)
The Adventures of Edda Manby published 1934-35.
    Hulbert Footner (1879-1944)
No claims made on public domain material.
Cover image: Woman in window © Ysbrand Cosijn

CoachwhipBooks.com

ISBN 1-61646-469-0
ISBN-13 978-1-61646-469-1

CONTENTS

Lady Can Do

Samuel Merwin

1929

To Lenny

PART I

1

Elsie's first surprise was the chauffeur. He proved to be a Chinaman.

The limousine was one of those incredibly costly and luxurious imported vehicles. She had never seen or felt such upholstery. The wide seat fairly enveloped her. The interior had fascinating little gadgets; cut-glass domes for the lights, and more cut-glass holding fresh flowers . . . orchids, actually. A card-case and ash-trays and a mirror and what not. She nearly laughed out loud as she settled back. The Chinaman was so gravely polite. And she just Elsie Penn, with the rather battered suitcase and typewriter that she'd lugged through the vast areas of the Grand Central Station. It was fascinating, being met with all this grandeur. And it was funny.

Rolling smoothly out of the village into a pleasant, dusky countryside, she fell to putting together in her mind what Miss Virtue had said. Miss Virtue conducted the college agency, and had seemed to interest herself in Elsie. "You will find the Cuppys really delightful people, Miss Penn. In spite of their vast wealth. Mr. Cuppy, you understand, is a great Orientalist. N. Jonas Cuppy, you know. He inherited enormous oil fields in California. I am told that his collection, outside of the Freer Gallery and the Metropolitan and South Kensington Museums, is probably the finest in the world. And Mrs. Cuppy is said to be a fascinating personality. They do not go about much in society. Mrs. Cuppy appears to prefer to gather interesting people about her. Artists and such. She really maintains a salon. She is said to resemble Madame Récamier. . . . Your work, Miss Penn, will be, I believe, to serve as a companion and social secretary to Mrs. Cuppy, and also to take care of her husband's correspondence. You may find it necessary to use a little tact and skill in dealing with Mr. Cuppy. His wealth, I have gathered, leads him into a certain measure of self-indulgence . . . these things are rather inevitable, I fear . . . but I am assured that he is kindly, that he is really generous in the extreme. When Miss Hinson was there she—er—"

"Why did Miss Hinson leave?"

"Oh, she married. In any event, Miss Penn, I feel certain that you will find little difficulty in meeting the situation. A girl of your intelligence. and training. And your native dignity. You are the mental type, distinctly." (Elsie had on, at the time, the sort of straight little frock you wore to business.) "I wouldn't think of recommending an inexperienced little thing of the sensory type, for this position. Living right there in the house and all. . . . You will be treated virtually as one of the family." Elsie giggled. Then caught herself. That Chinaman couldn't hear through the front glass, but he could see. He had one of those tittuppy little mirrors over the windshield.

They turned in through a Chinesy arch of carved wood, red and blue and green, into a curving driveway. A long driveway. Stopped under a *porte cochère*. It was rather disappointing to find that the house wasn't Chinese in architecture. It was just a Long Island mansion. But before the dim doorway swallowed her, her quick eyes glimpsed through the twilight a Japanese rock garden with stone lantern posts and arching wooden bridges. Within a middle-aged woman met her, saying—"I am Miss Briggs, the housekeeper"—and led her off up a broad flight of stairs. But those eyes of hers, windows of a sensitive imagination, caught vivid confused impressions . . . cabinets set in the walls, with glass shelves and cunningly hidden lights, full of exquisite carved objects in ivory and crystal and jade—junks and animals and vases and quaint little people. A stately Chinese servant in a long blue gabardine but with a cropped head ("He ought to have a pigtail," thought Elsie) moved through the hall with a tray of cocktails. She heard voices far away, chatting and laughing.

Miss Briggs conducted her to a pleasant room on the third floor. Another Oriental, also in a blue gabardine, brought in her suitcase and typewriter. Elsie, her eyes sparkling with a curious sense of excitement in the air, looked about, exclaiming softly—"How awfully nice!"

"Mrs. Cuppy is having a house party," said Miss Briggs. "Here is the costume she wishes you to wear."

Elsie stifled a girlish squeal. For, laid out on the bed, were Chinese garments in green satin, with embroidered patterns in artfully contrasted colors and swirls of gold thread and pictorial borders on the wide sleeves depicting houses and gardens and people. It simply couldn't be real. "I will help you dress and make up," remarked Miss Briggs dispassionately. And swiftly, deftly did so. Elsie found herself in long coat and flapping trousers and embroidered slippers and green gilt cap, with a roguish red-and-white face smiling at her out of the mirror. Her honest, pleasant mouth was now a vermilion bud. She felt like pirouetting.

"You had better go right down, I think," said Miss Briggs, and led her to a spacious room on the ground floor that was like an apartment in a museum . . . softly lighted, with carved cabinets made of some dark wood and full of priceless objects. In a corner, between two stands of Japanese armor, and partly hidden by a huge bulging blue-and-white vase that was at least six feet high, she saw a table in that same dark wood and two Chinese chairs with bent arms.

"This will be your desk," said Miss Briggs, and left her.

A rather high-pitched, rippling voice called, "Has she come, Miss Briggs?" Then—"Oh, here you are, my dear! I am Mrs. Cuppy."

A small person, quite as small as Elsie herself; slightly plump, but pretty. The eyes were large and round, pale blue in color, and tending to bulge. She seemed young. Or youngish. You couldn't tell. Forty, perhaps; or less. Anywhere in the thirties. That rippling voice was the sort that might easily coo and even gush. She, too, was in embroidered coat and trousers. A great deal of color and design on a base of blue satin that matched her eyes. Tiny feet and hands. Considerable grace of movement. A light, quick person. Probably, back of the cooing voice, a determined person. All this Elsie took in, and then focused her attention on the lady's cap. It was an amazing structure of open-work silver-gilt, completely covering the head, and so built up with flowers and butterflies and interwoven symbolic objects that it looked almost like a floral mound. Innumerable pearls were strewn about in the complicated design, the largest and most oddly shaped that Elsie had ever seen; while from each side hung five loops of matched round pearls, clear to the shoulders.

"You are looking at my cap, my dear. Isn't it wonderful? My husband bought it for me only the other day." She turned to a mirror that was set in a carved frame of red lacquer. "It belonged to the old Empress Dowager. Looted from the Summer Palace in 1900, during the Boxer trouble." Elsie didn't know what the Boxer trouble was, so she kept discreetly silent. The cooing voice rippled on—"All these beautiful Chinese things are brought to my husband eventually. The Chinese merchants positively live off him. What a history this old cap could relate! Do you know, my dear, it didn't come to us through the usual channels. Two strange Chinamen drove out here one evening in a flivver. Imagine! They had the cap wrapped up in a newspaper. And my husband tells me he bought it for a song. He is still chuckling over it. Some strange, dark story there. Most fascinating! Don't you love the romance that clusters about

these beautiful old things?" She smiled complacently into the mirror, and ran her little fingers
in among the looping strings of pearls. "It would
bring not far from a quarter of a million at auction. And I'm sure my husband didn't pay twenty-
five thousand. Isn't it amazing! . . . Now, my
dear, stand out here in the light and let me look
you over. . . . Why, you're charming! A jade image come to life!" She clapped her hands. "You're
perfectly charming! You must come and meet my
guests. Such fascinating people! I want you to feel
quite at home, quite as if you were one of us. We
are very democratic, you know. . . . Ah, here is my
husband!"

Elsie found herself before a large, stout mandarin. She saw a graying mustache, and puffy, tired
eyes. Rather a stupid face, she thought. Merely
having money didn't make people interesting, of
course. He had been drinking. She could smell it.

"Our new secretary, Jonas. Miss . . . Miss Penny."

"Miss Penn," said Elsie, with an uncomfortable
sensation of being afloat on a strange and very
wide sea.

Mr. Cuppy's big, soft hand closed about hers,
and held it a little longer than necessary. His wife
caught his arm, with a "Come, dear. We must go
back to the other room. I want to show Miss Penn
the adorable portrait Mr. Dane has made of me."

She moved briskly, lightly away. Elsie looked down at herself. The green costume was exquisite. The padded slippers peeped out from the bottoms of her satin trousers. Queer, all this. She'd have to feel her way. Perhaps she wouldn't stay. It certainly wasn't what you'd term a businesslike atmosphere. Not easy to be properly impersonal here.

That blue gabardine appeared with the tray. She saw Mr. Cuppy pause and take a glass. He poured it down his capacious throat at a gulp, and then rolled his tongue back and smacked his lips. With a "Thank you, Sin," to the tall figure in the blue gabardine. She didn't drink, herself. And she wouldn't. She'd have to keep her head. As it was, she felt drunk with beauty. She lingered to look at the single lantern on the desk. It was a six-sided vase of eggshell porcelain, brilliantly decorated in floral designs with greens predominating. The electric light within shone softly through.

She felt an arm about her shoulders and started: then stood as if frozen. Mr. Cuppy's voice, at her ear, murmured—"Nice bit of porcelain, that lantern. K'ang Hsi period. Late seventeenth century. I paid six thousand for it." The arm gave her shoulders a squeeze. They were hidden from the door by that huge vase. "This is what Miss Virtue meant," thought Elsie, shivering slightly, and moving away. "I'll certainly have to watch my step. Mrs. Cuppy has had her troubles with this man. He's just a boob."

"Come along, you two!" called that lady, from the door.

Elsie hurried to join her. Funny way for her to put it . . . "you two." A distinct touch of self-consciousness in her tone. Elsie hoped her high color wouldn't show through the paint. She'd probably better not stay. Too bad. It had sounded like an unusually promising job.

N. Jonas Cuppy. A name to which the newspapers always paid the profoundest deference. Money did that. She wondered what the "N" stood for. Something comic, surely, or he'd never lean so pompously on the "Jonas." Nehemiah, perhaps.

2

The spacious living-room glittered with color and (to Elsie's aloof ears) cackled with sound. Perhaps a dozen folk, all in Chinese costume. The cocktails had loosened their tongues. She found herself being casually introduced, and as casually, if firmly, placed . . . "My new secretary, Miss Penn. Isn't she a dear!" . . . It was no use trying to keep the individuals straight—these painted, exquisite ladies, and the mandarins.

"You've heard of Emily Eames, my dear." Heard of Emily Eames? My word! There was no more famous young actress in the English-speaking world. A languidly smiling, slender young creature who gave her a non-committal hand. . . . "This is Mr. Ettlethwaite, the novelist. You've read 'Burnt Fingers.' Isn't it the most adorable book! . . . Mr. Stromberg, Miss Penn. My new secretary. But I tell her she is to feel herself quite one of us. Mr. Stromberg does the most delightfully adventurous things, my dear. Climbed the second highest mountain in the Himalayas. He's leaving soon for darkest Tibet. The Stromberg-Cuppy Ethnographical Expedition . . . . Isn't it fascinating to have all these wonderful people about one! Just a little group of friends! . . . Oh, yes, you must know Mr. Delos. The music critic, you know. Mr. Delos, Miss Penn. . . . And Mr. Dane. John Dane, you know. Come right over here and see his portrait of me. You never in your life saw anything so fascinating. But oh, so flattering!"

Elsie found herself looking up into a pair of keen, inscrutable gray eyes. A tall young man, John Dane, with the faintest hint of an amused smile playing over a lean, handsome face. Then the three of them stood before the picture; a pastel drawing of Mrs. Cuppy in her Chinese dress set in a lacquered frame. It was charmingly done. And it did flatter the lady. What fascinated Elsie was not so much the portrait as the expression on John Dane's face. What could he be thinking? Probably you'd never know. Compared with the rest he seemed sober. That capacious tray appeared just then at his elbow. He said quietly (she liked his voice: it was rather deep, and quietly controlled), "No more, Sin, thanks. Reached my limit."

"You'll have a cocktail, Miss Penn?" Mrs. Cuppy's purring voice.

"No, thank you. I never drink."

"Never drink? How quaint! But perhaps it's just as well . . . Wait, Sin! I'll have another."

Elsie, a few moments later, found herself on a sofa with Mr. Delos. He had reached the argumentative stage and seized on her for an audience. Music, he said, was in imminent danger of passing, along with painting, into sheer degeneracy. Eastern Europe was the seat of the trouble. Those Eastern Europeans. They burrowed. Sapped and mined. Attacked our culture. Fought insistently, clamorously, to destroy a standard of art that they could not understand. . . . Elsie thought, "It's like a lecture." . . . Every few moments, as he talked, he was interrupted by an extraordinary human gargoyle in a yellow robe who strode about the room with a violin, playing themes from orchestral compositions. This person would rush upon

them, wind up a theme with a bold flourish of his
bow, fix madly glittering eyes on the impressive
Mr. Delos, and cry nasally, "What's that? What's
that, eh? What's that one?" Delos, turning each
time with a mounting impatience, would reply,
"That . . . er . . . why, that's César Franck." Or—
"Don't be absurd! It's . . . er . . . third movement
of Beethoven's Fourth Symphony." Or—"Boris
Godunoff, of course. From the coronation scene."

A little later, just as dinner had been announced,
Elsie, escaped at last from the harassed lecturer,
saw John Dane catch the yellow-clad gargoyle's
arm, and ask, with a note of dry humor in his
voice, "What on earth have you been doing to that
poor critic?"

The gargoyle chuckled. His eyes did look mad.
The nasal voice cackled, "He got two right. Two!"

And John Dane laughed, right out.

He walked down the hall with Elsie. She asked,
in a low voice, who the gargoyle might be . . .
"that funny little man with the bald head and the
queer eyes."

"Oh, the perfect nut? He's either a great com-
poser or a lunatic. God alone knows which. He's
been fifteen years on a symphony. Tells everybody—tells the world—that he's going to revolu-
tionize music. Utterly. But he never seems to get
anything done. The Cuppys staked him for years,

but got sick of it and cut him off. He simply lived off 'em. He'll tell you. Tells everybody. Hasn't the slightest self-respect that I can see. I didn't think he'd ever come here again. He didn't for a year or so. But here he is! He may really be a genius. *I* don't know. He's very comic on the subject of critics. Loathes them. Thinks they should all be killed."

At dinner claret was served with the fish, Burgundy with the game, sauterne and champagne after that, cognac with the coffee. It was a curious experience to sit there, icily sober, and note the effects of this flow of liquor. She'd never seen anything like it. The Chinese serving men moved gravely about, pouring, pouring, pouring. Elsie wondered what they could be thinking. Descendants of the oldest civilization in the world, catering to the idle pleasures of the newest. The one they called Sin particularly interested her. The tall one. Evidently the butler. She noted that John Dane merely sipped. Thank God, there'd be one reasonably sober person to talk with later in the evening. Mr. Cuppy, on the other hand, drank and drank and drank. Everything that was put before him. And held it amazingly. His eyes seemed to grow gradually deader and more puffy. The lines in his face appeared to deepen. His double chins bulged out over his collar. And his skin took on the yellowish tinge of parchment. Mrs. Cuppy talked a little thickly, but lost none of her vivacity. The actress, Miss Eames, leaned on Mr. Ettlethwaite, her arm about his shoulders. A man across the table, whom Elsie hadn't met, called, "Don't let her vamp you, Etty!"

"Vamp me? She can go as far as she likes. I'll tell the cock-eyed world this is my idea of Heaven."

Promptly, at this, Miss Eames drew his head over, kissed him, and murmured, "Isn't he sweet!"

When they rose from the table. Elsie considered the possibility of escaping. She could slip out. Very likely they wouldn't know. Perhaps just go up to her room. But she knew, from a nervous tightness that had seized on her, that it wouldn't be easy to get to sleep. She felt oddly unhappy. A sensation not unlike a poignant homesickness. If she went to bed she'd just lie there and cry. She thought of the rock garden she'd glimpsed through the *porte cochère*. A dim, cool spot. She decided to flee out there. On the way, she saw those Chinamen carrying the now recumbent Mr. Cuppy into a den behind the Chinese room. They were perfectly matter of fact about it. She paused by the door, an unsteady hand pressed to her quick-beating heart, and watched while they laid the lumpish thing on a sofa. Wondered again what their thoughts might be. You couldn't tell. Their faces told nothing. . . . Then she fled.

The rock garden did offer sanctuary. She mounted one of the high-arching bridges. It pleased her, that bridge. She didn't know why. Excitedly, at the point of giggling (that would be sheer nerves), she went back over it. Six or eight times she crossed it. The last time she leaned on the wooden parapet and looked down at the darkly dimpling water. She saw a goldfish, faintly. Watched it move slowly against the current. Then, with a catch of the breath, she wandered along and sat on a stone bench, looking up through the foliage at the sky.

She heard a step. A tall mandarin came over the bridge. John Dane.

"Room for another stray?" he asked.

She moved over and he sat beside her. He didn't appear to think conversation necessary. She felt grateful for that. You could see that he was an understanding person. And he wasn't drunk. He pushed back the black cap he wore, drew a handkerchief from his wide sleeve, and mopped his forehead; then stared moodily at the twinkling light in a stone lantern across the path.

"It's beautiful here," said she.

Before replying he lifted his head and sniffed the night air. "If only it didn't smell of oil," he said.

She laughed softly. "Aren't you a little naughty?"

"Always was. Can't help it. You see, I've been living here a week. While I was making that drawing."

"The Cuppys are friends of yours?"

He considered that. "I never heard that they had any friends."

That surprised her. "But all these people . . ."

"Oh, Hazel collects 'em. People. That's her game. Always getting new lots. Throwing personalities at each other, real ones and fakes. People live off her, of course. Take Stromberg. There's an adventurer for you. . . . No, I didn't come here out of friendship. I came for exactly five hundred dollars."

"Oh . . . you . . ."

"The price of my services. One pastel portrait, five hundred. I'm leaving to-morrow. Take my check and go on my way."

That was, vaguely, a disappointment. With this man gone, there wouldn't be . . . well, anybody.

She felt his quizzical eyes on her. "How about yourself? Think you can stick it?"

"Well . . . I . . ." Really, she must be careful. Secretaries mustn't talk. But one rather pointed question escaped her. "Mr. Cuppy . . . is he . . ."

"Yes?"

"Surely he isn't always . . . well, like this?"

"Oh, more or less. Always pickled, if that's what you mean. Oh, he doesn't always pass out."

"But . . . I'm afraid I'm a bit bewildered . . . I supposed he was rather a great man."

Dane screwed up his face comically. "Jonas Cuppy? A great man! My eye!"

"Well . . . perhaps I mean a great"—what was the word—"Orientalist."

"He isn't anything. Not anything at all. That's Hazel again. She's full of energy, you know. I suppose, when she found she'd married him, she had to do something to put him across. Organize him. She would."

"Well!" Elsie sat still a moment. "Frankly, I don't know whether I can stick it or not."

"I can't help hoping you won't. It isn't so good. If you don't mind my saying it, my guess is that you aren't the type at all."

"Still," said she honestly, "it is a job."

"Oh, yes. A job for a hard-boiled little devil who'd play up to them. You and I don't know each other, of course. But if my offhand judgment is any good at all, I'd put you down as anything but hard-boiled. I'd place you as a sensitive, essentially decent sort of person."

"Well . . ."

"And if so, I'm afraid you're in wrong here."

"They pay well."

"Oh, yes. I know."

"And after all, a girl who works for a living has to meet life. It can't all be pleasant."

"No, it can't." He rested his elbows on his knees; leaning moodily forward, gazing again at that stone lantern.

"Fortunately I'm the mental type."

He sat up. "Mental type? My eye!"

"Well . . . really! . . ."

"You're nothing of the sort."

"How can you. . . ."

"Oh, listen now! You're probably considerable of a dear. Oh, I saw the excitement, in your eyes when Hazel brought you into the room. And while Emily Eames was high-hatting you. Mental, nothing! You're young and impressionable. I'd bet five dollars you're full of romantic thoughts. My God, you're positively naive!"

"Of course, if you . . ."

"Oh, come! Here we are, in these absurd costumes . . . I can't speak for myself, but you're enchanting in yours . . . sitting out in an exquisite Japanese garden. It's a fake, but it *is* lovely to the eye and to the senses. And you sitting here and trying to tell me you're the mental type. It's simply too good! Why, bless your heart, don't you see that that sort of girl would never be out here at all? She'd have gone straight up to her room and shut herself away from that loony bunch in there."

"Well . . ."

"I'm romantic, and willing to admit it. Just a fool artist. Never will have any money. Never will get anywhere. When they all get educated to pastel portraits I'll be painting water-color landscapes that nobody wants. I'll be perverse about it, too. . . . Why, hasn't it occurred to you that it's all I can do to keep my hands off you? Surely you realize that to sit out here, the occasion being what it is, and not make love, is pure waste. Just a delightful opportunity thrown away. No, you're not safe anywhere here. Take my advice and pull out. You're not safe even with me. If I weren't in such a ticklish situation here . . . the damndest mess, just to-night . . ."

Elsie remarked primly, "I don't do those things."

He stared at her. Then, deliberately, gently in a way, gathered her into his arms.

She ought to stop him. Struggle. Fight him off. She knew he wouldn't use force. But she didn't fight him. Oh, she murmured some feeble protests . . . heard herself saying, "Oh, please!" . . . but what good was that?

She pushed him away. "Somebody's coming!" Her nerves were on edge. Very close to outright hysteria. The fact that he stirred her so, that she liked him, was no more than a part of that inner confusion.

A dainty Chinese figure was approaching. Mrs. Cuppy! She mounted the bridge. Swaying a little as she walked, and steadying herself by groping for the rail. Over she came. Laughing inanely. "Oho! Here you are! So you thought you could hide from me, John Dane! You come right along with me! Right straight back into the house. We're not going to have any of this sort of thing!" There was laughter all through this, but it wasn't pleasant laughter.

Dane, with a queer look on his face, rose without a word and moved toward the bridge.

Mrs. Cuppy leaned over Elsie. Or tried to. She'd have fallen if the girl hadn't steadied her. Smiling, in a fuddled way, and lowering her voice, she said, "You're a very pretty little girl. Very pretty and very sly. But take my advice, my dear, and look round a little more carefully before you try steal a man. Might be the wrong one. Might be somebody else's man. Just a frien'ly warning, my dear. Just a frien'ly warning."

Dane was lighting a cigarette. The woman joined him, caught his arm, and led him back over the bridge. Elsie dropped her head on her arm and cried. It was good to cry.

3

A car drove in under the *porte cochère*. It looked like a station taxi. A man got out, and the car went away. Elsie moved over to the stone lantern for a glance at her wrist watch. It was a little after eleven. She'd been alone out here more than an hour. Better go to bed. She could slip quietly upstairs. Probably she'd get very little sleep, but no matter. In the morning she'd catch a train back to town. If Mrs. Cuppy insisted on two weeks' notice, she'd simply waive the question of pay. Waive it anyway. She didn't want their money. For that matter, they'd all be sleeping late. She'd just go. Who could stop her?

She walked slowly to the steps and let herself in. Far away (it seemed) in that big living room, they were pounding the piano and screaming a popular song out of tune. One of the men kept roaring out a misplaced top note.

Miss Briggs appeared. "Oh, Miss Penn," she said, "I've been looking for you. It's a matter I imagine you'd better take hold of. Mr. Wong is here."

Elsie could meet this with nothing more than an inquiring look.

"Wong Long Ti," Miss Briggs added. Then—"I supposed you'd know."

"I never heard of him."

"Well, he's the biggest Chinese merchant in New York. Really quite a friend of Mr. Cuppy's. He often visits here. We'll have to put him up. The last train from town has gone. I'll confess I don't know where. The bedrooms are all occupied. The only thing I can think of is to put him in Mr. Cuppy's room. You see, he's . . . ."

Elsie indicated the door to the den. "Still in there?"

"Oh, yes. He won't know. We could just leave him. We'd have to really. The boys could never carry him upstairs. He's pretty heavy. I suppose we could explain to Mrs. Cuppy"

"Where is this Mr. Wong?" asked Elsie. She'd take hold, as best she could.

"In the dining-room. I put him in there."

"All right. Thank you. I'll talk with him."

He stood by a window. An elderly Chinese gentleman. It was amusing, in a way, to note his business suit and the derby hat he held. In her bizarre costume and with all this paint on her face, she felt incongruous. She wondered, in a flutter, if John Dane, in that queer, disturbing moment, had smeared her face; and stole a hasty glance at a mirror. He hadn't.

"How do you do?" Thus the visitor, courteously. He took her costume quite for granted. Doubtless he knew Hazel Cuppy's ways.

"I am Miss Penn, Mrs. Cuppy's secretary. Is there something I can do for you, Mr. Wong? Won't you sit down?"

He seemed unable to do that. She saw now that the kindly face looked old and worn, and that there was confusion in the slanting eyes. His fingers, too, fumbled about the brim of his hat.

"Thank you," he said. "I am in great trouble. I must, if I can do, see Mr. Cuppy." His English, if quaint, was clear enough.

"I am sorry. Mr. Cuppy is not . . . not well . . . and has retired."

"It is very important."

"I am sorry. He couldn't possibly see you to-night."

The limp fingers fumbled along the brim of the derby hat . . . turning it, turning it. The old face worked. He sank into one of the chairs by the table. "I am not very well," he murmured, apologetically. "It is, I think, my life."

"Oh!" was all Elsie could say to that. He was smiling now, in a pathetic, tremulous way. The only course she could pursue, obviously, was to persuade him to speak out. She couldn't deal in mysteries. So, after some meditation, she came out with it. "If you care to explain it to me, Mr. Wong, I will be glad to do whatever is in my power. I am afraid there is no one else you can talk with to-night. Really no one."

He sighed. Then smiled again. It tugged at her heart, that smile. He was a gentleman. "Very well," he said. "Maybe you know if Mr. Cuppy has got a cap of the Empress Dowager. A very wonderful pearl cap."

Elsie hesitated. The man was, after all, a dealer. And it wasn't her business to give information. "It is something, this pearl cap, of interest to you, Mr. Wong?"

"Too much," said he; and sighed again. "I will tell you this, I must buy that cap. I will pay much. All I have in the world, if necessary. I am not a poor man. I must have the cap to-night. And perhaps, then, Mr. Cuppy, as a friend, an old, old friend, would send me back to New York in one of his cars. I must do this. If you will tell Mr. Cuppy it is not a question of price. He will say the price. I will pay. I must buy the cap." He seemed to choke slightly. And then he said in pidgin English, as if, in this moment of emotional stress, his labored, quaint English failed him, "Lady can do? Maybe?"

Elsie knit her brows. "Am I to understand, Mr. Wong, that this is a matter of life or death to you?"

"It is, I know, my life."

No one could look into that simple, kindly old face and doubt the man's sincerity. He was, unquestionably, at some desperate pass. She might speak to Mrs. Cuppy. It wouldn't be pleasant. She shivered unhappily at the thought of entering that living room.

Dreaded what she might see there. This was tackling the new job with a vengeance. On this first bewildering evening. Still, it was the job. That was a steadying thought. It was something to do.

"If you will wait here, Mr. Wong," she said, "I will see what I can do for you."

She hesitated in the wide doorway. They were making a good deal of noise. There was liquor all about, on tables and on the piano, glasses and bottles and siphons. Still that flow of liquor. At the piano, the critic and the gargoyle in the yellow robe were hammering out jazz, four-handed, and singing. The irrepressible top note belonged, it appeared, to Mr. Delos. Miss Eames and that author, Mr. Ettlethwaite, were dancing, in a close embrace. From all sides voices rose discordantly. Some of the men, in a corner, appeared to be arguing hotly about religion. Elsie's unquiet eyes sought Mrs. Cuppy. There she was, on a sofa, but not with John Dane. It was Stromberg, the explorer, who talked with her, holding one of her hands and patting it as if for emphasis. A thin man with keen, handsome features and bright eyes

that were set too close together. The Manchu cap
on Mrs. Cuppy's pretty head had slipped to one
side, giving her a roguish air. Her free hand ca-
ressed those amazing strings of pearls. . . . John
Dane sat sprawled in an easy chair, soberly looking on. He gave her one of his quick, quizzical
smiles, which she didn't return. During her hour
of solitude in the rock garden she had decided to
put him straight out of her mind. It was the only
clean way to handle that sort of episode.

As Elsie crossed the room Mrs. Cuppy and
Stromberg rose as if to join the dancers. The woman steadied herself, standing there, by clinging to
the odd-looking European. She looked moody;
really rather cross, Elsie thought. The cap had
slipped further awry, so that the strings of pearls
fell across her face. She brushed them aside; then
carelessly tossed the cap on the sofa.

Elsie picked it up, as she said guardedly, "Mrs.
Cuppy, may I have just a word with you?"

"Oh, run along." It was unpleasantly fascinating to watch that pretty mouth shaping itself deliberately and with difficulty about the words. "I
wanna dance. Don' bother me." Then to the grinning Stromberg, "Don' let this li'l devil vamp you,
Gustaf. She's the sly one."

"But Mrs. Cuppy . . . please! . . . just a moment . . ."

"Oh, don' bother me! Run along!" And as she whirled unsteadily off she called back, "Throw tha' cap away. Keep it yourself. I don' care. It gets in my eyes." And then clung to her partner.

Elsie stood holding the cap. She hadn't an idea what to do. She saw one of the other men hit Stromberg jovially on the back and take the woman away from him.

The only place she could think of to put the cap was in the Chinese room. She walked quickly out into the hall. Then she heard a quick step, and Stromberg's voice fell on her ears. "What it is that you do with the cap?"

She turned. The expression about his narrow eyes, and his grin, disturbed her. He had a tall glass in his hand. She said, rather crisply, "I am putting it away"; and hurried into that dim, beautiful room.

Hearing steps behind her, and supposing it still to be the European, she turned with an exclamation of impatience. She must watch her nerves.

But this time it proved to be John Dane.

"What are you going to do with that thing?" he remarked. "It really ought to go into a safe, but I don't know where Cuppy's safe is, or how to get into it. It is priceless, you know."

"Of course," said she, remembering her decision to be short with him.

"I'll tell you . . . there's a sort of secret drawer in the table over here. Cuppy showed it to me. Let me see." He led the way around that huge vase and felt along the under edge of the table-top. "Here it is," he said, at last, and drew out a shallow tray.

Elsie, hearing a muffled sound, turned with a start.

"What is it?" asked Dane.

She lowered her voice. "Well . . . I think somebody else is in the room."

He stepped around the vase. "No," he said, "nobody."

She laid the cap flat in the drawer and closed it.

"Will you sit in here a little while?" he asked. "I'd like to chin a little more."

"No. If you'll excuse me. I'm pretty tired. I'm going right upstairs."

"Well . . . I *would* like to say that I've felt disturbed. I'm afraid I rather took advantage . . ."

"Please!" She simply couldn't say more. Stromberg was sitting on a carved chest in the hall. He grinned and waved at her. She ran upstairs. Ran with a curious sensation of panic. She'd slip out early in the morning. Carry off her suitcase and typewriter on foot, if necessary. Though doubtless she could call a taxi. There was a telephone in the side hall that led to the *porte cochère*.

It wasn't until she reached the second floor that she thought of the distressed Mr. Wong. She stood, then, for a long moment, thinking out what she might do. Certainly she couldn't let him have the cap. It didn't belong to her. But she must do something. She couldn't make herself go down those front stairs again; not into that part of the house. So she looked about until she found the servants' stairway and descended.

Mr. Wong was standing by that window in the dining-room. A patient little old man from a faraway land. She wondered what he could have meant in saying that his life was at stake.

"I'm sorry," she said. "Nothing can be done to-night. But you will stay here. And perhaps to-morrow . . . I will send Miss Briggs . . ."

She hurried out and looked up the housekeeper.

"I'll take him up," said that person, with a sigh of utter weariness. "I put out the light in the den. Mr. C.'s snoring in there. I opened the windows a little, and shut him in. It's all I can do."

She had been only a moment in her room when she heard a tap at the door. Opening, she found the Chinese butler standing there . . . tall, grave, respectful. He bowed.

"Maybe I can speak to Miss," he said.

"Certainly. What is it?"

"I dunno jus' what I do. I worry about Mister Cuppy."

"Oh, I imagine he will be all right. Let me see—your name is Sin, isn't it?"

"Yes, Miss. I am Sin. You think maybe I better try wake Mr. Cuppy up? Take him upstairs?"

"Why . . . oh, you can hardly do that. Miss Briggs is putting Mr. Wong in Mr. Cuppy's room."

"Oh . . . Mr. Wong." He looked puzzled.

"Yes. He came a few minutes ago."

"But Mr. Cuppy . . . he is not well . . ."

"I'm quite sure he'll be all right. Miss Briggs told me just now that she'd opened the windows in there and shut the door."

This appeared to disturb him. Watching him, reflectively, Elsie found herself entertaining the, to her, curious notion that this Chinese servant might be something of a person. His face had much of the simple honesty of Mr. Wong's. Faithfulness she sensed, and a deeply ingrained courtesy and kindliness. She'd never, before this strange evening, thought about the yellow people beyond an occasional glance at a laundryman. It hadn't occurred to her that there might be different types of Chinamen. "After all," she thought now, "there's hundreds of millions of 'em. I'm going to read something about 'em. They did make beautiful things. And they've had great poets. Interesting!"

He was speaking again, with the gracious respectful air that stirred in her an odd sensation of crudeness, of newness. After all, it was an old, old race. "I worry, Miss. Miss Briggs shouldn' open windows on first floor. We always lock. Maybe burglars."

"Oh, do you think so? Away out here?"

"I dunno. But I worry. Mr. Cuppy has so much." He moved his hands in a graceful gesture as if to include the whole house. "So much. Too much. Money can't buy." He stood, considering.

"Well . . . I'll confess, Sin, I don't know what to say. I'm so new here, you see. I'm afraid I can't help you."

His face still wore that intent expression. "I worry. I don' think I sleep. But"—with a note of gentle apology, this—"I musn' trouble Miss." He turned slowly away, and she heard him repeat "I don' think I sleep." Then, "Good-night, Miss."

"Good-night, Sin."

Closing the door and moving slowly over to the dresser, Elsie decided to look up books on the Chinese people as soon as she could get back to New York. The Public Library would advise her. Well, these queer Cuppys had certainly opened a new world to her. Or an old world. She owed them for that— "Fancy my liking Chinamen!" she thought, as she considered her excitingly painted face in the mirror. "Mr. Wong, and now this butler!" And then, aloud, in a rather shaken, husky voice, came this widely inclusive expression of a complicated mood—"Some evening! *Some* evening!"

It was a long time before she could close her eyes. She was awakened . . . hardly a moment later, it seemed . . . by a tapping on the door. A tapping that seemed to have been figuring in her troubled dreams. As if it had been going on for some little time. Bright sunlight was streaming into the room. She rubbed her eyes and looked at the watch on her wrist. It was a quarter to nine. She'd meant to be on her way by this time. Confused, feeling rather upset, she put on her slippers and went to the door.

It was Miss Briggs, in an old gray and gold kimono and slippers. An ashen, trembling, staring Miss Briggs. She came in a bewildered way into the room and dropped into a chair.

"I'm shaken," she said querulously. "They've gone."

"Who have gone?" asked Elsie shortly.

"Sin always brings me my coffee at a quarter to eight. I woke up at quarter past and realized that he hadn't come. So I put on this wrap and went downstairs. There wasn't anybody there. Not anybody. Not even in the kitchen. I went up to their rooms then. They've gone. Run away in the night. I called up the garage but nobody answered. So I went out there. Both the chauffeurs are gone, too.

The queer thing is, they've left their things. Their bags. Clothes hanging in the closets. All that."

So she rattled nervously on. Elsie listened rather impatiently. It was, all said and done, nothing to her. Impatiently, swiftly, she dressed. After all, it was an emergency. She'd have to help as much as she could.

They went downstairs together, and into the side hall. There Miss Briggs stopped abruptly, with an "Oh!" and caught at Elsie's arm.

"What is it?" asked Elsie.

"The door!" She was looking toward the den. "I left it shut last night!"

Together they moved toward it and looked within. And they saw what had been Mr. Cuppy, lying in a sprawling heap on the floor. His head had been crushed in as if with an axe, and lay in a pool of blood and brain.

Miss Briggs screamed.

"Wait!" said Elsie. "That's no good!" Her own knees were giving way, and she was aware of a pang of nausea; but her mind was the sort that clears in emergencies. "Wait!" she cried again. She hadn't an idea for what. But the cap was in her mind. She made her way to the Chinese room. Miss Briggs, sobbing hysterically, followed.

The secret drawer in the table behind the huge vase had been pried open. The cap was gone.

PART II

4

The doctor's name was Obry. Elsie was fully ten minutes in getting that bit of information out of the now wholly ungoverned housekeeper. She telephoned, and then cajoled Miss Briggs into helping make coffee. All those queer persons upstairs would be roused before long. Roused and shocked. They'd want breakfast. And there were no servants. An oppressive sense of horror seemed to fill the house like some noxious gas. Shortly Dr. Obry arrived and took charge. He'd have to tell Mrs. Cuppy. Then the local Chief of Police appeared, with a sergeant and others. Then the Coroner. Big fat men. Political type. Two men in civilian clothes said they were from the State Police barrack near by. A tall, spread-eagly young man proved to be an assistant District Attorney. A Mr. Atkinson. One curious fact—they picked up a pillow in the side hall. Lying on the floor. A regular bed pillow in a white slip. That notion of running away filled Elsie's mind. She couldn't, of course. Not now. Not with an unexplained dead body in the house. The doctor was a long time upstairs. Having his troubles, doubtless, with Mrs. Cuppy.

Police officers went through the house, waking the guests. Shortly these straggled downstairs, some fully dressed, others in bathrobes or kimonos. Miss Eames, the actress, had evidently forgotten, in her excitement, to rub off the cold cream that covered her face. Without their Chinese costumes and their paint the women were hard to identify. Mechanically Elsie set out the coffee and toast. Not one of them appeared to recognize her. She caught John Dane taking her in with a puzzled expression. But a moment later he coolly asked her for a spoon. . . . Funny! She'd forgotten all the spoons!

She found herself looking much at Mr. Wong, who had slumped down in his chair at the end of the table. Others were looking at him too. Rather suspiciously. Of course. They hadn't seen him before.

Mr. Delos leaned back in his chair and beckoned. Elsie bent over him. "What on earth does it mean?" he whispered. "Police and all! Treating us like this! What's happened?"

Elsie, who'd thought herself cool enough, found great difficulty in speaking. But then suddenly her voice broke through, "Mr. Cuppy has been—well—murdered."

Mr. Delos cried out, "Good God!" And the others gasped.

Elsie, as suddenly and intemperately as she had spoken, burst into tears and ran out into the butler's pantry. For the moment she was as weakly useless as the overwhelmed Miss Briggs. But only for the moment. It was merely nerves, of course. Reaction to a shock. She wasn't the weepy sort.

The officials were sitting, for what appeared to be a sort of preliminary hearing, in the Chinese room. A policeman led Miss Briggs in there. She wept all the way.

An undertaker's wagon appeared; and the Coroner left the Chinese room long enough to supervise the removal of the body. Then he went back.

Elsie had to do something, so she set to work carrying out dishes from the dining-room and stacking them in the butler's pantry.

A nurse arrived, by taxi, and went upstairs. A caterer appeared and took charge of the kitchen.

The spread-eagly Mr. Atkinson made a speech from the dining-room doorsill. "We regret the necessity of putting you all to inconvenience. But I

assure you we will not detain you longer than is
absolutely necessary. Until further instructions,
nobody is to leave the property." With which he
hurried back to the Chinese room.

The guests sat moodily about, after that, talking
a little, the women lighting cigarettes, the men
cigarettes or pipes. They dropped matches and
flicked ashes, carelessly, about the rug. Elsie wondered, in dismal idleness of brain, who'd clean up
after them.

The policeman brought Miss Briggs (weeping)
back to the kitchen, then came for Elsie. Meekly
she followed the big blue back. Her turn now, eh!
They went out into the main hall. There the officer, observing that the door to the Chinese room
was closed, offered her a chair and himself drifted
off a few steps to chat in low tones with a fellow
who appeared to be watching the front door. Bits
of their talk came to her ear—"I see the District
Attorney's got a man here already. Whadda you
know about that!"

"Oh, sure! Atkinson. Lives here in town, you
know. Out Myrtle Avenue."

"Stepping right into it, I'd say."

"Well, it's a big case."

"Oh, sure! N. Jonas Cuppy! Tough."

"I'll say so."

"Funny about that pillow that was found in the hall down here."

"Yeah. They couldn't 'a' killed him with that, hardly."

5

That door opened, and still another policeman beckoned her within. There the various representatives of authority were assembled, seated about the center table. The Coroner indicated a vacant chair. Mr. Atkinson explained, "It is our duty, Miss—Miss Penn, to get the story of every person who was in the house last night. Please tell us yours. As we understand it, you arrived early in the evening to begin work as Mrs. Cuppy's secretary. Please tell us exactly what happened from that moment. What you saw and heard and did."

That shouldn't be difficult. In direct, simple language she recited her narrative. Matters that were merely personal, she omitted. There seemed to be no object in dwelling on Mr. Cuppy's fuddled attempt to embrace her, or on the queer little scene with John Dane in the rock garden.

"Mr. Cuppy"—one of the State officers speaking; they addressed him as Mr. Carlock—"Mr. Cuppy drank a great deal during the evening, I gather."

"Yes. A great deal."

"When did he lose consciousness?"

"I couldn't say exactly. Dinner was at eight o'clock, about. I would put it at somewhere between nine and ten."

"Then the Chinese servants carried him into the den and left him there on the sofa?"

"Yes."

"After that you went out into the rock garden. Were you alone?"

"I was then."

"Not later?"

"No."

"Some one joined you there?"

"Yes."

"Who?"

"Mr. Dane."

Mr. Carlock consulted a paper. "Mr. John Dane, the artist, eh?"

"Yes."

"Had you known him before?"

"No. Never heard of him. I didn't know any of these people."

"Why did Mr. Dane go out there?"

"I haven't an idea, unless it was to get a breath of air. He found me, and sat down on the bench. We chatted for a while."

"About anything in particular?"

"No."

"What was your idea in going out there alone?"

"Well . . . I wanted to think."

"What about?"

Mr. Atkinson broke in here. "You understand, Miss Penn, that by answering our questions freely and completely you will be helping us, perhaps more than you or any of us realize at the moment. What we are trying to get together now is a rough survey of the background. I should like to ask one or two questions, if Mr. Carlock will permit me . . . Thank you. . . . Miss Briggs has told us how she put out the light in the den, opened the windows—a little way, she says—and then shut the door. Do you know anything about that?"

"Only what she told me this morning. Substantially as you put it."

"Then this morning, when you came downstairs with her—did you happen to notice that one of the den windows was wide open?"

"No. I merely looked in through the door; saw the—the body; ran in, here, thinking of the Chinese cap—"

"Because it had been left in your charge?"

"Yes."

"Mrs. Cuppy, you have said, gave you the cap. Told you to throw it away or keep it yourself?"

"Oh, that! I didn't pay much attention to that. She wasn't . . . herself."

"What happened after you found that the cap had been stolen?"

"I made Miss Briggs give me the name of the family physician."

"Miss Briggs, I imagine, was in a rather hysterical state."

"Decidedly. I called Dr. Obry, and then tried to steady Miss Briggs down enough to get a little breakfast ready for the guests. We were at that until Dr. Obry came."

"Did you, at any time last evening, observe any actions on the part of the Chinese servants that might suggest ill-feeling? Understand, we do not, at the present time, seriously suspect them. It is quite likely that they fled in a panic when they discovered the tragedy this morning. That one wide-open window in the den suggests that the murder was committed by outsiders. Possibly Chinese gunmen, who knew of the pearl cap. From your interview with Mr. Wong, that seems anything but improbable. And your talk with the butler, Sin, evidently impressed you favorably. But we must consider everything. How about those servants?"

"They behaved perfectly, as far as I saw. I remember watching them as they carried Mr. Cuppy into the den, and wondering what they could be thinking of us white people. But you couldn't tell a thing from their faces."

"Thank you. Now, if you don't mind, tell Mr. Carlock what it was you went out into the rock garden to think about."

"Well—I felt rather uncomfortable about the situation here. As a job, I mean."

"Why?"

"I didn't . . . didn't like the atmosphere of the house."

"Why not?" Carlock, quickly.

"Oh, I don't know. The liquor, partly."

"Were they all drinking?"

"Oh, yes. All but Mr. Dane. I'd noticed that he hadn't taken much."

"Perhaps he didn't like the atmosphere either."

"No. He said he didn't. He asked me if I thought I could stick it."

"Had you been drinking?"

"No. I never drink at all."

"And you were thinking you perhaps couldn't stick it."

"Yes. Before I went to bed I'd about made up my mind to slip out in the morning before they were up and go back to town. I didn't like it at all."

"Why not, exactly?"

"Well—must I answer that?"

"If you will be so good."

"I didn't like either Mr. or Mrs. Cuppy."

"Why not?"

"Well . . . Mrs. Cuppy seemed to me rather artificial and insincere."

"And Mr. Cuppy?"

"I don't like to speak unkindly of the—the dead—"

"Naturally."

"Well—he put his arm around me. Just after we were introduced. Over there, behind that big vase." There! She'd told that, after all!

"Who introduced you?"

"Mrs. Cuppy."

"Where was she at the moment?"

"She'd gone to the door. She thought we were following, I suppose."

"And why weren't you?"

"I'd waited there a moment because I wanted to look at that beautiful lantern. I thought Mr. Cuppy had gone out with his wife. He came up behind me."

"I see. Did he have anything more to say to you, after that?"

"Nothing. I didn't see him at all, except at the farther end of the dinner table, until they carried him into the den."

"How long were you and Mr. Dane together in the rock garden?"

"I don't know. Perhaps twenty minutes."

"Then you returned to the house?"

"He did."

"Left you out there?"

"Yes."

"Wasn't that a little odd?"

"I don't know." She was being drawn in pretty deeply. But these men, after all, represented the law. She mustn't try to evade them. "The fact is," she added, "Mrs. Cuppy came out there looking for him."

"Looking for Mr. Dane?"

"Yes."

"Had Mrs. Cuppy been drinking?"

"Well . . . yes. Decidedly."

"How do you know?"

"I saw it. She'd had quite a lot. And as she came over the bridge near where we were sitting, I could see that she was unsteady on her feet."

"What did she say?"

"To him?"

"To anybody."

"I . . . I rather hesitate to tell little matters that have no bearing on the murder."

The Coroner spoke. "You will have to let us be judge of that side of it, Miss Penn. But first we want all the facts. All of 'em!"

"Very well," thought Elsie, "I'll just let it go, then." And she did. Firmly. "She said just about this—'Oh, there you are! So you thought you could hide from me, John Dane! You come right back with me.' . . . Then, when he'd moved off a little way, she came to me and leaned over me. I had to hold her up. And she said—'You're pretty, and you're sly. But take my advice, my dear, and look around a little more carefully before you try to steal a man. Might be somebody else's man. Just a friendly warning.'"

"Mr. Dane had been staying in the house longer than the others, hadn't he?"

"I believe so. He'd been making a pastel portrait of Mrs. Cuppy."

"Very good, Miss Penn. Thank you. That is all for the present."

Mr. Atkinson spoke. "You have given us your whole story now, Miss Penn?"

"All I can think of."

"As we understand the matter of the pearl cap—Mrs. Cuppy, considerably in liquor, simply left it in your hands when she wished to dance. You had gone to her to tell her of Mr. Wong. She refused to listen. You didn't know what to do with the cap, but took it into the Chinese room. On the way across the hall you saw only Mr. Stromberg and Mr. Dane. Mr. Stromberg you brushed aside. But Mr. Dane followed you into this room and told you of the hidden drawer. You and he put the cap away there. You thought you heard some other person in the room. Mr. Dane looked and assured you that there was nobody. As you went out you saw Mr. Stromberg sitting in the hall. And excepting for a few words with Mr. Wong in the dining-room, you saw none of them again until this morning. That is about the gist of it, is it not?"

"Perfectly."

"Just one more question—where did you leave Mr. Dane?"

Elsie knit her brows. "I really don't know. I felt nervous and tired, and my one thought was to get upstairs by myself."

"You didn't say good-night, even?"

"No. I suppose he followed me out of this room. But if . . . if you are thinking . . . well, that Mr. Dane might have . . ." She shivered a little.

"Oh, no, Miss Penn. We're merely trying to piece this whole background together. It's something of a picture puzzle. . . . By the way, it occurs to me that you must be a stenographer."

"Yes. I am. . . . I just meant to say about Mr. Dane, as a mere first impression, that he seemed to me to be the one decent, really civilized person in the house."

"I see. Now, Miss Penn, it would help materially if you would consent to remain here and take down what the others have to say. There would be no hurry about transcribing it. But at some later time we might find it useful to look over all these stories as they were taken down word for word."

"I shall be glad to help you in any way that I can," said Elsie.

"I'm sure of that. And while we're sending for Mr. Delos, I'll ask you to glance over these rough notes of Miss Briggs's story. If there's anything there you can't make out, ask me about it. Thank you." Then to the policeman at the door, "Bring Mr. Delos!"

Elsie looked at the scribbled pages. A fairly detailed, if condensed, story. Only one of the notes eluded her eyes. She pointed it out to Mr. Atkinson. "Simply," explained that keen young man, "that Miss Briggs had to stay up to lock doors and windows and clean up a little after they all went upstairs. About two o'clock. Everything in confusion. Mr. Stromberg asleep on couch in living-room. Decided not to disturb him. Went to bed."

Elsie hurried upstairs to her room for notebooks and pencils. It was going to be a relief to be occupied. She felt that. Returning downstairs, on the lower landing, she encountered Mr. Stromberg running up, carrying his overcoat and hat. He stopped and quickly smiled. "Just gathering

up my things," he said. "I suppose they'll let us
go soon?"

"Haven't an idea," said Elsie, and went on down.

6

One by one the sleepy, cross guests gave their
stories. Mr. Delos sputtered indignantly over being treated as a suspicious character. Miss Eames
yawned as she languidly, briefly, answered the
questions. The Gargoyle proved to have theories,
and cackled excitedly until the Chief shut him
off. Not one of the lot had

any really illuminating facts to offer. The evening had been and would remain a good deal of a
haze in their minds.

Gradually Elsie found herself catching something of the impersonal atmosphere in which
these determined then were going at their task,
and even found herself, during the brief rests,
while the officials were talking, mentally piecing
together the odd bits of evidence that came to
light here and there. Toward noon the sergeant
entered and announced that the reporters had begun to arrive from New York. He brought, also, a
blood-stained hatchet. They had found it in the
shrubbery under the den windows. It was the sort

that can be bought at any hardware shop. Chinese gunmen might have brought it, or it might have been picked up in the Cuppy cellar. You couldn't say.

"Keep those reporters out," said Atkinson, as he examined the hatchet. Carlock looked it over next, through a pocket microscope.

"That goes," remarked the Chief to the sergeant. "Keep them clean of the place. If you need more men, call up headquarters."

Mr. Wong was brought in. Again, as Elsie considered the elderly figure and the crushed expression on the round wrinkled oriental face, she felt simplicity and honesty in the man. That Mr. Carlock again took up the burden of question.

"You arrived here late last evening, Mr. Wong?"

"Yes. So I did. I have come on the ten-forty train from New York."

"And you rode out here in a taxicab from the local station?"

"Yes, sir."

"Why did you come? You had not been invited to the house party?"

"No. But I have had a telephone call."

"From whom?"

"I don't know."

"Man or woman?"

"It was a man. A Chinese man."

"What did he say to you?"

Mr. Wong sat motionless for a long moment, thinking. The men about the table watched him intently. Finally he said, "If I can do I will tell the story."

"In your own way, you mean? Very well. Do so."

"I am interest', much of us in this country are interest', in the Nationalist Party of Canton. The party of Sun Yat Sen and Chang K'ai Shek. I have give money. For it is war in China. Men feel." He put his hand on his heart. "Men are excite'. Chang is at the Yangtze River. But he must have money. More and more money it is all the time. Men of our Party in this country give too much. A little time ago I am told that Hung Lo . . . he is Shanghai man now . . . Hung Lo sent to Ting Pao . . ."

"Who is Ting Pao?"

"New York man, Ting Pao. Very big man."

"And connected with the Nationalist Party?"

"Oh, yes! Hung Lo send the wonderful pearl cap of Empress Tzu Hsi . . . what you call Empress Dowager. He has ask' Ting Pao to sell the cap because New York is city of too much money. Ting Pao has talk' with me. Because I am merchant. He has said I am man who finds rich buyer. And then Ting Pao send the money to Hung Lo in Shanghai. And Hung Lo give money to Chang."

"Then the pearl cap was to be sold to raise funds for Chang's military campaign?"

"Oh, yes!"

"And this pearl cap was really of considerable value, Mr. Wong?"

"Oh, yes!" The Chinaman's hands fluttered upward. "Very great! Maybe two hundred thousand. Maybe three hundred thousand. I have said I will sell for most possible. And I ask no commission. It is a matter of great hurry. No time. I think of Mr. Cuppy. He buys so much Chinese beautiful things. All the time he buys." The slanting eyes swept about at the cabinets full of carved jade and nephrite and rock crystal that stood about the walls, at the long scroll paintings that hung, under glass, above them, at the richly ornamented screens, the old bronzes, the exquisite porcelains, the snuff bottles, the carved furniture. "Last night when I am eating my dinner, I am thinking about Ting Pao. The pearl cap must have come. I wonder. Then I sit a while. Then I am called to telephone, and the man tells me that if I do not give back the cap before midnight, I am to be killed by hatchet-man. That I cannot escape, the voice tells me. Naturally I am surprise'. I cannot think what he means. I ask him to tell me, for I do not know. He says to me I do know. That I am liar. But I make him tell. He says to me after long talk that men steal the pearl cap and sell it to Mr. Cuppy. He says to me I know these thieves. He says I make them do it and keep all the money myself." Mr.

Wong struck his breast with both hands. Trembling hands. "Never before do they say this. That I too am thief. Never in my life do they say that of me. And they say I will give back the pearl cap before midnight or I am killed by hatchet-men. So I take the train here. I try to see Mr. Cuppy. But Mr. Cuppy is sick. In there." He pointed excitedly to the den. "And no can see Mrs. Cuppy. I think I will buy the cap. I think of myself. And I think of Chang K'ai Shek, too. I am not rich man. I have my home. And I have bonds. Maybe one hundred and sixty-seventy thousand. I get all my bonds. They are in my safe. I bring them here." He struck his chest again. "I give all my bonds to Mr. Cuppy if he will give me the pearl cap. No can do. They take me to sleep in his bed because he is sick down here. That is all I know."

"You think these hatchet-men followed you here, Mr. Wong?"

"Oh, yes! I think so."

"But why should they kill Mr. Cuppy?"

"I cannot think. But maybe they think he is me. Maybe they come in by the open window. . ."

"Oh, you know about the open windows?"

"Oh, yes! All this morning I hear the people talk. Too much talk. Maybe"—eagerly, this—"Maybe they climb in the window. They hear a man sleeping. Maybe it is me. They kill him." He was keen, this old Chinaman; despite the tragic emotion in his breast his brain was clear. "Then they hunt in this room. They find the pearl cap and take it away."

"Why do you think the servants all ran off?"

"These boys? Oh, they find the body of Mr. Cuppy. They are scared. They run. They think the police arrest them. You see, Chinese man never takes responsibility, never, if can help, because if he do take it, then must keep his word until they kill him. These boys are afraid. So they run."

"You know these boys of Mr. Cuppy?"

"Oh, no. Only one. Often, I am here. They know me. I speak to them. But Sin I know. He work for me. Until last year. I have give him to Mr. Cuppy last year."

"Do you think you could find him?"

Mr. Wong looked doubtful. "It will be very hard. I do not know."

"Is he, in your judgment, the sort who would run away?"

"Sin? I do not think so. Oh, no! I do not understand that."

"Thank you, Mr. Wong. That is all."

"Then I can go. It is very important. I must go home."

"Not quite yet. By evening, perhaps. As soon as we have cleared up our work here."

"Thank you. Thank you too much." At the door he hesitated. Turned back. His face worked. There were tears in his eyes. "It is time too hard, too dangerous, in China. Chinese men in America are too excite'. There is, we say in English, hot blood." With which, brokenly, slowly, he went out.

When the door had closed on his bent figure, the men looked at one another.

"A rather interesting theory," remarked the Chief.

"Still," said Carlock, "there was no ransacking of the place. Whoever took the pearl cap knew where it was. Nothing else was so much as touched. I have sent that table in town to be examined for finger prints. We may find a lead there."

"A curious angle," observed Atkinson, "is that we have learned so far of only two persons who knew where the cap was hidden. One is Dane. The other"—he turned, courteously enough, to Elsie— "is you, Miss Penn. And, frankly, I haven't the slightest suspicion of either of you. Or, naturally, you wouldn't be here, in our confidence. I know something, too, of John Dane. I happen to know one or two of his friends in town. I have long admired his work. I am quite willing to accept him as a gentleman."

"There is still"—Carlock—"the possibility of a third person in the room when Miss Penn and Dane hid the pearl cap."

"Yes, there is that. We'll keep an eye out for developments there. But let's get on with our questioning. We have—let me see—three left. Mrs. Cuppy, Stromberg, and Dane. Dr. Obry, how soon will Mrs. Cuppy be able to talk?"

"Certainly not until later in the day, if then," replied the physician. "She is in a pretty bad way. I have given her a bromide. And I have a nurse up there."

"We'll have Stromberg in." The attendant officer left the room. "This fellow is an odd one," said Atkinson. "A Dane or Norwegian or North German. Hard to place. An adventurer, I rather think, who had worked round the Cuppys. They finance these expeditions of his, I've understood. Some of you may remember the queer publicity when he was lecturing last year on his Thibetan show. He claimed to have climbed some tremendous mountain out there. But stories drifted back that he didn't climb it. And there was a story got round that his motion pictures, presumably taken from the peak, really showed a familiar view from another and much lower peak that a lot of people have climbed. Some expert even figured out that he couldn't possibly have carried the picture machine up there, along with other supplies and the oxygen tanks, with the number of porters he had."

"And wasn't there," asked the doctor, "some trouble about a member of his expedition that died under unexplained circumstances?"

"That's right. That English boy."

The door opened. A police sergeant appeared. "Chief," he reported, "the pillow that was found in the hall belonged on the bed of Sin, the butler." The Chief merely nodded. And Elsie made a note.

A moment later Stromberg was ushered in.

7

He was tall, lean, strong, and moved with the grace of a wild animal. But Elsie didn't like his face. It was thin, and very keen. She considered the close-set, bright eyes, as they took in the circle of officials. A good deal of sharp thinking went on, surely, behind them. But he told his story well enough, in a slightly foreign accent, of the evening party, the costumes, the collapse of Mr. Cuppy. About the sequence of minor events he exhibited a measure of confusion, but admitted that he had drunk a good deal. At about two o'clock, he said, they all went upstairs. Of what may have happened after that he knew nothing until he was roused by a policeman. Once or twice he looked directly at Elsie, but plainly didn't know her. His room, he said, was on the second floor, in the rear, next to that of John Dane. They shared a bath.

Mr. Carlock asked, "Do you recollect seeing Miss Penn when she put away Mrs. Cuppy's pearl cap?"

"I remember meeting her in the hall. I had been dancing with Mrs. Cuppy and was cut out. I wandered into the hall, with a glass in my hand, I think. Miss Penn came through with Mrs. Cuppy's cap in her hand and went into this room. Dane followed her. I sat down in the hall and finished my drink. Then I went back to the living-room."

Dane was called. Elsie found herself bridling a little. It had seemed, at breakfast, as if he should have recognized her. He'd certainly seen more of her than Stromberg. He'd talked with her, looked at her, kissed her. At the thought a touch of color crept into her face. She hoped these men wouldn't notice. They apparently didn't. She must compose herself. This flutter of the nerves was absurd.

He took his place without so much as looking at her. Took her for granted. She might have been a piece of furniture. "Well," she thought, bridling again, "I like that!"

Dane's story was the simplest and clearest of all. He knew precisely what he had and hadn't seen during the evening; and he seemed gravely eager to help. Elsie noted the distinctly good impression he made on the men about the table.

There was an interruption while the Chief spoke to the sergeant, at the farther end of the room. The officials relaxed in their chairs. Dane turned to Elsie.

"I beg pardon," he remarked, "but aren't you Miss Penn?"

She nodded, with more than a trace of brusqueness.

"Of course I should have recognized you. I'm sorry."

Mr. Atkinson spoke up. "Isn't it rather odd that you didn't, Mr. Dane?"

"I don't think so. The ladies were all in costume, and were painted up in the Chinese manner. Miss Penn arrived late, and I didn't see her until she appeared in that getup."

"There's one rather odd little matter, Mr. Dane. We have no wish to pry into merely personal affairs that can have no bearing on the case. But when Mrs. Cuppy found you in the rock garden she addressed a rather peculiar remark to Miss Penn. Something to the effect that she was a sly girl, and that she'd better not undertake to steal a man until she'd looked around and made sure whose man it was."

"I didn't hear what she said to Miss Penn. I had moved away."

"But do you know what she meant?"

"No."

"Has there been . . . but I'll put the question this way: When you returned to the house with Mrs. Cuppy was anything said by either of you that might throw light on the remark?"

Dane plainly hesitated. "I suppose, Mr. Atkinson, that I really should speak with the utmost frankness, even concerning my hostess."

"It is imperative."

"Well, Mrs. Cuppy was not at all herself. She had drunk a good deal. I had not. The whole situation had, by that time, become distasteful to me. As I told Miss Penn, it was my intention to leave at the first possible moment. I'd planned to go to-day. Mrs. Cuppy did say a few rather foolish things. She is a pretty woman with all the power that wealth brings, and accustomed to having her own way. I took her straight to the living-room, drew Mr. Stromberg into conversation with her, and left her with him."

"Thank you, Mr. Dane. That is all, for the present."

Dane went out.

The Chief returned to the table with a small parcel rolled up in a newspaper. Solemnly, impressively, he laid this on the table and looked about him at the others. All leaned forward in quick responsiveness. Slowly, with that hushed, impressive manner, he unrolled the newspaper, and there lay the pearl cap. "Gentlemen," he remarked heavily, "here it is."

They stared. Elsie's nerves tingled and crinkled, clear to the roots of her hair. The Chief turned to her. "Can you identify it, Miss Penn?" And pushed it toward her. She took it up, mechanically, and turned it round and round in her hands. But at the moment she couldn't speak. Her excited thoughts were all out of hand. Here they had found it! Here in the house! Then . . . ! Her unsteady fingers fumbled with it. Felt those amazing strings of matched pearls that had disturbed Mrs. Cuppy by getting into her eyes. Felt the big oddly shaped single pearls that were set into the rich ornamentation of the crown; oval pearls, oblong pearls, several of fascinatingly irregular shapes. Never in her life had Elsie seen any so large or of such fine iridescence. Gathered, each a gem in a hundred thousand, from the farthest shores of the Indies to please an Empress. She was turning the cap round and round, a confused misty excitement shining in her eyes, her color high, her lips slightly parted. . . . Partly hidden in the filigree work of silver gilt, she spied an empty setting. One of the single pearls was missing. She recalled one, the largest of all, shaped like a pear, that had hung among the silver-gilt leaves. It was gone. She was about to point out the empty setting . . .

"It was found," went on the Chief, "in the closet of John Dane's room. Tucked away behind an extra blanket on a shelf."

Elsie's nerveless fingers dropped it to the table. For the moment she couldn't breathe.

The men looked at one another. Atkinson spoke up. "Hmm! Well! Pretty extraordinary, that! It does appear to fix the murder right here in the house. What have you done about Dane, Chief?"

"Held him. I told the Sergeant to get him away very quietly."

Elsie's thoughts were clearing. These men had the right idea. Take everything as it came. Take it as a job. Let a fact stand as a fact, without emotion, without color. She could do that, too. She was the mental type. Anyway, John Dane was nothing to her. Nothing!

She didn't know that Atkinson was intently watching her. His abrupt question, when it came, startled her. But hardly more than her own abrupt reply. Her brain was clicking now. She could be quick. As quick as any of them.

"Miss Penn," said he brusquely, "what do you make of all this?"

"Mr. Atkinson," said she, "I should like very much to have a look at Mr. Stromberg's overcoat. I saw him carrying it upstairs a while back. Couldn't you have an officer bring it from his room?"

The officials were all watching her now. Atkinson said, "Certainly!" The Chief nodded to the attendant; who went out and returned shortly with the coat. Elsie spread it out on the table and went through the outer pockets. Frowned impatiently.

"There'd be an inside breast pocket," remarked Atkinson. Elsie was flopping the coat over, when Carlock, who was feeling along the bottom of the skirt, cried, "Wait a minute! Here's something!" But Elsie's quick hand was already in that breast pocket. "It has been cut along the bottom!" said she; and slid her whole arm down inside the lining, feeling along the hem of the skirt. Her fingers closed on the lump that Carlock had felt through the cloth. She drew it out . . . a pear-shaped pearl not far from an inch in length . . . it fitted nicely into the setting and completed the design.

"A very neat bit of thinking," said Atkinson, with a friendly nod.

"Oh, no," she replied. "They have adjoining rooms, you know. I suppose Mr. Stromberg did follow Mr. Dane and me into this room, then slipped into the hall. He told you he went upstairs with the others; but Miss Briggs found him asleep on a couch in the living-room, after all the rest had gone up, and she left him there. Somehow or other, during what was left of the night, he got the cap. He cut this inside pocket and dropped the cap down inside the lining. When he finally did go upstairs he left the coat hanging down here in the hall."

"Might have, at that," said Carlock. "He knew he couldn't hide it in his bedroom. Not too successfully. And we might have looked at those coats and wraps all day without giving them a thought."

"Then, you see," Elsie resumed, "whatever his reasons, he took the coat upstairs this morning. He even seemed to want to explain, when we passed on the stairs. But I wasn't interested then. From his room, it was a simple matter to take the cap through the bathroom they shared into Mr. Dane's room. As you gentlemen know, I never saw Mr. Dane before last evening. He is nothing to me. Nothing to me at all! But if my judgment is worth anything, he is not a thief and he is not a murderer."

"Plausible enough," mused Atkinson.

Dr. Obry, with a remark about having a look at Mrs. Cuppy, left the room.

"Mike!" called the Chief, "tell the sergeant to come here!" Then, to the assistant District Attorney, "Do you want to hold Dane, Mr. Atkinson?"

"No."

To the sergeant, thus the Chief, "Let John Dane loose, Jim. Nothing there. Just have him stick around with the rest of 'em."

"We went through his waste-basket, Chief. Found a torn-up letter. Torn up mighty small. Henry Beall's piecing it together. Take quite a while. Part was burned. In the soap dish, I'd say. From the looks o' things, as if he'd started to burn it and then changed his mind and just tore it up. Or maybe he'd burned one page."

"Very good, Jim."

"How about arresting Stromberg, Chief?" asked Atkinson.

"I was thinking we'd better not. He can't get away. Better have him in again. Don't let him suspect we know a thing. Maybe we can snarl him up."

"I'd suggest a bite of lunch, Chief," said Atkinson. "It's after two. We've covered a bit of ground these four hours. Then we can take up Stromberg again, and Mrs. Cuppy. You'd better stir around, Miss Penn. Step outside if you want air. It's confining work." This assistant District Attorney was making it clear that he'd taken a liking to her. Odd

how quickly you always caught that undertone of
the personal in a man's speech and manner. She
was inclined to believe that the other men sensed
it too. Have to watch her step. You always had to,
with men around. She felt suddenly lonely. Easy
to grow pretty bitter about that sort of thing.

Dr. Obry reappeared. "Gentlemen," he said, "I
believe we can talk with Mrs. Cuppy this afternoon. But not all of us. Two or three at the outside. Miss Penn, I'm going to put you behind a
screen in the doorway of an adjoining room. You
must keep perfectly still. I shall carry a notebook
myself to cover what rustling you may be unable to
avoid. You see, gentlemen"—he was looking about
the circle, very gravely. For the first time Elsie
became aware of a tension among the officials . .
. perhaps it was that suggestion of limiting their
number . . . were they all, in a way, watching one
another . . . But Dr. Obry was talking on—"You
see, Mrs. Cuppy seems to me to be in a frame of
mind that may—I am not certain, but it may—
lead us into a worse tangle than anything that has
come up yet. I have preferred that you hear her
for yourselves and form your impressions at first
hand."

Elsie slipped out at that point. She couldn't
eat. Not just then. Her head ached. She couldn't
face those chafing, spiritually bedraggled guests
of the house. She wandered out through the *porte*

cochère and crossed the driveway to the rock garden. By dim pools and craggy little banks she
strolled. Over that almost semi-circular bridge.
Here was the stone bench where she had sat in
the evening. Here John Dane had spoken darkly
of some sudden, secret difficulty—"If I weren't in
such a ticklish situation here . . . the damndest
mess, just to-night" . . . why had he said that? Oh,
well, she wasn't responsible for him.

She saw him approaching. From the house. He
came on over the bridge. He'd ridiculed her when
she had told him she was the mental type. Well,
she'd show him. She could be a brisk enough little
person on occasion. She'd show him.

He stood before her. He looked older. He'd been
hurt. Of course. It isn't heartening to be arrested
on suspicion of murder. Even of thievery. Something sobering, haunting, about his gray eyes.

"I haven't the faintest notion what it's all
about," he began, in a slow, low voice. "But from
what those policemen have dropped, I've gathered
that nothing but some rather remarkable bit of
quick thinking on your part has saved me from
being rather seriously involved in this dreadful
case. I'm not going to ask what it was, but I must
thank you."

There was an odd moment, following that
speech, during which he appeared hesitant about
sitting beside her on the bench. He even rested a

knee on it, and then stood rather awkwardly. Just
stood there. He seemed to be breathing fast. So
was she. And she could feel her pulses in her temples, pounding. Her mouth was dry. He slid, with
a self-conscious, almost apologetic manner, down
to the seat. And then, dazed, she found his arms
about her and her hands clinging to his coat and
he was kissing her and she was crying.

He tore her hands away and sprang up. "Of
course," he said, unsteadily, "we're completely unstrung. We can't go plumb to pieces. Must keep
our heads until this dirty mess is straightened
out."

That was all he said. He went back to the house.

She knew her face was flaming. It wouldn't do.
She dipped her handkerchief in the pool below
and laid it on her cheeks and forehead. She was
angry. He needn't have rushed off like that!

PART III

8

The Chief and Dr. Obry stood in the *porte cochère,* each with a copy of a pink newspaper. The "Planet," of course. A journal that fed notoriously on murder and scandal, on any gross sensation of the moment. Elsie glimpsed headlines three or four inches tall; nothing else. The Doctor remarked that the latter part of the afternoon would be best for the interview with Mrs. Cuppy. Four o'clock or later. The Chief looked at him—cold eyes set in a face that was weather-beaten and was nearly square in shape, a massive, expressionless face—without a word. Dr. Obry hesitated a moment; then folding his paper with a slight motion of impatience, went within.

But the Chief spoke to Elsie . . . in a low, faintly wheedling voice that stirred surprise. A personal note, distinctly. She caught that, with a little flash of resentment. These men. . . .

"Mighty quick work," said he, moving the paper within her vision. "Wonderful how they do it. One of the motorcycle men brought 'em out just now." And he smiled, complacently.

She read: "HOUSE GUEST SUSPECT IN CUPPY MURDER—*Chief Urquhart Makes Sensational Disclosure—Brilliant Work By Local Police.*"

"Let me give you a tip, girlie," he went on, guardedly and still with that smile. "If you pick anything up, just slip it quietly to me. There's too many cooks on this broth. It's a straight police job. Don't let that fellow Atkinson get too close. He's just a politician and a publicity hound. And not the type for nice young girls to play with. A slick one, that fellow. Safest thing for you'll be to come straight to me."

Elsie inclined her head noncommittally and stepped within. She felt tired and wretchedly uncomfortable in spirit. How long was this miserable business to continue? How long must she serve these men? Not one among them a gentleman. Mr. Carlock, perhaps, you could trust; he was quiet and businesslike and impersonal. But the others—Mr. Atkinson, the Coroner, the Chief, stirred feelings of disgust. Fighting among themselves for publicity. Not much majesty of the law about it. And the newspapers already plunging into it as into some ghastly orgy. She'd heard and read of these travesties on justice. Her head ached. For a cent she'd run away from all of them, and from John Dane. She simply couldn't trust herself to behave rationally in this appalling atmosphere.

Mr. Atkinson was at the telephone. He turned to say quickly, "I'd like to speak with you, Miss Penn. In the Chinese room. I'll be there in a few minutes."

She nodded and went on into the main hall. Had he seen that pink newspaper? She wondered. The Chief had stolen a march there. And was grinning like a pig.

She had to pass the wide doorway that gave into the living room. At a table near the door four of the unhappy guests were playing bridge. Miss Eames lay wearily on a couch, with Mr. Ettlethwaite sitting beside her. Mr. Delos, at another table, was playing Canfield. Stromberg stood in the bay window, staring out. That Gargoyle person roamed about the far end of the room drawing gloomy, deep-toned themes from his violin. With his bow he seemed to be giving voice to the oppressive horror of the day. The tremolo notes throbbed in the air. One or two of the card players looked around impatiently. A man called, "Oh, shut up!" But the Gargoyle played on.

Mr. Ettlethwaite saw her, there near the doorway, and started up. She moved away. She didn't

want him or any of them talking to her. But he
came hurrying out. She didn't like his nose-glasses
with their pendant double tape of black silk, or
his loose bow tie, or his drink-bleared eyes, or his
air of self-conscious vanity.

"Really, you know," said he, in a confidential
tone that stirred resistance in her, "these boobs are
making an awful mess of this thing. They ought
to consult with me. All this is right up my street.
Perhaps you've read my mystery stories, 'The Trea-
sure' and 'Number Thirteen.'"

She hadn't, so she didn't say anything; merely
looked at him. She must control this feeling of
hostility. Her nerves were on edge, naturally. But
it was nothing to her.

"I know who committed this murder."

Still she was silent.

"It was that Chinaman Sin. A dozen bits of evidence point to him. He hated old Cuppy. And he
wanted that cap. Find Sin and you settle your case
in an hour. If they'd just consult me . . . the first
move must come from them, of course . . ."

"I'm sorry," said Elsie. "I'll have to ask you to
excuse me." And moved off down the hall.

Mr. Atkinson was still at the telephone. She
glanced into the dining-room. Mr. Wong was in
there, sitting alone at a window, a small, crushed

figure of a man. Impulsively she entered the room. He didn't look up until she reached his side.

"Mr. Wong," she asked, "I heard you say that the man Sin used to work for you."

"Oh, yes."

"Do you think he would commit murder?"

"Sin? Oh, no, Miss! Sin good boy. Very good boy." Curious how he pronounced his "r's." He didn't say "velly," not quite, yet the "r's" bothered him. He went on, in his patient, broken way. "Nobody so honest, so faithful, as good China boy. Sin good boy."

"Thank you," said she.

He resumed his moody watch out the window. Elsie returned to the hall.

There she met Mr. Stromberg. His narrow eyes fastened on her. "I'm going to ask a favor," he said, quick and low. "I've been thinking over what I told them. Will you ask if they will be so good as to hear me again? I have something more to say."

"Certainly," she replied, moving off. But he caught her in a quick stride. "I saw John Dane follow you into the garden. If I were you, I wouldn't let him talk to me. Very smooth, this Dane. But they're not through with him yet. He's in deeper than you or they know. You will see. You're too nice a girl to . . ."

What was the matter with these men? Did they think her responsible for the case? She went into the Chinese room. The Doctor was there, and Mr. Carlock, and the policeman they called Mike. The Chief and the Coroner appeared, and took their seats at the table. The Coroner was smoking a big cigar, twisting it about with unpleasantly mobile lips. Then Mr. Atkinson came rushing in, with a copy of that pink newspaper which he spread dramatically on the table. His face wore a strained, white look. He glared at the Chief, who glared back—solid, square-faced, complacently impassive.

"This is your work," he said, with heat. The Chief merely looked.

"Build yourself up all you like," cried Atkinson, "but show me just one more such leak as this and I'll make you all the trouble you want. You're asking for it, and you'll get it."

Elsie noted Carlock's thoughtful eyes on the two men. The Chief still took it without a word. You couldn't tell what was in his mind. "He's as inscrutable as those Chinamen," thought Elsie.

"Do you propose," Atkinson, "to have the newspapers running this case for us?" Then, with a little snort of impatience and a muttered, "Just try it once more! You'll see!" he flung himself into his chair.

There was a long silence. Dr. Obry tapped nervously on the table.

Elsie caught her breath, then said timidly, "Mr. Stromberg asked me if he might come in here again."

They all looked at her.

The Coroner spoke quickly, around his cigar. "Look here, Miss, you're not letting any of these people draw you into talk about the case, are you?"

She couldn't help flaring up at that. "Certainly not!" He might at least take that cigar out of his face when he talked.

"Let's have him in now," said Carlock. "We've got an hour or more before we go upstairs." He glanced at Stromberg's overcoat, which lay on a chair.

"Put that coat in the den," he said to the policeman.

The European took the seat at the foot of the table.

"You have something further to say?" asked Carlock.

"Yes." The narrow, quick eyes flitted about from one stern face to another. The man had, undeniably, considerable distinction. Many would think him handsome. He knew places and people. He had lectured widely. "Yes. I was greatly troubled when you called me before. I really did not know what to say to you. Of course, I was not under oath."

The Coroner removed the cigar now, as if to make a blustering remark.

"We quite understand that," said Carlock, courteously but quickly.

The Coroner flicked off a long ash on the silken rug—an exquisite piece of weaving in creamy gray and pale rose—and replaced the cigar in his mouth.

"You wish now to correct your statement?" asked Carlock.

"I do. I feel that I must tell you the whole truth."

"That we must have, Mr. Stromberg."

"Certainly. I realize it now. No matter what the implications may be. No matter whom it may hit."

"Certainly."

"I gave you to understand that I went upstairs when the others did, at two o'clock."

"And that was not accurate?"

"No. I evidently fell asleep on a couch in the living-room. They must have left me there when they went up. At least that is where I found myself."

"At what hour?"

"It must have been almost exactly two-twenty. I remember looking at my watch when I did get upstairs, and it was two-twenty-five then. Evidently I had hardly more than fallen asleep. Something awakened me. I do not know what it could have been. But I found myself lying on the couch. The room was dark. I remember that I distinctly heard some one moving. Something. I felt alarmed, got up at once and tiptoed to the door. Then I realized that there was light in the hall, some light, not very strong. I peeped through the portières— that is, I stood beside the doorway and moved the curtain away a little. The door to this room, the Chinese room, stood open. A person was in the hall, somewhere near the front door. I couldn't see him then. But after a moment he came back to this door, reached in to switch off the light, closed the door, and went upstairs. At that moment, before he switched off the light, I saw him as distinctly as I see you gentlemen now. He was in bare feet and wore a bathrobe. He had a pocket-knife in his hand, which he closed and dropped into the pocket of his bathrobe just before he switched off the light. Then he tiptoed upstairs in the dark."

"How do you know he tiptoed? You could see him?"

"No. I mean that I could hear him moving very slowly and carefully."

"You recognized the man?"

"Yes."

There was a pause. Elsie's nerves were taut again. Her temples felt as if they would burst.

"Who was it?"

"John Dane."

There was a long silence. All Elsie could do was to sit motionless. But crazily, as a confusion of uncontrollable thoughts raced through her brain, the phrases ran through them, "He's nothing to me! Absolutely nothing! Absolutely nothing! I simply don't care!" Meanwhile she was writing on. Her trained hand did that, mechanically. At least they weren't watching her. They were watching Stromberg. All but Mr. Carlock. She looked up once, and caught his eyes on her.

"What did you do then?" Carlock pressed on.

"I went up to bed."

"You heard or saw nothing that might throw any direct light on the murder?"

"Nothing. I didn't dream of such a thing. But this morning, after breakfast . . . if I may go on . . ."

"Do."

"Well, after breakfast I went out into the hall to get my pipe from my overcoat pocket. I felt some-thing bulging in the skirt of the coat. I couldn't think what it might be. It was away down inside the lilting. I felt in the side pockets. You see, I couldn't imagine how it could have got down in there. There were no holes or tears that I knew of in the lining. Even then I didn't think of Dane. Really, I hardly remembered the experience of the night. It was like a confused dream. But I felt in the breast pocket and found that it had no bottom. It had been cut. I reached down inside and felt a curious object. I couldn't make out what it was until I drew it partly out and saw that it was the Manchu cap. I found myself completely bewildered. Then I grew very angry. If I had met Dane at that moment I should certainly have struck him. I took the coat upstairs to my room. I couldn't make the thing out at all. Why Dane should go to the trouble of stealing the cap only to hide it in my coat was and is a mystery to me. No small part of my bewilderment was due to the fact that it was difficult to imagine Dane doing such a thing. I'd never dreamed he was that sort. He is, or had seemed to me, an attractive and decent person. Certainly a most plausible person. Oh, of course, I'd observed certain things . . . little things . . . but . . ."

"What little things?"

"Well, really . . ."

"Having gone this far, Mr. Stromberg, I'm sure you will readily see the importance—to yourself, if to no one else—of coming clean. If you are thinking of sparing the feelings of others, let me advise you that we are far past such a point. We must have every ascertainable fact, every fact, no matter where it may lead."

"Well, of course Dane has been living in the house for a week. He is known to be attractive to women. Well . . ."

"You imply that a woman is involved in this. What woman?"

"Oh, not in this. I know of no connection. But . . ."

"But what? We have no time to waste, Mr. Stromberg."

"Well, I think that all of us in the house had noticed that something was going on between Dane and . . . well, Mrs. Cuppy. Something had been going on, before we arrived. It was very noticeable."

"An affair, you mean?"

"I had no means of knowing how far it had progressed. It was simply noticeable. Miss Eames saw it right away and spoke of it to me. Mr. Ettlethwaite mentioned it in a way suggesting that he took it as a matter of course. Others hinted and smiled over it."

"I see. But you have found nothing in that which might tend to explain why Dane should steal the cap and hide it in your coat?"

"As to that, sir, I must confess myself completely baffled."

"What did you do when you took the coat up to your room this morning?"

"Well, I have admitted that I was extremely angry. I knew then, of course, of the murder. I was horrified at the thought that Dane should play such a ghastly trick on me. At the moment, in my anger, it seemed simply an issue between myself and him, whatever he might have been up to. I knew that he was downstairs. I went in through the bathroom we use in common to his room and put the cap in the closet there, behind a spare blanket. If you have not already searched the room you will find it there. Unless he has moved it. It was wrong of me, of course. But he had planted it on me. I planted it back on him. To get even, I suppose."

"Not an unnatural impulse, of course. What did you do next?"

"I came back downstairs."

"Where is the pipe you got from the coat?"

"Here." He produced it from a side pocket. "Why had you left the pipe in your overcoat?"

"Because I had smoked it while driving out from New York. Naturally I didn't smoke it at the party last night."

"I see. Where is the overcoat now?"

"In my room. At least, I left it there."

Carlock turned to the policeman. "Go up to Mr. Stromberg's room," he said, "and bring his overcoat down. Don't go through the hall. Go through the den and use the back stairs."

The officer went into the den and closed the door.

"Now, Mr. Stromberg, why didn't you tell this story in the first place?"

"I hardly know. I was still angry and very confused. I simply couldn't think clearly. The implications were more than I could comprehend. At the moment, I felt a horror of possibly throwing suspicion on Mrs. Cuppy. And even then I couldn't face the possibility of John Dane being implicated in a murder. Probably, too, I shrank from becoming entangled myself. I'll admit that. It looked like a very difficult sort of thing to explain. Since morning, however, I've cleared it up in my own mind. I realized perfectly that my course this morning was not the right one. But now I have no business considering myself. I place myself entirely in your hands, gentlemen."

"You are willing to sign and make oath to the truth of the statement you now make?"

"Certainly. I will do anything that may help to clear up this dreadful business."

"Thank you. Now as to your own relations with Mr. and Mrs. Cuppy. Have they always been pleasant?"

"Oh, perfectly. Why, they were my greatest benefactors. To them I owe everything."

The officer returned at this point with the overcoat. Stromberg exhibited the cut pocket, and all gravely examined it as if they'd never seen it before.

After that, Stromberg was excused.

9

The Coroner looked at the Chief. Both inclined their heads.

"We'll arrest Dane," said the Chief. "Hang on to him this time. And lock up Stromberg and Mrs. Cuppy as material witnesses."

"Just a moment on that," said Carlock, "if you don't mind, Chief. We've got them all here. They can't get away. What can we possibly gain by showing our hand?"

The Coroner removed his cigar, spat toward the fireplace, and spoke. "Funny he'd force that drawer. He was the one that knew how it opened."

The Chief glanced at him, and snapped out, "Cover. He's just the one that would."

Atkinson, who still wore an angry expression, asked, leaning toward Carlock with an air of rather ostentatiously ignoring the Chief, "Any report yet on finger prints?"

"I've talked with Lieutenant Estivier over the phone," replied Carlock. "He seems to think it's going to be pretty difficult."

"Why?"

"He has found too many. Dane's, I suppose—he must have left them when he opened the drawer for Miss Penn. Probably hers too. Perhaps Mr. Cuppy's. And more, I gather. It wasn't cleaned or dusted this morning, of course. Likely as not the man who forced the drawer wore gloves. He would have, unless he was an utter fool. Or even wrapped his handkerchief around his hand."

"How about the hatchet?"

"That didn't go in town until later. I have no report on it."

Dr. Obry, at this point, entered the room from the den. His appearance gave Elsie a start. She hadn't seen or heard him leave the room. So deeply, so terribly, had Stromberg's story absorbed her.

"I think we may talk with Mrs. Cuppy now," said the Doctor. "But it seems to me my duty, as her physician, to warn you again that unless the interview is conducted with the greatest consideration I cannot be answerable for the consequences. Mrs. Cuppy lies at the threshold of utter prostration. Naturally the shock of this murder has been a crushing one. Realizing that you might find it necessary to question her I have felt I had no right to give her an opiate or any drug that would stupefy her. As a result, while she has drowsed a little during the morning, her brain is still abnormally active. She is far from herself. But we may as well get it over with. I must urge on you, however, the importance of sparing her as much as possible. If, that is, her feelings and her extremely nervous condition are to be considered. It is quite necessary that I should be present. It would be much the best thing if only one other accompany me. I am sure, with Miss Penn taking down her statement word for word, you will all have the picture."

The Chief, without a trace of expression on his big, blocked-in face, rose deliberately to his feet. "I will go," he said.

Instantly Atkinson sprang up. "I must insist!" he cried. "As the only representative here of the District Attorney's office, it is my duty!"

Then the Coroner got up, without a word. Plainly, he meant to be present.

Carlock rose last, gathering up some notes he had been jotting down. "I'm sorry, Doctor," said he, "but it looks as if we'd all have to go. I'm sure, however, that every effort will be made to handle it quietly."

Dr. Obry spread his hands in submission. He looked slowly from man to man. But the Law had spoken. He was helpless.

"We'll take the back stairs," said the Chief; and led the way into the den, clumping heavily in his thick-soled boots. You saw that he wouldn't know what it meant to show consideration for anybody. The four others trod lightly.

Elsie went out into the hall. She wasn't going through that den.

They were still playing bridge in the living-room. And the Gargoyle's violin still throbbed like a doom. She ran up the stairs.

She heard a step. This as she reached the landing, exactly at the spot where, in the morning, she had encountered Stromberg carrying his overcoat. She looked up. It was John Dane, coming down. She decided, in a crazy flutter, not to speak. Simply to rush by. But instead, she stood motionless. Her knees were almost giving way. And her cheeks flamed. She caught at the railing. She felt all soft inside. She'd be crying if she didn't watch out. Mustn't do that. Those men . . .

Dane stopped. She heard his low voice. She couldn't look at him—simply couldn't—but his voice sounded tired. Did he know or suspect the sinister web that was weaving round him? Pity surged in her breast. "Just one thing." This was what he was saying. "Just this one thing. Please give me your home address."

"I live with my aunt." She said that. It wasn't an answer, of course.

"Where? I must know! Where?"

She simply couldn't speak. Couldn't frame another word. Her body sagged. With an effort she ran weakly on up the stairs. At the top she faltered, and with fumbling hands dabbed some powder on her face. Then, with another effort, pulled herself together and went along the hall to where those five men were standing in a silent group. The thing to do was, at the first moment possible, to escape. Get out of the house, off the place, away from this swamp-like air. Here you could hardly breathe. It was a spell that wove hideous dreams into your waking thoughts. Once back in the city she'd shake it all off. John Dane, too. All of them. "Why," she thought, impatiently, "I don't even know the man! Don't know a thing about him."

Dr. Obry was waiting to take her into the secret place he had prepared for her. But before she tiptoed into that adjoining room she saw a policeman come up the hall and hand the Chief a folded paper; saw him open it, look it over in his wooden way, and put it into an inside pocket of his coat.

The physician left her. Went back to the hall. She slipped noiselessly into the chair that had been placed in a doorway behind a screen. She

could hear Mrs. Cuppy turning restlessly in bed
and breathing hard. A woman's voice made a sooth-
ing remark; the nurse, doubtless. Then the door
in the sickroom opened, and the five men filed in
and took chairs, the Chief clumping heavily. She
could see them as they came in. And when they
were seated she could see Dr. Obry, Mr. Carlock,
Chief Urquhart and the Coroner. Mr. Atkinson
was hidden by the screen.

Mrs. Cuppy was crying now; sobbing in an uncomfortably spasmodic way, very low.

10

Elsie, still trembling, held her pencil poised. "After all," she told herself, "it's a lot better to be
kept busy, even in this awful business, than to sit
helplessly about like those others downstairs."

What were they waiting for? The hush was
painful. It seemed to run with a prickling sensation along your nerves. She heard that Coroner
clear his throat. The woman in the bed turned and
sobbed.

Then Carlock spoke. In a kindly, low voice.
There was something of the gentleman in that
State police official.

"We are extremely sorry to disturb you, Mrs.
Cuppy. I assure you we will be as brief as we can.

But there are a few questions we must ask." The
sobbing swelled out a little louder. There was a
distinct touch of hysteria in it. Curious, in a way.
You could understand sorrow, the crushing hand
of tragedy. But this was an ungoverned woman.
Beside herself. Surely she hadn't loved that hulk
of a husband so intensely. Why, she couldn't have!
Carlock pressed on, quietly enough, but firmly.
"Will you try, please, to tell us when and how you
came into possession of the Chinese cap?"

Mrs. Cuppy was slow to answer. She made one
or two false starts, still weeping uncontrollably.
But finally she cried out, "I don't know! My . . .
my husband gave it to me!"

The voice had none of the rippling, cooing
quality that Elsie had noted in it at their first
meeting. It was a broken, shaky voice, hoarse from
the paroxysms to which she had been surrendering
herself.

Now, abruptly, she screamed, "Where is my
secretary? Why hasn't she come to me? She's a sly
girl! She stole that cap!"

"We have the cap, Mrs. Cuppy," explained Carlock. "But we must learn how it came into your
husband's possession. Do you know? Try to think
clearly."

"Oh . . . how can I . . . he bought it."

"Can you tell us from whom he bought it?"

"I? How should I know?"

"Did he bring it out from New York?"

The woman merely sobbed.

"It was a common thing, was it not, for the Chinese merchants to come out here to show their wares to Mr. Cuppy?"

Another outburst of grief. Then, "Yes! Oh, yes! Of course!"

"Was the cap brought out here in that manner, by one of the regular merchants? By a man with whom he was in the habit of having dealings?"

"I think so. How should I know? I wasn't there, I tell you." Then, a thought more steadily, "He bought it for a surprise for me. I wasn't there."

"He told you nothing about that side of the transaction?"

"No! No!"

"He didn't tell you how he bought it, or from whom?"

"I tell you, no!"

"And he didn't mention how much he paid for it?"

"Of course he didn't! It was a present!"

"Then you know nothing whatever of the transaction?"

"Haven't I told you I don't? Why do you ask me these questions? Why do you come in here like this?"

"I'm sorry, Mrs. Cuppy. I'm sure we all are. But it is our duty to ascertain the facts. Now will you tell us, please, exactly what you did with the cap last night, before you went upstairs?"

"I don't know what I did! I will not be questioned like this! Who are all these men, Doctor? Why did you bring them into my room? Send them out!"

"They are all officers of the law, Mrs. Cuppy." Thus Dr. Obry. "I'm afraid I have no power to send them out."

"Just a minute." This was the Chief, speaking for the first time, in a hard, raspy voice. "You don't remember asking Miss Penn to take care of the cap?"

The sobs began again.

"Answer me! You had been drinking, had you not?"

Elsie, startled, looked up. The Chief was leaning forward, his stony eyes fixed on the wailing woman behind the screen. Carlock was watching him, his lips compressed.

"He's torturing her," thought Elsie. "How awful!"

"Really," Dr. Obry put in, "I doubt if it will be of any use to . . ."

"Be quiet!" The Chief's voice suddenly took on body and force. "Isn't it the fact, Mrs. Cuppy, that by that time in the evening you were too drunk to know what you did or didn't do?"

Elsie, horrified, looked up again and saw Dr. Obry's shoulders twitch in a sort of shiver. But he merely clasped his hands tightly on his knees and stared down at them. He was, as he had intimated, helpless.

The Chief drove remorselessly on. Elsie thought fantastically of a grim gray warship stripped for deadly action. "Tell me this, Mrs. Cuppy, were your relations with your husband pleasant or otherwise?"

Dr. Obry's shoulders twitched again. But he didn't lift his heavy eyes.

The sobs swelled into a sound not far removed from screaming. But the Chief raised that big voice of his. "You are perfectly able to answer me. These hysterics aren't going to get you anywhere. Not anywhere at all. I'm going to stay right here until you make up your mind to drop this non-sense. Answer me! Now or later!"

A chair moved. There was a step. Atkinson appeared within Elsie's range of vision, standing over the Chief, sternly.

"This can be done at some other time," he said tartly.

The Chief ignored him. "Mrs. Cuppy, did you love your husband?"

There was a breathless hush. Dr. Obry, looking up now, at last, stared unhappily. The sobbing and sniffling started up again. And she wailed, "Oh, yes! He was the dearest, the most generous man that ever lived! We were utterly happy together! He lived only for me and I only for him!"

"How long have you had John Dane here?"

Another hush. Then a sudden scream that froze Elsie's blood. And a rustling sound, as if the woman were sitting up in bed. And a queer soft pounding. Was she beating a pillow? "Is that man still in my house? Throw him out! I won't have him here!"

"And why won't you have him here?" the Chief thundered.

"He's a monster! He had pursued me! I had to tell my husband! He gave me no peace! He tried to compromise me! He outraged my hospitality! My husband ordered him to leave the house this morning! Why is he still here? I won't have him here! Throw him out!"

This was screamed out incoherently, broken with sobs and hysterical quick intakes of breath. Then more screaming, and that frantic pounding sound. And Elsie wrote it down. Or her hand did.

"So you loved your husband dearly?"

"Oh, yes! Yes! Always!"

"And John Dane annoyed you?"

"He did, I tell you! He did! He did!"

"And you didn't respond to his advances?"

"How dare you suggest such a thing!"

"Wait just a minute now! Wait just a minute!" Deliberately the Chief drew that folded paper from the inside breast pocket of his coat. Spread it open on his big knees. Quite as deliberately removed a pair of spectacles from their case and put them on. Atkinson was still standing over him—in an almost threatening manner—and he had to look out around the thinner figure of the assistant District Attorney to glare (over his glasses) at the woman.

"If you weren't inclined to respond to John Dane's advances then why did you write him this note?"

"I never wrote him a note! Never! Never! Never!"

"You not only wrote it, but you weren't so drunk but what you had a pretty good memory of it this morning. That's why you're staging this dramatic scene. Thought you could throw us off the scent by accusing Dane, did you? . . . You wait a minute, now. I'm going to read it to you. You listen to me! Sooner or later you'll listen! Here, now, is the cool little note you wrote last night to the man you despise—'John you darling' . . ."

There was a sudden scraping of chairs. All the men sprang up excepting the Chief. He sat motionless, with the faintest imaginable flicker of a smile on the wooden face. . . . "She has fainted!" Dr. Obry's voice. "Lower her head! Quick!"

"I wouldn't worry, gentlemen." The Chief, dryly. "She'll come round when she's made her point. After all, we're in no great hurry. Let her play her scene out."

Atkinson came back at him. "If I were you," he said, in a suppressed voice, "I'd watch my step. You can't get away with this third-degree stuff. Not with people like the Cuppys. You'll find yourself in some pretty damned hot water first thing you know. But then"—he spread his hands—"you've spilled the beans already."

The Chief looked up at him now. "I'll take care of the beans, Atkinson. And I'm not asking your advice. I've got her. Got her cold . . . There! See? She heard me. Really, gentlemen, you better just lay her on the bed. And you just sit down. I'm going to read you this letter. Don't worry about her. She'll hear it, all right. She'll hear it."

He readjusted his spectacles and turned the paper toward the window. "'John you darling— Come to my room to-night. It's perfectly safe— Old Cuppy'll be snoring his stupid head off downstairs—I'll leave my door ajar—oh, I'm crazy about you—Crazy—Crazy—Crazy—Hazel' . . . It's just scrawled, you see, in pencil. Must have scribbled it the minute she got upstairs. And either took it or sent it to his room, for that's where we found it. And it's all here. The paper Dane burned must 'a' been just the envelope. Then he likely thought that was going to look pretty messy so he just tears up the note, very small. But we got it. And it's all here."

Through all this there was not a sound from the bed.

"Well," said Atkinson acidly, in that same suppressed voice. "I've warned you. You can't handle rich and influential people the way you'd handle a bum off the street. Likely it'll cost you your job. Anyhow, it's not our business, this stuff. Even if there was a little of this sort of thing going on. Rich people do these things. You can't do anything about that. It may mean something and it may not, but for God's sake . . ."

"Not our business? Then what is our business?"

"To find the murderer or murderers of Jonas Cuppy."

"The murderers of Jonas Cuppy are in this house." Impressively he said that. And complacently. Suddenly then, with an agility astonishing in so large a man, he sprang up and pointed at the bed.

"There!" he thundered. "See that? She moved! She's heard every word of it!"

The silence that followed this bellow came upon them like a stunning force. Elsie pressed a hand to her breast, struggling to breathe.

From the bed came a faint whimpering.

PART IV

11

The five men filed out into the hall. Mrs. Cuppy was whimpering on. The nurse stepped methodically about the room, moving chairs.

The door behind Elsie opened, slowly and very softly. She turned with a start of something near panic. Luckily she made no sound. Funny, her hand was pressing, almost painfully, against her breast. And her toes were curled tightly within her shoes.

It was Mr. Carlock. Uncertainly Elsie smiled. Might as well smile. He was beckoning. Very carefully she slipped out. And in that same cautious way he shut the door. The other men must have gone directly back downstairs; they were not in this upper hall. She walked with Mr. Carlock toward the stairs. It was odd, but the situation had taken on so intense an air of drama that it had begun to recede a little way (but a very definite way) from

reality. It might almost have been framed within
the proscenium of a theatrical stage. Certainly,
at the present moment, moving slowly along the
hall with this very quiet-spoken Mr. Carlock, she
didn't feel as if she had the slightest personal part
in the tragic mess. She might have been sitting
in an orchestra chair looking on. Pretty soon the
act curtain would drop, and she would stroll out
to the foyer and chat with friends. "I suppose,"
she thought, "I'm fed up. Something snaps then,
somewhere in your nervous system, and you just
automatically relax."

Then a thought she hadn't known she was entertaining flashed out in indignant words that
were real enough for anybody. She stopped short.
"Mr. Carlock, Mrs. Cuppy said she didn't know
anything about how the cap came here."

He stopped, too, and fixed his thoughtful eyes
on her. "Yes, she said that. Isn't it true?"

"Certainly not."

"How do you know?"

"She told me. Told me all about it. Listen! I
can give you almost her exact words. It was that
first evening . . . when was that? . . . last night?
Funny, it seems years ago." She didn't know she
had caught Mr. Carlock's sleeve tightly in her fingers. "She said this . . . I was looking at the cap,
you see; she had it on . . . she said—'You know,

my dear, it didn't come to us through the regular channels. Two strange Chinamen drove out here one evening in a flivver. Imagine!' . . . She said just that. And then, 'They had the cap wrapped up in a newspaper. And my husband tells me he bought it for a song. He is still chuckling over it. Some strange dark story there. Most fascinating.' And this—'It would bring not far from a quarter of a million at auction. And I'm sure my husband didn't pay twenty-five thousand.' . . . You see, she knew perfectly well that it was stolen. Oh, do you think those thieves might have . . . have committed the murder?"

"Not likely." How cool he was. And how quietly impersonal. Now she saw her hand on his sleeve and removed it. "You see, they got their money. They'd hardly stick around here. For one thing, they'd be afraid of those other Chinese, the war party. Their lives wouldn't be worth three cents. Most likely they're in Mexico by now."

"But why shouldn't Mrs. Cuppy tell the truth?"

"She knows how valuable the cap is. As stolen property it would have to be returned to Ting Pao."

"She didn't act last night as if she cared about it. The way she was throwing it around. She even gave it to me. Actually!"

"She wasn't sober then."

"Oh! No. That's true."

They were going on down the broad stairway
when they heard some one running down after
them. Carlock turned. It was John Dane. She saw
that he carried a letter. And she saw somber eyes
in a white face. Then her own eyes fell.

"I beg pardon, sir," he said. There was an intent, almost burning note in his voice. "I have
written a note to Miss Penn. Have you any objections to my giving it to her?"

"Certainly not, Mr. Dane."

Again she felt that softness within. And again,
she knew, the revelatory color was flaming hotly
in her cheeks. She appeared to have simply no defense against the emotional appeal of this man . . .
"John you darling!" So Mrs. Cuppy had written.
A wild new sort of anger surged in her breast.
She couldn't speak. Yet it was all she could do to
keep still. For a cent, right in front of this police
officer, she'd turn on John Dane and give him a
piece of her mind . . . But she mustn't . . . Not a
word. . . . Hotly she decided she wouldn't touch
that note. Wouldn't have anything to do with such
a man. He was nothing to her. Nothing. If she
could only get away. Only have a chance to think
. . . to breathe. . . . She took the note. It shook in
her hand. And then John Dane ran on down the
stairs and disappeared within the living room.

Vaguely (her tired confused brain was racing so crazily) she knew that Mr. Carlock led her down and around behind the stairs and into the den. She couldn't very well refuse to go in there. Anyway he couldn't make her look down at the rug where that awful . . . she shivered.

He was speaking. "I'm going to ask you to read that note, Miss Penn."

Fumblingly she tore the envelope. Her eyes were filling, making it difficult to see clearly. She found her handkerchief, and somehow read:

This I must say to you. You have every right to think me a trifler. I am not. You enchanted me last night. Today, without that costume and make-up, as your honest little self; you have enchanted me even more. I don't know about love at first sight. Perhaps that's just rot. I simply don't know. I'm all mixed up. I do know that you are honest and real and simple and adorable. One doesn't find so many real people nowadays. And I know you're not the sort to be let loose in this ugly world. I know this, too—I've got to square myself for the way I seem to have begun with you. Won't you give me that chance? Oh, I'm head over heels in love with you! You wouldn't give me your address. But I'll find you—somehow— the minute we get out of this frightful mess. And I'll show you—I've simply got to find a way to show you—that I'm decent. I've got to have a chance. Maybe the police will give me your address. They're friendly enough with me now, thank God! Overnight I've come to realize this—that I'm going to put up a fight for you. I've got to. We're the same sort. Why, good God, we can't be together two minutes without flaming up! It must mean something.

Oh, I know this is just a crazy, incoherent note. For God's sake, let me know where I can find you! I will find you! I *will!*

And anyhow, it's a relief just to write this. I'd rather write it than say it. I want to be put on record. I want to be tied. I don't know what love is—it's a lot of different things, I suppose, with different people—but whatever it is, I've got it. And I'm going to win you if I can. But first I've got to win your respect. That's my job now. I must.

JOHN DANE

To Miss Elsie Penn.

She was crying. She moved to a window.

Mr. Carlock spoke. "It is my duty to ask you, Miss Penn, if there is anything in that letter that might bear on the case."

She couldn't answer; could only twist the paper in her hands.

"Your own position, I'm sure you realize, is rather delicate. If it were found that you were in private communication with any of the guests in the house I'm afraid you'd find yourself in pretty serious trouble."

She thrust out the crumpled note. He took it and read it.

That phrase about the police blazed in her brain . . . "They're friendly enough with me now, thank God!" . . . He knew nothing of his present terrible danger. Chief Urquhart came to mind—strong, stony, implacable, rushing like a beast of prey to the kill. She saw again his complacent grin when he'd read his own name in the headlines. She couldn't so much as pass a friendly warning. Not a word.

Mr. Carlock returned the note. She stood, every nerve in her body taut as a bow-string, folding and refolding the paper into a compact little square.

She shivered again. A thin querulous voice that appeared to be her own remarked, "It's getting cold."

"I'm afraid," said Mr. Carlock, glancing out at the long late-afternoon shadows, "that nobody's thinking about heating the house."

"If you don't mind"—her own voice again—"I'll run up and get my coat."

"I'll come with you," said he.

So! She, too, was to be watched. The thought hurt. She wouldn't so much as speak to John Dane. Or would she? How could she tell what she might do? They went up the back stairs together. Mr. Carlock stood at the door while she was in her room. She got her coat from the closet and slipped it on. She put the note in a capacious side pocket of the coat; then drew it out again and kissed it passionately. But she caught herself. "No sense in blubbering like a baby," she thought; and rejoined Mr. Carlock. Together they went down. And all the way her hand, deep in that pocket of her coat, clutched John Dane's wadded note.

Mr. Carlock spoke of it, on the stairs. "Shall you be sending him any reply, Miss Penn?"

She was flushing again. She'd simply have to get hold of herself, somehow. She must speak quietly. But she couldn't. Her voice broke out hotly, "Certainly not! Why, I don't even know the man!"

"If you should," said Carlock, in his grave, even voice, "I must warn you to be extremely careful."

That angered her. What was he, after all, but another of those policemen!

In the Chinese room the other officials were in their chairs about the table. Dr. Obry sat with his head in his hands. Once, when he lifted it, she saw that he looked gray and old. Chief Urquhart sat firmly, massively upright, like a wooden idol. Mr. Atkinson was speaking angrily . . . "So you're doping it out as another Snyder case. Well, you're wrong. It's not so simple as that. Not by a damn sight!"

The Chief didn't so much as look at him. He sputtered on for a moment or two, then sat back sullenly.

The Coroner spat on the rug.

Mr. Carlock, slipping quietly into his chair, reached for paper and pencil to jot down a few brief notes. Two beams of yellow light streamed through the western windows and illuminated the cabinets against the opposite wall. The policeman called Mike walked over and raised the blinds. His heavy step was the only sound. Elsie's gaze roved, nervously alert, about the treasure-house of a room. Those beams of amber sunlight, alive with millions upon millions of dust-motes, gilded the ivory carvings, glinted upon the figurines in rock crystal, lighted prettily the green and rose and

tawny and creamy mutton-fat jades. On a carved
and lacquered green table, over in the corner
by the fireplace, lay the pearl cap, still casually
rolled up in that bit of newspaper. Nobody, passing through the room and glancing at it, would
give it a second thought.

Faintly, beyond the closed door and the hall,
came the throbbing sound of a violin, playing
eerie, monotonous strains with hardly a trace of
what a policeman or an assistant district attorney
or a coroner could be expected to recognize as
a tune. The sustained tones fell unpleasantly on
Elsie's nerves. She shivered. And then she saw that
Mr. Atkinson was twisting in his chair and tapping with his long fingers.

Mr. Carlock spoke. At the first sound of his
quiet voice, all started as if he had broken a spell.
"Dr. Obry," he said, "you examined the body, of
course."

The physician, roused out of his painful, bewildered reverie, lifted his head and replied with
a simple "Yes."

"At what hour would you put Mr. Cuppy's
death?"

"Well"—Dr. Obry cleared his throat—"It must
have been about a quarter past nine this morning
when I first saw the body. At that time he couldn't
possibly have been dead more than four or five

hours. Everything considered, I would put it not earlier than between four and five o'clock."

"Could he have lived for any time after the attack?"

"With his head crushed in like that? Hardly. No, death must have been very nearly instantaneous."

"You would fix the moment of death, then, positively, as later than four o'clock?"

"Yes."

"Thank you."

The violin drew nearer. Just outside, in the hall. Throbbing on. Suddenly the jumpy Mr. Atkinson banged a fist on the table and cried out, "Stop that noise! Officer! You! Tell that bird if he doesn't lay off I'll break his damn fiddle over his bald head!"

Mike stepped out into the hall. Abruptly the music stopped. Voices sounded near the closed door. Angry voices. Then, as abruptly, the violin began again, right outside the door; in a minor key, deep, penetrating; utterly mournful and musically aimless wanderings up and down the G-string; but much louder and with a more intensely vibrato throbbing.

The policeman stepped quickly within and leaned against the door. That lugubrious, deep-toned wailing filled the room. To Chief Urquhart the officer addressed himself. "Do you wish

I should adopt rough methods, Chief? He says, 'To hell with the District Attorney! What does he think he is'—he says—'a critic? Tell him we got one in the house already'—he says—'and that's too many!'"

That Gargoyle person was scraping off chords now, very loud chords, of a cacophonous modernistic sort. Atkinson sprang up, shoved the policeman aside, and flung the door open. There stood the queer little bald-headed musician with the long nose, scraping away, thrusting it upon them exactly as a naughty child might have done; grinning with an angry leer, his eyes staring and rolling. It wouldn't surprise you to see him stick out his tongue. Elsie's toes were again curling tightly within her shoes. There seemed to be, in the man's appearance as in his music, something deranged, something perversely, primitively violent, something almost maniacal. Perhaps he'd committed the murder. Why didn't they think of that?

But Mr. Atkinson merely snatched the violin, thrust the sputtering musician away, slammed the door, and dropping the instrument on a chair resumed his seat, breathing heavily.

The Coroner muttered, "Crazy as a bedbug, that bird!" And spat.

And then Chief Urquhart announced, grimly, with one huge hand spread flat on the table, "We're going into conference now. Dr. Obry, we'll excuse you if you don't mind. And you, Miss Penn."

12

Elsie walked along the hall with the Doctor. In the living-room those bridge players were still at it. Mr. Delos was playing Canfield; unaware, of course, all of them, of that dreadful scene in Mrs. Cuppy's room, as of the present grim conference. The actress still lay on the sofa, wearily, with Mr. Ettlethwaite still seated beside her. Talking about himself, of course. John Dane sat alone near the bay window. Stromberg lay sprawled in a big chair. So much she caught in a fluttering glance.

"You'd better lie down until you're needed, Miss Penn," said Dr. Obry gently. "Those brutes are putting you through a terrific experience."

"I think I need air more," she replied wanly. "I couldn't sleep anyway."

They walked out into the *porte cochère*. "If I could only bring myself to realize what they're up to."

"It is terrible, Miss Penn. You do see, of course . . ."

"Well, I . . ."

"Chief Urquhart has his case nearly built." The Doctor's voice broke slightly. "He's going to accuse John Dane and Mrs. Cuppy of the . . . the murder. Oh, it's unthinkable! Why, I've known Hazel from the moment she was born! Admitting that she is a spoiled child, that she is wilful, that she has done foolish things . . ."

"Oh, they didn't . . . they never . . . I can't believe . . ."

"I've known Jim Urquhart a long, long time, too, Miss Penn. He's crude and rough. Sometimes he's stupid. But he's stubborn. And he's strong. Can't you see that he's in complete command of the situation? Atkinson is a child in his hands. A reed. Just a young fellow with a political job. And believe me, there's politics enough in this county. Plenty of it. That Coroner's nothing but a hanger-on. Used to run a livery stable."

"But Mr. Carlock, he's . . ."

"I've been watching for him to take hold. But he doesn't seem to. I can't make him out. As a lieutenant of the State Police he could really exert almost as much authority as he might choose. You see, he has the State behind him. And he is widely known as an expert in these cases. He and that sergeant of his work a lot with the District Attorney's office in the city. New York. George Carlock—the name even—carries weight. Authority. These local men usually feel that. But I can't make him out."

"Mr. Urquhart"—Elsie broke out nervously with this—"the Chief, he's working for himself!"

"Oh, yes."

"He's after the publicity!"

"Yes. And he would be. Jim is ambitious politically. I know that. And it's the publicity I dread most."

"You mean . . ."

"Don't you understand, Miss Penn, that this story is going to burst out in the papers to-morrow morning? Jim Urquhart will see to that. Trust him! And once the story breaks—Hazel and John Dane, her lover, accused of the most sensational, really the most important murder in years—rich, important people, all that can't you see that once the story breaks they are ruined for life? The newspapers will simply crush Hazel. They'll hound her to death. I really think it will kill her. And as for Dane, where will he be? Whatever new developments may arise, his name won't be worth a snap of the fingers. He may as well go out to Tahiti and stay until he dies."

Elsie whirled on him. "Mr. Stromberg lied. He said it was two-twenty this morning when he saw Mr. . . . saw that . . ."

"Saw Dane in the hall?"

"Yes. He fixed it positively. Said he was up in his room at two-twenty-five. Yet you fixed the

time of Mr. Cuppy's death, just as positively, at a
time hours later."

"Hm! That's so! Your mind is keener than mine,
Miss Penn. I never thought of that. Why didn't
you speak out?"

"Oh . . . I guess I was just too worn out. Besides, Mr. Carlock got it. Why else did he ask you
those questions?"

"Even so, Stromberg's story will land with terrific force on a jury, I'm afraid. He tells it con-
vincingly."

"Oh, why doesn't Mr. Carlock *do* something!"

"I wish I knew, Miss Penn. As I tell you, I can't
make that man out. Well"—the Doctor sighed,
and then brushed off, with a tired hand, a few
beads of perspiration that had appeared on his
temples—"well, I must go up to Hazel." He sighed
again; stood a moment lost in his own tragic
thoughts. "The awful thing about it"—he was now
like a man so unnerved that he talks aloud to himself—"the horrible thing is that Jim Urquhart can
ruin Hazel . . . ruin them both . . . without even
approaching a conviction. The newspapers will
seize on the love affair, broadcast it, wallow in it.
There'll never be a chance to explain. Six truths
can't overtake one lie." Unsteadily he turned and
entered the house.

Elsie, hardly knowing what she was about, descended the steps and crossed the road toward the Japanese garden. Twilight was settling, but there were no lights in the lantern posts of carved stone. There was nobody about the place now to attend to such matters.

She mounted the high-arching little bridge. Leaned on the railing and looked down at the dim, lazy goldfish; but as she bent her head her eyes filled, and she couldn't distinguish much of anything in the dimpling water. Her mind was a jumble of queerly confused memories. Her hand, deep in the pocket of her coat, clutched John Dane's note. That man couldn't have committed a murder. Nor was he a thief.

Those policemen, back in the house, were the law. All the law there was. Blundering on. Politics. Publicity. Primitive, ruthless men fighting one another to build reputation and success on a foundation of broken lives. It was disheartening.

She heard a car in the driveway and turned. A State policeman sat at the wheel. She could just make out the straps crossing over the shoulders and the cap. A small figure of a man appeared from the house and entered the car. Mr. Wong. They were letting him go, then. Driving him into the city, probably. They'd better. He wasn't out of danger. Pure intuition told her that. In a curious way she was sorry to see him go. He was one man you could believe.

She descended the farther slope of the bridge. Here was the stone bench where she and John Dane had sat. Twice. Her pulse raced crazily. Again she found herself pressing a hand to her breast—her free hand; the other, down in that coat pocket, still held the note. Extraordinary the blunt power in Dane's hastily scribbled words. They'd had the force of a blow when she read them. It was a love letter. In her thoughts those words stung and glowed. Oh, why wouldn't life let her alone! That was all she wanted (she thought)—to be let alone.

She hurried past the bench, following the winding path along the brook-side. The twilight deepened. The heaped-up rocks, which had been placed with an apparent carelessness that was subtly art, seemed in the dusk like miniature shadowy mountains. There were mosses and ferns. Twisted cedars grew there and deepened the shadows. The house was out of sight now. The path led to a tumbled-up boundary wall of rocks and there twisted off to the left. She stopped, looking about. She didn't want to go back by that bench. Perhaps if she followed the path it would lead her back another way.

"Do you want to make fifty dollars?"

Elsie caught her breath. That crazy pulse was pounding against her temples. A man's voice. From nowhere, apparently. Low and cautious. She looked; frightened, but with every faculty almost abnormally sharpened. Her eyes searched the leafy top of the wall. At last, in the deepest of the shadows, she glimpsed a face.

"Don't be alarmed. It's all right. I'm from the 'Morning Earth.' Here's a note for Mr. Delos. And here's a fifty-dollar bill. Will you take the note in to him? That's all I ask."

A nightmarish feeling that she couldn't move had seized upon Elsie.

"Will you do it? Perfectly proper, really. Needn't involve you in the least. The local police are slipping everything to the 'Planet.' Getting good pay for it, too. It isn't on the level."

That was probably true enough. But she wouldn't speak.

"Then look here, if you won't take the note will you do this—tell him that if he can possibly get a story out here to me I can wait until half-past nine to-night. Until ten, as a last resort. Be right in this spot. Have a car waiting. Tell him it's Andrews—Ben Andrews."

Elsie found now that she could move. She turned and walked back. The voice died out.

By the stone bench she paused. Just stood there. If only she could think! But she couldn't. Her mind was a tangle of indecisions and memories, of the horror that hung over the day, of hurt pride and jealousy, and of an unnerving pity for John Dane. His kisses were still on her lips. They'd just flamed up, the two of them. He'd said that. It was true. She'd flamed too. A sudden bitter hatred of Hazel Cuppy surged in her breast like a pang. She'd made love to him. He was an artist. Sensitive, of course. A man of temperament. Elsie was mothering him now. She couldn't help it, however much it hurt. Even if he'd . . . whatever might have occurred . . . Oh, it was all that woman's fault! And now she was crying again.

She sat on that bench. A queer thing to do. But all at once she'd wanted to. Well, that was how it was!

Mistily she could see the dark shape of the house. It was lighted up within. Over the windows of the Chinese room, in the nearest corner, the blinds were drawn.

A man came over the bridge. Her nerves were on edge again. John Dane . . . No, that other State officer in citizen clothes; the one that had come with Mr. Carlock in the morning.

"Will you please come into the house, Miss Penn?" he said respectfully. "Chief Urquhart wishes to see you."

Funny, he knew precisely where to find her out here, in the dusk. Perhaps he'd happened to see her go into the garden.

13

Mr. Carlock sat at the telephone in the side hall; listening intently and jotting down notes on a pad. Elsie hurried by, and went on around the stairs into the main hall. Even before she reached the entrance to the living-room she heard voices . . . "One spade" . . . "Double" . . . "Two spades" . . . "Three hearts" . . . "Three spades" . . . "Four hearts" . . . "Double!" . . . How *could* they?

A policeman in the hall let her go into the Chinese room. She quietly resumed her chair. At least none of these men could suspect what was going on inside her head. Oh, perhaps Mr. Carlock . . . But what of it! She felt defiant.

Chief Urquhart stood by the fireplace, talking in low tones with the Sergeant. Elsie looked over her pencils. All needed sharpening. And her note-book was nearly full. She picked up another and broke the back so it would lie flat.

Mr. Carlock came in and dropped his notes of the telephone conversation on the table. After a moment the Chief returned to his chair.

"That was New York headquarters," said Mr. Carlock. "They've got a bit of news. Five of the Chinese servants have given themselves up."

"Is that all of them?" asked Mr. Atkinson.

"All but one. The butler, Sin, seems not to be among them."

The Chief asked crisply, "What's the story?"

"Their story, the servants', is that when they came downstairs this morning they couldn't find the man Sin. And he wasn't in his room. I gather that they were in some confusion over that. Sin was in the habit of giving them their orders for the day. Then the boy whose duty it was to clean up in the front part of the house discovered Mr. Cuppy's body in the den. After that they all ran away. Simply in a panic. Very much as Mr. Wong suggested. They say that they walked across country to Jamaica, caught a train to New York, and hid in the basement of a curio dealer on Pell Street. This afternoon they decided to surrender themselves."

"And you believe that?" asked Atkinson, with a sneer.

Carlock shrugged. "For the present. It is common experience that this sort of Chinaman, the regular domestic servant, is truthful and faithful."

"Even so, where is that butler . . . Sin? No, it's fishy."

"At the moment I haven't a notion where Sin is," said Carlock. "He may be hiding. He may be dead."

"Oh, then you believe in him, too!" Atkinson.

"I'm inclined to. Mr. Wong recommended him to Mr. Cuppy. I have not been able to pick up the slightest bit of color against him. What little data I have would appear to make him out a particularly steady and honest sort."

Atkinson kept at him, "And you trust this man Wong?"

Carlock looked steadily at the Assistant District Attorney. When he was ready he replied with the single word, "Perfectly."

Atkinson snorted. Lit a cigarette. With a beaten-back expression fell to scribbling notes.

Chief Urquhart brought down his big hand on the table. "All this is beside the point, gentlemen. We've got some real evidence before us. And we know where we're going." He moved his chair back and around, turning his massive front directly toward Elsie and taking her in with a firmly fixed gaze.

Elsie's wits fluttered. So it was, at last, her turn. She thought . . . she was still, it is to be noted, in that confused phase . . . "What's he up to now?" She tried to meet those cold eyes but couldn't quite. Nervelessly she fingered the pencils before her; twisting them about, then laying them side by side in a neat row. Not before, even during the scene in Mrs. Cuppy's room, had she felt the full strength of the man. At least it hadn't then come to her as a personal experience. The wheedling tone, that rather disgusting suggestion of the man-and-woman business, was gone. No foolishness now. He meant business. She could think of nothing but an enormous, tireless bulldog.

"Miss Penn," he began, in deliberately measured words (Oh, those eyes!), "you told us this morning of a talk you had with John Dane in the garden. I want you now to go back over all that. He was out there with you about twenty minutes, you said. A good deal can be said in twenty minutes. I want you to straighten it out in your mind and tell us everything he said. Everything."

Elsie sat motionless. If only she could *think!* As it stood, she couldn't. Not yet. . . . Was there anything she'd kept back? The very thought suggested that there was.

"What was the first remark he made?" pressed the Chief.

"Well, he . . . oh, he came wandering out there. I was sitting on a bench. He asked if there was room for another stray. I moved over on the bench and he sat down."

"Then what was said?"

"Well, I . . . oh, something, just talk . . ."

"What talk?"

"I think I made some remark about it's being beautiful there in the garden."

"What reply did he make to that?"

"Well . . . if I can recall it . . . oh, yes, he lifted his head up and sniffed the air and said something like—'If only it didn't smell of oil.'"

"Oh, he said that?"

"Yes, sir."

Elsie was doing pretty well, she felt. Talking evenly enough. Only Mr. Carlock knew that the Chief was beginning to torture her almost as savagely as he had tortured that wretched woman upstairs. Then and there she made up her mind that not one of those others should so much as glimpse the truth. Whatever the crazy truth might be. As for Mr. Carlock, let him think what he might. She couldn't help that. She saw clearly enough how closely he was watching her. But let him! There was nothing she could do about it. And the experience, whatever it might turn into, had to be lived through. Somehow.

"Then what?"

"I . . . I think I asked if the Cuppys were friends of his, and he replied that he'd never heard of their having any friends. I spoke of the guests in the house and he said that Mrs. Cuppy collected personalities and was always getting new lots and throwing them at each other. People lived off her, he said. Especially Mr. Stromberg. He said that he himself, I mean Mr. . . . Mr. Dane, didn't come out of friendship but for five hundred dollars."

"What did he mean by that?"

"The price of his services, he said. For doing that pastel portrait of Mrs. Cuppy. And that he was leaving in the morning." She was speaking more readily now. "Most of what followed after that I have already told you. He asked if I thought I could stick it out and all that. We talked a little about Mr. Cuppy then. I asked if he was always like that . . . I meant drunk . . . and he said, 'More or less. Always pickled, if that's what you mean. Oh, he doesn't always pass out.' It was after that that he advised me not to try to stay."

"Just how did he put it?"

"Oh, he . . . well, I remember his saying, 'I'm afraid you're in wrong here.'"

"Did he explain what he meant by that?"

"I don't think so. I don't remember. I'm really trying to tell you everything, but it isn't easy. To remember, I mean. I was pretty excited. I was dressed in a beautiful Chinese costume and my face was painted up and . . . and then I'd never been in a millionaire's house before and with famous people all around. I do remember that we talked a little about how you couldn't always choose your associations if you were working for a living."

"Was anything personal said? About himself and yourself?"

"Oh, a little, I suppose."

"Well . . . what?"

"Why, when we were talking about jobs, that way, I told him that I . . . that fortunately I was the mental type."

"What did he say to that?"

"He said, as I recall it—'Mental type? My eye!'"

"He must have said more than that."

"Well, only that he'd watched me when we were in the house and that I was just a . . . a romantic girl."

"Oh, he did!"

"Yes, sir."

"Go on. What else did he say about that?"

"Oh, nothing much . . . I mean . . ."

"What did he *say?*"

Elsie was fighting back the color again. This terrible man kept at one so! "Really, nothing much. You see, Mrs. Cuppy came just about then and . . ."

Mr. Atkinson broke in at this point. "Miss Penn, you have been in our confidence all day. We have had a right to assume that you are an honest, straightforward young woman. But you are raising doubts in our minds. You are keeping something back."

"Oh, no, Mr. Atkinson! Really! It's harder than you seem to realize to . . ."

"Oh, come!" boomed the Chief. "We know all about that. Speak out!"

"Well, I remember his saying that he was romantic and willing to admit it. And then he said that I wasn't safe anywhere here. 'Even with me!'" Her voice had dropped almost to a whisper.

"So! He said you weren't safe with him!"

"Yes, sir." What on earth were they getting at?

"Then what?"

"Why, Mrs. Cuppy came."

"I see. And that is all?"

"I . . . why . . . yes, I would say so."

There was a long, tense silence. No one moved; and she could feel their eyes on her. The strain was pretty nearly unendurable.

Suddenly the Chief's voice boomed out again. So suddenly that she jumped in her chair. A big voice with a merciless dry twang in it. "Now, Miss Penn, just one more question. When you were sitting on that bench with John Dane, discussing your romantic nature, did he make love to you?"

She couldn't, at the moment, forestall a low, quick, gasping intake of breath. The room seemed full of eyes. She began to cry. For just an instant the perversely impish thought popped up that she hadn't cried so much in one day since babyhood. What was the matter with her, anyway? Were her nerves just completely shot?

"Answer me!" thundered the Chief. "Did he, or didn't he, make love to you?"

"I . . . why . . . a little . . ."

"Speak up! Louder!"

"Why . . . a little . . . I . . ."

"Oh, he made love to you a little. Now just what do you mean by that?"

"I d-don't know."

"You don't know? That's peculiar. Did he take you in his arms?"

"I don't know . . . I—guess so . . . I . . ."

"You guess so. Hmp! Then he did take you in his arms?"

"Y-yes."

"I see. He took you in his arms. Did he kiss you?"

Elsie summed all that was left of her sadly scattered native sense and character. This man was, of course, simply breaking her down. A little healthy anger came unexpectedly to her aid.

"Did he kiss you?"

Elsie looked straight up at him, wiping her tears away, and said, firmly enough, "Yes."

"Very good! He kissed you. You permitted it?"

No answer. But she was still looking at him.

"You knew, at the time, of his affair with Mrs. Cuppy?"

"No! I did not!"

"But he had told you, bluntly, that you weren't safe with him. You made no attempt to leave when he said that?"

"No."

"Very good. That is all, I think."

The tension broke. A chair scraped. Carlock, who hadn't uttered a word (in a confused way she felt a flicker of gratitude for that) set to work on those interminable notes of his. The Coroner spat and lit a fresh cigar. Elsie slumped back in her chair. She even felt a measure of relief. It might, after all, have been worse. There was nothing shameful in an honest kiss, whatever unpleasant construction might be put upon it by the vile minds of these men. She hated them all. Loathed them. Even, in a measure, Mr. Carlock. He might (she thought now) have stopped the odious probing. He hadn't lifted a finger.

This was the moment, a grave but distinctly relaxed moment, that Chief Urquhart chose to whirl on her. Really to take her breath away. Speaking rapidly, in a sort of roar.

"We have your word that you've told us all of it—everything that might bear, even remotely, on the case?"

He caught her in a moment of exhaustion, completely off her guard. She bit her lip. Looked about her in a sort of panic. A little color crept into her wan cheeks.

"Ha! I see! You haven't told us!"

"Oh, but I . . ."

"I see! All but a few really important little things that you'd just as soon we didn't know about!"

"Oh, no, Mr. Urquhart . . ."

"Come out with it, then! He said something else. What was it?"

Elsie nerved herself. She was caught. Her small hands gripped the sides of her chair. She wouldn't tell them an out-and-out lie. She couldn't do that. Again she looked straight up at him. And now there was a glint of something like steel in hers. It is doubtful if the Chief saw it. She looked very tired, very frail.

"Mr. Urquhart," she said, "it is really difficult to reconstruct a fairly long conversation. Especially if you had reason to be excited and confused at the time. Besides, I'll admit that my emotions have been stirred. We can't help these things. Of course, I haven't wanted to tell these intimate happenings. And I haven't wanted to tell things that might help you to build your outrageous trumped-up case against Mr. Dane."

"You dare say that? You've been here, all day, completely in our confidence, hearing all the evidence and . . ."

"Yes, I dare say it."

"So you've deliberately held out on me! Like a crook!"

"No." Wearily she explained. "Not deliberately. If you knew just a little about human nature you'd understand that people who feel deeply, people who are torn with emotions they can't understand, don't always think straight. I told you everything that came into my head this morning." She sighed. "But I suppose, with all of us, there are times when the heart keeps a good deal of what it knows from the head."

"Are you trying to tell me I don't know my business?"

"I'm perfectly sure you don't." (Was there, just for an instant, a faint twitch at one corner of Mr. Carlock's mouth?)

"Well, I'll be damned!" roared the Chief.

And Elsie, more than a little beside herself now, flashed straight back at him with "I'm perfectly sure you will."

14

Before he could sputter out a reply to that inspired thrust, Mr. Carlock took quick command.
Indeed, for the first time all day he showed what
he might be when he chose. "Miss Penn," he said
briskly, "just what was that one further remark of
John Dane's?"

"It was after he warned me that I wasn't safe
with him. The rest of it was—'If I weren't in such
a ticklish situation here . . . the damndest mess,
just to-night . . .' That was all. There was just a
foolish word or two. Really nothing. Then he—
kissed me. I heard somebody and made him stop.
It was Mrs. Cuppy. You've had the rest."

Her heart had known vaguely that this admission must damage John Dane in the eyes of these
heavy-handed officials. But she hadn't thought it
so important as it now seemed. The effect of the
quietly uttered words was electrical. Even Chief
Urquhart, who was still apoplectically purple
about the neck, sat up with a jerk. Mr. Atkinson,
convinced at last, stared. The Coroner dropped
his cigar and had to pursue it, puffing hoarsely,
about the rug.

"You're very sure that that was all, Miss Penn?"
This from Mr. Atkinson, hot on the scent.

"Perfectly sure."

"He gave you no inkling as to what lay back of the remark?"

"No."

"You had then no notion as to what he meant?"

"No. Not then."

"Later?"

"Yes. I know now."

"Oh? You know now what he meant?"

"Certainly. Mrs. Cuppy was after him like a crazy woman. He was in a very embarrassing position. He couldn't quite slap her face. Just as he can't try to save himself now by attacking her character. A situation like that must be extremely difficult to a man who happens to be a gentleman. Mr. Stromberg, I presume, was an earlier lover of Mrs. Cuppy's, and that would be a complicating . . ."

"And just why do you presume that?" snarled the Chief.

"Because she prefers to keep him in Tibet." At this point she met Carlock's eyes full. There was understanding in those keen eyes. But also a hard aloofness. Even he wasn't a man to confide in.

The Chief banged the table. "This is enough!" he bellowed. "Young lady, we won't trouble you for any more of your opinions. We're here to deal with facts."

Elsie promptly got up and went over to look at the marvelous carved jades in a wall cabinet.

"Better bring Dane right in here," whispered the Coroner. "Put him through the hoops. Sweat it out of him."

"Not here," said the Chief, more complacently.

"Why not?"

"Because the sergeant took him over, half an hour back, and put him right where he belongs."

"Locked him up?"

"Sure. I've got him this time and got him good."

Elsie's eyes widened, but she didn't look around.

"What's more"—still the Chief—"I'm going down there right now and give him the God-damndest riding he's ever even heard of. Yes, sir! When I get through with that bird high hats'll be worth about two for a nickel."

Elsie stood rigid; but didn't turn.

"We'll all go," said Carlock, in his brisker voice. Promptly then, full of it, they all gathered up hats and coats, stuffed their various collections of notes into their pockets, and left. A moment later she heard two cars drive off.

She walked quietly over and sank down into her chair. Thinking. In swift blinding flashes. That man Sin kept popping into her mind. He knew something. If he was alive. Mr. Wong would help.

He'd be back in his New York home soon now. And there was the one they called Ting Pao. The pearl cap belonged to him.

The policeman called Mike was edging over toward her. She didn't look up. If something could be done . . . something quick, sharp, decisive . . . she glanced at her watch; not yet seven-thirty; amazing! . . . there was still, surely, at least four hours in which to forestall that terrible blow in the morrow's papers. . . . Down, in the town police station Chief Urquhart would soon, any moment now, be hammering at John Dane, breaking him down, breaking him down . . . oh, didn't she know! . . . Her right hand felt gropingly for that boyishly outspoken letter of his, deep in her coat pocket. Her left, as if to distract attention from its fellow, played among those pencils.

"You mustn't take it too hard, Miss." Mike, who had, now you came to think of it, been bursting with speech, was breaking out at last. "He's rough, he's hard as nails, Jim Urquhart is, but believe me, Miss, he's got the heart of a child beating in his breast. The heart of a child . . . Couldn't I point up them pencils for you, Miss? I see a sharpener in the next room."

"Why, thank you, Mike. It might help."

He gathered them up. Moved toward the door. Paused. Struggled for a moment with a choking, nearly silent laugh. "I was just thinking, Miss. You sure did toss him a couple of hot ones." After which brief tribute he went into the den, and the door swung to after him.

Up to that moment Elsie, though she knew that she was going to do something and do it with all her feverish might, had seen no clear way. But now her quick eyes rested on the paper parcel in the corner. The pearl cap . . . Mr. Wong . . . Ting Pao . . . Sin! A queer, confused train of thought. She got up; stepped lightly out into the hall. The living room was empty. Of course! They'd be eating. She went around to the *porte cochère*—walked right out. She wouldn't sneak. They could stop her if they wanted to. She crossed the road and picked her way through the dark garden to the end of the path. Spoke, guardedly, "Mr. Andrews."

He was there, waiting.

"I want you to take me to New York," she said. "Don't worry about your story. Before the evening's over I think you'll have all you can handle." A nervous, soft laugh came. "In fact, you're in it."

PART V

15

"Where is it you wish to be taken?"

Elsie jumped. Mr. Ben Andrews had thrown an arm over the back of the front seat and was looking around. He spoke respectfully. Rather good looking, he was, with an air of being a bit of a personage in his own circle. A big youngish man, with quite a lot of black hair bulging out beneath the brim of his hat. The other, a wizened little person, rather older (with a face like one of those queer caricatury fish in the Aquarium), drove the car. Dimly, casually, she seemed to know that the fish was named Phil. . . . Funny! Yes, the pair of them had talked together a little, in the front seat. But they hadn't disturbed her. She was curled up alone in the rear, sitting on her foot; and the foot was asleep. Funny, that fish-person. He was silent now, but she recalled a husky, croaky voice that went perfectly with the face. Her right hand kept pressing deeper and deeper into her coat pocket, down against John Dane's letter.

"Why? We're not in already? My word, it's the Queensborough Bridge!" Her voice sounded natural enough. Fortunate, that, for her brain was a crazy tangle of racing wild thoughts . . . the obscene picture of that murdered man on the floor of the den—Mrs. Cuppy sobbing and pounding her pillow—the pitiless energy of Chief Urquhart—the tortured look in John Dane's eyes and the sting of his kisses on her lips—the crushing threat of the morning papers, only a few quick hours away—testy, bored people playing bridge— the throbbing gloom of the Gargoyle's violin— goldfish in a shadowy, dimpling stream . . . exaltation was hers, and terror, and a confused dread, and an unreasoning, fighting instinct to carry on. Time enough to slump when the job was done.

The car sped down through the plaza at the New York end of the bridge, crossed the Avenue, and stopped at the curb in Sixty-First Street.

"Well," asked Ben Andrews, "how about it? What now?"

"I've got to find Mr. Wong at once," said Elsie. Funny, she couldn't conceivably have explained herself, yet there was something in the back of her head, something firm and strong (almost like another personality that she didn't know very well) that appeared to understand precisely what it purposed doing.

"But he's back there at the Cuppy house."

"No. They let him go. A policeman drove him. He must be home by now. Better stop some place and telephone his house. He'll surely be in the book. Tell him Miss Penn must see him at once. Must."

She saw the two of them exchange a quick glance when she gave her name. Of course, they'd all figured in the afternoon papers. But it didn't matter.

It was Ben Andrews who went into the glaring white drug store on a corner. She watched him elbowing his way through the crowd at the long soda fountain and entering a mahogany booth. She held her wrist watch around to the light. A minute . . . two . . . three . . . five . . . Why didn't he hurry! . . . Out he came. If he knew what she was living through he'd run. She felt irritated. That was silly, of course. There was no time for personal emotions. As there was (confusing, this!) no time for anything else. Here he was!

He stepped into the car, slammed the door, and mopped a wide and rather pleasant forehead. "Well," said he, as if thinking aloud, "what do you know about that!"

"About *what?*" cried Elsie, tapping an impatient foot.

"It wasn't easy to talk with that Chinese servant. But I made out that Wong had telephoned he'd be home almost an hour back. Hadn't appeared. They were worried. I had me a hunch then, called the paper, and got the story. Our man at police headquarters phoned it in. Some men in another car attacked Wong out near Woodside. Crowded his car off the road and shot it up. As a result, Wong is on the danger list at the Long Island City Hospital. The cop who was driving him was shot through the left wrist. He got his gun out and put up a fight. Drove 'em off. They probably mistook him for a chauffeur. They got clean away, of course. And that, Miss Penn, appears to be that."

It was a blow. Elsie sat motionless. Nice little Mr. Wong! . . . But that other personality was stirring restlessly in the back of her head. "Tell me," she broke out, "have you ever heard of a man called Ting Pao?"

"Ting Pao? Sure! He has a curio store on Mott Street, with a big restaurant upstairs. The boys from the paper eat there quite a lot."

"Would he be there now?"

"Almost certain to. These big Chinese fellows never stop working, you know."

"Chairman of the New York Committee of the Chinese Nationalist Party," croaked Phil. "His name's been up in this case. The police questioned him this noon, but didn't hold him. He couldn't or wouldn't tell anything. Quite a responsible man, you know."

"Please go there!" said Elsie.

A wide, bright stairway. An enormous room, lighted in red and yellow and blue. Chinese chairs and tables in exotic filigree work, inlaid with glistening nacre. A cashier's desk that suggested the five-and-ten. Walls of incongruous blue-and-white tiling. Queer white people dining; couples that eyed each other couple guardedly. A nickel-in-the-slot piano grinding out a current jazz tune. Soft-shod Chinese waiters with cropped, bristling heads. Ben Andrews asked for Mr. Ting. Finally he came, a short, stout man; shorter and stouter than Mr. Wong. Younger, apparently. More vigor. Shrewdly quiet eyes in a round strong face.

The reporters waited for Elsie to speak. She did so. "I have something very important to talk over with you, Mr. Ting Pao," she said. "Will you be so kind as to take us somewhere where we can't be overheard?"

If Ting Pao had been a white man you'd have said that he hesitated. But in his case hesitation is not quite the word. He simply stood motionless, looking at them, taking them in. The nearest

thing to a flicker of expression on the round face
had been the first look he gave the two reporters. You sensed that he knew them. Elsie glanced
quickly at her watch. But Ting Pao was unhurried.
Finally, in his own good time, and still without a
word, he led the way to a private room and closed
the door. They sat about a square black table with
a marble top and with carved legs and sides inlaid
with that characteristic nacre.

"Well," asked Ting Pao—to Elsie's surprise in
easy, natural English—"what can I do for you?"

"I," said Elsie (and it was startling to sense how
firm was her purpose and how clear her words, for
that conscious region she had always supposed to
be her mind was still at the mercy of those crazily confused, racing memories and thoughts) . . .
"I am Miss Penn, Mrs. Cuppy's secretary. I have
had a strange, really a terrible experience to-day.
I discovered Mr. Cuppy's"—a very brief pause—
"body this morning. Since then, all day, I have
been helping the police officials by taking down
in shorthand all the testimony of the people in
the house." It was beginning, already, to be a long
speech, but it all had to be said. The reporters
were watching her with a puzzled interest. And
Ting Pao's slanting eyes with the drooping lids
never wavered from her face. How still he could
sit!

"So it happens, Mr. Ting Pao, that I have had to pay close attention to every detail of the case. I suppose I—well, I know all that is known about it." Here, for an instant, her breath caught. She didn't know what Chief Urquhart might at this moment be doing to John Dane in that country police station! "I'm not going to talk about that. I was acting in a confidential capacity, and have no right to. But I have also talked privately with Mr. Wong. Last night, very late, he came out to the Cuppy house to get the pearl cap. You know something about that, I believe."

Ting Pao didn't move.

"Well," Elsie went on, with a quick little touch of vehemence, "I do." . . . She seemed to be speaking in the manner of those police officials. Funny! A good deal of Mr. Atkinson and Mr. Carlock; something actually of Chief Urquhart. Evidently she hadn't for nothing spent the whole day sensitively, even morbidly, absorbed in that inquisition. It had done something to her. Had done this. . . . "I know that it was shipped to you as head of the Nationalist Party here in New York. It was stolen, however, before it reached you, and sold to Mr. Cuppy. I don't know your attitude toward Mr. Wong. His life was threatened, you know. And this evening he has been shot and perhaps killed." She watched the round face, but ever the eyelids were motionless. Though he simply couldn't have known. "He had been asked to help, Mr. Wong had. He had already given money to aid your war in China. Now he was asked to find a buyer for the pearl cap. It was natural that he should be asked. He is a very influential merchant. But the cap never reached him, because it never reached you. It must have reached New York, because it was sold to Mr. Cuppy several days ago. By the thieves, undoubtedly. Those men got their money, and escaped. But the men who killed Mr. Cuppy and the men who shot Mr. Wong haven't escaped, and they won't. You see that. No Chinese could leave the city to-night without being seen and suspected.

"The first Mr. Wong knew of all this was last evening, when he was threatened, by telephone. He came out at once to try to buy the cap from Mr. Cuppy and deliver it to you. He offered his whole personal fortune. I know this, because I am the one he talked with when he came. I have heard his story and I believe it. I am sure that Mr. Wong is not a thief. He never hired thieves to steal that cap. I am convinced that he has the interests of your party as deeply at heart as you have. He was as anxious as you, as anxious as Hung Lo in Shanghai, to convert that wonderful cap into money to help your armies. He knew, too, that there was no time to be lost. Do you agree with me?"

There was a long silence. But at last Ting Pao spoke. (Elsie had made up her mind that she could sit as patiently as he.) . . . "I don't know," he said. "I don't know anything about all this."

"Forgive me, Mr. Ting Pao, but that isn't fair. I am laying my case before you as frankly as I possibly can, and for a reason. I'll give you that reason in a minute. But I do hope you will decide to be as frank with me."

"But I don't know what you mean. I am sorry."

"You knew about the cap."

"I have a letter from Hung Lo in Shanghai and a telegram from San Francisco. Two men, the telegram says, are bringing the cap. It does not come."

"You knew that Mr. Wong had been told of it."

"No."

"I am sorry . . . you did. It was you yourself who asked him to sell it for the party."

Another silence. "And you know, Mr. Ting Pao, exactly who you did and didn't talk with about this cap. Don't you see what I mean? *You are the only one that did know!* You had the letter and the telegram. You asked Mr. Wong to undertake the sale. Very well, then, it stands to reason, doesn't it, that the men who threatened to kill Mr. Wong when they found that the cap had been stolen, must have heard of it from you? You know, then, who threatened Mr. Wong, what man or men."

"No."

"Yes. And you know who is really responsible for the attack on him to-night."

"No. I don't know."

"Wait a moment, please! I don't want you to misunderstand my purpose in coming here. I'm not representing the police. I'm not here to get you into trouble. I'm here for a definite reason, and I've got to win you to my view of the situation if the thing can be done. These gentlemen are reporters, but I think you know them and I believe you can trust them. I'm going to make you an offer, Mr. Ting Pao. An offer that I hope will make you think it worth your while to help—to help justice, to help prevent a tragic blunder from being made by the police. Listen! You know all about this cap business. You must! I don't believe you're a murderer. You know Mr. Wong. You must believe him to be a man of honor. Tell me, do you trust him or don't you?"

Silence. Finally, "Oh, yes. Wong and I are old friends. He is an honorable man."

"Certainly. I haven't known him quite twenty-four hours. But I know I could trust him. You, too, Mr. Ting Pao, are spoken of as an honorable man. You have a business. You are respected. I believe, if you will let me, I could trust you as I would trust him. But first you must be frank with me."

"But I don't know."

Elsie sighed. She didn't catch the fact that those searching eyes of the two reporters were now studying her pallor and the red spots on her cheeks. That person in the back of her head was keeping mercilessly at her, driving her on. She glanced at her watch.

"Let me see if I can't make it easier for you," she said. "You are really in a position that makes it just about impossible for you to admit anything. To say anything, even. I find I have something of the picture in my mind, pieced together from things Mr. Wong has said. I'm sure that neither you nor Mr. Wong would have anything to do with either thieving or murder. But there are men in your party councils, here in New York, who are a lot more excitable than you and Mr. Wong. The great march of the Southern armies has driven them half wild. They cannot always be controlled. Perhaps they are frightened, too. Perhaps they didn't mean murder. But they did mean to get that wonderful cap, and sell it, and hurry the money out to Shanghai. Probably they can't control their people. And now that it has resulted in one murder and perhaps two, they don't know what to do. Is that a fair picture of it?"

Silence.

"Listen! To-night the police, I know, are about ready to accuse two persons of that murder. Two innocent persons. One of them is simply incapable of doing such a thing. The other is a gentleman. It is unthinkable that he could be guilty. There is some circumstantial evidence. They can never be convicted. Never in the world. But if the story that country police chief has to tell, because he wants the publicity—no other reason, just that filthy hunger to push himself—if that story appears in the papers to-morrow morning those two persons will be ruined. Are you willing to sit here and let them be ruined?"

"But what has all this to do with me?"

"By keeping silent you are shielding the real murderers."

"Oh, no! I am not doing that!"

"Wait, Mr. Ting Pao . . . you know who these firebrands are. You know all about Chinatown. Don't forget that Mr. Wong was threatened last night and shot to-night. You know who you've talked with about this cap. And you know exactly how they feel. So I say, by keeping silent you are shielding murderers."

Silence. It lengthened. Elsie looked at her watch. There was a breathless sense of drama in the room.

Suddenly Ting Pao dropped his head into his hands.

16

"You know, don't you"—Elsie, thrusting her argument home—"that some of your Chinese people went to the Cuppy house last night to steal back that cap?"

Slowly, wearily, Ting Pao lifted his head. In that long moment, her nervously alert faculties caught the abrupt change in the round face. It actually appeared to have lost its fullness. There was a haggard look. He settled back, like an utterly tired man, in his chair. His plump but strong hands fell nervelessly across his thighs. He raised those hands a little way as if to make a gesture of protest; but let them fall again.

"I will tell you," he said, in an unsteady voice. "I do not know all that you think. But it is true that I am in a terrible position. It is true that some of our people seem to have lost their heads. I don't know who stole the cap from the two messengers. I am sure they themselves had no hand

in such a crime. The cap was taken from a handbag, here in Chinatown, the night they arrived.
So they have told me. Now about the murder of
Mr. Cuppy. I do not know who killed him. It may
be, as you say, that he was killed by men of my
race who went out there during the night to try to
recover the cap. And I do not know who attacked
Wong. I have no idea. But there has been great
trouble in our Committee—the New York Committee of the Nationalist Party—over the loss of
the pearl cap. It represented such a large amount
of money. I have known that there were men on
the Committee who did not look at this trouble
through my eyes."

A croaking voice sounded. Elsie started. Up to
now not a word had come from the reporters. "Mr.
Ting, tell us, did you hear any threats against
Wong in the Committee when the theft was being
discussed?"

Another of those silences. Ting Pao considered
the fish-faced one, then turned his gaze deliberately back to Elsie. "No," said he, "I heard no
threats. Nothing so strong as that."

"But"—the croak persisted—"you heard suspicions voiced?"

"Yes."

Elsie leaned forward. "Just a minute, please!
Mr. Ting Pao . . . I want to tell you what is on

my mind to do, and to try to persuade you to do. Listen! Do you know a man, a servant, called Sin? That is the only name I know. Just Sin. He was butler at the Cuppy house. Before that he worked for Mr. Wong."

"Yes, I remember Sin."

"If you have read the papers you know that the Chinese servants all disappeared early this morning. Well, five of them gave themselves up this afternoon. All but Sin. The truth appears to be that they found the body and simply ran off in a panic. During the day they thought better of it and returned. Their story is that they haven't seen Sin at all. He had vanished before they came downstairs this morning. Nobody knows where he is, or whether he's alive or dead. Mr. Wong assures me that he's an honest, faithful man . . . Now, Mr. Ting Pao, Sin, if he is alive, knows something about that murder. Perhaps he saw it. I believe that he was carried away by the murderers. I simply can't get him out of my mind. I mean, after listening all day long to the stories of those people, after writing down every word, every single detail, until it all seems to be etched into my brain, I come back to Sin. If we can find him we'll learn—something. It may be only a hunch, but I believe it. I feel it so strongly that I'm going to make you a proposition."

Ben Andrews shifted his chair nearer. Mr. Fish-
Face sat, elbows on the marble top of the table, his
almost chinless face propped between two skinny
fists, his pale eyes staring. Elsie herself was grip-
ping the edge of the table with both hands.

"I realize," she went on, "that perhaps you cannot do what I'm going to ask you to do, without
running some real risk yourself. You have to deal
with hot-headed, terribly excited men. But if you
refuse to do it you will be in the position, as I
have said, of shielding murderers."

"No," said Ting Pao, brokenly, "I will not do
that."

"I suppose you don't know, now, where this Sin
is."

"No, I do not."

"But you know Chinatown. If he is, as I believe,
shut up there somewhere, you could find him."

"Yes. I believe I could."

"Remember, Mr. Ting"—this was another eager, excited croak—"the police couldn't find him
in ten years. Not if he's locked up underground in
Chinatown."

"No. I don't believe they could."

"Then," pursued Elsie, before Fish-Face could
croak again; she didn't want him talking . . . "then
here is my proposition. Find Sin. Now. Right
away. I've got to keep ahead of the newspapers.

Find Sin. You will know where to go, whom to ask. Give me your word that you will deliver him within an hour, alive and able to talk, and I believe I can put the pearl cap into your hands."

"When?"

"That I can't say exactly. The cap has been found. The police have it. If, as I believe, Sin can clear up this mystery, the police will restore it to you. Isn't the chance worth taking?"

A long silence. Then, "Yes." Ting Pao rose. "I will have to go myself. Oh, five minutes, ten minutes. Not long. I must not telephone. You will please wait here." And he left the room.

Fish-Face sprang up and paced the floor. But Andrews tap-tapped on the table. Tap-tap-tapped. "Miss Penn," he broke out, "if I had my hat on I'd take it off right now and make you a low bow. That was a wonderful job! An amazing job!"

Elsie shook her head. She couldn't talk about that. Her eyes sought her watch. They felt strained and tired. It took an effort to focus them on the watch. Specks of light were dancing round the edge of those eyes.

She started and shivered, with a low sound of fright. Some one was pawing at her from behind. It was Fish-Face, groping for her hand. He wrung it; hurt it; turned away. He didn't speak. The exaltation that had inspired her, driven her, carried her, was dying out. It had been like a performance, like a highly pitched scene, played under terrific stress. Now it was over. That other personality that she'd felt she didn't know very well had possessed her. It was fading now. Leaving her alone with herself and two reporters in a back room of a Chinese restaurant. She'd be crying in a minute. Just all unstrung. But she couldn't humor her weakness. The job wasn't finished yet.

How those precious minutes were clicking away!

A step sounded in the passage. The door opened. Ting Pao entered. "He is here. Not far.'"

"Sin?"

"Yes. Ten minutes and I will get him. They will give him up."

Ben Andrews rose. "Need any help, Mr. Ting?"

"No. It is best that I go alone. Sin has been hurt. His arm is broken. But I am assured that he can travel."

Elsie had been struggling to speak. Now some of her voice came.

"You are giving me your word, Mr. Ting Pao?"

"Yes. I am giving you my word."

"You will bring Sin no matter what the cost? Even if they try to kill you?"

"Yes." He sighed. Wiped a beaded forehead. Then, with a quiet "Wait here, please," went out again.

Elsie dropped her head on her arms and sobbed. She didn't see or hear the whispered words that passed between Ben Andrews and Fish-Face. But the latter moved to the door. She caught that. And the door suddenly opened; and a voice she knew remarked crisply, "What's going on here?" Mr. Carlock! Here!

Ben Andrews called, "Why, hello, George! You're just in time!"

The croaky voice husked out something or other . . . "Just going to get her a bracer, George. All in, poor kid. But Jesus Christ! Believe me, George! She's . . ."

"Get aromatic spirits of ammonia, Phil!" Carlock's voice, low, authoritative. "None of this bum liquor!"

17

Mr. Carlock, seated at the table, stirred the faintly opalescent fluid. The spoon clanked in the glass. He had sent the reporters out into the restaurant and closed the door. "Here, Miss Penn, drink this. It will buck you up."

She lifted her head. Dried her eyes. Pushed the glass away. "No. I don't want it."

She looked at him, and he at her. Her spent nerves were rallying, as they had rallied under

Chief Urquhart's probing. That fatalistic strength was returning. Once again she was beginning not to care.

"So!" said he. "You ran away."

"No. I walked."

"Why?"

"Because none of you were doing anything."

"You know nothing about that."

"I know enough. You—even you—were going to let that awful story go out in the morning papers."

"About Mrs. Cuppy and John Dane?"

"Yes."

"But what did you think you could do?"

"I rather think I've done it."

"Indeed? Well—suppose you tell me just what it is you've done."

But Elsie, white now, and calm in a tense way, slumped back in her chair, was thinking. She came out with this: "How did you find me?"

"Really! You didn't think you could wander around without being seen?"

"Oh! You mean I've been watched?"

"Certainly. Every minute."

"Every min . . ." A touch of color fluttered in her cheeks. Those crazily mixed memories again. That moment in the garden with John Dane!

"Every minute. Since ten o'clock this morning. My instructions to Sergeant Stafford were to permit you to move about freely but not to let you get out of his sight. He obeyed literally. Almost too literally. When you asked Ben Andrews to drive you into the city, he simply jumped on his motorcycle and followed you. You came here to Ting Pao's. He telephoned me. So much for that. Now I'm going to ask you to explain."

"Well"—she had to pause in a desperate effort to arrange her thoughts—"well, I think I just felt that something had to be done, and done quickly."

"How did you get away? Where was that officer . . . Mike?"

"He'd gone into the den to sharpen my pencils."

"I see. And you walked out."

"Yes."

"I notice you didn't stop to get your hat."

"I didn't stop for anything."

"But where did you pick up these reporters?"

"Mr. Andrews had spoken to me earlier in the evening. When I was walking in the garden."

"Hmm! I see. That explains something Stafford didn't quite get."

"He offered me money to take a note to Mr. Delos. Fifty dollars. I didn't answer then."

"That's right. Delos writes for the 'Morning Earth.' I see. Well, I wonder if you realize just what you've done."

"Oh, yes." Wearily she said that.

"You were pretty outspoken with Chief Urquhart this afternoon. He's a very determined man. And a stubborn man. You've seen that."

"Oh, yes."

"He never forgets a grudge. And he has some power. He can make it pretty unpleasant for you."

"Oh, yes. But he's—oh—oh, just all wet."

"I'm afraid you're hardly in a position to sit in judgment over him, Miss Penn. You were in the position of being detained as an important witness. You ran away. That is serious business. Very serious. And it gives him a hold on you."

"I suppose so. But—oh, I've got eyes, and ears, Mr. Carlock! I'd been sitting there all day, taking everything down. It was clear enough what Mr. Urquhart was driving at. And he was wrong."

"Oh, he was wrong?"

"Certainly. And you weren't lifting a hand."

"Never mind that! Just what was your idea in coming here?"

"To find the murderers."

"And just who are they?"

"The Chinese who went out to the Cuppy house last night to get the pearl cap. Mr. Wong sensed it. They were after him, and killed the wrong man. You heard him, this morning."

"Yes, I heard him. So you thought you could come right in here and find the murderers?"

"No. Not at all." Astonishing how her spirit could still flare up. Lucky, too. She welcomed it. "But I believed I could find a man who would know the truth."

"And just who is that?"

"Sin."

"The butler?"

"Yes. He is a trained, faithful servant. He'd never take part in a murder."

"How do you know that?"

"Mr. Wong told me so. And when he talked with me last night, I liked him. I know he is honest."

"And because you liked Sin, and Mr. Wong told you that he . . . Quite delightfully simple, isn't it?"

"Mr. Carlock, can't you see that those officials out there are simply believing the wrong people?"

"You don't know that."

"I know that I wouldn't trust that man Stromberg out of my sight."

"Why not?"

"I don't like his eyes."

"Oh! Really!"

"You heard him lie about the time he went upstairs. You *heard* him! Doesn't that mean anything to you? Exactly two-twenty-five when he was in his room, he said. He took pains to fix that. And Dr. Obry is positive that the murder took place after four. How about that?"

Carlock knit his brows. Then abruptly, he said, "Let's get back on the main topic. You came in here because you thought you could find Sin in Chinatown, did you?"

"Certainly not. But I'd thought of a man who could."

"Who?"

"Mr. Ting Pao. I tried to get in touch with Mr. Wong first. But he'd been shot."

"Oh, you know of that."

"Mr. Andrews called up his paper."

"I see. But where is Ting Pao now?"

"He has gone to get Sin."

"To get Sin? Hmm! And how did you persuade him to do that?"

"Oh . . . I can't tell you, Mr. Carlock. My head's swimming. I talked pretty hard. I think I made him see that he was shielding murderers and permitting innocent persons to be accused. And I told him that the cap has been found, and that if Sin, as I believe, could clear up the case, I felt sure that the police would be willing to restore the cap."

"You proposed a trade, then?"

"Yes. Just that . . . They dragged Sin out and kept him prisoner. They hurt him. Broke his arm."

"Well . . . really, Miss Penn, this is an extraordinary situation. I suppose I shall have to believe that you have acted from natural enough human motives, however unwise. I must try to make it clear to you that you are in a pretty delicate position. Of course, if this man comes through, if he delivers Sin, and then if Sin turns out to be a real witness, say an eye-witness . . . and there you have a couple of pretty big ifs, Miss Penn . . . why, it is just possible that we may be able to keep Urquhart from making things very unpleasant for you. But if there's a slip anywhere, or if Sin doesn't know . . . well"—he spread his hands—"I'm sorry, that's all. I'm afraid you'll have to take your medicine." He sat very still, thinking this over, gravely. "But why, Miss Penn, in Heaven's name! Why didn't you tell us out there what you were thinking instead of taking this wild plunge?"

"You wouldn't have listened."

"We might have. We listened when you ran down that matter of Stromberg's overcoat."

"You'd have felt that I was simply all out to save John Dane."

"Possibly . . . well, of course . . ."

"I suppose I was, in a way." She sighed wearily. "And then Mr. Urquhart drove me clean out of myself. *He'd* never have listened! He is all out for a conviction."

"I understand that, but . . . See here, Miss Penn, my duty is clear. I've got to send you back there. At once."

Elsie went limp. "Oh . . . !" It was hardly more than a weak breath.

"I'm sorry. It isn't so pleasant out there right now. And your standing with Mr. Urquhart is none too high. He's not the sort that can endure much back talk. He may lock you up. He can. This is the biggest thing he's ever got hold of. He'll stop at nothing. But out you go! There's no delaying that." He opened the door and called guardedly.

Elsie covered her face.

Mr. Carlock returned to the table. "I'm sorry I can't say much of anything that would cheer you. It's a grim business. . . . Well, my advice to you is to sit very, very tight. Don't talk at all. I really doubt if I can do a thing for you, but . . . Tell me, is Ting Pao supposed to be bringing that man Sin back here?"

"Yes, Mr. Carlock. Right away. Any moment."

"Very good. I'll wait. Give him a fair chance to make good . . . Oh, Stafford!"

The sergeant appeared. Still a quiet-appearing young American in civilian clothes. He inclined his head courteously toward Elsie.

"Take Miss Penn back to the Cuppy house. You've got your side car?"

"Yes, Lieutenant."

"Very good. Go ahead."

Elsie dragged herself to the door. Caught at the knob. Hesitated. "Mr. Carlock. About Mr. Ting Pao. He knew something. I think he was really in a pretty difficult position. And I'm sure it took a lot of courage for him to go out to that other crowd of his people and arrange to deliver Sin. You see, they'd never have dragged him off except to protect themselves. I hope you won't be hard on him. On Ting Pao, I mean. And please see that he gets the pearl cap."

"If he comes decently through I think you'll find that he won't suffer, Miss Penn. There's some common sense, even a little humanity, in policemen. About the cap I promise nothing. Oh, if Sin was an eye-witness, if he can clear it all up, fine! But that's a pretty long chance."

Sergeant Stafford offered, rather clumsily, to take her arm. But she pulled herself together, said, "I'm all right," and went out. Passing through the restaurant she contrived a wan smile for the waiting reporters. The sergeant helped her into the side car. They roared off uptown toward the Queensborough Bridge and Long Island. And all the way Elsie's right hand, deep in her coat pocket, gripped with nervous intensity a wadded-up note.

18

It was night. The streets were gorges. The bridge was a black path into a gigantic, ominous spider's web. Out on the island highway shapes of houses and trees slipped by in a dark blur. Thousands of lights rushed and glared; thousands upon thousands of lights; like pairs of blazing eyes on roaring monsters that came endlessly at you and almost got you. Almost.

They swung through the Chinesy arch into the winding driveway. There was the dim mass of the house, with lights in it; the *porte cochère;* the shadowy depths of the rock garden. Were those people still playing bridge? She shivered. She simply couldn't step again into that house. But she must. Must perhaps, even, enter the Chinese room and face that stupidly, stubbornly adamantine Chief and that Coroner who'd formerly had a livery stable and who spat on an exquisite Chinese rug. Yes, she was out of the machine, she was quietly mounting the steps. She was inside. In the side hall. In the den (she kept her eyes up). A door opened. The sergeant (in the doorway) asked if they wished Miss Penn in there. The Chief's voice replied, with a rasp, "Certainly." So she entered, and Sergeant Stafford slipped back and shut the door.

Her heart sank. She had really forgotten something of the power of these men and the personal force of Chief Urquhart. But here they were!
Here they sat, about the table, looking. It helped
a little to see Dr. Obry. There was a queer hush
in the room. A fire blazed in the fireplace, but
didn't look cheerful. Funny how they all looked at
her. Their faces seemed rather tired and haggard.
Did they know? Or had she merely interrupted the course of some tense talk? What on earth
were they thinking? She hadn't a notion what she
ought to do. But still they didn't say anything.
Not one word. She certainly had nothing to say
herself. And Mr. Carlock had ordered her not to
talk. She slipped out of her coat and took her
seat. Her pencils, neatly sharpened, lay in a row
before her. She looked up. The policeman called
Mike was leaning against the mantel. As if nothing untoward had happened. He winked. And she
found herself acknowledging that wink with the
ghost of a smile. She felt like a ghost. It might
actually be that they didn't so much as know she'd
been off the property. Heaven could testify that
they'd been engrossed in their own ugly business.
The personal problem now was to make the scene
come real. She'd wrenched herself, for an hour or
two, out of it; and now couldn't get back in. Just
a nightmare!

Chief Urquhart brought his big hand down flat on the table.

The silence continued a moment longer. Dr. Obry rose. "I suppose, then, you will wish to go up there again."

"No," said the Chief, with finality. "No!"

"She is"—Dr. Obry—"in a state of genuine hysteria. That extremely unpleasant scene this afternoon left her in a pitiable condition. Since then she has heard nothing from you. She has been left to her own devices, to her own thoughts. The result is heart-breaking. If this treatment is to be kept up—this system of solitude interrupted by brutality—I feel that I cannot answer for her health or even for her reason. I am not sure that you wish for any statement of opinion from me, Jim . . ."

"Not particularly, Fred. You tend to your business and I'll tend to mine."

"Very well." Dr. Obry's tired face flushed perceptibly. They were speaking of Mrs. Cuppy. Elsie's jaded brain had caught that. And Dr. Obry was putting up a bit of a battle for her. His name, it appeared, was Fred. The Chief was Jim, of course. Two middle-aged citizens of the town. They knew each other, those two. Fred and Jim!

The Chief again banged down that big hand. "Bring her right down here!" he commanded.

"Here?"

"You heard me."

"I must protest against that, Jim! She is really ill, with a temperature . . . a woman of delicate sensibilities . . ."

"Mike"—the Chief—"go right up and bring Mrs. Cuppy down. Tell the nurse to throw some clothes on her, and be quick about it. Something more to say, eh? All right! She'll say it, and she'll say it right here in this room! She's had her chance, that one!"

So they were back at it! And brutally as ever. Milling round and round in that same disheartening, morbid mess. Round and round and round. But more ploddingly now. The keener interest of the morning and afternoon—the response to vivid fresh drama that stirs even a policeman's blood at first—was gone. Worn out. Elsie drew in a quick breath. Even the air was stale. Why didn't they open the windows, blow it out. Thick, syrupy air. Dead cigars—a half moon of them about the hearth where they'd been carelessly tossed—stinking there. Dust on the furniture; ashes strewn about the rug . . . already the beautiful room was filthy. Like the case. Like the minds of that Coroner and Mr. Jim Urquhart.

Mr. Atkinson, who had been leaning forward with his head on one hand, breathed heavily and shifted his head to the other hand. He looked wrung.

Dr. Obry squared his shoulders. "Very well, Jim, but I can't let this ugly business go on without a protest. The name of Cuppy means something in this town. You seem to have forgotten that. Mr. Atkinson there has warned you once today. There's a limit to your sort of . . ."

"That'll do, Fred! I'm in charge here. The less you say, the better!"

"But it won't do, Jim. And God help you if you're wrong!"

"Hey, Mike!" Urquhart was roaring now. "What are you gawking at? Can't you understand a plain order?"

The policeman muttered, "Yes, Chief," and moved toward the door. Dr. Obry, with deep lines in his gray face, said quickly, "I'll go with you." The door closed on the two of them.

The Chief sat immovable. Waiting. The Coroner spat. Mr. Atkinson shifted his head to the other hand; then picked up a pencil and fell to drawing aimless diagrams on the pad before him, painstakingly shading the lines and then adding rows of dots and curly-cues. Elsie, in a state of painful fascination, watched the moving pencil.

The clock on the mantel ticked loudly. Minutes passed. Minutes and minutes. Elsie wrenched her gaze away from that swift pencil and looked at the clock. Chief Urquhart's wooden face turned toward her now and then. She could feel his eyes. Ten minutes of ten. The papers would have to know within an hour or so. Probably midnight would do. They'd wait up to the last possible minute, of course. At least those "Morning Earth" men knew something of what they had to wait for. Thank God they were with Mr. Carlock! He'd have trouble shaking them off now—Ben Andrews and Fish-Face. They'd stick.

The Coroner spat.

This waiting was horrible. Five minutes of ten. Just waiting.

Elsie was staring down at her pencils; endlessly arranging and rearranging them in a neat row. Why didn't the Chief say something to her? What was he trying to do? Break her nerves by making her wait? Well, he couldn't. When he finally moved his big body around in his chair, she felt rather than saw the act. A glance along the table-top corroborated her senses. Those implacable eyes were fixed on her again. She felt them.

"Well, young woman!" Yes, it was that unpleasant stern voice. Slowly she lifted her eyes. She bridled at the phrase, "young woman." That spirit of rebellion was rising again. Mr. Carlock had cautioned her against talking. "Sit tight," he'd said. Very well, she'd sit tight. He'd be returning, sooner or later. Possibly he'd help her. In so far as he could. It was a fluttering hope. But surely he'd meant something when he said it. Something.

"Where have you been?"

She looked straight at the Chief, compressing her lips. His big fist banged on the table. "Where have you been? Answer me!"

She simply looked.

"Well . . . are you answering, or aren't you?"

"I'm not." Curious how the angry resistance this man stirred in her breast overrode her fear of him. Though the fear was there too. But he needn't know that.

"See here, young woman! I'm willing enough to treat you decently, as decently as you'll let me. But you are making it difficult. I'll give you one more chance. If you won't answer, I'll lock you up in a cell as a material witness. And I'll keep you there a while. How do you think you'll like that? Just think it over. . . . Now listen here! You put yourself in a bad light a while back. You undertook to hold out an important bit of evidence. We're not through with you yet on that count. And now, the minute my back is turned, you try to run away. That'll take quite a lot of explaining. You knew that you were under orders not to leave

the property. Are you ready to tell me a little about
it? Or aren't you?"

"No."

"That State officer brought you back. Where
did he find you?"

No answer.

"Now you're simply foolish. Do you think I
can't find out? Mike! Bring that State sergeant in
here!"

Atkinson raised a hand. There was a shuffling
sound in the den. And voices. The door opened.

The Chief lowered his voice. "All right, young
woman! You'll keep. Just make up your mind that
I'm a long way from being through with you. You'll
be singing another song before morning."

Mike entered and held the door back. The nurse
hurried in with a blanket. She moved an uphol-
stered chair nearer the fire and spread the blanket
over it. Finally appeared Dr. Obry with Mrs. Cuppy in his arms.

They'd thrown a dainty negligee about her.
Blue, with white fur. Nobody'd given a thought
to mourning costumes, this day. And in their hurry, upstairs there, they'd just caught up the first
handy wrap. Her pretty little feet, shod only in
furry slippers, dangled below the doctor's arm.
She was whimpering weakly, like a hurt animal.

Dr. Obry placed her in the chair, and the nurse drew the blanket about her. Her head sank back. The face was deadly white. Her hands fluttered up over her eyes and the dazzling rings on them were incongruous.

"Well"—thus the Chief, harshly, speaking out of a wooden face—"so you've got something more to say!"

The only sound in the room then was that whimpering. It grew a little louder. Then the woman gasped for breath. Elsie thought, for a moment, that she might be strangling.

"Come out with it. What is it?" The Chief's voice thundered.

Oh! It really was a relief of a sort, to hear her voice . . . "I can't! I can't!" It was a relief, too, to be making notes again. Elsie's pencil flew over the page with nervous speed.

"You can't? Then what are you taking up our time for? What is all this about?"

The whimpering became a sobbing.

"Now see here, Mrs. Cuppy! We had quite a scene with you upstairs to-day, and we're not interested in having any more of 'em. You seemed to think you had something more to say. Well . . . *say* it!"

"I—I . . . oh, God . . . !"

"Going to play it right out to the finish, are you? Very well, we'll try a few questions. You've admitted, by your own proposal to talk, that you know more than you told us upstairs. Well, what is it?"

Sobs only.

"Something about John Dane, maybe. You had a little to say about him the other time. He was pestering you. Making love to you. Maybe this time you're ready to admit that you were making love to him. That it?"

"Oh, no, no! How dare you! I loved my husband with all my heart!"

"And so you wrote John Dane begging him to come to your room. You said old Cuppy'd never know. Snoring his fool head of downstairs."

The jeweled hands came down from the ashen, tear-stained face. The blue eyes widened. Stared. They looked really bewildered.

Elsie, pencil poised in air, tried to puzzle that out. Had the shock of the other scene, followed by the hours of waiting alone, turned that flighty brain? Had she, perhaps, really fainted when the Chief was reading her scribbled note aloud. At best she was a fool. You felt that.

"Oh, come!" The Chief went grimly, contemptuously on. "We simply have no time for this stuff.

If you've got anything to say, say it! If you think now that maybe you haven't got anything to say, after all, I'll just send you down to a neat little cell in the station house and you'll have all the time you want to think it over. Mike, tell Joe to bring my car around."

Dr. Obry started; but held his tongue. Mike left the room.

Mrs. Cuppy, after one wild look, did an odd thing. Simply dropped her hands into her lap and knit her brows. Her breast still moved convulsively with her breathing. She was still crying. But the tears ran unheeded down her cheeks. She kept drawing her brows together. With some difficulty. She'd frown tightly, and then the muscles would appear to slip and the frown would relax. She'd look puzzled and then frown again. You could see that she was trying to think her way out of the web she was caught in. Her mind was really confused; no doubt about that. But she seemed at last to have caught the idea that pose and hysterics couldn't help her. She'd been knocked down to some sort of rock bottom.

Outside, you could hear Mike calling. And then the lights of a car glanced by the windows. Joe was ready.

"I'll tell," said Mrs. Cuppy. The sobs started up again, but she contrived to get it out. "It was a little talk I had with Mr. Dane. Just before the crowd went upstairs. Just a few minutes. In the dining-room. He drew me through the doorway. It was dark there. He said . . ."

"Go right on."

"He said"—a few sobs—"he said, 'We've got to do something about your husband. Get rid of him, somehow.'"

"Was that the first thing he said?"

"Yes."

"Came right out with it, didn't he?"

"Yes."

"It was just a short talk, eh?"

"Oh, yes!" Eagerly this. "Only a few minutes. You see, my guests would have missed me if I . . ."

"What then?"

"Oh, I told him that I must go back to my guests. You see . . ."

Mike reappeared. "Joe's ready, Chief. At the porte cocheerie."

"Very good. You wait here. . . . Now Mrs. Cuppy, as I understand this, you were together several minutes. Quite a little more must have been said. What was it?"

"Oh, I . . . we just talked a little. Nothing important."

"Hm! I see. You just talked. What about?"

"I can't remember every word!"

"No, I suppose not. You agreed with him, did
you?"

"Agreed with him? I don't understand you!"

"That something must be done about getting
rid of your husband."

"Certainly not! How dare you!"

Urquhart pursed his lips. Deliberately pushed
back his chair. As deliberately walked around the
table toward the fireplace. Mrs. Cuppy, shrinking
back in the big chair as he drew nearer, never took
her staring, confused eyes from his bulky figure.

Dr. Obry, his face set, moved forward protect-
ingly.

"It's all right, Fred," remarked the Chief. "I'm
not going to hurt her. I just want to be sure we've
got this straight." He stood squarely over the
cowed, struggling woman. "Now, Mrs. Cuppy, as
you've put it, John Dane drew you into the dining-room. The first words he said were a proposal
to do something about getting rid of your husband. And you listened!"

"Oh, no, I . . ."

"Yes, you did! You let him say it. You stayed
right there and let him say it! Chatted with him.
About getting rid of your husband. Only left him
because you really felt it might be thought rude
not to rejoin your guests. And then you went upstairs and wrote that cute little note, begging him

to come to your room. What kind of a wife do you call yourself, anyway? You didn't run away from him as a murderer. You didn't even strike him. Just stayed there and chatted about things so unimportant that you can't even remember. Little things. Oh, killing a husband and things like that. Don't you realize what you've been saying? Good God! . . . Mike! Tell Joe to pick up a couple of men and fetch John Dane here. Tell him to step on it. Needn't take five minutes. Bring him right in here."

Mike left the room. A moment later the car rushed off by the windows, and Mike returned.

The Chief stared down at that pitiful figure in the chair. "I'm going to get to the bottom of this," he said, "if it takes all night. You meant this for a charge against John Dane. Didn't you? *Didn't you?* . . . Been lying up there in your bed thinking up neat little stories. Trying to save yourself. But you can't do it. You can't do it! You're not good enough at the game. Making a mess of it. Just a poor thing, aren't you? In over your head. Floundering." He bent over the chair, his big hands resting on the two arms. "Why don't you come clean, Mrs. Cuppy? Why don't you tell the truth? Haven't you any courage, any heart? Your husband, the man that's done everything in the world for you, lies dead in Bill Deem's undertaking shop downtown. His head all crushed in with a hatchet." He paused. Simply took his time. Then, with a deliberate, dramatic force—with a quality not altogether removed from a crudish sort of majesty—added (his eyes probing her squirming, pitifully evasive soul)—*"You know who swung that hatchet!"*

Dr. Obry cried out in anguish—"Oh, Jim, for God's sake! She doesn't know a thing that happened last night. She was . . ."

The Chief cut him off with a curt—"Shut up, Fred! I'm dealing with murder. You keep out of it!"

The tragic little figure in the chair was nearly hidden by his huge form. It was the nurse who cried out, "Doctor! She has fainted!"

Instantly, once again, Dr. Obry took command. This was his province. He caught her up in his arms, rested the limp body across a bent knee, and lowered the loosely swinging head. For a few moments he and the nurse worked over her. Then he carried her to a sofa, and gave her a dose of something from one of the bottles in his bag. Held her head and put the bottle between her nerveless gray lips.

The Chief followed them. Stood menacingly, silently over them. You felt that he'd spring again, the minute her eyes opened. Spring like a tiger.

And Elsie, sitting tensely on the edge of her chair, looked on. A queer sad sort of fire seemed

to be consuming her body. They were bringing
John Dane. . . .

19

He looked years older. The presence of tragedy
had touched, softened, deepened his face. His eyes
were dull, set back in shadowy hollows. Such a
weary, weary face! Feeling that if she let a muscle
move she'd run to him, cry over him, caress him,
Elsie sat motionless. With a sensation of clinging
desperately to her chair.

He declined to sit. Stood lounging at the end of
the mantel, with an elbow on it. Rested his cheek
against his hand. Slowly, soberly (with the look of
a man whose thoughts have mined too deeply to
be concerned with the surfaces where words are
found) took in the scene. The big Chief, standing,
dominating the room. Mrs. Cuppy on the sofa.
Dr. Obry holding her head while the nurse slipped
a cushion under it ('She has come out of it, then,"
thought Elsie). The Coroner and Mr. Atkinson
and Elsie at the table. Mike and the two policemen who had brought Dane.

Dane's eyes rested a moment on Elsie. In that
same deeply grave way. No smiling, no movement
of the facial muscles. He simply looked. Her eyes
met his, and again that fire blazed. Her face was

hot. But she didn't care. And anyway, the others
weren't looking at her. She did feel rather terribly exposed. But she couldn't help that. How hot
it was! Stifling! And the room swarmed with immense blue policemen! Thousands of 'em! No . . .
three. But . . .

The Chief speaking. (Oh, God, the merciless
rasp in that voice—how it kept at you!) "Mr.
Dane, Mrs. Cuppy has made up her mind to come
through with some evidence that directly con-
cerns you. I've had you brought here so that you
can face your accuser and give us your version of
what took place, if you have another version. Mrs.
Cuppy has been a little upset, but I think she'll
hear all we may have to say among us. . . . Now,
Mrs. Cuppy, just tell us again . . ."

Said Dr. Obry sternly, "No!" Then—"Let Miss
Penn read her transcript."

Elsie went limp. She hadn't foreseen this. She
looked up at John Dane. Simply couldn't look
anywhere else. The confused thought came that
he had somehow found himself. Down there at
the jail, perhaps during the grilling he'd had to
endure. Something gallant there, just in the way
he stood, quietly waiting, as if he'd worked it all
out and was willing to let them rave. For that
matter, hadn't she, in her earlier turn, found
herself? Under the Chief's grilling, too. Found

herself, and leaped into desperate action. But she'd got nowhere. And then she'd slumped. Lost her hope. Worse, she'd lost her faith. All vision gone. Blacked out. She could hardly make it come real in her thoughts that there was a Lieutenant Carlock; or that if there was he'd very really get hold of Sin; or that Sin could possibly have the real truth. So speedily had she been caught up again in this web. That was the hell of being a woman. Emotionally unstable. No getting round it. Women were so. Men weren't. Not in that tricky, moody way. They carried on. John Dane, standing quietly there at the end of the mantel, was pretty splendid. Could she buck up to some appearance of steadiness? Doubtful. Yet she must.

They were looking at her. She realized abruptly that the Chief had been speaking and her inner ear hadn't caught it.

He spoke again. "Read it, please! Mrs. Cuppy's statement as to what took place in the dining-room. Nothing more. None of my questions or her replies. Simply her statement of what took place."

And then Elsie found herself doing so. With even a measure of self-control. Evidently the human creature, when under real pressure, could endure a lot. A lot. More than you'd dream. Elsie read aloud, very low, but steadily enough, "It was a little talk I had with Mr. Dane. Just before the crowd went upstairs. In the dining-room. He drew me through the doorway. It was dark in there. He said . . . he said . . . 'We've got to do something about your husband. Get rid of him somehow.'"

"That'll do!" cried the Chief. "Just that!" He turned on Dane. "Well, sir, what have you to say to that?"

There was a long silence. Elsie sat as if frozen, looking down at the table.

Finally Dane answered, "Nothing."

"You confess it?"

"No. I say nothing."

"You admit that such a conversation took place?"

"We had a few words in the dining-room. Yes."

"Just before the party moved upstairs?"

"Yes."

"You discussed the possibility of getting rid of Mr. Cuppy?"

"I have nothing to say about that."

"No fencing, now! Was the subject mentioned?"

"Why . . . yes."

"By you?"

No reply.

"I'll give you just one more chance to answer that question. Did you bring up the subject?"

Dane didn't move for a full minute. The silence grew heavy, thick, painful, unbearable. Finally he glanced over toward the all but inert blue-and-white figure on the sofa (she was beginning to whimper again, very weakly); shifted his position slightly; shrugged his shoulders. That was all. Not a word.

"So you refuse to answer?"

Dane simply stood there.

"You realize that this amounts to a confession?"

Silence. Then this, from Dane, wearily, "Why is it that I am not permitted to call up my lawyer?"

"You're going to have time enough for lawyers. Believe me! . . . Now we're going to act out that little scene here. Exactly as it happened. Mrs. Cuppy, stand up!"

Dr. Obry muttered something.

"First, however," that indomitable Chief again, turning on Elsie—"I want you to read a few words more. The little thing that John Dane said to you in the garden. We'll see if we can refresh his memory. . . . Come on, read it!"

Elsie was trembling, as her fingers fumbled through the leaves of the notebook. "I don't know that I . . ."

"None of that stuff! You know well enough! Just the confession he made. The important little item you tried so hard to keep from us. Read it!"

Somehow she did. Huskily. ". . . if I weren't in such a ticklish situation here. The damndest mess—just to-night." Her lids fluttered up. She couldn't help looking at John Dane. She was glad, in a confused way, that the Chief had accused her of keeping it from them. At least, he'd see . . .

Urquhart was back at Mrs. Cuppy. "Come on now! Stand up! . . . Dane, you come here! Stand as you stood when you talked with Mrs. Cuppy in the dining-room."

Dane didn't move. He was looking straight down at Elsie. As if he hadn't heard.

Urquhart whirled on him. Gripped him by the shoulder with a "Damn you! You do what I say or I'll . . ."

The door opened and Carlock stepped quietly into the room. For the moment Elsie's breath stopped dead. She was pressing weak hands against her breast. Very cool he was, stepping easily, briskly into the scene. He spoke calmly enough. They might have been sitting about the table, Chief Urquhart and all.

"Oh, Dr. Obry, you'd better get Mrs. Cuppy upstairs. We shan't need her now. Out through the hall, please. I don't want her going through the den. You'd better have your men take Mr. Dane out, too, Chief. But keep him handy, here in the house. I may want him, a little later."

Jim Urquhart stood motionless. Here, behind the unobtrusive personality of Lieutenant Carlock, authority loomed. Something was coming from him that would have to be listened to. You felt that. Even (as Elsie put it to herself) this big bully felt it.

Dr. Obry didn't so much as wait for a word or a nod from him; simply picked Mrs. Cuppy up and left, the nurse hurrying after with his bag and with that blanket caught up under one arm. Before Jim Urquhart so much as turned around—slowly—taken clean aback (you caught that)—they were gone. He was frowning. But he recovered, after a moment more, something of his habitual wooden front and nodded to the policemen who had brought Dane. "Take him into the dining-room," he commanded, sharply, "and shut the doors. Don't let him talk to anybody."

"That's all right, Chief," Carlock broke in. "We needn't worry about him. Just keep handy, Mr. Dane, if you'll be so kind."

The Chief glowered. But the situation had been swept out of his hands. And he had no answer, no attitude, ready. So, frowning on, he marched—massively—back around the table and resumed his chair.

Carlock rested his hands lightly on the farther edge of the table. "Gentlemen," he said, "before I go on with this, it is only fair to say a word about the extraordinary thing Miss Penn has done."

Elsie, struggling against an up-surging of relief so stirring that it might easily have mounted into

hysterics, felt the hot color rushing again from
her toes all the way up through her spent body
and into her face. It was only by lowering her
eyes and holding tightly the arms of her chair that
she was able to keep from laughing, or crying, or
something.

Carlock went quietly on. "With a touch of in-
sight . . . perhaps genius would be a better word
. . . that went straight to the heart of the problem,
Miss Penn realized that Ting Pao, the Chinese
leader to whom the pearl cap had been consigned,
must be made to talk. That, as you know, is not
always easy in dealing with these Chinese. Indeed,
it is very difficult. The New York police, to-day,
were unable to get a word out of him. They were
inclined to believe that he really didn't know. But
Miss Penn firmly believed that he did know. That
he must. I won't go into the details of that story
now. We must bear it in mind, however, that Miss
Penn had been with us all day. She knew everything that we knew. Perhaps even a little more.
Her imagination was caught by the fact that the
butler, Sin, didn't return with the other servants.
Also by their statement that he was already gone
when they came downstairs this morning. Mr.
Wong had informed her that Sin had been his butler for years and that he was a faithful servant, incapable of wrongdoing. She leaped intuitively at

the conclusion that Sin had either witnessed the murder or had been drawn into it, and that the Chinese hatchet-men who entered this house last night for the purpose of recovering the stolen cap had carried him off for their own protection. To keep him out of the way, as a witness. She sensed, as well, that Ting Pao, as a leader in Chinatown, could find the man if any human being could. Her idea was to go straight to Ting Pao and persuade him to talk. She knew that he was desperately eager to come into possession of the cap, so she hit on the scheme of offering to trade the cap for Sin. I gave her her head. More fully than she herself realized. There was a chance that a woman might succeed where men had failed. It was not a matter for discussion or debate. She was either right or wrong. Acting under my instructions, therefore, she proceeded to New York by automobile. And . . . well, she accomplished more than our friends of the New York police department were able to do—she got the truth out of Ting Pao." He went over to the den door and opened it . . . "Sin! Come in here!"

Elsie didn't stir. Didn't lift her eyes. She caught it all now. Mr. Carlock (she could have hugged him) was doing a great deal more than protect her from that Jim Urquhart. He was telling her (as well as those men) what her story was. Before she could say any of the thousands of possible wrong things. "Before" (so ran her racing thoughts) "I can gum the works." Very good. This was her story.

A curious figure appeared in the doorway. If Mr. Carlock hadn't spoken the name she'd have met with some difficulty in recognizing him. He had no coat; indeed (she saw now) he wore only a shirt and trousers. The shirt was torn. His feet were bare. His left arm was curiously bent, with something projecting through the shreds of the sleeve above the elbow; he held that arm by the wrist, in its bent position, with his right hand. His face was gaunt and dirty; and there was a bloodstained bandage about his head, with unkempt black hair bushing out above it.

"Better sit down, Sin," observed Carlock; but the Chinese merely compressed his lips and remained standing. Carlock then turned back to the table. "As you will note, gentlemen, this man has had rather a tough time of it. His left arm is broken. A piece of bone is projecting through the flesh. He appears to have been badly beaten up about the head. I wished to have his arm set before undertaking the ride out here, but he flatly refused. His one thought was to return to the house at the earliest moment possible and tell his story. So here he is. . . . Now, Sin, suppose you tell us exactly what happened in the night. Don't be afraid of these gentlemen. Tell it just as you explained it to me. Come up here by the table where we can all hear you."

20

"Las' night I can't go to sleep. I worry about Mr. Cuppy downstairs in the den. I speak to Miss"—he indicated the staring, flushed Elsie—"an' she tell me Miss Briggs open windows in den. So I worry some more. We always lock downstairs. But Miss"—again that courteous inclination of the battered head toward Elsie—"she dunno what to do. I dunno what to do. I think maybe I come downstairs an' wait. Maybe Mr. Cuppy wake up. Then I help him upstairs. But Miss say Miss Briggs have put Mr. Wong in Mr. Cuppy's room. I di'n' know Mr. Wong come here. So I just dunno. Bimeby I hear all people come upstairs. After two o'clock. I think an' think. I get up. I put on shirt an' pants. I come down and lie on floor in side hall. Right by door of den. I bring pillow down."

The men at the table looked at one another. Sin resumed, "I lie down there on floor an' try to sleep a li'l'."

"Just why did you do this, Sin?" asked Carlock. "I want you to make everything clear to these gentlemen."

"Oh, I worry. I don' like windows open on first floor. An' I worry about pearl cap Mrs. Cuppy have got. I hear China boys talk about that. So I worry. Oh, lots o' things. An' maybe Mr. Cuppy wake up. Then I help him. That all right?"

Carlock nodded. "Yes. Go ahead."

"Maybe I sleep some. I dunno. But I hear noise. Window."

"A window opening?"

"Yes, sir. In den. I hear men moving. Very careful. Very quiet. I think burglars. I get up. I go very still—toward telephone. Before I can do, door opens."

"The door of the den?"

"Yes, sir. Men come out, very careful. They see me."

The Chief interrupted crisply, "Was there a light in the hall?"

"In front hall, sir. Not in side hall. Always light in front hall, every night. Can't see much. Dim. Very dim. But I see a li'l'. They run at me. There's four men. China men. Beat me. I fight. I know about that. Then I dunno."

"You mean you became unconscious?" asked Carlock.

"Yes, sir. I think. I dunno quite. I get mix'."

"Naturally. Go on."

"When I know again . . ."

"You mean when you came to?"

"Yes, sir. Then I dunno at first what they do. My head hurt. Very mix' up. I am tie' up. My han's. An' something in my mouth. All tie' up."

"You were gagged?"

"Yes, sir. I am on floor in dark place. I feel coats aroun' my head. Pretty soon I know. In coat closet."

"That is directly opposite the door of the den, isn't it?"

"Yes, sir. Jus' opposite. We are all there. Very dark. Three—four men in front. One man step on my foot. They look at something. Door open, but not much. Jus' li'l'. They look. But bimeby I look too. I look through their legs. One man hold something agains' my face. Revolver. But I look all I can. I see something. A man. All white. Has got no clothes."

"Naked, you mean?"

"Yes, sir. Has got no clothes. He go in den. He has got something in his han'. I can't see much. But I think it is hatchet. And he has got something else in his han'—piece of cloth."

"Wrapped round his hand, you mean?"

"Yes, sir. Afterwar', when I hear the men talking I know they hear cellar door open. That is why they are scare' and hide in coat closet. Then the man go in den. Doesn' shut door at all. An' they open door a li'l' wider. I hear Mr. Cuppy snore."

"The door of the coat closet, you mean?"

"Yes, sir. I see a li'l' more. Not much. But I hear. There is noise—thump—thump! Then more noise. Funny noise. Crack—crack! Then Mr. Cuppy don' snore any more. He is murder', I think. He kill'. That all-white man. I feel terrible. The China men are scare'. Awfully scare' now. They whisper. They think people blame them for murder. An' then I know why they come. They come for pearl cap of Tzu Hsi. They don' want to be in trouble for murder Mr. Cuppy."

"What else did you see and hear, Sin?"

"Di'n' see much. But more noise come. I can't think. Maybe he jus' jump aroun'. Maybe he dance. I dunno. Then bimeby he come out. He laugh to himself. He hasn' got hatchet now. An' he jump aroun' a li'l'."

"In the hall, you mean?"

"Yes, sir. Then he go."

"Where?"

"I can't see. I think maybe to front hall. Pretty soon it is all quiet. The China men are awfully scare'. They whisper a lot. Mos' of them wanna run away. One man say no, they mus' get the pearl cap. I know him, that man."

"Who was he?"

"Jim Lee, he was. He work here a li'l' time last year. When I firs' come. He is no good. A gambler.

I sen' him away. He don' like me. I know he has
say he makes trouble for me some day. Yes, sir,
Jim Lee say they mus' fin' the cap of Tzu Hsi, but
all the others are too scare'. They say they don'
wan' electric chair. They think nobody believe
what they say if they tell the truth. Anyway, they
break in. Jus' awfully scare'. So they make Jim Lee
open the side door. They tell him to be very still.
But he can't help make some noise. When he shut
the door. One man run. Two men grab me. Then
I think maybe, if they're so scare' of noise, they
won' dare shoot, so I get away. I try to run. I can't
make noise because that thing is in my mouth. It
hurts. An' my head hurts where they beat me. Well
. . . then I dunno. I think maybe they knock me
off steps. I dunno what happens. When I know
anything next time we are in automobile. I wake
up there. It is cold. My arm hurts pretty bad. I
feel sick. My arm is broken. They take me to New
York an' put me in a cellar. They don' give me
anything to eat. The way they talk, I think they
don' know what to do about me. They are scare'
I will tell somebody they were in the house when
Mr. Cuppy is killed. No, they dunno—they are
rattle'—so they leave me in cellar. They untie my
hands. There are rats. I am very unhappy. It is
a long time. Oh, long, long time. Then a man
comes—a China man—an' he say—'Come with

me!' He takes me to back door of Ting Pao's place.
You are there. So we come out here. I am glad."

Not a person had moved during this extraordinary recital. Elsie hadn't made a note. Nobody seemed to even think of that. Not an eye had strayed from the bloodstained face under the bandage. The Coroner broke the hush by spitting, and then muttering a bit of amazed profanity.

"Very good, Sin," Carlock was speaking. "Now tell us—when the murderer came out of the den, were you able to see him any better?"

"A li'l', sir. Not much. Not his face much. Oh, jus' a li'l'—jus' once."

"Could it have been John Dane?"

Sin laughed softly, apologetically. "Oh, no, sir! Not Mr. Dane. Not so big. I know Mr. Dane."

"Or Mr. Stromberg?"

"No, sir. Not so big."

"Better have all the men in, Chief," said Carlock, in his brisk way. "Line them up. Perhaps he can identify the man with the hatchet. Sin, you come over here!" He led the way to the portieres that hung at the sides of the tall front windows. "Stand in here. Be careful not to let them see you. And don't speak. I will call off the names, one by one. Just try to fix them in your mind as I say them. Then, after they are gone, you will tell us what you can." With which he produced a pocket knife and cut a small opening in the thick velvet. "Look through that, Sin."

Policemen brought them all in, a hushed, puzzled lot. All but Dane and Stromberg. Mr. Delos was sputtering under his breath. The Gargoyle leered, grinning. Mr. Ettlethwaite wore a worried expression. The three others were men that Elsie hadn't, during the evening, been able to identify at all. But two of them, she thought, were the bridge-players. They were ranged in a line with their backs to the fire.

Carlock, from a list he'd had in his pocket, read off the names slowly, one by one, pointing at the proper individual as he did so. "Mr. Green . . . Mr. Ettlethwaite . . . Mr. Maybach" (This was the Gargoyle. Funny, Elsie'd never thought of him as having a name!) . . . "Mr. Delos" . . . and so on. Then they filed out and the door was closed. Sin came out from his hiding place.

"Extraordinary thing!" remarked Mr. Atkinson, in a subdued voice . . . "that naked business. Explains why your men haven't found any blood-stained clothes, Chief."

"But he had something wrapped round his hand," observed the Coroner. "A cloth. That, if we find it, will be the nearest thing to evidence."

"Sure." Atkinson. "Far as the rest of it was concerned, all he had to do was to pitch the hatchet out the window and then go upstairs and take a bath."

Carlock had brought Sin back to the fire. "Well," said he, "how about it? Think you could pick one of them?"

"I think, sir"—Sin—"Mr. Maybach."

"Mike," said Carlock, "bring Maybach in here. Better take Sergeant Stafford with you. He's in the den. I'm not sure of this fiddler. Don't know just what he may pull." He took Sin by the right arm then, gently, and led him into the den. Elsie could hear him sending for Dr. Obry.

They brought the Gargoyle in, each officer firmly holding an arm. He was still grinning, rolling his eyes from one to another of the group. Carlock returned; went directly to him; with deft, swift hands felt everywhere about his body. The Gargoyle tried to shrink back, but the two officers held him. From a hip pocket Carlock drew a rumpled handkerchief. Spread it out. Tossed it on the table. There were unmistakable dark stains on that handkerchief.

"There's your evidence, Chief," said Carlock. "I'll turn him over to you now."

21

So his name was Maybach, this leering, grinning, quite mad musician. A slender, insignificant little

man, notable only for the glint in his staring eyes
and for his quaint ugliness. Elsie stared at him,
convinced yet unbelieving. Her thoughts whirled
round and round. She'd been right—and wrong.
She was exultant, bewildered, unhappy. She wanted to laugh—and cry. Here was drama. Tragedy. Yet
it was almost unbearably grotesque. Anger welled
in her breast against Hazel Cuppy. The spoiled,
pretty woman, caught in the mesh of her own dis-
organized life, driven by a profoundly ignoble
panic, had turned and twisted and lied weakly,
shamelessly, frantically, in a bitter effort to save
herself. For that she would eagerly have sent John
Dane to the chair.

Chief Urquhart's voice boomed out, "Bring him
over here!"

Mike and Stafford dragged him toward the table. He was resisting. Shouting epithets in his
cackling high voice. Carlock stepped forward to
take a hand.

The scene that next took place was unbeliev-
able. It developed so swiftly, so confusedly, that
Elsie was never to be able to reconstruct it in her
mind in an orderly sequence. The man looked
so small beside those police officers, so weak—a
pallid, stooping little figure—that apparently he
couldn't possibly have done what she, with her
own startled eyes, saw him do. He knocked Carlock flat on the rug. You couldn't even figure out

how he ever wrenched himself away from those two officers. It was an exhibition, of course, of the desperate energy and the amazing quickness and concentration of purpose that is the peculiar gift of the maniac. Then (and it seemed still the same instant in time) he was bounding down the room toward the den door. Stafford caught him, only to be whirled against a cabinet of carved jades. His shoulder crashed right through the glass. The exquisite bits of loving workmanship were tumbled into heaps. Mike was after him with a rush. But Mr. Carlock, rebounding (it seemed) from the floor, leaped upon his back. The Chief sprang up from the table and ran at him. But the little man struck, dodged, ran to another corner, screaming profanely, in a frenzy. The Chief cornered him, swinging a massive fist and raising a welt over his cheek bone; but with the speed and force of a terrorized animal the Gargoyle butted the Chief in his one vulnerable spot, the stomach, and drove him back gasping and covering up. The little lacquered table in green and gold fell with a crash. Mr. Carlock tripped him and then dove down upon the sprawling figure. They rolled over and over upon the rug. Mike and Stafford dove too. They beat him nearly to insensibility; beat him until he moaned. There was a click. Somebody had snapped handcuffs on him. They jerked him to his feet. One eye was swollen shut. His lips were puffed and bleeding. As he stood there, the purpling Chief, his eyes blazing with savage rage, gave him a terrific kick. Elsie covered her eyes. It must have been at about that moment that she heard Mr. Atkinson say, rather breathlessly to the Coroner (the two of them seemed to be standing almost at her shoulder), "But where's the motive? How about that?"

To which query the Coroner responded with, "Yeah! And who stole that Chinese cap? How about that now?" And spat.

Elsie uncovered her eyes. Now her brain began to cooperate (however ineffectually) with her ears. The cackling voice screamed, "Well, I did it! Sure I did it! It was coming to him! Stupid old ass! I'm a genius! He cut me off! Wouldn't support genius! I decided to give him one last chance. I put it up to him. Yesterday. What else was he good for! Tell me that! Sure I did it! Smashed in his stupid old head! He said he couldn't do another thing for me. So I finished him. Of course I did. And then I danced! Danced all round him! Naked I danced! Don't you wish you'd seen that, eh! God, but I capered! I was happy! I'm happy now! I'm right! It was justice! I'm God! Put that in your pipe and smoke it! I smashed in that soft old head! Oh, pineapples!"

They were pulling and pushing him toward the den. Extraordinary how they puffed over it. Pulling and pushing at that little, beaten-up, rumpled man.

"Oh, go ahead! Do what you like with me! What of it! Think you can send me to the chair? Well, you can't! Do you know why? Because I'm crazy! Crazy as a bedbug! You can't execute a crazy man! Look up your law! You can't do a thing to me! Not one damn thing! Just shut me up in the loony house! You'll have to feed me! I'll finish my symphony, that's what I'll do! It'll be grand . . . quiet . . . nobody disturbing me . . . I'll do my symphony . . . !"

Then this, from the doorway. The hot, high-pitched words and phrases rattled out like bullets from a machine gun—"How about Stromberg? How about that bird, eh? What you going to do about him? He stole the Chinese cap! Hid it in his overcoat. I saw him! Kept out of sight in the hall! All naked! God, it's a scream! He thought nobody knew! Heard the rumpus in the den and thought they'd blame it on burglars! Or say, maybe he heard those other men! They ran out. Quite a party! Stromberg thought he'd get free of Hazel Cuppy! The skate has lived off her for years! Oh, I know him! Read him like a book! Thought he could get away with it! And all the time I was the burglar—little naked me! Boy, it's funny!" And the room reverberated with his cackling laughter.

The door closed on him.

22

Slowly, wearily, Elsie came down the stairs, in her coat and hat, her suitcase in one hand, her typewriter case in the other. They'd all been told they could leave. It was going on eleven. There was just time to catch the last train into the city. She was wondering, wearily, if somebody would drive her down to the station. Surely there'd be cars.

She saw the actress, Miss Eames, pale, cross-looking, hurrying through the hall, with Mr. Ettlethwaite hovering solicitously.

She put down her burdens a moment to rest her hands and get her breath. Balanced them on a step stooping over. In the front hall, near the coat closet, John Dane and Mr. Carlock were talking; quietly, as if nothing had happened. They had their hats and coats on. She wished she'd taken the back stairs. She simply couldn't face John Dane. She *couldn't*. Perhaps he wouldn't look around.

But Mr. Carlock saw her, and said something, with an earnest air. Then he smiled. Actually smiled. She hadn't realized that he could be so good-looking.

She picked up her luggage and went on down, as briskly as she could. But Dane came quickly to meet her. He took her things. She resisted somewhat, without a word (she couldn't speak)—but he got them away from her. He still looked haggard and dull of eye. And his manner was stiffly distant.

"I wonder if you'd mind . . ." he began, awkwardly. "I know you're a wreck . . . we all are . . . but I thought maybe we could talk just a little. Oh, sanely, I mean. There are a few things I simply must . . ."

She could only stand there.

"I was calling up for a taxi, but Lieutenant Carlock heard me and said nothing doing. He insists on sending us to town in a police car."

"Us?" She did manage to get that out, rather sharply.

"Why . . . yes." How gloomy he was. "Do you mind? Very much?"

"Oh . . . I suppose . . ."

So they went out together to the *porte cochère*. Mr. Carlock followed with what appeared to be Dane's bag. One of those big, handsome English Gladstones in very heavy, soft yellow leather. He'd have nice things, of course. The car was waiting, with a policeman in front. A little car, with curtains up. That was good. They'd be right in there with the driver. There couldn't be anything . . . well, personal. Not very well. Mr. Carlock said some nice things, she hardly knew what; and then the car rattled off, past the rock garden, along the shaded driveway. The two bags and the typewriter, piled in there, crowded their knees and feet uncomfortably close.

After a moment of oddly embarrassing silence, Dane remarked, in that same stiff voice and manner, "I'm taking only this bag with me now. Sin is sending my trunk on by express."

She almost sniffed aloud. Who cared what he might do with his trunk! What would he say next? That it was a charming evening?

And then, without another sound from either of them, without a hint or a warning, she was in his arms and her arms were clinging about his shoulders and he was kissing her and she was crying. She was aware of the rather awful thought that she must have simply grabbed at him. What on earth was the matter with them, anyway? Couldn't they be together two minutes without flying up this way? Did he think she was that sort?

She was snuggled down within his arm. In a minute she'd draw away. But the warmth and the strong protectiveness of it was most unnervingly tempting.

Suddenly he chuckled.

Now she did sniff.

"I was just thinking . . . something Lieutenant Carlock said, there in the hall, a minute or so back. He said that if I didn't . . . well, ask you to-night to marry me, he'd be strongly tempted to break my head."

This was so startling that all Elsie could contrive to say was, "Oh!"

He sobered. She certainly didn't mean to snuggle closer, but somehow it happened. "Will you marry me, Elsie? It does seem to be sort of . . . well, the next thing."

"I suppose . . ." she heard herself saying (that driver might have been on the planet Mars for all she knew or cared), "I suppose . . . the way it seems to be, that we'll have to do . . . something . . ."

Alice Royce, Girl Detective

A Series of Stories of a Clever Girl's Extraordinary Experiences

Charles Somerville

1912-1913

(Newspaper Serial)

No. 1—The Clue of the Little Horseshoe

This remarkable detective story and others equally fascinating to follow are drawn from real life and the only thing fictitious about the heroine of their thrilling adventure is her name. She is a real person.

For the protection of the confidence reposed in her by her many clients, and in order that a greater freedom might be given the author in telling of the strange cases in which Alice Royce has been engaged, the actual names and locations of the stories have been frequently changed and also the names of the human characters who figure in the mysteries.

Alice Royce is now in her early twenties. Her advent into detective work was caused by David Belasco, the eminent dramatic author and director, to whom she once submitted a play. He was interested to the point of sending for her. He told the girl that her play showed imagination and a remarkably precocious knowledge of stage technique. But he said her people were not real. "They are dream people.

You do not know life. Learn life, and then, I think, you will write a good play."

How better to learn life than in detective work— to learn the most intimate and the strangest phases of life at first hand?

Alice Royce had been employed by prominent detective agencies, by the New York Police Department, and on matters of great secrecy and delicacy by the Standard Oil. Her reputation has grown quietly in influential circles.

In her work, the pretty, dark-haired, brown-eyed young woman has shown courage befitting a man, an intuition sometimes almost uncanny; skill unwonted. Her work has carried her into criminals' dens and desperate situations; into the business and social worlds—the luxurious world, generally called "Society."

John Craig, the youthful manager of the Union Bank Note Company, looked up from his desk in surprise at the young woman who stood before him. Then he glanced back at the small card in his hand. He read again: "A. Royce, Investigator."

"Are you A. Royce?" he demanded quizzically. "Are you the detective?"

The girl smiled and slipped easily into a chair beside his desk.

"I'm Alice Royce," she said. "I'm the detective."

John Craig had heard that there were such crea-
tures as female detectives. They were, he thought,
invariably women of forty or more, with hard,
shrewd features and angular bodies.

Miss Alice Royce, Investigator, however, was
scarcely more than a girl. His stare changed to
frank expression of approval at her trim little figure in its smart tailor-made gown of blue cloth,
the graceful hands clad in tan gloves folded in
her lap over a black leather, gold-mounted bag,
the heavy coils of chestnut hair framing her rosy
countenance, the fascinating prettiness of her
small, half-uptilted nose and the freshness of her
gracious, winsome mouth. He also saw that her
large, brown long-lashed eyes were alert, splendidly intelligent.

However, he brought his mind back to the serious sinister affair that had caused him to appeal
to the famous Blaney Detective Agency for aid.

"Frankly, Miss Royce," he said, "the Blaney
Agency have given you a most difficult problem.
I only hope you will be able to succeed, that you
will be able to restore David Raynor to his wife
and children and to us."

He paused and passed his hand over a frowning
brow.

"The thing is such a black mystery," he said.
"All my theories and efforts in the case have come

to nothing. David Raynor has disappeared as utterly as if a great hand had reached out of the sky and snatched him from the earth."

"Just who is David Raynor?" asked the girl quietly. "Tell me what you can about him—everything, no matter whether some of the details seem important to you or not."

"Raynor, Miss Royce," continued Craig, "was our 'star' man—one of the most expert engravers in the United States. He has been with this company for fifteen years. His salary was $7,000 a year. He is now about forty years old, a slender, mild-mannered man. He lived with his wife and two children in a pretty villa in Mount Vernon, well beyond the town itself, out on the old Eastchester road, with his home facing Seton's woods. I think you will find that his life was in every way exemplary; he was devoted to his work here, to his home, his wife and his children. His life was indeed an open book, simple, sober and kindly. Neither his wife nor any of his associates can imagine the possible existence of an enemy, and his actions prior to his disappearance were altogether normal. He appeared to have nothing weighing on his mind to its fear or discomfort. And—well, in short, there you are."

Miss Royce produced from her handbag a little gilt-edged morocco bound note book.

"According to the facts furnished me by Mr. Blaney," she said, "it is now seventeen days that Mr. Raynor has been missing, and that on Thursday, the day of his disappearance, he left his office as usual, met no one, and was seen by his fellow commuters on the train to Mount Vernon and was further seen to alight there?"

Craig nodded.

"Mr. Blaney stated to me," said Miss Royce, "that on Monday Mrs. Raynor had come to you to beg you to take the matter in hand, report it to the, police and use your influence to stir them to take extraordinary measure to find her husband?"

"Yes."

"And you had consented to this most readily, but that a few minutes after she left your office she returned in great excitement to beg you not to do anything of the kind but to go on with only a private investigation of the case?"

"Exactly. At the very entrance to this building as she was departing a man, who was a total stranger to her, a dark-skinned, full-bearded man whose speech suggested Italian origin, came suddenly upon her. He told her that if she valued her husband's life she must not take the matter to the police, that her husband was alive and well but that his future well-being depended solely on her remaining quiet, discouraging investigation and awaiting such time as he would be restored to her."

"There was no demand for a ransom?"

"No, not then or at any other time since. No Black Hand letters, you know, or anything of that sort. Of course it was this threat passed to Mrs. Raynor that so thoroughly aroused me to a determination to do everything possible to learn what fate poor Raynor has met. Up to that time I leaned very much to the theory that Walsh, the foreman, had insisted must be the real explanation."

"And what was that, Mr. Craig?"

"That Raynor's close attention to his duties, the night work he had been doing for weeks in order to meet our contract for the delivery of new sets of plates for a South American republic's bonds and paper currency; the eye-strain and nervousness which frequently afflicts engravers had brought on an attack of aphasia and sent Raynor wandering, to return home, perhaps, when a period of rest cleared his mind. Even now Walsh says his theory is probably the right one."

Craig paused. Suddenly Miss Royce lifted her eyes to his face, brushing back a tendril of soft brown hair with a tan gloved hand.

"Where did that interview between you and Mrs. Raynor take place?"

"Right here—in this office."

"Was anybody else present?"

"No—er, that is, not at first. Walsh came in while we were talking, to extend his sympathy to Mrs. Raynor."

"And heard you promise to do your utmost to make the police take a keen interest in her husband's case."

"Yes, he was here when he heard me promise to stir the authorities up to taking earnest action in the case."

"Which left the office first at the end of the interview—Mrs. Raynor or Walsh?"

"Walsh," answered Craig positively.

"Some time before?"

"Yes, for after he went away I looked up Raynor's account and made out a check to Mrs. Raynor for the money due him."

Miss Royce walked to the broad window and stared a few seconds at the towers of the skyscrapers. Then she turned decisively and said:

"Mr. Craig, kindly have Walsh come in here."

He entered the office lumberingly—a huge, big-handed man with a round head whose red hair was closely cropped. His face revealed rough, brutal features, lightened, however, by small, cunning, darting green eyes. When he was asked by

Craig to tell Miss Royce all he could of Raynor and the circumstances of his disappearance, he stared at the girl and laughed.

"You are a detective?" he grinned. "A sort of suffragette detective! Say, what's the Blaney Agency doing anyway, Mr. Craig—stringing you? What can a girl like this do in the case. It's just as I thought—they can't make head nor tail of it themselves and so they send this kid around as a bluff. You ought to send this girl back to her knitting."

"Still," interrupted Miss Royce smilingly, "you might do me the favor of telling me what you know."

"What's the use?' retorted Walsh. "I'm tired talking about the thing anyway. And you'll see—in the end it will be just as I've said from the first. Raynor got played out working long hours and got a little hazy in the head. He's wandering somewhere and he'll turn up in time all right."

"But how about the man who met Mrs. Raynor and threatened her husband's life if she sought the aid of the police?"

"Hysterics," snorted Walsh. "She's gone a little off, too with the worry of the thing. I don't believe there ever was any such man. Imagined it, that's what she did."

He turned angrily and lumbered out of the room.

"Miss Royce," began Craig, "I must apologize for"—

"There's no need of it, I assure you," she said easily. "He may be right, of course. I think I'll go now and see Mrs. Raynor."

One fact stood sharply out in the mind of the young detective as she left the offices of the Union Bank Note Company—the presence of Walsh at the interview between Craig and Mrs. Raynor. He had heard Craig promise to set the police hard upon the hunt for Raynor. Walsh had left Craig's office several minutes before Mrs. Raynor's departure. In that period of time the object of the distressed woman's visit to Craig had become known. At the very threshold of the Union Bank Note Company had stood the dark, black-bearded man who accosted her and threatened the life of her husband if the police were called to investigate his strange disappearance. How had the black-bearded man learned so swiftly of what had passed between Mrs. Raynor and Craig? The evidence pointed straight at Walsh.

In driving up to the Raynor home at Mount Vernon she noticed particularly its isolation, the stretch of woods separating it from its neighbors, no building near but an old, deserted church. It was a pretty home, with well-ordered lawns and the neatness and comfort of the furnishings within spoke favorably for the little, sorrowful woman, the missing Raynor's wife. That she was suffering keenly was noticeable, but she spoke quietly and coherently and there was no evidence of a nervous condition.

"After this man had spoken to you, what did he do?" asked Miss Royce.

"He walked quickly to the curb where a taxicab was waiting. He turned just before he got into it to look back and frowned savagely at me. Then he jumped in the cab and before I really had realized what had happened, the cab was gone."

Miss Royce seated herself at Raynor's desk and sorted the papers. Receipted bills from tradesmen, the fire insurance policy on his home, these and other papers of like nature were all that came to her hand until she paused holding an envelope with no enclosure save a small dark green object deep in one corner. Miss Royce shook it out, looked at it carefully and finally held it up for the gaze of Mrs. Raynor.

"Is this an emblem of any secret society to which your husband belonged?" she asked.

The object held up was a tiny horseshoe fashioned of a metal that somewhat resembled oxidized silver. It was a perfectly made little horseshoe, very carefully curved with the end deftly turned up and was complete even to little perforations to serve for the insertion of nails in affixing the shoe.

Mrs. Raynor smiled sadly as she looked at it.

"He belonged to no secret society," she answered. "That little horseshoe was sent to him for luck," her eyes filled with tears, "for all the good that's come of it. It's rather odd about the little horseshoe though. It was delivered to David the day before his disappearance."

"There is no stamp on the envelope," observed Miss Royce. "Was it delivered by hand?"

"Yes, a uniformed messenger brought it to him at the company's offices. What puzzled Dave was that there was no note or card from the sender. We talked it over, however, and decided that whoever it might be, the sender had simply in absentmindedness failed to inclose a note or card."

"An A. D. T. boy?"

"Yes."

An hour later and she was sitting in the office of the general superintendent of the A. D. T. service.

As a result Miss Royce not long afterward was interviewing Jimmy Smith, A. D. T. 1524 at one of the downtown offices of the company.

"He was a dark guy," the boy said; "with a black beard. He met me right outside the office here when I was coming in from delivering another message. He gave me the letter and walked around to the Union Company Building with me—just a couple of blocks. He says I'm to be sure not to give the letter to anybody but Mr. Raynor himself."

II

"Good God!" cried "Billy" Fenton of the United States Secret Service, leaning far over a table in the Grosvenor restaurant and staring at the youthful Alice Royce; "where did you get that?"

The girl held up the little green horseshoe so that it was very near his eyes. He took it from her swiftly and looked at it more closely.

"That little horseshoe seems to have a special meaning for you, Billy Fenton," she said.

He looked up quickly.

"This is no case for you, Alice," he said gravely. "A girl's got no business in this. Alice, this is leading you up against the worst gang of counterfeiters in the country—counterfeiters and murderers, too. That little horseshoe is the sign of the gang. You know where I saw a thing like that last? I saw it in the hand of Jim Hillary in a little hut up in the mountains in Pike County, Pennsylvania. Poor

Jim was stretched dead on the floor with a bullet through his brain and the Secret Service had lost one of its best men. He had grown too hot on their trail. First they sent him a letter inclosing one of these little things—nothing more. And then they left a little horseshoe in his dead hand as a warning to the rest of us."

"Billy," said the girl; "I've found the black-bearded man who Sent that horseshoe to David Raynor."

"How?"

"Followed Walsh, the Union Bank Note Company's foreman. They had dinner together at a little Fourth avenue hotel where 'black beard' is stopping. He is registered as John Romano. He's leaving the hotel to-night. The porter has had his baggage checked and his berth purchased for Asheville, N. C. He goes on the 10 o'clock train from the Pennsylvania."

"Well, wherever he goes—at the end of the route, we'll find Raynor. I can't tell you little lady how grateful I am that you thought to let me in on this; that you figured out a missing engraver might have something to do with a counterfeiting plot. I can see the game right now. Raynor's straight as a die, but they've got him down there making him work on the finer touches of their counterfeit plates—making him work at the point of a pistol. They've probably promised him a safe return home after he has delivered the goods to them. But if that gang isn't landed before Raynor finishes his work—well, Raynor'll never see his wife and kids again. He'd know too much."

"Do you think they'd"—the color left the girl's lips as she halted on the question.

"They'd kill him like a dog and leave his body to the vultures somewhere up in those Carolina mountains. I tell you it is the worst gang that ever operated—Romano, 'The Wolf,' they call him, and another Italian, 'The Rat,' a German, two Spaniards and a Greek. They've flooded half the countries of Europe with bad money. They've established some sort of Southern connection— we had a vague line on that. But now, thanks to you Alice, we may be led straight to their hidden mountain 'plant.'"

"And Raynor?" said the girl who, for all her courage, grew half sick at the thought.

"Billy" Fenton reached over the table and patted her hand.

"I don't suppose there's any use," he said, "asking you to keep out of this?"

"Billy," she said; "my assignment is to find David Raynor, and at any risk to myself to try and restore him to his family alive and well."

Pleasant-faced "Billy" Fenton nodded.

"I was pretty sure you'd say that." Then he added more gravely: "They've had Raynor down there about three weeks now. They've probably gotten out of him all they want or nearly so. There's only one thing that looks hopeful. If sentence of death were passed on Raynor I hardly think it would be executed till 'The Wolf' got there. And we'll get there when he does—get there, I hope to God, in time."

At first the trailing of Romano, "The Wolf," was easy. They were his companions on the train to Asheville, and also when he changed cars there to board a little branch road whose terminal was at Murphy.

The serious setback came when Romano alighted at Murphy village. To escape observation they hung back in the little station waiting room watching as he strode impatiently up and down the platform, every few seconds anxiously peering up the road. Suddenly down the mountain path in a cloud of dust came a swaying, rattling buckboard drawn by two sleek, spirited, hardy mountain horses. With a shout of reproach at the driver for not having promptly met the train, The Wolf clambered to a seat beside the driver, a flaxen-haired, gaunt mountaineer; there came a cut of the lash across the horses' flanks and they went fairly galloping up the hill.

It took twenty minutes to locate a farmer who could supply them with a horse and buggy.

It was half an hour before "Billy" Fenton and Alice Royce started up the mountain. There had been a shower in the morning and the fresh wheel ruts of "The Wolf's" carriage were easily to be followed until after an eight-mile drive along the loneliest of highways. "Billy" Fenton drew rein in front of a little hotel at Clyde, just over the North Carolina border into Tennessee. There the crossing of half a dozen carriages had so crisscrossed the track that further pursuit of "The Wolf" was hopelessly cut off.

On entering the hotel, Fenton walked up to the tall, dark-visaged man behind the desk and said as he registered:

"I guess I'll be here for a few weeks. I found a young lady at the station at Murphy trying to get over here so I gave her a lift. She's very pretty. Do you know her?"

The landlord looked sharply at Alice Royce as she entered and shook his head.

"I was hoping," smiled "Billy" Fenton, "that I might get an introduction."

This little talk was in pursuance of the plan that Alice and he had made on the way over. "Billy Fenton let it be known among the hotel loungers that he was an engineer studying the practicability of establishing a trolley road from Murphy to Clyde and Greenville. Alice Royce informed the landlord's wife who seemed curious about her, that she was an artist, who had been told that rare scenic subjects were to be found in the neighborhood of the little Tennessee town. This served a double purpose, for it made seem wholly natural the long walks that the young woman took morning and afternoon with a little paint box and a light easel under her arm.

But a week passed and their reconnoitering had brought them no actual clue of the whereabouts of the counterfeiters' den. On the third night, however, Fenton showed her in his open palm four bright, new silver dollars.

"Counterfeit," he said, significantly.

Discouraged, Alice Royce came in from a fruitless walk over many miles of the mountain paths. She wearily ascended the stairs to change her dusty walking garments for a house gown. But as she was about to enter her room she halted. She stood with the door knob tightly clutched in a hand that trembled. For tacked on the outside of her bedroom door she saw a little green horseshoe—the duplicate of the one that David Raynor had received!

She drew back, glancing swiftly up and down the hallway. Then she moved swiftly down to the end of the hallway and peered at the door of "Billy" Fenton's room. It was tacked there also—the tiny green horseshoe!

So "The Wolf" knew them—knew their errand at Clyde? Yet how could he have known? Only Craig knew the whereabouts of Fenton and herself. Could Walsh have wormed it out of him and sent the information to Romano? It seemed the only explanation!

In any event she and Fenton were marked.

To her relief when she descended the stairs and stood on the little piazza it was to see "Billy" Fenton ride up on a tired pony, smiling and unharmed. He heard with a grave countenance the news she had to impart.

"Alice," he said, "this is mighty serious business. I had hoped to run down this gang myself. But with ourselves threatened and poor Raynor—God knows what may have happened to Raynor by this time!—to be rescued if he has not been already murdered, I have called Harkness and his Revenue men over from Asheville to help us. He can be of the greatest use. He and his men were born to these mountains and woods, you know. I'll ride over to Murphy's to-night. Harkness should arrive there by that time."

He paused and laid his hand in brotherly fashion on her arm.

"Little lady," he said, "you must promise me that you will not move away from the hotel to-night. No prowling about on your own account. It is important for me to meet Harkness, but unless you promise me you'll stay in the hotel every hour and every minute to-night, I will not leave you."

"All right. "Billy," she said, and they shook hands.

"In case of danger?" he asked. "Are you armed?"

She patted the bosom of her gown.

"I've thought of that," she said. "It's a 0.32-calibre."

She watched Fenton ride away.

Wearied from her long day's tramp on the mountain it was only a little after nine o'clock when she decided to retire.

She stopped short, startled. She was conscious of another presence in the room. Her eyes could distinguish no shape, but she was certain that she had heard the sharp intake of a bated breath.

The cry that Alice Royce tried to utter was strangled by a huge, powerful arm sweeping swiftly around her neck. It closed against her throat with sickening, choking force. She tried to raise her hands to tear the terrible, powerful arm away, but she was already losing consciousness, and there resulted only a feeble flutter of her hands.

Vaguely the girl realized that she was being borne over mountain roads in a rickety-ramshackle carriage, that she was blindfolded and gagged and her arms bound to her sides. The ride seemed to last for hours. Vaguely she knew that the carriage had come to the journey's end. Powerful arms lifted her at her head and feet, and she was carried up a stairway and knew a minute later that she had been laid at full length on either a bed or a lounge. Then supple fingers worked at the knots of the ropes binding her arms, the gag slipped from her mouth, and lastly, the bandage was whisked from before her eyes. She raised herself on an arm still numb from the thongs that had bound it and stared—straight into the face of "The Wolf." He held out to her a glass of water which she took and drank eagerly. Then he stepped back and threw himself in an indolent posture into a big, old-fashioned arm-chair.

The girl saw that she was in what had been the grand salon of an antebellum Southern mansion. There, seated at a big, square table in the glare of three big student lamps sat David Raynor. She knew him instantly. More than fifty times she had studied the photograph his wife had given her. It was surely David Raynor. He sat working at a bronze plate with a slender instrument. And on a chair near him was a rugged, yellow haired man with a great scar across his low, bulging forehead. And this man just then looked sharply at David Raynor.

Then the girl looked back at Romano. She looked at him squarely, without flinching.

"Well?" she demanded finally. "What do you mean to do with me?"

"I could have you killed," he said sharply. "I could have you killed here and your body never be found."

"You would have to answer to the Government," she replied steadily.

"The Wolf" laughed, showing great white teeth between his black beard.

"The Government—what does it amount to in this wilderness? There is no government here but me—I'm the government. You see, lady, what you have led yourself into. Perhaps you are relying on Fenton. Don't. We will have Fenton here to-night and—has Fenton told you what happened to Jim Hillary? Ah, yes—I see from your eyes that you know. The same will happen to him."

"And me?" asked the girl.

He arose, moved over to her and seized her roughly by the arm. In a flash the girl's hand went to the bosom at her dress. But she dropped it again, conscious of the uselessness of the gesture. She had realized that the revolver was no longer there.

He led her up the broad, old-fashioned hallway
and to a big, square windowed room.

"You will stay here," he said. "And who knows"—
he bent toward her and smiled—"who knows but
maybe we become very good friends?"

She drew away from him then in greater fear
than she had before shown. But he did not follow
her. He laughed and made a ridiculously elaborate
bow, turned and the old stairs creaked under his
heavy footfall at he descended.

Alone in the room the girl struggled and labored, dragging the heavy old bureau and bed-
stead near the doorway to be wielded into a barricade if "The Wolf" or other of the gang sought
to invade the apartment. Once or twice she closed
her eyes in uneasy slumber, but only for a few
minutes at a time. At dawn she went to one of the
big windows and looked out. Beside a tree a lanky,
red-bearded man stood looking up at her, a rifle
in his hand. He leered and she drew quickly away
from the window. An ashen-haired, shoulder-bent
woman brought her a breakfast of corn bread, eggs
and coffee.

Nightfall found the girl near the end of her
nervous strength. Finally she had flung herself on
the bed and given away to tears. She looked out
at the great mass of giant trees and in the pale
moonlight could see in a haze the far-away peaks.

Suddenly she heard a cry—a cry from her guard beside the tree trunk below. And then his gun flashed out. A dozen flashes answered it not fifty feet away. She heard the man below groan and a second later the sound of his fall. Next came shouts and yells from Romano summoning all the gang to barricade and guard the door. The roar and smash of battle followed. A great crash came. The big Colonial door had been beaten and splintered. Men fired blankly, almost into each other's faces, as the besiegers came rushing over the barricade of chairs and tables.

Then there was silence.

Alice Royce went tottering out into the hallway, laughing and crying in her relief and joy, for through the smoke-filled house came the high clear voice of Billy Fenton shouting:

"Alice Royce—Alice, are you here? Are you safe?"

"Oh Billy Fenton, God bless you!" she answered as she saw his face through a rift in the powder smoke as he came rushing up the stairway.

Two of the counterfeiters were dead and Romano desperately wounded. The seven other men of the gang, securely handcuffed, were sent to the county jail in a big mountain stage the next morning. The investigators found evidences of a most complete counterfeiting plant, even to a huge crucible, bales of silk threads and the materials for the making of paper notes. Romano died the night after receiving his wound. In the end he made a complete confession. It implicated Walsh of the Union company. Walsh, because of his business connection, was able to buy implements and material for the counterfeiting scheme without exciting suspicion, and sold these things to Romano at exorbitant prices.

But of the manner in which Billy Fenton with Harkness and his men were able to trace Alice Royce to the criminals' rendezvous the Secret Service man said:

"You see, when I got back to the hotel and found that you were gone and saw that your effects in your room showed plainly there had been no intention on your part to leave the hotel, and remembering too the promise you made me, I knew that your disappearance was a matter of the 'little horseshoe.' I found that morning another horseshoe on my door. My trip to Murphy had also brought me information that the hotel proprietor at Clyde was a distributing agent of the counterfeiters and otherwise hand in glove with them.

"It was kind of tough," laughed Billy, "on an itinerant preacher who had a room on the same floor with me, but I took the horseshoe off my door and tacked it up on his. Then I sent a messenger to Harkness to steal into Clyde at nightfall with a picked group of his revenue men—and waited. Sure enough, when the clergyman retired to his room about 9 o'clock he was overpowered, bound and gagged and driven out here. It was the easiest thing in the world for Harkness's trained mountaineers to follow the carriage and—well, you found Raynor all right and I've done the biggest job the Secret Service has known in the last twenty years."

As for Raynor, he told his rescuers that he had known very well the significance of the little horseshoe that had been delivered to him, but had evaded telling his wife what he knew, fearful of the distress that it would cause her. Agents of the Romano gang had dogged his steps for months offering him large sums of money if he would join them and use his superior skill in putting on the finer touches in the counterfeit plates. When he threatened to expose them they made counter threats to the effect that they would kidnap and murder his children. He had taken Walsh into his confidence and Walsh had cautioned him to silence, saying that the threats of the gang were not by any means to be disregarded. Finally he had received the horseshoe.

The cuff buttons that Alice Fenton wears with her shirt waists now are tiny horseshoes washed in gold. A scarf pin of the same design is affected by handsome Billy Fenton of the Secret Service.

No. 2—The Mystery of the Blue Glove

This is a true story, "Alice Boyce," the relation of whose remarkable adventures and still more remarkable work began with "The Clue of the Little Horseshoes," is a genuine woman. Her name, like the names of all others concerned in this series, is changed at her own request. This is to protect her business and her clients. The actress about whom this story revolves is now playing on Broadway. "Mrs. Loring" and her daughter are living quietly on the Continent. "Captain Marx" is dead. "Robert King" will be easily recognized by the members of half a dozen clubs; the manner of his death alone will identify him as the central figure of this hitherto hidden tragedy—"The Mystery of the Blue Glove."

Charles Somerville

Alice Royce had been working all day at what she laughingly called a "police job." In this instance it had been something in which her heart was concerned—the gathering of evidence against the fortune-tellers, clairvoyants and other charlatans who so persistently prey upon the poor and credulous. At seven o'clock she entered her pretty Riverside apartment to be met breathlessly by Annie, her black-haired, blue-eyed Irish maid.

"All day long the dear lady have been telephonin' for ye and could hardly talk for cryin'," said Annie. "'Tis something terrible that's the matter!"

Many such excited calls came to Alice Royce's apartments, but Annie, being actively emotional, never grew hardened to them.

"Of course, you took the lady's name and address?" her young mistress asked.

"Oh, yes, miss. An' who—*who* do you think it is?"

"Well, Annie?"

"'Tis Dorothy Anderson, the great actress, Miss Alice. She says please will ye come to her the minute ye get her message—up to the Arlington Hotel, if ye get the message in time, or to her dressin' room at the theatre if it's later."

Lively interest flashed in Alice Royce's fine brown eyes at the mention of this new client, for Dorothy Anderson was a woman of rare beauty and temperament; of a talent that really approached genius. The young detective quickly consulted her watch. It was half-past seven—too late to see Miss Anderson at her home. She would have started for the Palladium Theatre by that time. So Alice Royce threw off her wraps and ate the dinner Annie had prepared for her.

The end of the first act of the new and celebrated society comedy at the Palladium found the girl detective in Dorothy Anderson's dressing room. The curtain had fallen on an audience vastly charmed and smiling over the actress's delightful portrayal of a witty, winsome character. But the dainty smiles with which she had faced the audience, answering repeated curtain calls, fell instantly from the star's lips as she made her way to her dressing room. On the way her maid met her with Alice Royce's card. The famous actress faced the young detective with her magnificently luminous eyes, large and pleading.

"Miss Royce, Mr. Scott, the dramatic agent, has told me of the wonderful cleverness you displayed once in working for him. I hope you can help me. A frightful—a hideous mistake has been made. It must be righted. The memory of a good and splendid man—the man I love, Miss Royce—must be righted. It stands now under the stigma of self-destruction. I know that's a lie. I know that Robert King did not—could not have killed himself! Yes"—the handsome woman stepped over

to her dressing table, took up an afternoon newspaper and handed it to Alice Royce. "Yet you see
here," she pointed to the particular headline "that
a coroner's jury has brought in a verdict declaring, his death to be a suicide. Robert King—a
suicide? How can I believe that? A few hours before his death we had named the day of our wedding; we had spent an entire happy Sunday evening planning our honeymoon trip; we had talked
every minute of nothing but the future. He was
a virile, healthy, brilliant-minded man, intensely
interested and in love with life and"—the actress's
eyes became suffused and she ended heartbroken-
ly—"in love with me. It is an outrage to believe
that he killed himself!"

"Could there have been any motive? Business
troubles?"

"Positively none. He was a man of leisure, a
retired British army officer in more than comfort-
able circumstances. Why, the detectives found by
his bank books that he had more than $100,000
deposited in several New York banks. He had been
a lonely man, he told me, until our meeting on
the *Kron-Prinz Wilhelm* when I was returning to
America last autumn. He told me there was no
member of his family living save some distant
cousins."

Gently Alice Royce asked the beautiful, distressed woman to recount to her the circumstances of Robert King's death as she knew them. There was no hint of pseudo-emotion in the manner in which Dorothy Anderson's lips trembled, and her rich, soft voice sank or grew vibrant as she gave this gruesome information.

"Robert," she said, "lived alone, save for a valet. His bachelor apartments were in the Crandall, in Fifth avenue, near the Central Park plaza. He left me at eleven o'clock Sunday night. We had planned for a motor ride and a dinner on Long Island the next day. He showed no signs of depression. When he did not call for me at noon I telephoned his apartments. No answer could be had. The telephone boy said Mr. King's valet had left on Saturday to fetch from Connecticut two saddle horses which his master had purchased. Thoroughly anxious and certain that Robert would not have slighted me, I went to the Crandall and begged the superintendent of the apartment house to have the door forced open.

"It was not necessary. We found the door opened to a turn of the knob. Robert"—the actress covered her horror-stricken eyes with her hands—"was sitting in the library. He was fully dressed—in evening clothes—just as he had left me the evening before. He still wore the boutonniere that I had arranged for him from the bouquet he had sent me. There was not the slightest sign of a struggle in the room. He was sitting in the big Morris chair. His mouth drooped queerly. His eyes were staring. I knew instantly that he was dead!

"There was no wound on his body, and, save at his lips, not the slightest discoloration of his face. A faint door, queerly pungent, of peaches was in the air. On a table near his hand were two glasses. One was half filled with a colorless liquid—simply water. But the other glass was empty and over it was the faint yet biting odor of peaches. There was no letter—nothing."

Outside the dressing room door came the piping cry of the callboy: "Miss Anderson—Miss Anderson. Curtain—curtain!"

The actress turned swiftly to her mirror. A dab of powder on her forehead, the swift touch of a pencil to her eyes and she swept out of the room. A moment later Alice Royce heard her clear laughter ringing from the stage.

II

After the play the girl detective questioned her client more closely. The results were few. At times King had been subject to moods of depression.

But he had held a vigorous contempt for suicide. Leaning a little toward theosophy he had believed that for a man to kill himself was to destroy not only his body, but his soul. All this was negative. Alice Royce listened to it, made a few notes and proceeded to the next logical step.

This was a visit to Inspector Langley, chief of the New York detective bureau. It had fallen within his province to handle the case from its inception. In a few crisp, analytical sentences he imparted to Alice Royce his findings. Briefly, they were that there had never been a clearer case of suicide. King had entered his apartments at midnight. The negro hall boy had heard no disturbance. There had not been the slightest evidence of a struggle. Nothing whatever of an outwardly sinister nature had happened from the moment King had closed his door until the time he was found dead, with two glasses beside him, one full of water, the other smelling of cyanide. A mistake? No, the odor of cyanide would have warned him. Anyway, what would the poison have been doing there?

"Now," concluded the Inspector, "can you see anything in it except suicide?"

"No," admitted the girl detective, "it would really appear that Miss Anderson's refusal to believe in her fiancé's suicide was based purely on sentiment.

However, she has employed me to make as exhaustive an investigation as possible. You would have no objection, Inspector, to my examining Robert King's rooms?"

"Go as far as you like, little lady," smiled Langley. "You will find the rooms exactly as they were the morning the body was found. In the event of possible developments I gave the superintendent of the Crandall apartments strict instructions to admit no one; to disturb nothing. Go ahead—and good luck to you."

III

It was evident to the eye of Alice Royce that King's apartments had been in no way disturbed and that, indeed, the police examination of the rooms had been no more than cursory. The body had been removed to an undertaking establishment, and the funeral held in a chapel connected with that establishment. There had been a brief ceremony, attended only by such acquaintances as the dead man had made at the clubs and hotels. One of these was his attorney, Alexander Hall. Alice Royce had talked with Hall that morning over the telephone. He had said that he knew nothing of his client's foreign affairs. King had made no will, the lawyer was sure.

The wealthy bachelor's rooms were carpeted with rare rugs. The library-living room was furnished with massive chairs, a centre table of mahogany, and a splendid old buffet, well stocked with fine wines, liquors and much delicate glassware. There were engravings of battle and hunting scenes on the walls, and Remington and Barye bronzes on the table, mantel shelves and pedestals. Books in fine bindings lined the walls. The bedroom was undisturbed. In her minute search of the rooms the girl detective did not hesitate to go carefully through the contents of the desk. She forced open a locked compartment and found a packet of Dorothy Anderson's letters. She took the liberty of scanning these, but read in them no line to suggest anything but the beautiful young woman's deep love for the dead man.

But the aspect of the big, broad, silver-mounted blotter on the desk caused the searcher to look at it closely. There were several lines of writing crisscrossing each other on it. She picked up the blotter with the idea of holding it before the mantel mirror to decipher the reverse impression. Then she paused. In the spot where the blotter had rested lay a sheet of large, heavy stationery. On it were three lines of large, rugged handwriting. The young detective read:

Sunday, —.

Dearest Dorothy:

Forgive me for the pain I am about to inflict upon you, my darling. But it is better that you should learn—

For an instant, as Alice Royce sat studying this significant, incomplete writing of the dead man it seemed only to confirm the police theory of suicide. Robert King had been in trouble; there was something painful, perhaps disgraceful, concerning himself that he had felt bound to reveal to his fiancée. Yet why had he broken off suddenly in the writing of the letter! If he had at first meant to write her a communication before destroying himself and had changed his mind, deciding to leave no word behind, surely he would have destroyed the letter he had begun, and not slipped it into an obvious hiding place under the blotter.

Alice Royce arose, intending to finish her search of the apartment with a close examination of King's bedroom and all the pockets of his clothing. Heavy portieres hung between the library and the bedroom. As she thrust one of them back, stretching out the folds by the movement, a little cry of surprise escaped the girl's lips. She bent swiftly and arose, holding up to scrutiny a glove—a woman's glove! It was a long, soft glove.

Most notable, however, was the color, decidedly unusual, the girl detective decided, for the leather was dyed a dark or navy blue. Of course, there were cloves of that color to be purchased in nearly any store, but the choice was uncommon—white, black, tan or gray being the shades generally in use.

The possibility suggested itself that this blue glove might be the property of Dorothy Anderson, something King had treasured as a memento. Alice Royce went to the telephone and was soon in communication with the actress. Her reply had an unusual interest.

"No," Miss Anderson said, "the glove is not mine. Did you say it was a blue glove? That is strange. One of Mr. King's peculiarities which I failed to tell you about was a marked aversion to the color of blue."

Turning then to a further examination of the blue glove, Alice Royce had the satisfaction of finding stamped quite legibly on the inside of it the name of the manufacturers. It was that of a domestic firm with main offices in New York City. At the manufacturers she was told that the consignment of blue gloves had only recently come from the factory and that only one retail firm in New York had as yet any of them on their counter. The name of this firm was readily supplied. Alice

Royce, half an hour later, was engaged in questioning the girls at the long glove counter there.

The first three girls were able to tell her nothing save that none had sold a pair of blue gloves. There was no demand for the color, they explained. But the fourth girl, after pondering a little, said:

"Why sure, I remember selling a pair of long blues, the only pair I did sell. I remember the customer well, because—well, the poor lady was blind. She was a pretty, slender woman about forty, I guess, although her hair was almost white. But her face was young, and her big, closed, blind eyes looked awful pitiful. She was with a young girl—her daughter sure. They looked a lot alike. She asked particularly for blue gloves and I couldn't help noticing that the gloves she had on were blue, and that her dress was blue, and her hat was a toque made of blue velvet."

"Did you send the gloves to her home?" asked Alice Royce eagerly.

"No," said the girl. "I'm sure she took the parcel with her."

"Perhaps she charged them. Has she an account with the store?"

"She paid cash," replied the girl, positively.

All that the young detective, knew, therefore, was that the woman of the blue gloves was blind, middle-aged and had a daughter about seventeen years old. But surely she had been a visitor to Robert King's rooms—or, that is, at least some woman owning a blue glove had visited there. If it was the blind woman the hallboys must certainly remember her because of her very affliction. The police had said that there had been no visitors on the night of the tragedy. But Alice Royce had decided to inquire more carefully into it, remembering also that the police had missed the letter and the blue glove. She was wholly unprepared, however, for the startling revelations that awaited her at the Crandall. She went there about nine o'clock that night, that she might see the boy on duty at the telephone and doorway in the hours just before and after midnight on the date of King's strange death.

In the first place, close questioning produced marked confusion in the colored boy. She had found him gossiping with another young negro, whose brown uniform indicated he had come from a neighboring apartment house. The Crandall boy's was green. The other lad stepped aside only a little way and openly listened to the conversation between the Crandall telephone boy and Miss Royce. By the shifting of the latter boy's eyes and his stammering replies the investigator became certain that he was concealing knowledge of importance.

"Jim," she said suddenly to him, "don't you know that if you hide anything you might be suspected yourself of killing Mr. King?"

"Yas'm," said the boy with downcast eyes. "Yas'm, I reckon maybe I better tell. But I'm mighty scared to do it, miss. Jes' about twelve o'clock Saturday night—mebbe a little later—there come a man an' a lady an' a girl askin' for Mistuh King. I phoned to him and he says for 'em to be shown right up. Dey was dere mebbe three-quarters of an hour. You knows de room is jest up one flight, but I didn't hear no loud talkin' or queer sounds or nothin'. When dey come out—da man and lady and girl—de man come up to me and he slipped me ten dollars right in my hand, and he said no matter who asks me I mustn't say nothin' 'bout him and his friends bein' up to see Mr. King. De little girl was lookin' white and scared, too, an' she could hardly walk along leadin' de other lady."

"Leading the other lady?" Alice Royce asked swiftly.

"Yas'm, de other lady was blind."

"Huh!" interjected the boy in the brown uniform, "dat's funny. Dere's a blind lady living where I work."

"Where's that?"

"Right around the corner, lady. De back wind-ers looks right over de court inter de winders of dis yer house; yas'm."

IV

Tremulous with anxiety, Dorothy Anderson made her way—at the call of Alice Royce to the Harmsworth apartments in West 7—th street. The girl detective over the telephone had said:

"When you arrive at the Harmsworth ask for Mrs. Jane Loring. It is from her lips that a full ex-planation of Robert King's death is to come. I fear it may be a painful recital to you. However, she refuses to clear the mystery until you get here."

Alice Royce, facing the distressed, blind Mrs. Loring and her slender, beautiful daughter, Grace, awaited therefore the coming of the famous wom-an who had been betrothed to Robert King.

With the use of a liberal tip it had been an easy matter for the girl detective to learn from the negro hallboy of the Harmsworth the identi-ty of the blind woman, and, in turn, to have the boy make inquiry of Mrs. Loring's maid. This girl remembered the fact that her mistress had lost a long, blue glove. Possessing this knowl-edge, Alice Royce had presented herself in the Loring apartment.

"It is true that I lost the blue glove," said the blind woman. "But I know nothing of a Mr. King and was certainly not in his rooms. It is highly probable that I dropped the glove in the street and that the gentleman picked it up and carried it into his apartments."

Alice Royce studied the other woman keenly.

"I notice, Mrs. Loring," said she softly, "that you seem invariably to wear blue."

"Why do you mention that?" demanded the blind woman, sitting suddenly erect

"Robert King hated blue," replied the investigator sharply.

"Hated it?" faltered Mrs. Loring. "Then he remembered—"

Too late she tried to check herself. The girl at her side trembled and began to sob.

"Mrs. Loring," said Alice Royce kindly, "you have betrayed yourself. You knew Robert King. You know something of his death. I have proof that you and your daughter and Captain Marx were in his rooms within an hour of this mysterious tragedy. Miss Anderson, his fiancée, has retained me to clear this matter up. You had better confide in me."

The blind woman had arisen and stood gently swaying, her daughter's arm supporting her. But she was silent.

"Mother," spoke the girl in a husky whisper, "why not speak? It really doesn't matter now. You know the news we received only this morning. Captain Marx has only a few hours to live. He is unconscious even now." Grace looked toward Alice Boyce. "We were just about to start to Captain Marx's rooms," she said. "He is dying."

The woman in blue sank slowly back into her chair.

"Grace is right," she said finally. "I had best tell you everything since Captain Marx is dying. But I think it is only just to Miss Anderson that, as the one vitally interested, she should herself hear my story."

"It would be best," agreed Alice Royce. When she returned from the telephone, however, she uttered the question uppermost in her mind. "Mrs. Loring, did Robert King commit suicide?"

"He did not."

"Then he was murdered?"

"He was not." The blind woman hesitated. "The law perhaps might call it something like that, but morally, no, he was not murdered."

In brooding silence the woman in blue sat throughout the fifteen minutes that it took Dorothy Anderson to arrive from her own apartments.

"Miss Anderson is here, mother," said Grace in a whisper, bowing slightly to the handsome woman who had been admitted.

Mrs. Loring began immediately to tell the manner of Robert King's death. "His right name was George Loring," she said, "and I was his wife, Grace his daughter. He was formerly Colonel of the — Dragoons, stationed in India. My father was a British army officer. I had lived in India from early childhood. At seventeen I was engaged to a handsome, brave officer, Captain Ellwynne Marx. He was slated for promotion, but when Colonel Loring, a dashing young officer of precocious achievement, took charge of the post he evinced a quick prejudice to Marx. He secured the captain's removal to a distant post.

"You may imagine the anxiety I suffered when, from the time of this assignment of Captain Marx, I had no word from him. Then slanderous stories began circulating about him—about his affairs with native women. I turned from all thought of him in disgust, and when Colonel Loring began to shower attentions on me I was flattered by them— in brief, within two years after the Captain's silence had begun I was Colonel Loring's wife.

"Then one day on the piazza of our bungalow—three years afterward—I was confronted by Captain Marx. It was a frightful, shocking story he had to tell me of Loring's perfidy. The letters of our engagement days had been intercepted by Loring. My husband, during an insurrection, had assigned Marx to lead a scouting party. Bribed hillsmen had captured him. For three years he had lived as a slave among savages. His health irreparably broken, his heart seared by the belief that I had been utterly false to him, he had nevertheless contrived his escape and made his way to our post to reproach me for my infidelity and demand satisfaction of Colonel Loring.

"I was enraged to the point of hysteria when I heard the Captain's story. I did not attempt to dissuade him from his purpose of revenge on Loping, but I demanded that first my husband hear his condemnation from my lips. I was beside myself. I spoke with frightful bitterness. I told him that he was a disgrace to the uniform he wore—his was a blue regiment—and that whenever he looked at it it should remind him of his treachery to me and to Ellwynne Marx, if Marx did not kill him, as he richly deserved. It made no difference to me then that he was Grace's father. I upbraided him fiercely—so fiercely that in wild anger he struck me—struck me across the eyes and I fainted. There came a seizure of brain fever and the awful result was that I suffered paralysis of the optic nerves and was doomed to hopeless blindness.

"My husband did not stay to face Captain Marx—could not. He deserted his regiment, fled from India, never appeared in England and appears to have found refuge in America. All these years Captain Marx sought trace of him and finally found him. He sent for me then, saying that it was a matter of life or death between him and Loring, and it was only right that I should see Loring before he died in order that my daughter, Grace, should not suffer in the inheritance of her father's fortune. So I came. Captain Marx apprised Loring of my presence in this country late Saturday night—when he returned to his apartments. This conversation was over the telephone, Loring not knowing who his informant was. The Captain waited until that late hour so that we would be sure of an interview undisturbed."

Alice Royce remembered the unfinished note found under the blotter in Loring's rooms. Realizing his wife's presence in America meant the end of his new romance, he had evidently decided to make a clean breast of affairs to Dorothy Anderson.

"I don't remember—I can't remember all that was said. I could not, of course, observe the expression in my husband's eyes when he recognized in our escort the man he had wronged mercilessly and wretchedly. I heard his cry of astonishment at sight of his daughter, and I know he kissed her and I heard him sob.

"The men spoke lowly together for a while, but then Captain Marx's voice, thin and strident from his long illness, rose:

"'You know, by God, Loring, what is expected of you as an officer and a gentleman. You know what the men of your command in India would have done if you had remained to face your just dishonor. They would have sent you a revolver in silence. If you are not lost to all sense of shame, of honor among soldiers, you will make now the reparation that I demand!'

"'But, Marx, before my own child?'

"Then I heard the Captain speaking very slowly, each word measuredly spoken:

"'On the child's account alone I will give you one chance with me for your life. I have here a bottle of deadly poison. Get me two glasses of water. Put them here on this table.'

"Loring obeyed, spellbound by the other man's intensity.

"'Turn your back,' said Marx coldly. 'In one of these glasses of water I will pour a poison that will mean certain death. When I give the word, Loring, if you are not utterly a coward, you will turn and choose one of these glasses, drinking its contents to the last drop. On the other hand, I will promise you to drink the glass that's left. If you escape you will no longer have me to fear.'

"'It wasn't death I feared when I ran away from India,' Loring retorted. 'I simply could not face the hatred and shame of you—and Jane. I'll show you, Marx, now whether or not I can meet death like a man. Give the word.'

"'Now!' cried Captain Marx, and Loring wheeled and faced the table on which stood the two glasses—one containing harmless water, the other deadly poison. He hesitated only the small fraction of a second over the choice—so infinitely brief a time that as my daughter Grace ran toward him with arms outstretched, uttering a little, piteous cry, she was too late to stay his hand. He had taken up one of the glasses, lifted it to his lips, and in a single gulp had poured its contents down his throat. He fell back in the big chair, grasped the arms of it rigidly and in that instant was dead."

"Alice Royce," said the actress, Dorothy Anderson, unsteadily, "please take me home!"

No. 3—The Missing $100,000 Necklace

In the matter of the reported robbery of the $100,000 diamond necklace belonging to Mrs. Ada Vantine, wife of Richard H. Vantine, the silver and copper king, and taken from their $20,000-a-year apartment at the St. Lazar Hotel on Fifth avenue, New York, Alice Royce, girl detective, was called to the office of the Blaney Detective Agency of world-wide reputation one morning in December last year and immediately admitted to the private office of the famous James W. Blaney himself.

The chief arose, extended a hand in greatest cordiality toward the brown-haired, rosy-cheeked, gypsy-eyed young woman whose skill in past cases had won his professional admiration. When they were seated he approached rather curiously to the matter in hand.

"Vantine," said he, "is a handsome man of fifty with a youthful face against his iron-gray hair and mustache, dresses very well, is genial, likable and keenly interested and in love with life. Mrs. Vantine is a beauty and very much younger than her husband—not quite half his age I should say. You will certainly recall her, I think. She was, up to her marriage to Vantine six months ago, Ada Romaine of the musical comedy stage, just about due to receive a star part. But after her marriage to Vantine she gave up the stage entirely—seemingly without any regret whatsoever. As far as we can find, she has been as genuinely in love with her rather elderly husband as the millionaire is with her."

Blaney paused and smiled.

"I suppose you are beginning to wonder what all this has to do with the robbery of the $100,000 necklace. Frankly, perhaps nothing in particular. At any rate, never mind my ideas. Go to the case yourself with a free mind.

"In every one of the apartments de luxe at the St. Lazar there is built in the wall—usually one of the bedrooms—a small steel, fireproof safe with a combination lock for the deposit of guests' valuables. Mrs. Vantine kept her jewels—the principal article of which was the $100,000 necklace, which the mine owner gave her on their wedding day—in such a safe in their rooms.

"Three nights ago when the couple returned from the opera Mrs. Vantine broke the clasp of the necklace when removing it. This happened in the presence of her husband. He expressed sympathy, of course, and offered on his way to business next day to leave the necklace for repairs at Daroney's. There it had been made, matched and purchased. She urged rather insistently at the time that he go to no such trouble—she would take the $100,000 ornament to Daroney's herself. Vantine, having an early business engagement the next morning, arose before his wife, breakfasted alone in the sunparlor, then bethought himself of the necklace and decided it were better for him to take it to Daroney's rather than risk his wife, unattended, carrying so expensive a piece of jewelry. The wall safe being in his own sleeping room, he opened it and abstracted the necklace without awakening his wife.

"Now, Vantine in later years had become something of a connoisseur on precious stones. He wears very little jewelry himself, but for years past had collected gems and then, when he married, took keen pleasure in having them set in rings, pendants, tiaras and otherwise for the adornment of his young wife's person. Sitting in the privacy of his motor car he drew out the necklace to examine the injury to the clasp. He uttered an involuntary exclamation of astonishment. He stared again—closely—and knew he had made no mistake. For in the cold, clear morning light he saw that, splendidly skillful in workmanship though they were, the stones of the necklace he held in his hand were not genuine diamonds—were, in fact, fakes—paste!"

Then, according to Blaney's further account, Vantine, utterly forgetting his business engagement, turned the car back for the St. Lazar, dumfounded by the storm of conjecture and doubt that swept over him. It was out of the question that a house like that of Daroney had foisted an imitation necklace on him. Besides, it had passed over the counter directly into his own hands at the time. From his own knowledge the necklace then received was genuine. Yet where but at Daroney's could have been fashioned of false gems so perfect a replica? Could his wife have disposed for money of the original and ordered this substitute that he held in his hand? But why? She knew his financial resources to be practically unlimited; her every wish his greatest desire to fulfil. He flushed to have even thought of this explanation. He went with rushing steps to his wife's chamber to announce his discovery. She sat up suddenly in bed—her beauty undiminished by the disorder of her golden hair and the drowsiness of her large blue eyes. Then to his astonishment she gave way to an outburst of tears and admitted that she knew the necklace to be false.

"Oh," he laughed with reassurance, "I think I understand. You thought the better to protect my wedding gift by using a paste duplicate for ordinary occasions. You have the genuine necklace in the safe?"

"No," she stammered. "The real necklace is gone. I've—I've been robbed!"

"Not of all your jewelry, surely?"

"No—only the necklace. It—it happened two months ago."

"But why did you say nothing to me?" cried Vantine, speaking angrily for the first time to his girlish wife. "Why was I kept in ignorance? Why was I not told so that the police and private detectives could be set to trace the thief?" He yielded to sudden bitterness. "You must have thought pretty lightly of my gift."

"Oh, Dick—Dick, dear," she pleaded, "I simply could not tell you. I felt so ashamed to have been robbed of it."

She raised her fair, slender arms toward him and Vantine's reproaches passed swiftly to words of comfort and endearment.

So then the Blaney detectives had been sent for. Their inquiries led nowhere. Mrs. Vantine could give no slightest hint of how the theft might have been committed. Only she and her husband knew the combination of the safe. He was able to state with certainty that every night his wife had worn the costly necklace he had taken it in his own hands and locked it in the safe in his own sleeping room.

The suggestion was made that Lucy, his wife's colored maid, might perhaps have effected a sleight-of-hand substitution of the imitation necklace for the genuine during some few seconds when her mistress had spread it on her bureau while dressing or retiring. Young Mrs. Vantine became nearly hysterical with resentment of this idea. She declared Lucy to be most faithful and honest, brought herself from her old home in Georgia. Indeed a rigorous investigation not only of Lucy's habits, associations and movements but those of every other servant who might have had access of the rooms lifted suspicion from all of them.

There was then considered the fire-escape running up the north side of the hotel—the possibility of a thief entering in the night into Mr. Vantine's sleeping room. But the combination lock of the safe gave no mark and, even presuming the thief to have been one of those ultra-clever criminals who can "feel" out a combination by a wizardry and refinement of touch, the rungs of the fire-escape showed the scrape of no foot on their rungs, freshly painted only a few months back, to say nothing of the foolhardy daring of a thief who attempted such a thing practically under the glaring lights of the avenue.

Blaney then told Alice Royce that search had been made in every pawnshop in every city and town in the United States and of the capitals of Europe without trace being found of the necklace as a whole or the finding of any diamonds of the odd size and "cut" of the missing gems.

II

When Alice Royce had been made acquainted with these baffling circumstances in the case of the missing $100,000 necklace it really first appeared as if every possible avenue of investigation had been treaded and in vain. Yet, underlying, she found one subtle suggestion. On this she acted promptly when, leaving Blaney's office, she went directly to the Vantine apartments in the St Lazar and was presently face to face with the former musical comedy beauty.

The sight of young Mrs. Vantine momentarily put to flight the thoughts that had entered Alice Royce's mind. An exquisite creature she was surely,

with a wondrous charm of slender youth, bright-
ness of eyes and rosiness of lips. When she learned
the girl detective's errand, however, there came a
sudden, impulsive drooping of her mouth and an
evasion and weariness in her eyes.

"They have given you a most hopeless task,
Miss Royce," she said. "Something tells me that
my necklace will simply never be found. I know
it. Just as there appears to be no possible information as to how it was stolen, there isn't the
slightest clue to lead to its recovery. Detectives
have been going and coming—going and coming.
What good have they done? I am perfectly willing
to answer all questions, but what can I possibly
tell you, Miss Royce, that I have not already told
the others?"

And, indeed, half an hour's patient questioning
gave Miss Alice Royce no more information than
she already possessed.

"Mrs. Vantine," said the girl detective then,
"when your husband first discovered that the
necklace you were wearing was paste the genuine
necklace had been missing all of two months. The
imitation necklace is almost perfect. How did you
make the discovery that it was paste?"

"Oh, I don't know—instinct, I suppose. One
day when I was looking at it I felt in doubt of it."

"Did you take it to Daroney's to make sure?"

"Oh, no. I just instinctively knew it was not the original necklace of genuine diamonds."

"Did Daroney make this particular imitation necklace?"

"No—the detectives have already inquired there."

In her general observation of the room Alice Royce's eyes had noted a delicate bird's-eye maple escritoire with the lid down. She quickly, however, transferred her gaze to Mrs. Vantine's pretty face.

"I have been told," she said, "that the safe combination shows no marks whatever. May I ask you to be so good as to show me your jewel case?"

"Certainly," said the millionaire's wife. "If you will excuse me a minute I will go to Richard's room. It may take me a little time—I have to fuss a dreadful while before I can work that combination."

With something of a qualm at the action she was taking, but spurring herself with the consciousness of the strange duties that her work sometimes required, Alice Royce stepped swiftly over to the dainty little desk. On it was a double blotter, the pad fastened with silver corners. Swiftly she abstracted the two blotters and substituted fresh ones that were fortunately at hand in one of the pigeon-holes. In view also was a bankbook that she took up hastily. She noted that it was rather

old and in the name of Ada Romaine, and scanning its entries she saw that they marked deposits
in the sum of a few thousand dollars made prior
to the actress's marriage to Richard Vantine. And,
what was more interesting, that since her wedding there had been several heavy drawings on the
slender account. The last had been about three
months before and only a few weeks prior to the
date given by Mrs. Vantine as being that on which
she discovered the substitution of the spurious
necklace for the genuine.

When Mrs. Vantine entered it was to find Alice
Royce seated in the chair where she had last seen
her. A cursory examination of the ivory and gold
jewel case was followed by a negative nod of the
detective's head.

"Mrs. Vantine," she further inquired, "you frequently have visitors—friends of your old profession?"

"Yes, but none of these are possibly to be suspected. Why, I never have allowed the necklace to
pass out of my hands hardly—surely never out of
my sight."

Alice Royce arose.

"It would rather appear as though I had taken
up your time uselessly," she observed. "I'm sorry."

But the millionaire's young wife was most gracious in her manner of showing her visitor out,

and it was with a certain hesitation that later, at luncheon in a nearby restaurant, Alice Royce drew a tiny vanity mirror from her handbag and with it the two blotter slips she had found on Mrs. Vantine's desk. Under the reflection of the mirror she deciphered several scraps of names and words on one of the blotters. The names were all feminine. But on the other was a single name and the impression was easily legible. "Robert J. Mallory jr.," she read and then below a blur ending "—nta, Ga."

Further writing there was on this blotter. Patient examination with the mirror disclosed "—rest Bob" and "—dying to see you" and "greatest love."

Alice Royce ate lightly. In fact, she surprised the waiter with a generous tip that did not seem to coincide with a luncheon half-eaten.

The bankbook she had seen on Mrs. Vantine's desk directed her to the Gibraltar Trust Company. To her card, reading, "Alice Royce, Investigator," she added the word "Urgent." This she sent to the President and was soon standing before that slim, elderly chief director.

She hesitated only an instant. That which was to be done—flatly it was her duty.

"Mr. Preston, Richard H. Vantine's compliments, and I am instructed," said Miss Royce, "to ask you the exact sum privately loaned by you to

Mrs. Vantine with her diamond necklace as secu-
rity."

"Why, fifty thou—"

Mr. Preston suddenly adjusted his glasses.

"But, see here," he said indignantly, "the transaction was in strictest confidence between Mrs.
Vantine and myself and"—

"The draft was sent to Robert H. Mallory jr. at
Atlanta, Ga.?"

"I did not say so," retorted the President, rapidly whipping off his glasses and starting to polish
them feverishly with a spotless white linen handkerchief.

"Oh, it's all right, Mr. Preston," said the girl
detective with a friendly smile. "It's simply Mr.
Vantine's desire"— she paused.

"Naturally," said Mr. Preston, "with me it was
simply the desire to oblige a client who seemed
somewhat distressed. And, of course, Mr. Vantine
will understand that the necklace is in my own
confidential keeping and to be redeemed at—er—
the usual rate of interest."

"Naturally," said Alice Royce, and departed.

III

She thought then that she had practically reached
the end of the case. And yet gentle, womanly

pity touched her strongly on behalf of beautiful, youthful Mrs. Vantine. The first impression had been that a blackmailer—some man or woman of her early stage days who had knowledge of her life which she would dearly pay to keep from her husband—had attacked the wealthy mine owner's wife. But the writing on the blotters—the translation of "—rest Bob" to "Dearest Bob" had been so obvious, coupled with "dying to see you" and "greatest love," convinced Alice Royce that, the location of Robert J. Mallory being Atlanta, Ga., she had to deal with some lover of Ada Romaine's girlhood days whom she still adored and who, on her having achieved marriage with a millionaire, was so unscrupulous as to plead his poverty, to perhaps hold over her the exposure of an old betrothal; even, were he of so contemptible a bent, to threaten a breach of promise of marriage suit against her. Such suits had been brought with men as plaintiffs. It would only take the mere threat to have caused Ada Romaine to go to any length to avert such a situation. The investigation by the Blaney detectives of her whole stage career had shown that if she had ever been drawn out of the way of proper and decorous living the adventures had been most secretly performed. No evidence of it was extant. It was known that her acquaintance with Richard H. Vantine began through the medium of an introduction at the home of a famous playwright where she was a guest, and that the subsequent courtship had been enacted quite conventionally under the chaperonage of the playwright's wife.

The girl detective recoiled from the thought of carrying her knowledge to Richard H. Vantine. Rather, she decided it were best to admit to him a failure to solve the mystery of the missing necklace. But she would see Robert J. Mallory jr. and she would hold out to him the unpleasant prospect of exposure if he persisted in efforts to mulct the millionaire's bride. This would be, after all, doing Vantine the best turn, and what she knew of James W. Blaney and a certain admirable quixoticis in his nature, made her believe that the famous detective might see it also in this light.

In any event, she took the first available train to Atlanta, arriving there at nightfall. The city directory showed both a Robert H. Mallory and Robert H. Mallory jr. residing at a number in Vine street. There she found a poor, antiquated frame house with sparse shrubbery struggling hopelessly in front of it, steps awry leading to the piazza and rotting, crooked pillars supporting its roof. The house was empty—deserted. Inquiry in nearby houses made Miss Royce smile, but not happily. The Mallorys had suddenly come into

money and had moved to a beautiful new house
in Peachtree street—"right up in the newest and
prettiest part!" Spick and span, smelling, indeed
of fresh paint, was the Peachtree street house into
which the Mallorys had moved. Spick and span
and awkward in her new black gown, white apron
and cap was the negress who answered the door-
bell. Spick and span and all glossy with fresh var-
nish were floors and furniture in the parlor into
which she was shown. Quite clearly she heard the
maid upstairs saying: "Dere's a Yankee lady downstairs to see you, Mistuh Rob. Heah's her cyard."

"What?" she heard a young voice exclaim. "A
client already?"

A minute later and Mallory entered the room.
He was little more than a boy—a smiling, very
good-looking boy as well. He must be even younger, Alice Royce concluded, than the wife of the
millionaire.

"I have come to see you," said Miss Royce and
then halted. The quickest way was best. "Mr. Mallory," she said, "you know Mrs. Ada Vantine?"

"I reckon I do," he said. "Have you a message
from her, Miss Royce?"

"Hardly—from her. But"—

His youthful face grew suddenly grave.

"Has anything happened to my sister?" he demanded.

"Your"—

"Sister."

Alice Royce's cheeks grew rosier than ever. She looked into the honest, handsome, anxious eyes of young Mallory and felt ashamed.

"I thought her maiden name was Romaine," she faltered.

"The name she took for stage purposes," said the boy, staring and puzzled at her confusion.

One more glance at "Bob" Mallory and Alice Royce took him completely into her confidence. It was his turn to blush—more furiously than she had done. But the young fellow, recovering his composure, arose and slowly pacing the obviously newly furnished room said:

"The truth is mighty soon told, Miss Royce. Yes, I received the $50,000 draft from my sister. The purpose was the purchase of this house and its furnishings. You see how it is—like many other families in the South we've been wretchedly poor since the war. Why, my father has worked all his life as a bricklayer and my other sister is a stenographer and I've—well, I've been a soda water fountain boy while I've been working my way through law school. That little house in Vine street was the best we had. Ada, from the time she was a little girl, had made up her mind to go on the stage. Nothing that father or mother could say served to discourage her. She did join the chorus of a road company that played here. We, of course, looked upon her as lost, but in about a year we heard from her—affectionate, pretty letters that showed her quite unchanged, and with them clippings to show she was really making an artistic success.

"Then came her announcement of her marriage to this Yankee millionaire—a quiet ceremony, she said, at the 'Little Church Around the Corner.' It's a quaint name, isn't it? Then—she confessed it all to me in a letter, that she had been as reticent as possible with her husband concerning her family, not that she was ashamed of us you know, but ashamed to tell the poverty that had afflicted us since the civil war, ashamed of the humble occupation father was forced into through necessity. However, knowing that inevitably some meeting must take place, she forwarded me this money so that when they got here next month to visit us Mr. Vantine would find her family in surroundings that would not embarrass her."

Young Mallory halted in his pacing of the room.

"Of course," he said, "I had no idea how this money was raised. It was sister's request and we put it into effect. We had heard that her earnings in the last two years had been very large and despite the fact that she had sent mother money frequently and myself also to help me along in my law studies, we really thought that the $50,000 represented the remainder of her own savings. Why, everything here stands purchased in her own name and"—

"Please promise me, Mr. Mallory" said Alice Royce, "that you will change nothing; keep everything as it is until you hear the contrary from your sister."

"Yes, Miss Royce," said the youth. With native courtliness he escorted her down the lawn pathway and to the old-fashioned public carriage awaiting her.

On her way back to New York the girl detective debated what her course of action would be, but before the train had stopped in the Pennsylvania station in Manhattan she had made up her mind. She went straight to the office of Richard H. Vantine. She told him the whole story. The kindly smile that appeared slowly but steadily on his lips, the tenderness and relief that came into his eyes proved that her judgment was right.

"Poor little girl—poor little girl," he said gently. "Why—it is so easy to understand now. Miss Royce, you've made me very happy. I cannot tell you what thoughts and doubts came into my mind. I would hate to admit them to myself now. Poor little woman."

Then Vantine, his handsome face glowing, caught the girl detective's hand.

"Miss Royce, that wretched $100,000 necklace is completely forgotten—it never existed. Do you understand? She is not to know that I even knew about—about Atlanta."

"A client's orders are always strictly obeyed," smiled the young woman.

"Thank you," said the millionaire, and bowed.

No. 4—Alice Royce and the Assassins Club

Alice Royce ran swiftly from the living rooms of her apartment into the hallway, startled by a cry of alarm from her maid, for the girl on opening the door in response to a sharp, sudden rattle of the electric bell had been almost carried off her feet by the inrush of a wild-eyed man seemingly half crazed with excitement, who shouted:

"Mademoiselle Royce—Mademoiselle Royce! I must see her! I must see her quickly—for God's sake—please!"

As Alice Royce guided her queer visitor into the front room of the apartment she observed that the man was all of a tremble, that his teeth chattered as crazily as his eyes rolled.

He was a short, wiry man of forty years or thereabouts with a bush of black curly hair over a thin, sallow face. He affected a small black mustache and goatee; the mustache evidently designed to be worn uptwisted in military fashion, but now, with its drooping, sprayed ends, adding to the general disorder of his appearance. In a vague way the girl detective was aware that she had seen her visitor somewhere before.

He tossed himself into the chair she offered and sat for some seconds crazily twisting the soft felt hat he held clutched in his shaking hands. He was so evidently on the point of hysteria that he tried repeatedly to speak, but could the words through his chattering teeth.

The girl placed a calm hand on his shoulder.

"Come—come," she said in slow, low tones. "Try and bring yourself together. What have you to fear?"

"My life, mademoiselle," said the man before her. "My very life is at stake. Unless on this very day I myself commit a murder—Dieu!—I myself will be killed! I am not insane, mademoiselle. These are the facts. I must destroy a human creature or be myself destroyed—unless, mademoiselle, you perhaps can save me. I have come to you—in very despair I have come to you."

"You know me?" asked the girl detective.

"Yes, mademoiselle; you will perhaps remember the affair of the Vantine diamonds? It is I, mademoiselle, who furnished the imitation of the genuine necklace. It is I who am the expert in such things that you sought out, Mademoiselle Royce."

As he was speaking, the recollection of the man's identity had come readily to the young professional investigator.

For upward of an hour the Frenchman went on in explanation of his visit and his condition of terror. There were times when his English failed him completely and he arose, pacing the floor, speaking volubly in his native tongue. The girl became more and more deeply interested, and once she raised a hand to halt him the while at the telephone at her desk she called up Washington on the long distance telephone and was placed in connection with the — Embassy.

"This is Alice Royce," she said to one of the secretaries who responded. "I understand the Ambassador intends coming to New York on the 2 o'clock limited to-morrow. He must not carry out this intention. He would be in gravest danger in New York. Who am I? Speak to Assistant Secretary Blank at the State Department He will tell you that I am responsible and no mere alarmist. He will tell you that my warning must certainly be heeded. Meanwhile, please have the chief of your secret agents telephone me" (she paused and gave the number). "I assure you it is a matter of the gravest concern."

It was indeed an alarming, terrifying revelation that Anatol d'Montrat, the man before her, had made in the turmoil and rush of his excited speech. The while he talked something like contempt for the little frightened man had crept into Alice Royce's mind. His story disclosed him to be a pitiful little egotist who in an imagined desperation of character and purpose had permitted himself to be drawn into a dangerous, murderous group of political malcontents and then, when the realization of how deeply he had been enchained came suddenly and terribly upon him, had given way to complete cowardice—to hysterical fear.

For, in short, Anatol d'Montrat had I been designated by the "group"—"The Liberty Twelve" they called themselves—to commit no less a crime than murder. In the drawing of lots he had been "called" on the very night before the day he presented himself to Alice Royce to assassinate Count (let us say) Clarendon, Ambassador to the United States from (again let us say) Karomania.

He went into a full explanation of this "group;" the characters who comprised its membership and the manner in which he himself had been drawn into its rendezvous and had come to stand as a candidate for choice as the one who was to end violently the life of the Karomanian Ambassador. He said that the chief of the group was a queer little, florid, stout German whose source of income was mysterious but abundant. Evidently this leader of the band was really insane—a paranoiac who thought there had fallen upon himself a divine mission to destroy secretly the lives of the men who figured in the guidance of the world. His scheme looked toward the destruction of every ruler in the world, and not only the rulers themselves but their queens, their heirs and their most powerful and highly recognized advisers. Two of the other ten men were Russians embittered by prison terms served in Siberia. One of them had as a little lad witnessed the hanging of his own father in a Russian prison yard. His life was consecrated, he frequently averred, to a vengeance on Russian authorities to be so dreadful and sweeping that it would horrify the world.

Anatol himself had fallen under the influence of Herr Kruger, the little German chief, owing to nightly discussions of social wrongs that they held on a bench in Union Square. The acquaintance had been a chance one—as far as Anatol was concerned. He himself, although he had become an expert skilled workman in the fashioning of artistic jewelry, nursed the disappointment of grander ambitions. In his youth he had dreamed of a life to be crowned with fame as a great author, teacher and preacher. But the world had not listened to him. His literary products had been a failure. None, indeed, had ever seen the light. Gradually,

in his disappointment, he had turned bitterly against the world, and it had been on a night
when he sat on one of the park benches, darkly
brooding, that little Herr Kruger with his strangely bright blue eyes had ensconced himself beside
him and they had talked—talked for hours, in
which gradually his new found acquaintance had
painted, in a manner that fascinated Anatol while
it frightened him, his gigantic trouble scheme for
the establishment of world-wide anarchy through
world-wide assassination.

The next night Anatol had kept an appointment with Herr Kruger which resulted in the little
Frenchman being, after due caution to secrecy and
a frank avowal of the death that would befall him
if he betrayed the secret of the "group's" existence,
taken to the rendezvous of the Anarchist gang.

This proved to be on the top floor of an
old-fashioned brick house in one of the "Seven-
ties" between First avenue and Avenue B, New
York. There he met the other members. Save in
the case of the two Russians, who it appears the
German had invited to this country by correspondence, Anatol found that the other members of
the "group" had been gathered quite in the way
he himself had been come upon. Herr Kruger, it
seemed, haunted the parks with his half insane
blue eyes sharply casting about for men whose

demeanors of disappointment, dejection and
brooding suggested that they might be possible
welcome recruits to the organization by which he
meant to stain crimson the steps of thrones, even
the portals of the White House itself. Nearly every
nationality was represented in the membership of
"The Liberty Twelve." All were aliens to America.
The nightly discussion of their wrongs and disap-
pointments had brought them to a temper of ugliness in which they grinned as they chattered over
their pet schemes for achieving the assassination
of all the rulers of the world!

Anatol, it appeared, had been as free of tongue
as any of them, talking loudly and dramatically
of most ferocious deeds against society that he
meant to commit. Meanwhile Herr Kruger always
presided among them with the greatest calm and
avowed sensation of pleasure over the murderous
plots that he heard revealed. Incidentally, he also
most liberally financed the "club." Most of the
members had been men without occupation in the
first place. But those who had been practicing a
vocation in the beginning had, including Anatol,
abandoned their employment and taken to living
on the bounty of their German chief.

All this had gone on for several months, to Anatol's great enjoyment. While the plotting of assas-
sinations had remained merely bombastic talk the

bloated and voluble Anatol had been in all his
glory.

But—then! Three nights before Anatol confided to Alice Royce, Herr Kruger, with his blue eyes
dancing more brightly and wildly than ever, had
announced that the days of mere talk were at an
end—the hour for action had struck.

The destruction of the lives of all the "enemies"
of the society, Alice Royce heard with growing,
eager attention, did not devolve on the American
group alone. Kruger had, she learned, with mysterious financial resource and energy formed similar
groups in European capitals and the general plan
was to arouse fear and consternation everywhere in
the world at once. Kruger, d'Montrat stammered,
had drawn up in writing, in accordance with the
plans and agreements from the other groups, a paper setting down the time, place and manner of all
the contemplated crimes.

The Karomanian Ambassador had fallen as first
choice among the victims of the plot in America.
In his career it was known that from time to time
he had through his secret agents caused the imprisonment or deportation of many Anarchists
who had succeeded in edging their way past the
United States immigration authorities. According
to the big general plan of Kruger, as contained in
the paper he had drawn up and which d'Montrat

asserted he had seen with his own eyes, at the same time that his pistol rang out against Count Clarendon in twenty other cities of Europe prominent men had also been marked for death. But who these had been the little Frenchman said he was too excited and distraught to remember. He described closely, however, the section of the desk in which this sinister document was hidden.

There had been, he said, a night of bitter denunciation of Count Clarendon by "The Liberty Twelve" when finally Herr Kruger had announced the drawing of lots for the appointment of the diplomat's murderer. The German had joined the others in the drawing, but in the end out of the folded paper slips carelessly tossed into a hat the gruesome paper containing the words "Thou art the man" found itself between the fingers of little Anatol d'Montrat.

"Then they gave me this," sobbed the Frenchman, drawing from the inner breast pocket of his coat an ugly blue steel magazine pistol. "I am to be waiting," he said, "at the entrance to the Ritz-Carlton when the Count shall arrive from Washington. Then the murder must be done. One of the members will be waiting nearby in an automobile—one that looks very much like a taxicab. I am to leap in that and be driven off. If I am arrested the man driving the motor is to pretend he knows nothing of me, that he is only a hired taxi chauffeur. They have had me," continued d'Montrat, his voice rising shrilly, "practicing every day shooting at the dummy figure of a man precisely of the size and proportions of Count Clarendon so that I should not fail when the time came to aim at his heart!"

II

It seemed, after all, a simple matter enough to call the police over the telephone and expose the whole dangerous group. But from this measure Alice Royce shrank. The danger to the life of the little Frenchman would in such case be grave and imminent. "The Liberty Twelve" would of a certainty know that the betrayal had come from him. The other men were of equal murderous inclination as Kruger, d'Montrat had asserted; any that might escape the police would be as merciless as the German in carrying out the vengeance of the assassins' club.

And yet Alice Royce realized that action must swiftly be taken. Count Clarendon's life seemed safe enough with d'Montrat completely in a funk. At any rate he could be watched to see that he did not, impelled by the fear of Kruger and the "group," really attempt to carry out the New York assassination plot

But what of the other lives—the other men marked for assassination all in the same day—whose deaths were to sweep the world with a sensation of dread and alarm?

The paper on which all their names were entered and the time and place of the contemplated murders set forth were in the clubrooms of "The Liberty Twelve" in — East Seventieth street. To send d'Montrat back to the clubrooms for this document of such sinister significance was not to be considered. He would not dare the task, or if he did might he not fall back into the power of the other murderous eleven?

The girl detective decided she herself would undertake the securing of this paper and the cabling of swift warnings to those whom she might find named in it as prospective victims of assassins' knives and bullets.

"Have you a key to the clubrooms?" she demanded of the Frenchman. He shook his head negatively. Yes, there was a janitress of the building, but it would have to be a heavy bribe indeed that would induce the woman to allow any one—even the club members, save Kruger, into the rooms. However, Alice Royce, knowing human lives to be at stake on her success in entering these rooms, hesitated no longer than it took to put on her hat and otherwise arrange her attire for the street in clothing that should not be too new or suggest a more than neat stylishness, for the neighborhood where she was to go she knew to be one where a fashionably dressed young woman would attract undue attention. Before departing she slipped a revolver into her handbag. And on the street she sought out a hardware shop. The neatly wrapped parcel she carried with her on leaving the shop contained a brightly bladed hatchet, for the girl detective had decided that desperate cases demand desperate measures. She had determined on hacking open the door of the assassins' club in her effort to secure the paper which had such grave importance in the matter of many prominent lives. The hatchet would also come in handy for splitting open the locked drawer of the desk where the document was concealed.

Her quick observation, however, suggested a better manner of obtaining entrance to the assassins' club, for on her arrival at the address she saw that there was a sign on the old, shabby brick house announcing "Rooms to Let." The fat German woman who answered her ring was doubtful at first about hiring any of the rooms to the young and handsome fraulein. She averred that the lodgers were all men and save only herself and her daughter there were no women in the house. But on the girl investigator saying she was engaged in business downtown and would only be home at nights, and especially as she appeared quite satisfied at the figures named for rental of the various rooms, the woman consented to permit her to inspect the vacant apartments.

It was the rear room on the second floor that Alice Royce engaged. She paid the rental and was left alone for an inspection of her new quarters.

Only one thing interested Alice Royce about this apartment and she had observed this while talking to the woman of the house; it was, indeed, what had brought her to a quick decision to hire the room. She had seen through the windows the presence of a fire-escape. No sooner was she alone when she opened the window and slipped out on the iron platform; a similar platform overhead was just outside the window of the assassins' club.

But the question was—was the room above empty? Back into her own apartment she crept and waited patiently for fifteen minutes or more listening for the sound of any human presence in the room above. Coming to the conclusion that the room was vacant she climbed out again upon the iron platform and with a quick glance at the neighboring windows in the hope that she was not observed, ascended swiftly the rusty iron ladder to the platform above. Both windows of the club room were thrown wide open—an effort to clear the place of tobacco smoke, the stale odor of which was markedly present to her nostrils as she bent forward and stepped cautiously over the sill. The room was quite empty.

The furnishings were scant. There was an old desk placed near one of the windows and in the centre of the room was a big pine table and a dozen or more chairs stood about. An ice-chest that furnished refreshments for the conspirators in their long hours of wrangling and discussion was all else in the room excepting the pictures on the walls. These showed the portraits of Czolgosz, the assassin of McKinley; the regicide who murdered Portugal's King and heir apparent; Guiteau, Garfield's murderer, and there was a colored chromo of a painting depicting some of the guillotine horrors of the French revolution. On the centre of the table was a grotesque, gruesome object It was a human skull and set rakishly over the hollow edges was a crown of gilded cardboard. It was the idol of the assassins' club—King Death, the ghastly symbol which they worshipped in their infernal design of improvement for the world.

Without hesitation Alice Royce attacked Kruger's desk with the hatchet she had carried with her for the purpose. Then she saw she had further work to do. Only inconsequential letters and papers lay exposed in the drawer. But also there was in it a flat, black tin despatch box. This she shattered resolutely. When finally the lock was smashed her quickly moving hands soon brought to her eyes the prize she sought.

Kruger had worked with neatness and loving care, it would appear on this list of the first "batch" of lives to be taken. It had been elaborately prepared in red and black ink and was even decorated with death's head drawings, also in red and black.

The girl gasped to observe what was written there, the world-famous names of men marked for destruction. Her swiftly moving glance, however, reassured her. The warnings would surely arrive in time to prevent the crimes; d'Montrat had been right; each assassination in Vienna, St Petersburg, London, Rome, Paris and Madrid had been set for one and the same hour as the circumstances of trapping the victims or of securing the opportunities of approaching them would permit.

"YOU DAMNED LITTLE SPY!"

Alice turned quickly in recoiling amazement. She had heard no sound in the room. She had suspected no other presence. But evidently the splintering of the door of the desk and the breaking of its lock were sufficient sounds to smother the slightest noise that Herr Kruger had made in the turning of the key and opening of the door. For the man who had come in upon her was Herr Kruger, the head of the assassins' club. He stood looking at her with the flashing light of insanity in his blue eyes, his lips under his pale yellow mustache writhing, showing his tobacco-stained teeth. He lurched rather than sprang toward her, his hands outstretched, aimed at her throat.

She had laid her handbag upon the desk. There would be no time to reach for it, unclasp it and produce her revolver before she would be in his grasp. The desk stood near the window and the window sash was raised. The girl made up her mind to seek flight by way of the fire-escape. The man might have a weapon; might shoot her. But there seemed to be little choice. If she remained there he would strangle her. There was no mistaking the light in his eyes. It was maniacal.

Even as she came to this decision she saw that he had drawn a revolver.

"If you make a move"—he began. But already she had leaped to the window sill. This act alone saved her, for on that very instant Kruger had discharged a bullet at her. She stumbled and fell outside on the iron platform. The bullet that would have sunk in her body had struck her right foot with stinging force. She felt a sudden, sharp pain and then a numbness of the limb more frightening than had been the pain.

The girl detective was trying unsuccessfully to cry out for help, trying desperately at the same time to steady her reeling senses.

Then the door within came crashing down. Three men, one a great, stalwart Russian, entered the room pell mell. The big man the next instant had Kruger by the throat and in his grasp the little stout German was plainly powerless. He fought hard to retain and use his revolver, but it was torn from his fingers by a single wrench of the huge Russian's hand.

By nightfall Herr Kruger was on his way to an asylum for the criminal insane.

The secret agents of the Karomanian Government having arrived at Alice Royce's apartments after she had started on her dangerous quest found d'Montrat there still in hysterical fear. They had learned from him the haunts and address of the others of "The Liberty Twelve." Every one had been rounded up by the time Kruger was his way to the asylum. No charges were made against these men, there being no desire to advertise to the world on what slender chances sometimes the lives of royalty and of those great in statecraft frequently depend. Instead, the next morning on three ships leaving New York harbor the would-be

assassins of the anarchistic group were on their
way to deportation to their own countries with
word sent ahead to the authorities of various cities to watch out for them. Simultaneously in many
cities abroad anarchists were being rounded up
by the score, the cable having sent to the various
foreign governments the names contained in the
secret paper of Herr Kruger that Alice Royce had
captured.

It was some weeks before the wound in her foot
permitted the young woman again to resume activities. Meanwhile, however, by way of comfort
there arrived for her from the Karomanian Government a check in four figures and from Count
Clarendon a ring containing an emerald that had
once glistened in the headdress of an Egyptian
queen.

No. 5—The Blue Ridge Mystery

In the mail of Alice Royce there came one morning in December, 19—, a curious letter, crude in expression, ungrammatical, yet touching the heart of the girl detective to a quick response. Save for the injection of punctuation and capitalization, the letter is herewith directly reproduced:

Ramsay, Tenn., Dec. 12, 19—.
Dear Miss Royce: Bein' as how we all down thisaway knowed how you was the one that ketched the counterfitters here last year, and admiring you for a wonderful smart young lady, I am sending you on my bended knees this letter for you, please, for God's sake to help me. Miss Royce, my husband has been put away in jail for all his life for a killin' of Ralston Pendleton, which he never done—never, Miss Royce. I reckon as

how everybody most but me thinks he done it—him bein' found the way he was. But the day they took him away he swore to me, like he swore all along that he was innocent. Miss Royce, we were only married just a litabit a while, and Miss Royce I don't want that my baby when its born shall have its daddy a murderer to everybody's mind. Allen's innocent, Miss Royce. He didn't do no lyin' to me. He was found right beside the man they all said he killed; but he didn't. The quarrel they had was done finished and over long ago.

Miss Royce, my pap done lent me $15 to send to have you come down here, and after that I'll sell the ring that Allen gave me for our engagement that cost $20. I'm only a poor mountain girl, but I thought if you could help me in this awful trouble you all would do it anyway. All the time after I've sent the letter away, I'll be prayin' you'll come and help me. Please, Miss Royce, think of me thataway and come right away. Yours respectfully,

Laura Rose Bullen.

Far different in appearance than her crudely written letter was Mrs. Laura Bullen, the young mountain wife, whom Alice Royce saw for the first time when she alighted at Crandall, Ramsay being four miles away, off the railroads and in the heart of beautiful, if melancholy, Blue Ridge Mountains. She was a slender, flaxen-haired girl, sweet-mouthed and with an expression of suffering in her great childish blue eyes that was tenderly piteous. Her father, lean-featured, gaunt and shabby, but with a fine gentleness of speech and ease of courtesy tor all his rudeness of appearance, stood on the station platform with her, holding her hand for all the world as if she were but a child. Alice Royce found herself almost uneasy in the faith with which they looked upon her during the slow, mountainous drive to Ramsay and, when sitting in the low ceilinged room of the old mountain cottage, lighted only by a dim kerosene lamp and the glow and glare of a wood fire, she found herself regretful at first for having made the journey, for having by her coming instilled hope in hearts that had better, it would appear, attune themselves to resignation.

For the case of murder that the State prosecutors had made against Allen Bullen was very strong and clear; his guilt seemed indubitable. The trial that ended in his being sentenced to life imprisonment had been brief indeed.

Allen Bullen was only twenty-two years old and up to a year before when he inherited his father's small farm with its complement of sheep and hogs, his reputation had been one of wildness, though there had been nothing sinister in any of his escapades. But, following the customs of the mountaineers on certain occasions, such as market days in Crandall or sometimes when they journeyed to the fairs or "court week" at the county seat, Battletown, there had been excessive indulgences in the pale whiskey that the men of the hills manufacture in defiance of Uncle Sam's "revenuers." In the rude humor of the locality young Bullen's susceptibility to "corn liquor" had been a great joke. It was known that frequently on returns from such local celebrations he might be expected to act and talk queerly and vaguely with eyes curiously staring, like those of a somnambulist, and that in the middle sometimes of a word or a gesture ha had been known to fall into a heavy—a complete swoon. Such actions and, results, while by no means uncommon as forms of alcoholism, were decidedly unusual among the hardy, open-air mountaineers, the majority of whom could drink the raw, new liquor in repeated doses without qualm or visible effect.

But after his marriage to pretty Laura Mason in the springtime, Allen Bullen had gone "straight"— that is, until the day in August when with other mountain farmers he went to Crandall to dicker with the wool agents for the prices on the autumn shearing. Primarily, his happiness in his new state was his undoing for on that occasion in the Cran- dall tavern he had "met up" with Larry Hampton against whom he had held something approaching a feud over young Hampton's own former aspira- tions for the hand of Laura Mason. The youths had settled their differences in a friendly glass. Then Fred Hampton, Larry's older cousin, had joined them, expressed his pleasure at seeing them friends again and—young Bullen's resolution, which was that he would return home early and sober to his bride, died with the befuddling of his senses.

Fred Hampton had wisely shaken his head when Larry and Allen swung out of the tavern arm in arm to tramp jovially back the few miles to Ram- say. He said he would wait awhile and "take it quieter" on the way home. About fifteen minutes later he departed.

II

The pack of hunting dogs from their kennels in the rear of old Judge Grantham's home set up a wild baying in the lonely lateness of the night and the Judge himself, flanked by Henry and Martha, his negro house servants, came down the old broad stairway answering repeated thunderings on the door, coupled with sharp, excited cries of urgency.

Their lamplight flung its rays sharply on the white face of Fred Hampton.

"Judge Grantham," he moaned, "my cousin Larry's been murdered—by Allen Bullen. Poor Larry's layin' down the road apiece—near Crow's woods—right there on the road with his heart all hacked."

"Where's Allen Bullen?"

"Right there beside him."

"A duel?"

"No—a murder—plain murder. Larry's knife and revolver are in his pockets. Bullen's a layin' there alongside of him—dead drunk—you know the way he gets. And he's got the bloody knife in his hands."

Hampton's hand went up as if to shield his eyes from the horror of what he had seen.

"Your own hands are bloody," said Judge Grantham suddenly.

"Yes," answered Hampton, as suddenly staring at them, "they got that away when I picked Larry up to see if he was dead."

Old Harry, the negro, was sent to spread the alarm, and soon armed with lanterns and headed by the dignified old Judge the party made their way to Crow's Woods.

It was quite as Hampton had told it. The youth Larry was dead; there were five stab wounds in his left breast, all of which had penetrated the heart. Not even the clustered lights of the lanterns flashing fully on the face of young Bullen aroused him. It was seen that he was not injured. His right arm was outflung along the ground, and held half listlessly in his hand was a long-bladed, horn-handled clasp knife, such as are commonly to be found in the pockets of mountaineers. During the useless efforts made to revive him, cause him to face his victim and secure some statement concerning the ghastly deed, some one in the horrified group recalled the old rivalry in the courtship that there had been between the young men.

"And he pretended," said Fred Hampton bitterly, "that all that was past and Larry and him was going to be good friends again like when they were just boys."

As Fred Hampton had already stated there was no weapon in Larry's dead hand. His knife was in his trousers' pocket; his revolver on his hip, not a cartridge discharged. The youth's body was decently covered with an overcoat loaned for the purpose and carried to his home.

Bullen had also to be carried, but it was roughly he was borne to Judge Grantham's home. There, a doctor called from Crandall's succeeded in reviving him. When told of the charge against him, the youth was so shaken with horror that his talk was incoherent, but pieced together the statement finally stood that on their way home young Hampton had become so drowsy and uncertain of his steps that he had finally flung himself on the roadside and declared he meant to have a sleep there and then. Young Bullen declared he had done his best to persuade his companion to continue the journey, in the friendliest manner, and then suddenly he stated that he himself must have become unconscious. He could remember nothing further until awakening in the Judge's house.

And this, when the trial was held, proved all he had to tell the jury to offset the damning fact of his being found beside the dead man in the road with the bloody knife in his hand—all he had to say for himself save one thing. He swore that the knife found in his hand had not belonged to him. But the evidence was that he was searched on the night of his arrest and no other knife was in his possession. James MacNaughton, keeper of the general store at Ramsay, swore he had sold Bullen such a knife as was exhibited in court.

"But that is not my knife, I swear," the prisoner had cried; "my knife had a nick off one end of the horn handle and it had a broken blade."

"You mean," said the Prosecutor scornfully, "It had a nick in the edge of the big blade—that nick is there as you see, gentlemen of the jury."

"No—no," the prisoner retorted. "It was the little blade—the short blade—the end was broken right off."

But as a man's clasp knife is very much of a private possession, the only witness in substantiation of himself that young Bullen could bring as to the marks on his knife was his young wife, to whom the stern-faced jury of farmers listened kindly but incredulously. In fact, it took them only fifteen minutes to bring in their verdict, dealing a second degree verdict largely on the pretty child wife's account and because of the evidence of young Bullen's peculiar condition that had permitted him to drop in a stupor beside his victim. The defense had tried to make a point of this—had demanded whether it were possible for a man to murder another without becoming so sobered as to flee the scene of the crime. But the Prosecutor had replied with many citations from cases to show that murderers had frequently been overcome by sudden torpor and drowsiness immediately after the

commission of their crimes. Besides, they produced witnesses to prove that, when intoxicated,
complete unconsciousness had been known to
overcome young Bullen in the midst of the wild-
est pranks.

And these were the facts that Alice Royce heard
from the lips of the youth's pitiable child wife,
interspersed with tearful pleadings for assistance
in proving her husband innocent.

III

The activities of Alice Royce in the week following brought revelations astonishing to herself
and were destined to end in a thrilling, intense
and tragic scene. There were two days spent at
the scene of the murder, despite that months had
passed since the night Larry Hampton had lain
there with his life ended by five fiercely directed
stab wounds. There was a third day when she returned to the scene accompanied by the Assistant
State Prosecutor from Battletown; a day in which
she had talked to many citizens in Ramsay and in
Crandall; then she had disappeared from the vi-
cinity, but on the eighth day when she returned to
Ramsay, the State Prosecutor, a handsome, gray-
haired man of a fine dignity of demeanor and his
younger assistant accompanied her. They went

directly to the home of old Judge Grantham. Half an hour later an astounded, aged official sent old Henry for Deputy Sheriff Briggs. And when that official entered Judge Grantham's big office parlor the population of Ramsay followed after, for in those localities the rule of public court is strictly upheld.

"Judge Grantham," said the Prosecutor slowly, "it would appear that but for the brilliant reasoning and patient effort of this gifted young lady," here he paid Miss Royce a most courtly bow, "this State might have continued an enormous injustice to an innocent young man. I refer, sir, to Allen Bullen of Ramsay, now under a life sentence for the murder of Lawrence Hampton.

"The real criminal, Your Honor, I now firmly believe is in this very room." He paused, and then turning to the prisoner said deliberately, solemnly, "Fred Hampton, I charge you now with the murder of your Cousin Lawrence."

Hampton, his small, blue eyes lighting fiercely, shouted: "Why—what kind of talk is that? Everybody knows who killed my Cousin Lawrence!"

"Everybody thought they knew," said the Prosecutor coldly, "until this young detective brought the real facts to light. Your Honor, I will state what these facts are, and then the prisoner can insist upon a hearing or waive it—as he sees fit.

"Greed, Your Honor, not revenge or angry passion, was the cause of this crime as I will shortly prove.

"But first let us take up the circumstance of the knife—or rather knives!" The lawyer's voice rose on the last word and he held up to view two horn-handled clasp knives exactly similar until he had opened the blades. Then it was observed that there was a nick in the long blade of one knife rusted with its crimson life statin; that the short blade of the other knife was broken off almost at the middle.

"Miss Royce reasoned," continued the Prosecutor, "on this proposition: What if Allen Bullen's story were true; what if the knife he held in his hand were not his own? Then you have the picture of these two young men, victims of their foolish excesses lying in a stupor on the road. Upon them comes one who conceives a deadly purpose against Lawrence Hampton. How easy to murder Lawrence and cast the shadow of guilt on his unconscious companion! Had Frederick Hampton possessed a sufficiently cool nerve to abstract from the pocket of the slumbering Bullen that young man's own knife, murder Lawrence with it and then put the blood-stained weapon in Bullen's helpless hand; that poor youth would have paid most dearly for his night's debauch. The real murderer would never have been found out.

"But Frederick Hampton struck first; murdered first, thinking only to commit the crime and flee. But there came the after thought—the placing of his knife in Bullen's hand. There were no initials on it—it was the same sort of horn-handled knife that a dozen men in this room could produce—save only for the nick in the blade. If, however, Bullen's guilt was to be successfully established, he must rob the man of his own knife. And this knife must be done away with—hidden from sight. As it was he who must give the alarm of murder, it would not be wise for him to keep this knife of Bullen's in his possession for an instant. It was dark. He could not know but there was some brightly distinguishing mark upon it. Did he fling it away—as far in the woods as he could? Or did he hide it somewhere near the scene of the crime before giving the alarm? Ha hid it, Your Honor.

"Two days of patient search by Miss Royce revealed a spot twenty feet off the road where the earth had been disturbed and then pressed down by a human foot. In this tangle of shrubbery no other human feet had passed, and in the hardening and freezing of the clay of this Tennessee soil the footprint remained perfectly outlined.

The measurements were taken. Miss Royce before breaking this ground called on my office and my assistant accompanied her to this spot. Under that footprint, Your Honor, was found this knife with a broken short blade and a nick off the corner of the handle—such a knife as Allen Bullen swore was his!

"Next, Your Honor, Andrew Renfrew, who is here, will swear to the occasion when he saw Frederick Hampton while in the act of mending some old harness nick the long blade of his knife. Hampton was annoyed at the time, told Renfrew what he had done and showed the nicked blade. Then, Your Honor, thanks to Miss Royce's investigations, we will prove by Roger Agnew, the postmaster, that six days after the murder Hampton received a package from a mail-order cutlery concern in Cincinnati. Inquiry of that firm revealed that his purchase was that of a new clasp knife.

"As to the measurements of the footprint over the place where the knife was found, my assistant and Miss Royce took measurements of footprints that they actually saw Hampton make.

"They prove him to have been the man who buried Allen Bullen's knife.

"I said, Your Honor, that greed was the motive. I might add chagrin, too. Miss Royce's investigations of Hampton's affairs reveal the existence of an uncle in Virginia—a man of wealth. Three months ago this old gentleman's son was killed by a fall from a horse. This left Frederick and Lawrence Hampton as the only heirs. Although Frederick was the elder, the old gentleman had openly stated among acquaintances that Lawrence was his favorite, and that he had drawn up a will to that effect since his son's death. But if Lawrence was dead—this man here would be the natural heir-at-law.

"And this is the man who swore before his God, you remember, that he was the only witness to come upon the murder of Lawrence Hampton. He was indeed the only witness of that crime, for poor young Allen Bullen lay there unwittingly with his limp hand ready to receive the accusing knife."

The lawyer halted and turned to look fully at Hampton.

"Have you anything to say?" he demanded. "If so—arise."

But Hampton remained crumpled in his chair, passing a long hand over a livid face. Finally he spoke.

"Murder," he said, "murder will out!"

No. 6—The Mystery of Wilmot Gray

"Well, Miss Royce," came over the telephone in the hearty, jovial voice of T. W. Blaney, chief of the famous detective agency, "I've certainly got a funny one for you this time. I guess you might call it 'The Case of the Live Corpse.' If you please, Miss Royce, meet me at the office of President Blair of the Tower Insurance Company—you know, the building on Broadway, of course—at 2 o'clock this afternoon. I know It's a case that will interest you. Queer is no name for it. It's ghastly and ghostly."

Blaney was already there when the girl detective arrived, and he must have spoken flatteringly of the pretty young woman's record for skill and success in her profession, for President Blair, large and florid, arose pompously and made her a most elaborate bow.

"The case is such a strange one that it has been brought to my personal attention," said he, after settling down in his big revolving armchair. "Usually, of course, I leave all such affairs to our own investigating department. But this has proved too baffling a proposition for even our cleverest men. So I asked Mr. Blaney's aid, and he has told me that, in lieu of his own inability to take up the case personally at this time, he would offer your services as being the equal in every way to his own."

Miss Royce, having properly acknowledged the compliment with a short little nod and a vivid flush, Blair continued, consulting a memorandum:

"Two years ago a man of the name of Wilmot Gray, living at No. 1860 Ralmont avenue, in the Bronx, took out a $25,000 policy with this company. He was unmarried and lived with his mother. Together they kept a little stationery and cigar store at the address I have given you, occupying living rooms in the rear. The investigators at the time made the observation in their reports that it appeared to be a rather large insurance for a man in such modest circumstances to take on. However, they also stated that as he was only thirty years old, a man of temperate habits and in excellent health, the risk was one to be approved and taken on by the Tower Company.

"Right here, perhaps, it would be well for me to give you a description in detail of Wilmot Gray. He was about 5 feet 6 inches in height;

had light brown, rather curly hair, wore a pointed beard and mustache, was slim, but rather well built and weighed about one hundred and thirty-five pounds. He had a small scar on the forehead just over his right eye and another scar on his left foot, which he told his medical examiner at the time had come to him when a boy. He had been chopping wood and the axe head, slipping from the handle, had struck with its edge on his bare foot.

"Six months after taking out the $25,000 policy, Miss Royce, Wilmot Gray died. It was a brief illness—a few days; pneumonia. Such was the cause of death given regularly in the death certificate by Dr. Donald H. Wagstaff, a licensed physician, and as far as we know a perfectly reputable one. His offices are in Ralmont avenue, in the Bronx—a few doors away from where Wilmot Gray had his little shop. The regularity of the death certificate convinced us of the fact that Wilmot Gray was really dead, and there was further recorded the burial of his body in Greenwood Cemetery. So the claim was paid at the time without question."

President Blair paused and leaned toward the girl detective, his eyes lighting dramatically.

"Now comes the startling information to us," he said, "that Wilmot Gray is alive, in as excellent health as the day we insured him! And yet in the face of other very convincing facts I strongly doubt if the young man can be anywhere except in his grave.

"But listen, if you please, to the written statement of Dr. James Slear, who was formerly a medical examiner with this company, but is now in the employ of the Alps Insurance Corporation. Dr. Slear says:

"'On the 15th of this December I was detailed to make an examination of an Arthur J. Preston at No. 324 West 18—th street. Although, of course, in the nature of my practice I make countless examinations, I was struck with the idea that I had seen Preston before and that for some cause I had good reason to remember him. Something had happened, I was sure, to especially impress me with this man. But when I asked him if we had ever met before, he said he was certain that we had not. When requested to strip, he did so without hesitation. Then it was that memory startled me, for I saw the selfsame scar on his left foot that I now clearly remember as having seen on the left foot of Wilmot Gray. Gray I naturally especially remembered, as an insurance doctor is likely to remember a $25,000 risk which he passes who dies six months afterward. In the course of my further examination I had naturally a chance to subject the man to close scrutiny. I am sure that Wilmot Gray and Arthur J. Preston are one and the same.

Their height, features, even to the pointed brown beard; weight, and all other physical characteristics are the same. I remembered that Gray had a small scar over his right eye. So also has Preston. When I asked him his age he said he was thirty-two. Gray gave his age as thirty when I examined him, which was just two years ago.

"'In conclusion, I am so firmly and completely of the belief that Preston and Gray are the same man that I would suggest that the Tower Company make a rigorous investigation, even to the extent of applying to the courts for the exhumation of the body buried in Greenwood Cemetery, presumably as that of Wilmot Gray.'

"You will observe, Miss Royce, that Dr. Slear writes very positively, and a further coincidence is the fact that Preston is seeking insurance with the Alps Company in exactly the same sum that Gray obtained from us—$25,000.

"But"—President Blair dubiously nodded his head—"on the other hand, not a fact that could be ascertained by a dozen of our most expert investigators will show anything other than that Wilmot Gray is really in his grave. To be sure, his mother has absolutely disappeared. After the receipt of the insurance money she told her neighbors that she meant to return to her old home—a village in Connecticut—purchase a farm and retire there for the rest of her days. But to none of them did she name the village where she intended to go. Search for her has been fruitless.

"Nevertheless, our agents have rounded up fully a score of perfectly respectable and trustworthy persons who saw Gray in his coffin—who attended his funeral and took a farewell look at his countenance before the coffin was sealed. And there is the clergyman who officiated at funeral services and declares it was surely a dead man who lay in the casket over which he preached, and, finally, there is Dr. Donald H. Wagstaff—whose assertion cannot be controverted—that he attended Gray in an illness of pneumonia and that the young man actually passed away in his presence. Under such circumstances the Tower Company naturally hesitates to go before any court and ask permission to exhume the body of Wilmot Gray."

In token of helplessness, the official waved his hands.

"Yet when these facts," he said, "were put before Dr. Slear he nevertheless insisted that he could not be mistaken—that Preston was surely none other than Gray; that the Tower Company had in some super-clever fashion been cheated out of no less than $25,000. And there's where the case stands, Miss Royce. Will you undertake the exposure of Preston as a swindler or, failing that, guarantee forever to lay the ghost of Gray?"

II

When Alice Royce accepted the commission to investigate the curious and suggestively uncanny case it was after an agreement made with President Blair of the Tower Company that he would confer with the president of the Alps Insurance Corporation and arrange that Preston's application for the $25,000 insurance policy be accepted.

"For," said the girl detective, "if all the other facts stand as you have stated them—the testimony of persons present at the funeral, of the officiating clergyman and the attending physician, Wilmot Gray must have played an amazing trick in successfully posing as a victim of pneumonia and then as a corpse, to say nothing of his escape from his coffin afterward. If Preston is Gray—he'll try the same amazing trick over again. I will watch sharply to see if in the next few months he 'dies.' If he goes right on paying his premiums for years, it would be good proof that Dr. Slear was mistaken—misled by the similarity of the two scars—the one on the foot, the other over his eye. By the way, did Dr. Slear ask Preston how he came to get that scar on his foot?"

"Yes—to be sure. Preston declared the injury came about in a fall he had from a motorcycle. He said also, by way of not damaging his case as a 'risk,' that he had since completely given up that form of sport."

The first suggestion beyond that of lying in
wait for Preston's possible "death" that came to the
pretty girl was to seek out some of the old neighbors of Wilmot Gray and take them to where they
might have a sight of Arthur Preston. But this, she
concluded, presented a danger needless to incur.
Preston might observe these watchers and, were
he really Gray, be warned that he was suspected
and under espionage, at which, if he were a guilty
man, he might easily decamp, for there existed
no evidence whatsoever with which the police
authorities could be armed to prevent his disappearance. The thought that also she might, having
identified Preston, walk up quietly behind him
and speak to him in the name of Gray, watch the
effect of such a salutation and gain information
thereby, she also dismissed. Best was the scheme
to keep Preston in sight and await developments.

Meanwhile, however, there was no reason why
she should not see the man on some pretext and
secure the opportunity to draw her own conclusions regarding his character. There was an unex-
pected development when she arrived at Preston's
address in 18—th street. Here was something that
neither Dr. Slear nor the investigators had reported, or else President Blair had intentionally left
it out. Preston owned and conducted there a stationery and cigar store, as Gray had done in the

Bronx! Could it be that also, like Gray, he was unmarried and the only support of a mother? No; in this respect there was a difference. From the woman proprietor of a notions store in the neighborhood she learned that Preston was a married man. He had, however, no children.

"I thought perhaps," said Alice Royce to the shopkeeper, "when I heard that a Mr. Preston had a store in his neighborhood, it might be an old friend of mine. But it can't be. He had several children."

In this wise she displayed caution lest the woman be a friend of Preston and happen to tell him that inquiry was being made concerning him.

Sauntering into Preston's shop, she slowly looked over current magazines, under the eye of the brown-bearded, rather good-looking man who came out from the rear living rooms, and she was rather interested to note that the humble shopkeeper wore a flashing genuine diamond in his scarf and another in a ring on his finger. Beyond the fact that he was affable and could intelligently discuss his literary wares her talk with him brought her no profit of elucidation of his character. There was no positive expression of roguery in his countenance; in fact, he seemed only to be that for which he set up—a small shopkeeper; all save the glittering, costly jewelry that he wore.

But in the months that followed, Alice Royce by careful and nearly constant watching began to secure considerable enlightenment, in the course of which another important character came under her observation, so that in the end she was not in the least surprised when one morning, about five months after she had been called into the case, she read among the death notices in all the leading newspapers the following:

"Preston, Arthur J., beloved husband of Ella Preston, in the thirty-second year of his age. Funeral services at his residence. No. 324 West 18—th street at 2 o'clock Friday afternoon. Burial at Greenwood."

When she read this solemn announcement, its effect on Alice Royce was to make her smile, but when on Friday afternoon at 2 o'clock she presented herself at the funeral services she wore a becomingly serious expression; in fact, during the prayers and the brief funeral sermon, she was of those in the crowded little parlor who wept most conspicuously. The widow was not present beside the bier, it being announced that she was too utterly prostrated by her grief. When finally the line formed to pass the casket for a farewell glimpse of the deceased, Alice Royce paused perhaps longer than any of the others—so markedly, indeed, that the undertaker guiding the throng rather brusquely touched her on the arm to indicate that she was holding up the line.

Alice Royce observed that the lid at the head of the coffin was only partly lowered in its grooves, so that merely the face and throat of Preston were visible. His countenance looked very placid, and there was a flower in the lapel of his black coat. And when Alice Royce leaned far over the bier as though in devotion and did a rather horrible thing—jabbed a pin in the cheek of the placid face—it never changed expression. There was no twitch, no grimace of the features or start of the head. Immediately thereafter, concealed in her handkerchief, she passed over the lips and nostrils of Preston's face a little mirror. She was sure this action had not been observed or understood by the undertaker standing near, but it was then that he touched her on the arm as a signal to pass on. As she did so she lifted her handkerchief as if to stay her tears. In reality, she stared hard at the surface of the little mirror.

She waited outside the house in a group of morbidly curious women and children and watched the casket borne to a big automobile hearse. A single carriage followed, into which only two persons entered. One was, of course, the widow, her countenance completely concealed by her veil. With knowing eyes Alice Royce regarded the portly, elderly man in high hat and frock coat who escorted the woman. And when the little funeral procession moved rapidly off Alice Royce nearly as rapidly made her way to a taxicab awaiting her at the corner. In this she followed the hearse.

It was as she expected. The procession did not move out directly toward the Brooklyn cemetery. It moved due east, then slanted north and finally stopped before the undertaking establishment of the Reshwar Brothers in the Bronx.

At 4 o'clock that same afternoon Alice Royce called up President Blair in his offices at the Tower Insurance Company. "Wilmot Gray, Dr. Wagstaff, the woman in the case and the Reshwar Brothers were all arrested ten minutes ago and Exhibit A in the case of fraud will be a casket loaded with bricks," she announced.

III

Blaney, the celebrated detective, and Blair awaited the arrival of Alice Royce impatiently, eager to hear her explanation of the strange case of Wilmot Gray.

"It was really very simple," said the girl detective, "the minute I began to know something of Dr. Wagstaff. It seems that for years he has devoted himself to a study of hypnotism and became really an adept. Gray, who was in the beginning genuinely a shopkeeper, became one of Dr. Wagstaff's best subjects. He could throw Gray into a perfect state of catalepsy. Many of the neighbors had witnessed these exhibitions in the past, when Gray would, under the suggestion of the old doctor, remain for hours perfectly rigid, breathing so slightly that some of the more ignorant observers would fear the man was dead or dying and beg Dr. Wagstaff to restore him to normal consciousness.

"Then, when Preston died within a few months of taking out a $25,000 insurance policy and I found that, like Gray, he had died of pneumonia, and, as with Gray, Dr. Wagstaff had been his attending physician and made out the death certificate, I was altogether sure of my ground when I attended the funeral.

"Preston," laughed the girl, "certainly looked dead. His breathing was indeed imperceptible. I jabbed a pin in his cheek, satisfying myself that I was right in believing that the striking semblance to death was caused by his having been thrown into a state of perfect catalepsy, and then my mirror test gave me positive evidence by the moisture on it after I had passed it over the dead man's lips that Preston was alive and breathing. I watched the coffin carried out and saw that the head lid was only half-screwed down. This convinced me

that Preston was being taken elsewhere to be released. Of course, it would be dangerous for him
to have remained in the house; the possibility of
somebody seeing him alive after his own funeral
was too grave a menace.

"The coffin hadn't been carried into the Reshwar undertaking establishment half an hour before
Preston or Gray walked out with Dr. Wagstaff and
the woman, who is really, I understand, his wife,
and were arrested by the Central Office men who,
like myself, had, on my information, followed the
funeral procession. Preston had doffed his 'grave
clothes' for less solemn raiment, and he had also
shaved off his beard and mustache by way of pre-
caution. But he was easily recognizable.

"Indeed, five minutes after his arrest he was in
the midst of a full confession. He declared that
the schema had originated with the elderly doctor,
and that most of the proceeds of the first 'haul' he
had turned over to his mother. Wagstaff had convinced the undertakers that the scheme was one
not possible of detection, and all the conspirators
had entertained a not altogether improbable vision of securing vast fortunes through Wagstaff's
hypnotism and Gray's deaths."

No. 7—Alice Royce and The Motor Car Crime

Of course, it is understood that when the scene of this shocking crime of which Alice Royce was called upon to find the perpetrator, is laid in this account in a fashionable country house colony near Philadelphia, the actual locality really was far from that city. The reason for this secrecy will appear obviously before the strange story is completed. For the purposes of this narration, therefore, the stage is set at a place called Mansfield, Pa.

Of this country house community, Grace Ransom, youthful, beautiful and wealthy, was undoubtedly—at any rate to the young bachelors of the colony—its most attractive member. Scarcely one of these same young bachelors had not at some time or other offered complete and life-long devotion and their whole fortunes to the graceful, fresh-faced girl with her joyous disposition and fine health.

The one misfortune of her life had been the early loss of her parents. At their death she and her brother, Carl, full ten years her senior, had been left $2,000,000 each and in his twenty-fifth year Carl, according to the provisions of the will, had assumed guardianship of his young sister.

Even the young bachelors who had been hardest hit admitted the justice of Fate's decree when the announcement was made of the betrothal of Grace Hansom to "Matty" Andrews. Even as she reigned as belle, "Matty" stood as the "star man," riding, driving, shooting, on the links—to every sport to which he turned his hand. Tall, sun-tanned, with the laugh of a boy and the grip of a man, of quick wit, Andrews was a true sportsman and a clean fellow.

Conditions being thus it will be readily under-stood how powerful the shock and how keen the horror that was experienced when on the eve of what was to have been the wedding day of the most prominent young couple of fashionable Mansfield, the news was shot over the telephone wire to a hundred or more homes that young "Matty" had been found unconscious, beside his wrecked automobile which had plunged into a thicket of trees off the Randall Boulevard. The idol of the colony was dying, the reports stated. Several ribs and a leg had been broken and there was every indication of a fractured skull.

And yet more horrifying was the announcement that came from the young man's cot at the Oleanda Hospital, whither he had been borne in the ninety horse power flier owned by his friend "Mile-a-Minute" Briggs. This was that it was no accident but a deliberate and oddly ferocious attempt to murder Andrews that had caused the young man's injuries and the wreck of his car—an attempt that seemed certain of success. Restoratives applied by physicians at the hospital had vouchsafed the young man a brief period of consciousness. He had been able to stammer slowly and painfully a recital of the manner of the attack. Then he had lapsed back into a coma from which it was feared he never would emerge.

Weird in conception and execution, horribly cunning in its design, had been the attempt at murder. Had the blow aimed with the purpose of striking with such force as to cause instant death fallen true to its purpose; had it not been for the brief period of lucid consciousness given "Matty" Andrews; it surely would have been accounted that the young clubman died by a grievous accident for which none was to blame.

Andrews had been a dinner guest at the Ransom home on the night of the outrageous occurrence and left there shortly after 10 o'clock, he and his fiancée agreeing it would be a case of "early to bed" that the morrow might find them fine and fit to meet the great occasion in their lives. Alone in his low, two-seated motor car, he had swept away down the long avenue of trees stretching from the portal of "Ransom Hall," turned into the Randall Boulevard and toward his own home five miles further down the road.

In turning into the road, he had with ordinary caution observed that no other car was approaching in either direction. But only a few seconds after he had set the nose of his automobile down the Randall road he had heard the hum of another car. It was in the rear. From the sharp whine of its engine it evidently was going at top speed. He flung a look back over his shoulder. To his astonishment the car following displayed no lights. In the utter darkness of the tree-lined boulevard he could not even vaguely see the approaching car; saw nothing; heard only the sound of the engine, growing louder and louder.

Andrews knew that half a mile ahead there came a sharp curve in the road. As things were moving the car behind would overtake him just at this turn, so he put on greater speed, thinking it wise to make this turn before halting to allow the madly driven car to pass him. But just as he started to put this resolution into effect the other car dashed up to him on his left side.

The lightless, wildly moving car veered crazily toward his own and for an instant or more the automobiles went dashing along together with scarcely a half foot of space between them. As they plunged along side by side, Andrews noticed that the car had a single occupant. Andrews cried out above the swirling, choking dust:

"What the devil are you trying to do, anyway?"

The man in the other car made no reply. Instead there was a sudden swish! A great blow fell on the back of Andrew's head. His hands flew out wildly and helplessly as he toppled over the wheel and the car itself, without guidance or control, went veering and swaying at fifty miles an hour into the curve ahead, plunging off the road, crashing onto the stalwart pine trees that clustered at this turn of the highway.

Out of the shattered car Andrews was flung. It was nearly an hour later that he was found with huddled, twisted body and blank mind by his friend Briggs, as the latter in his big car came himself toward the particular curve in the Randall Boulevard. This curve that had shot Andrews's car off the road had served to draw the glare of the lights of "Mile-a-Minute" Briggs's machine, exposing to that young man's eyes the spectacle of the wreck.

Briggs took the limp and broken body quickly in his arms, staggered with it to his own car and then drew on the engine for every ounce of power, more than demonstrating by the swiftness of his journey to the Oleanda Hospital the cause for his sobriquet of "Mile-a-Minute" Briggs.

II

That very night the President of the Mansfield Country Club telephoned the Blaney Detective Agency, whose offices in New York are open twenty-four hours of every day, and because of the wealth and social distinction of the victim of the attempted assassination and his associates, added to the peculiar circumstance of the murder occurring on the night preceding the appointed wedding day of Matty Andrews and Grace Ransom, Blaney decided to work on the case himself and called upon the assistance of Alice Royce.

"The women folk may know something to help solve the mystery and there's where you come in," he told her. He also ordered four of his most competent men operators to report aboard the train which started at 7 o'clock the next morning for Mansfield.

Motor cars were at the station to meet the party of detectives and Blaney immediately despatched the four operators to the scene of the crime to hunt for the weapon—the bludgeon—with which Matty Andrews had been attacked. There was a strong likelihood that somewhere on the road the young man's assailant had flung the weapon away. The agency chief, with Miss Alice Royce beside him, ordered the other car to be driven to the Mansfield Country Club. A score of other automobiles, all of them dusty and otherwise travel stained, were drawn up before the colonnaded piazza of the Country Club, for members had spent the entire night and most of the morning scouring all roads in the hope of finding some trace of the mysterious lightless car and its murderous motorist.

There was some surprise in the eyes of the men at the Country Club at the sight of Blaney with a pretty, innocent-eyed girl, but these glances were changed to those of curious respect when the famous detective introduced Alice Royce as his ablest assistant.

In the hour's talk that followed only negative information regarding the startling attempt at murder was obtained. The obvious theory had been thoroughly threshed out before the arrival of the detectives—the theory that some crazed and disappointed suitor of Grace Ransom might have put into effect a mad resolution that if the beautiful woman were not for his possession none other should have her. Jack Haughton, one of the smitten, had been in Europe for the last six months, and it was known that he was still abroad. Vernon Whitehead, whose bid for Grace Ransom had been too open not to entail gossip in the colony, had very frankly come forward with a satisfactory account of his whereabouts the night before. With four other members of the little private poker game in corroboration, Randy Gresham, another of the unsuccessful candidates, had been in sight of his fellow members of the club all evening. Other names had been taken up as possibilities only to be dismissed when brief investigation had shown conclusively they could not have been involved.

The talk had reached this stage when the sharp blast of an auto horn sounded outside and a minute later, McNamara, one of Blaney's men, entered.

"Here's the club, sir," he said. "We found it about half a mile up the road—just a little way off, among the trees."

Alice Royce studied the weapon, leaning over the shoulder of the seated Blaney. It was indeed a ponderous weapon—five feet of a maple sapling, so thick that Alice Royce saw that it must have been cut down with an axe or hatchet, and just as

she made the observation, Blaney himself uttered
it:

He had to whittle down one end of it so that he
could get his hands around it.

Looking at the huge club, the bystanders nodded their heads gravely, hopelessly. A blow from
such a thing certainly must have fractured "Matty" Andrews's head. Finally Blaney lowered the
bludgeon and rested it on his knees.

"Of course, gentlemen," he said, "it is possible
that Miss Ransom may have information of an en-
lightening character—something so entirely private that you would not know of it, or something
the importance of which she might not herself
appreciate. Might I ask if she could bear the ordeal
of an interview? Or is she too utterly prostrated?"

The answer came from the President of the club
to the effect that, due to her splendid spirit and
vitality, Miss Ransom had been able to parry the
blow of the shock and had not collapsed.

"Indeed," he said, "she is most determined that
everything should be done to trace 'Matty's' murder—or rather, most probably his murderer. She
has called up on the telephone eagerly inquiring
for news throughout the morning and thanked me
warmly for losing no time calling it your aid. I
think you will find her both able and willing to
discuss matters with you and tell you all she may

know that would be of any service. Indeed, one of
the Ransom motors is outside now, assigned here
to be used in case of need. You can go there in
that."

"Miss Royce will see Miss Ransom," said Blaney.
"I have another line on which I wish to direct my
men."

The Ransom chauffeur was summoned and
he led the girl detective to a low, high-wheeled,
two-seated car, in color a dark blue, and whose
six-cylindered engine betokened a machine designed for speed.

The June weather made it unnecessary for any
covering save a dust rug, for the absence of which
the chauffeur apologized.

"I thought I had left it in the machine last
night, miss," he said "but after I started out this
morning found I'd forgotten it. But it's only a
short ride."

Miss Royce nodded and stood aside to allow the
young man to mount and take the wheel. Her eye
naturally fell upon the floor mat at his feet. Her
eyes suddenly narrowed to sharp scrutiny. As she
got on the step she suddenly uttered a low cry of
annoyance.

"Oh, excuse me—before you start," she said, "I
dropped my handkerchief. Don't bother. I'll pick
it up."

As she picked the handkerchief from the floor-board, the chauffeur, had he been of sharp observation, might have seen a half dozen swift motions of Miss Royce's fingers, in which she not only took up her handkerchief, but nimbly took up four or five very small objects lying within her reach.

"Were you at work last night?" casually observed the young woman as the youth sent the car smartly out into the Randall Boulevard.

"No, miss; Mr. Carl—I'm his man—gave me the night off."

"You didn't clean the machine this morning?"

"No, miss, there wasn't time; they woke me up at 5 o'clock and had me out on the roads in the other car."

As they swung into the tree-lined entrance to Ransom Hall, Miss Boyce looked toward her escort with one of her prettiest smiles.

"Just before I go in to see Miss Ransom—have you such a thing as a hatchet in the garage? You see, I've a theory that a jealous woman had something to do with this—that she, in fact, chopped down the sapling that made the club. I'd just like to get a hatchet in my hand to feel the weight of it—to see how it would feel to wield it. I might, you know, gauge the weight and size of the woman by such a test."

The young fellow looked at her in a puzzled fashion, but promptly replied:

"Yes, miss, there's a hatchet in the tool chest in the garage all right."

He entered the garage to get it. Whereupon Miss Royce took opportunity to pull out the seat cushions and was rewarded by the finding of two other very small particles such as the four of which she already was possessed.

When the hatchet was placed in her hand, she said again, smilingly:

"I will just take this to Miss Ransom, if you don't mind; in order to explain to her my theory." As she started toward the house, she halted suddenly and looking back inquired:

"Is there any other road leading out from the house to the Randall Boulevard—other than the one which we came up?"

The chauffeur nodded affirmatively:

"There's a narrower road back of the stables and the farm hands' houses. It comes out on the boulevard about a quarter of a mile above this main entrance, miss."

She gave him a gracious little nod of farewell and entered the house. In the pause in the doorway, while the butler was announcing her, Miss Royce brought out of her handbag a small but strong magnifying lens. She studied closely the edge of the blade and then as she further examined the instrument a quick smile came upon her lips. She took off her linen motor coat, wrapped the hatchet in it and then placed the coat upon a hallway chair with her handbag resting on it, by which time the butler had arrived to escort her to Miss Ransom.

Miss Royce found the society girl in full possession of her nerves, but in grief that at times could not be denied its expression in tears, as she recounted the hours just preceding the murderous attack on her fiancé.

"If I could only do something—throw some light on this dreadful affair; but, Miss Royce, I am utterly in the dark. Mr. Andrews dined here with my brother Carl and myself last night. It was just an informal little dinner with the men still in their golfing clothes; we had all been on the links in the afternoon. At 9 Carl retired, laughing as he went, saying he would not intrude on our 'last hours' as it were. At 10 or a little afterward Mr. Andrews got into his car and departed. I know of no one who could have desired to kill him—man or woman. I am sure he has taken me fully into his confidence regarding all his affairs. None suggests such a dreadful possibility. Yet, of course, some such state of affairs existed. He had not been robbed. It is possible that in the darkness he may have been mistaken for some one else. But, oh! Miss Royce, what am I to think?"

The girl detective paused before speaking, considerate of the woe of the beautiful young woman before her.

"Miss Ransom" she said finally. "I've a theory that some treacherous servant in your employ may have signaled from a window of the house when Mr. Andrews took his departure. Have you any objection to my making an examination of the house and talking to the servants?"

The society girl's answer was to press a button in the wall and when a maid responded she said:

"Morrison, please obey any requests Miss Royce may make."

As the detective turned to bow on leaving the room it was to see Grace Ransom deeply ensconced in a huge leather armchair, her face buried in her shapely hands.

Once outside, Miss Royce seemed to have a very definite thought in mind.

"Is Mr. Carl at home?"

"No, he had to go to New York—there were so many things to do about postponing the wedding."

"Is his valet here?"

"Yes, Moore is in. Shall I call him?"

"If you please."

Ten minutes of close earnest conversation there was with Moore, the man at times looking startled, but finally bowing in earnest assent to what the young woman told him.

Alice Royce rejoined Blaney at the Country Club, and together they motored to the railroad station. As they walked the platform awaiting the train Blaney said:

"We found the place where the sapling was chopped down. It's right on the Ransom estate."

"And something more," said Alice Royce. She showed him the little particles she had gathered from the Ransom motor car: showed him also the hatchet and told him of her inquiries for the day.

Blaney stopped suddenly short in the walk and stared at the girl.

"By heavens! Miss Royce," he declared. "I think you've solved it! A week's investigation ought to prove it!"

III

It was, as a matter of fact, ten days later when Alice Royce and Blaney arrived in the afternoon at Ransom Hall and found there awaiting them at Blaney's request Miss Ransom and her elder brother, Carl.

Blaney, in his blunt, direct fashion, fixed his firm eyes on Carl Ransom and said:

"You're the man who tried to kill young Andrews."

Ransom leaped to his feet, his eyes glaring, but his face was very white.

"It will do you no good to deny it," continued Blaney imperturbably. Ransom simply continued to stare.

"You gave your chauffeur the night off. You gave your valet the night off. You left your sister and Mr. Andrews at 9 o'clock. You pretended to retire. Instead you got in your car."

"I did hear a car then," said Grace Ransom suddenly. "'Matty' and I were afraid visitors were coming in on me!"

"You got out your car and with a hatchet from your garage went down the back road and chopped down a maple sapling. You carried it over to the car and sat there whittling one end of it down to a convenient size for a handle. You stayed along the back road until you heard Andrews start, and then with the lights out on your machine pursued him and, as you schemed, overtook him near the curve in the road so that when you struck him down his machine would go flying off the road."

Ransom suddenly found his voice.

"What hellish rot are you talking? How do you come to dare make such accusations against me."

"Maple wood chips and shavings found in your automobile; a maple wood sprig caught in the jointure of the handle and blade of your hatchet—the chauffeur away and you the only man with a key to get into the garage and get that hatchet. Similar chips and shavings that were caught in your golf stockings and brushed out by your valet next morning."

"What sort of poppycock evidence is that?" demanded Ransom, but his voice was shaking.

"And a thumb print on the hatchet blade," said Blaney. "I dare, you, Ransom, to make one right here for purposes of comparison."

The young clubman turned a quick, keen glance toward his sister. The girl was staring fixedly at him. But then she turned to Blaney.

"Why," she demanded, "should my brother desire to harm—to murder my fiancé, Mr. Andrews?"

"Because, Miss Ransom, as guardian of your father's estate he is obliged to render you an accounting and give you full control of your property on your marriage. Is that true?"

"Most certainly."

"Well, ask him how much of your property he's got left to turn over."

The girl faced her brother and gasped at what she saw expressed in his eyes.

"Why, Miss Ransom," continued Blaney, "our investigations have shown that, having lost his own fortune to the last penny in stock gambling, he dipped into your funds—for a mere $50,000 at first; but he's a million into them now. Don't try to lie out of it to her, Ransom," said Blaney sturdily; "I've got the records of your deals in my pocket to prove it right now."

But Ransom had only started forward to fall back into a chair, covering his face with trembling hands.

"Carl!" cried his sister.

"God help me," he answered, "it's true!"

In the long silence, the girl caught at her breast with her hands and shuddered.

"That was why in the beginning," she said slowly, coldly, "you kept bringing me all manner of nasty gossip about 'Matty,' calculated to disgust me with him utterly, if I hadn't taken the trouble to prove them all lies—so, that was why?"

* * * * *

Due to the vigor of constitution awarded by his outdoor life and the fact that the blow aimed to dash out his brains had really fallen below the

skull and at the nape of his neck, young Andrews
made a complete recovery.

Whereupon he and Grace Ransom decided so
completely to hide the hideous scandal which she
confided to him as being his right to know, that
they carried the plan even to the extreme of having Carl Ransom act in the brotherly capacity of
giving the bride away. But shortly after the wedding he went to Europe, where he has made his
home since, and that is now three years ago.

No. 8—Clew of the Army Sword

The swift manner in which Alice Royce detected the slayer of old John Austen, the rich recluse of Actonville, N. J., is yet a subject of comment in that community, although the tragedy occurred three years ago. The girl detective confronted what was regarded as an almost hopeless mystery.

(The name Actonville is a fictitious one. The real name of the town is withheld to spare the feelings of a good woman who was brought into most painful notoriety at the time.)

Of old Austen himself his townspeople knew little, although he had lived among them for twenty years up to the time he was found slain in the library of his home. He had arrived one day, a stranger. He engaged a carriage and was driven about the town until on Elm avenue, far back of the roadway and nearly entirely hidden by a grove of giant trees, he espied the deserted Graves mansion. He made note of the real estate agent's name and address as it appeared on the "For Sale" sign and was driven to that office.

The Graves mansion had once been the splendid social establishment of Actonville, but its owner had taken residence abroad, and long before the arrival of John Austen had given orders to the Actonville agent to sell the house to any person offering a fair price. Thus when Austen presented himself to the real estate dealer a bargain was soon made.

At that time Austen was about fifty-five years old, spare but ruggedly built. His features were sharp and his mouth was thin-lipped and tightly drawn under the closely cropped horseshoe-shaped mustache.

A man named Newton Spencer and his wife were engaged as his servants. He lived in utter seclusion. No visitors ever crossed the threshold of the mansion. He covered the old library walls with books, a few etchings and some old army swords and guns, suggesting that he had seen civil war service, converted an adjoining apartment into a bedroom and abandoned the remainder of the house to his servants. His meals were taken to him in the library, where he spent nearly all his time. His only diversion was an afternoon drive behind a team of handsome horses. This he took daily regardless of the weather. Frequently he returned with the horses coated with lather, panting and otherwise showing every indication of hard driving.

Sometimes—before she grew utterly deaf, as she had been in the last five years—old Mrs. Spencer would hear her master pacing the library, talking to himself. The tones were angry and rose now and then to sharpness, but the walls of the old-fashioned house were thick and no words ever reached the housekeeper's ears.

At times when she entered the library his eyes would be strangely bright and steadfast in an expression of brooding anger, though in no way directed against her. Toward his servants he was monosyllabic, even brusque, but never altogether rough or rude.

Austen made occasional trips to New York, but apparently the sole purpose of these was to fetch money with which to replenish funds he kept in a local bank for the liquidation of his tradesmen's bills.

II

The evening of the tragedy was brilliant with stars.

It was just at twilight that old Mrs. Spencer, walking the main pathway under the big trees, by way of escape from the kitchen heat endured in

the preparation of Mr. Austen's dinner, was surprised to observe a young man open the gate, pass
in from the street and up under the elms toward
the house. She supposed the stranger had mistaken
the place for some other person's home. But when
on account of her deafness he had fairly shouted the name of her master she turned readily to
lead him toward the door, there being no positive
orders forbidding callers. As she thus turned she
saw aged Mr. Austen standing in the long open
window of the library. And she made out a waving
gesture of his hand that was plainly an invitation
to the young man to enter.

Mrs. Spencer conducted the visitor to the door of
the library, and as her master opened it she turned
and repaired to the small room off the kitchen,
where she and her husband had dinner. Later in
the evening, when the old couple made their way
to their own sleeping rooms, they observed the
light from Austen's study showing sharply through
the keyhole and chinks of the door into the dark
hallway. Spencer, whose hearing was unimpaired,
was certain afterward that there was no sound of
conversation in the library.

At 9 o'clock the next morning when Mrs. Spencer, bearing her employer's breakfast, entered the
library she dropped the tray and a shrill cry of
terror came from her lips.

Stretched at full length, face downward on the floor, was John Austen. His right hand, folded under his chest, held a revolver and at his feet was a spray of glass chips from a chandelier globe that his bullet had shivered before imbedding itself in the ceiling. On her master's white head the old woman saw a ghastly suffusion of crimson and in front of him an empty sword scabbard. Near it lay the unsheathed weapon itself with its blade red stained. She tottered from the room, calling feebly for her husband.

When the Police Chief of Actonville and his assistants arrived and made further examination of the room they saw that the sword used by the slayer was one of the several that had hung on the wall. The pistol also was Austen's. Between bookcases was an old safe, the door flung wide. Papers were scattered over several feet of the floor in front of the safe and mixed with the letters and documents on the floor were yellow-back currency notes and a sprinkling of gold coins. Examination of the wound on the old man's head revealed that a single, ferocious blow had cloven John Austen's skull, killing him almost instantly.

Mrs. Spencer gave a fairly good description of the man who had called the evening before. A lean, broad-shouldered man of thirty or thereabouts, she said he was. "His face was most pleasant," said the old woman, "and when he saw Mr. Austen at the window he smiled and waved as friendly as could be." There was little, however, that was distinctive in his appearance, she went on to say. He was well dressed in a blue serge suit and wore a Panama hat and russet shoes. When he waved his hand she had observed that he wore a massive ring with a stone in it.

Such were the circumstances as far as known when the Police Chief of Actonville appealed to a famous New York agency for expert assistance and Miss Alice Royce was assigned to the case.

III

Alice Royce, accompanied by McNamara, one of the members of the New York agency, arrived at Actonville at 6 o'clock of the day following the tragedy. She spent half an hour on the premises of the old Graves mansion. Most of the time she was in the library, where, save for the removal of old John Austen's body, the room had been preserved by the police absolutely undisturbed.

At 6 o'clock the following evening Alice Royce entered the private office of the Police Chief of Actonville, followed by a tall, slender man who was pallid to the lips, whose eyes were wild, but who nevertheless walked firmly as one bent on executing a resolution. McNamara brought up the rear. The Chief was amazed when the girl detective said:

"Chief Foley, this young man is Chester Garside of Seatontown. He desires to make a full confession of the killing of John Austen."

The Chief turned a swift questioning glance at the young man, who nodded and said:

"That's correct. I killed John Austen. I know that whatever I may say here can be used against me, but I am anxious to tell how it happened, and I'm ready now."

Foley hurriedly summoned a stenographer. With the eyes of the interested auditors upon him Garside arose, paced the length of the room three or four times and finally spoke.

"Since I was sixteen," he said, "I have been known as Chester Garside. In reality my name is Austen and it was my father I killed. Chester Garside Austen," he added bitterly—"that is my name.

"My father was thirty-nine years old when he married—my mother a girl scarcely twenty. He had inherited a fortune and at forty-five he was a millionaire. My own boyish recollection of him was that he was a brooding, domineering man, who sometimes treated me with great severity, sometimes seemed to show an actual hatred of

me, but at other times suddenly would disclose
moments of tenderness toward me. All through
my childhood I remember bitter quarrels between
my parents. Frequently my mother would draw me
closely to her and sob:

"'Oh, my boy—my little boy—it is too wretched to bear!'

"As I grew older I understood the cause of her
anguish. My father was insanely jealous of my
mother. Insanity is the only way to describe his
wild suspicions and his ferocity of temper when
those suspicions were aroused. In Seatontown,
where our home has always been, everybody knew
how truly wild these suspicions were, how utterly
founded on trivialities. The nineteen years' difference in the ages of my father and mother was
a subject of morbid consideration with him, and
no younger man might meet my mother in the
ordinary manner of social intercourse without instantly incurring my father's anger."

Garside paused, stared hard at the little oblong
book of the stenographer and the poised pencil,
then squared his shoulders, thrust his hands in
the pockets of his blue serge coat and continued:

"The name of Chester Garside, it is needless
for me to tell you, is that of a famous artist—
an elderly man of fifty-eight now. He was reared
in Seatontown and there was a boy-and-girl love

affair between my mother and himself—a mere romance of early youth, you understand. Young Garside went to New York to pursue his art studies and this love affair subsided into simple friendship, which, however, proved enduring.

"Garside attended my mother's wedding and left immediately for Paris. When he returned a year and a half later he was Seatontown's celebrity, and was, of course, lionized.

"Meanwhile I had been born. My mother in natural admiration for the fame her old schoolday sweetheart had won conceived the romantic notion, as young mothers so frequently do, of conferring on me his name and inviting him to stand as godfather for her child.

"She had long before told my father of the adolescent romance. Now, to her dismay, when she broached the subject of my christening and told him the name and sponsor she had chosen, my father flung himself into the fiercest outburst of rage that he had ever exhibited. He snarled out the most outrageous aspersions on my mother. She had borne past scenes patiently, but this time her anger blazed, and with it came the determination to defy my father. She did.

"I was christened Chester Garside Austen and the young painter became my godfather. My father stood at the altar rail by my mother's side during the ceremony. After their bitter quarrel my mother had refused to speak to him, even to sit at the same table with him, and he had experienced a repentance for his conduct as abject as his outburst had been furious.

"But for all that the suspicion my father had conceived had been by no means wholly eradicated.

"From my earliest childhood I recall that next to my mother I adored Garside, and that my father held really a very small place in my heart. Garside, with his ability to enter into my childish thoughts, the toys and sweets he was forever handing out of his pockets for my delight, naturally won my affection.

"My father at times angrily protested to my mother, but she coldly turned those objections aside, declaring that friendship with a man of the character of Garside was the most admirable influence that possibly could come into a boy's life.

"This brings me to the time of the last painful scene between my parents. I was fourteen years old, had been ill of typhoid fever and was convalescent. Garside called to inquire of my condition and, hearing his voice below, I eagerly requested my mother to fetch him to my bedside. He readily responded. My mother and he were seated beside me. She was holding my hand and Garside was thrusting my hair back from my forehead with kindly fingers while he was happily outlining a canoe trip on which he promised to take me when I grew stronger.

"I looked up to see my father standing in the doorway. Following my glance, my mother, and Garside turned also and saw him. His heavy black eyebrows were gathered, his glance set in glaring anger.

"'What a pretty picture!' he sneered. Then, giving vent to his rage, he shouted: 'Don't talk! Don't try and say anything. I'll leave you two to your whelp! You will never see me again!'

"Nor did we. Although Seatontown is not many miles away from Actonville, my father had hidden himself completely and, besides, my mother made no inquiry whatever regarding him. She had property and we continued living in comfort. In the course of time she divorced my father for his desertion. Garside renewed his devotion to my mother and, in the end, they married—my mother in all confidence that her friends intimately acquainted with her past would place no false construction on the event, as I am sure they did not.

"I willingly dropped my surname and adopted Garside as a father. No boy ever had a better one. In the passing of twenty years the austere, sinister figure of my real father faded from my memory, save as now and then the recollection would come of his anger-blackened face staring into the door-way of my sickroom."

The pallid-faced man paused, thankfully took a swallow of water from a glass the Police Chief handed him and continued:

"There came last week a letter addressed to me, which I now surrender to your keeping. You will see that it came from my father, that it is written in friendly tones, speaks of the loneliness of his declining years and appeals to me to visit him.

"Of course I showed the letter to my mother and stepfather. Their rancor against him was quite gone; they expressed only pity and urged me to visit the aged man immediately.

"I arrived in Actonville night before last. Being assailed with some uncertainty as to how, after all, I might be received in my father's house, I registered at the hotel, left my grip there and then made my way to my father's residence.

"Mrs. Spencer has, I understand, told you of my arrival.

"'Good evening, Mr.—Mr. Garside,' he said with sneering bitterness as I entered the library.

"I took a seat before him, dropping the hand I had at first extended in friendship. He studied me intently for several seconds. His eyes were strange, uncanny, and the flash and glitter in them told me that years of solitude, of wretched brooding on a fancied wrong, had done their insidious damage to his mind.

"He told me that he had heard of my mother's marriage to Garside. He asked many questions regarding their life and whether or not my mother was happy. I could only truthfully answer that she was.

"'And you, I understand,' he observed, 'have also given her cause for joy; you have been dutiful and I hear are the leading young lawyer of Seatontown?'

"To this I only smiled. My father arose abruptly, went over to his safe and brought out an armful of papers. These he sorted over and passed to me as he rapidly sketched an inventory of his belongings. Having impressed me with the fact that his fortune amounted to nearly a million and a half dollars, he paused and chuckled wickedly. Not for an instant did I guess the infamous proposal he was to make me."

Garside stopped short. He bent his face closely to that of Chief Foley.

"Do you know what he wanted me to do?" he demanded. "He had conceived a subtle scheme for revenge against my mother.

"He offered me a half million dollars there and then if I would disappear, leaving no word whatsoever behind me, promising never in my lifetime

to see my mother or give her any information as
to what had become of me. Moreover, he promised
that the other million of the fortune would be
held in trust for me by the provisions of his will
and paid wholly over to me on my mother's death,
providing that in the mean time I held no communication with her of any kind. He chuckled crazily
over the contemplation of his revenge.

"I indignantly refused this offer, told him how
dearly I loved my mother and—yes, I didn't re-
frain, either, from telling him of my affection for
Garside.

"He stopped me with a cry of rage. Wildly stammering profanity and imprecations, he arose from
his chair and made his way to the safe. He drew
forth another paper. He waved it at me frantically.

"'This is a will,' he cried, 'that I have already
drawn up. This will go on the public records when
I am dead. And it contains the whole damnable
truth about your mother and that treacherous
painter. And you! I have set down my reasons here
for your complete disinheritance!'

"He thrust the paper back into the safe, moved
around the table as he spoke, opened a drawer and
was fumbling inside it.

"'Father,' I cried, 'you can't mean to libel my
mother and me! You certainly won't utter that
dirty lie from the grave!'

"His eyes were blazing wildly as he faced me.

"'I'll do it,' he shrieked hysterically. 'And I'll do more! I'm near the grave, but you will go to yours before me. Garside robbed me of my wife—I'll rob the pair of them of their whelp!'

"Then his hand came up from the table drawer, and in horror I saw that it held a revolver. Had it not been for the palsy of age, increased by the tremor of his crazy emotions, he would have killed me at that instant.

"I glanced around for a weapon—on the right on the wall I saw the crossed army swords. I seized one, tore it from its scabbard and in fear of my life struck at the insane old man. The single blow felled him. His bullet flew over my head, shattering a globe on the chandelier."

* * * * * *

Garside tossed himself into a chair, and there he sat, staring as if a moving film of pictures of the terrific scene was then crossing his vision.

"That is all," he said finally, "excepting that when my composure was somewhat restored I ransacked the safe, dragged out the infamous will and bore it away from the house."

IV

Chief Foley led Garside away to a cell, then returned quickly to his room.

"Miss Royce," he asked eagerly, "how did you go about it? How were you able in so short a time to find the slayer?"

"Easily enough," smiled the girl. "He is left-handed."

"What do you mean?" demanded Foley.

Then, as she went about adjusting her motor veil in a matter of fact manner, she added:

"There were many things to indicate that a left-handed man had slain Mr. Austen. You will remember the scabbard flung to the slayer's right, the sword to the left Mr. Austen's hand holding the revolver was crossed under his chest, the revolver pointing to the left; the shattered globe in the chandelier was toward the slayer's left; in short, the attack on him had come from the left. The wound on the old man's head showed a plain inclination of the cut from left to right."

"But how did you identify Garside?"

"It was evident from his open manner of approaching the house that when he came there he had no crime of murder in mind. Mrs. Spencer knew he was a stranger in Actonville. The baggage-man at the railroad station remembered directing such a stranger to the hotel—the Actonville

House. I looked at the registry there. Left-handed writing is easy to identify. The right-handed writer seeking to write vertically always achieves a decided backhanded result, but the lefthanded writer almost invariably achieves the vertical exactly. When I found in this manner of handwriting the name 'Chester Garside, Seatontown, N. Y.,' McNamara and myself went to the place indicated on the first train.

"Chester Garside was pointed out to us on the street. I hurried along and passed him, dropping my handbag I did so. He politely stooped and picked it up with his left hand. And on this hand was the large ring with the stone in it such as Mrs. Spencer told us John Austen's visitor had worn. Then McNamara and myself went to his office and questioned him. It was not hard to get him to tell the story. In fact, he was on the point that very night of making a confession."

* * * * * *

Six months later Chester Garside, supported by the testimony of his mother, told the same story to a jury. He was acquitted on the ground of self-defense.

The Adventures of Edda Manby

Hulbert Footner

1934-1935

(*Mystery Magazine,* Tower Magazines)

The Man with the Crooked Finger

Fred was sore. When they pulled up in front of Edda's boarding-house he broke out: "Absolutely heartless! Absolutely heartless. I'd give my life for you, and you ship me with a wisecrack!"

Poor Fred! thought Edda. He's a sincere boy, but there's a deficiency of lime in his composition. She said nothing.

"I'm mad about you!" Fred went on, "and all you want is to borrow ten dollars!"

"I'll pay it back," she said meekly.

"You won't get the chance! It's got to be all or nothing with me! You'll never lay eyes on me again!"

He embraced her with a kind of desperation. Edda submitted since it was for the last time. When he let go of her she patted her hair into place with a sigh. If he was going to take it like this it was impossible to beg him for the money. "Don't get out," she said, "I have my key."

She ran up the steps and waited in the vestibule
until Fred's car roared away down the street. Then
she came down the steps. The truth was she had
no key. It had been taken from her earlier in the
evening after a scene in the lower hall on her way
out. Also the suitcase she was carrying. She had
been told that she needn't come back unless she
brought something to pay on account.

Young Fred's love-making had been so cyclonic
she hadn't been able to tell him the situation.
Midnight was a little late to start looking for a
lodging. And a little model in oyster-white satin
with a bunny wrap, not much to face the world
in. There was nothing in her beaded evening bag
but handkerchief, cigarettes and compact. Not
one red penny! "Thank God. I have a friend." she
thought. "I'll just have to walk up to Mildred's
place. What if Mildred isn't home?" Brhh! She refused to face that possibility.

A man came charging around the corner from
Lexington Avenue. He pulled up short; raised his
hat. "You're too pretty to be out alone," he said.
"I'll walk home with you." Meanwhile he was rapidly turning up his hat-brim and throwing open his
overcoat, revealing evening dress beneath. Slipping
his arm through Edda's, he urged her forward.

Before she could adjust herself to the situation,
another man came tearing around the corner;
hard blue eyes; outsize feet. He stopped and ran a

suspicious eye over him. Edda's escort was saying
in an easy voice: "Ya-as, I'm dated up with the
Rumseys for the hunting."

"Did a guy just run by youse?" demanded the
plainclothes man.

"Eh, what? Oh, surely, officer!" said the man.
"I turned my head to look at him. He ran in an
areaway near the end of the block, this side."

The officer ran on. Edda's companion steered
her briskly around the corner. A taxi came trund-
ling up. "Hop in," he said, "I'll take you anywhere
you want." Edda lost no time in obeying. Here's a
bit of luck! she thought.

"Where to, Mister?" asked the driver.

"Just keep on," was the answer, "and step on it,
Sir Malcolm."

Edda took a look at her fellow-traveler. The
passing lights gave her flashes of a Times Square
grin; hard-boiled. "What was the trouble you
had?" she asked politely.

"Well, a fellow owed me some money, and I
went to collect it. We had words and he hollered
out of the window for a cop. It seemed easier to
beat it than to stop and explain."

Likely story! thought Edda. "I like policemen," she remarked, just to be saying something.
"They're so physical!"

Her companion, it appeared, did not share her feelings about policemen. Neither had he any opinion of their cleverness. He related several anecdotes to prove his point. "Aah!" he said, "as long as your money holds out, the cops can never catch you! All you got to do is register at a first-class hotel and have your meals sent up."

While they bowled along and made friends talking, he began to inch across the seat. Edda knew the signs. Finally he said: "What's your name, kid?"

"Edda Manby."

"Cute name! Mine's Jack Scanlan. . . . Kiss?"

"Nothing doing," said Edda.

"All right. Where do you live?"

"I'm going to a friend's flat on Forty-sixth around the corner from Lexington. You've saved me walking."

"What's the matter? You broke?"

"Abso-stony-lutely." She told her little story. Old stuff. No job. No job. No job. And always the grim necessity of keeping up the facade in order to get a job.

"You should worry," said Jack. "You have personality. You can always cash in on personality. Why don't you go on the stage?"

"I'd rather have a job," said Edda. "I'm strong for regular meals."

"With your looks you wouldn't have to pay for your meals."

"I know, but a girl gets tired of being bright at meal-times. I'd sooner be myself and pay for my own."

"I'm on the stage," he volunteered.

"Oh, yeah?" said Edda politely. She thought: It hasn't done much for you.

"First time I ever heard of a good-looking doll passing up the stage."

"I'm not passing up anything right now."

"I could put you in the way of getting an engagement."

"It would have to be quick."

"Well, maybe we can get hold of the guy I have in mind tonight. If he likes you you could touch him for an advance. Come on up to my place and we'll talk it over. . . ." Warned by the look in Edda's eye he quickly added: "My wife's there."

"Where is it?" asked Edda.

"East Forty-ninth."

Edda thought: Well, if I don't like the set-up, its near Mildred's. "All right," she said.

Jack gave the address to the driver.

It was an old-time walk-up house cast of Lexington, with a sporting flavor. The original apartments had been subdivided into many small flats

rented, furnished, by the week. Late as it was the
tenants were still going in and out; Lexington
Avenue stars. A landlady sat at a desk in the downstairs corridor looking them over. She was equal
to her job. From the temperature of her greeting
to Jack, Edda drew her own conclusions. Pretty
near zero.

In the lighted corridor Edda got her first good
look at him. The semi-darkness had flattered him.
Youthfulness was his line, but it was beginning
to pull at the seams. Thirty-eight, she decided.
There was a yellow look in his eyes that made her
cautious.

They climbed three flights under their own
power, and Jack led the way to one of the little
flats in the rear. He knocked in a certain manner;
knock, pause, three knocks, pause, knock. The
door was opened by a beauty-parlor blonde with
smoky eyes who had rather a fallen look without
her girdle. She was crabbed.

"Who the hell is this?" she demanded as they
walked in.

"Edda Manby," said Jack. "Helped me to stall
off a cop down in Thirty-sixth Street."

"So you fumbled the job!" she said bitterly.

"You can't always bring home the bacon."

"Ought to have gone myself," she muttered.

"Edda's broke and wants a job on the stage," said Jack. "I thought it might lead to something if we introduced her to the Colonel."

He was behind Edda, and the latter had a hunch that there was some conjugal signaling going on. However, she was not going to pull out just because there was a tang of danger in the situation. The blonde's name was Maud. Her animosity cooled, and she appraised Edda with the eye of an expert.

"Her figure's all right," she said, "but her map's a little out of drawing."

"A slight irregularity of feature is the essence of charm!" said Jack. "At least that's what they say."

"Oh, yeah?"

"And boy! I'll say she has spizz!"

"How do you know?"

"Didn't I ride up with her in the taxi?"

Maud suddenly became friendly. "Sit down, dear," she said. "Will you have some beer?"

Edda declined.

"It's a good thing," muttered Jack. "Beer's out."

"Well, you needn't exhibit our poverty," said Maud, smiling like a fond wife.

They all sat down. Under the guise of light talk Maud put Edda through a pretty stiff examination. In the bottoms of her smoky eyes she was doping things out. Edda, keen to find out what was coming of all this, gave her the answers she wanted.

Finally Maud said she would dress. In passing Jack she gave him a signal, and he followed her into the bedroom, while she waited. Edda's eyes strayed around the sitting room. It was furnished in the golden oak period when pillows had frills. From behind the closed portieres Maud flung out an occasional bright remark. In between Edda could hear whisper, whisper, whisper. Jack was getting his instructions.

Maud reappeared looking very svelte in her girdle and white evening gown. Edda wondered idly where she had checked the excess. Maud said:

"I'm going to round up the Colonel. You stay here until I phone." When she had gone, Jack drifted around the room looking at Edda out of the corners of his eyes. The walls were thin and there were plenty of people around. Edda didn't mind. After a while he said:

"That little crooked smile of yours drives me crazy!"

"Think of Maud," said Edda.

"Maud! Hell! She's a broad-minded woman. She wouldn't care unless it was absolutely forced on her attention."

"Nothing to it!" said Edda. "I have other plans."

"You don't know me," said Jack. He started for her.

She saw it coming, and already had the door open. "I'll wait for you down in the street corridor," she said. "You stick by the phone."

He followed her, pleading: "Aw, have a heart, Edda." He couldn't go down without making a fool of himself before the landlady. Edda left him at the top of the stairs, and descending to the street floor, took a seat in the corridor. The landlady gave her a dirty look, but Edda didn't owe her any money. She could bear it.

When Jack came along a while later his softer mood, if you can call it that, had changed. His close-set eyes were full of business now—bad business. "Come on!" he said out of the corner of his mouth. he added: "That other taxi got my last half-dollar. We'll have to walk. It's not far."

"Just how far?" asked Edda.

"Borneo Bicycle Club, a 'speak' in Forty-fourth. Maud and the Colonel will meet us there. The old man can't climb our stairs on account he's got a bad heart."

The club was east of Lexington in one of a row of old brownstone fronts that had seen better days. Crowded inside. No style to it. One of those alleged gangsters' hangouts that give Park Avenue dames such a thrill. The slick waxy-faced little guys sitting around might or might not have been

bona fide killers. Anyhow, Raymondo, the proprietor, was making a good thing out of it. This
Raymondo was a fat little Italian in a tuxedo, with
a face you could absolutely break rocks on.

Maud and the Colonel arrived almost at the
same moment. Edda suspected at a glance that the
Colonel was not in the theatrical business and never had been; he was too conservative. More like a
big banker who sat in his office all day with slaves
pussyfooting in and out on Oriental rugs. At two
o'clock in the morning in a shady speakeasy with
his top hat on one side of his head he was merely
a number one sucker.

"Meet the kid sister, Colonel," cried Maud.
"It's her first night in town!"

Gosh! thought Edda, is this intended to be
taken straight?

The rosy, white-haired Colonel rolled her hand
between his as if it were a lemon he was soften-
ing. "She's a duckling!" he said. He drew her hand
through his arm, patted it and surveyed the room
like a conqueror of the sex. "How about a little
drink?" he asked.

"Let's go upstairs," put in Jack.

To Edda, this was like the flash of a warning
signal. "Oh, not upstairs!" she protested. "I like
to watch the crowd."

"Nonsense, darling," said the Colonel. "It's a nasty crowd."

Edda found herself neatly separated from the Colonel, and swept up the stairs as if by an irresistible force. Everybody was talking and laughing. Her protests passed unnoticed. Raymondo ushered the party into a room at the back that was filled with dining-room furniture and an immense Chesterfield. A cynical looking waiter appeared carrying a magnum of champagne in a bucket of ice.

"It's chilled." said Raymondo rubbing his hands. "You can open it right away."

Raymondo and the waiter stole out, closing the door behind them as softly as a kiss. Edda noticed two things about the room; firstly there was a key in the door; secondly an iron fire escape outside the window. There was no let-up in the storm of speakeasy talk, which never asks for an answer. The Colonel drained his glass at a gulp, and Jack instantly filled it.

As time passed, his red face kept setting redder and his white hair whiter by comparison. Across from Edda he courted her in the flowery style of his youth. She got more and more uneasy. Not for herself but for him. Something was beginning to click in her mind. If there had only been some way of sending him a telepathic warning without words!

At about the fourth glass the Colonel demanded that Edda come and sit beside him. Maud, smiling, changed places with Edda. The Colonel dragged his chair close and put an arm around her. She did not repulse him. On the contrary, she affectionately rubbed her cheek against his. This brought her lips alongside his ear.

"Do you know these people?" she whispered.

Turning his head slightly he whispered back: "Never saw the woman but once before. Don't they belong to you?"

"No! They're crooks."

"What about you?"

"They just picked me up an hour ago."

From the other side of the table Maud and Jack looked on at the whispering with fond smiles. Everything going fine!

The Colonel whispered: "I'd better get out of here!"

"Suggest that we all leave," answered Edda. "Easy to shake them outside."

To her relief he proved less foolish than he appeared. He didn't break out and precipitate trouble. For a while the loud talk went on. Like dogs barking; big dog, middle-size dog, little mutt yelping. In the end Maud herself gave the Colonel an opening. She said:

"Can't drink another drop unless I eat something."

Jack put in: "You can order anything you want here."

"Don't let's eat in this joint," said the Colonel. "Let's go to the Conradi-Windermere. It's only a step."

"You can't get anything at the Conradi-Windermere at two in the morning," said Jack.

"I can," said the Colonel, slapping his shirt front.

"The Conradi's too grand!" objected Maud. "It's more folksy here at Raymondo's."

The Colonel made out to be a little drunker than he was. "I'm paying, ain't I?"

Jack made haste to smooth him down. "Just one more glass, and then we'll go. It's a shame to waste this good wine."

"Take it with us," said the Colonel. "Drink it in the taxi."

He pushed his glass across the table to be refilled. Jack's aim was uncertain, and he knocked the glass to the floor, smashing it. Laughing foolishly, he carried the bottle to the sideboard, and filling another glass, brought it back.

The Colonel started to drink it—and stopped. His drunkenness dropped away. He stood up so quickly that his chair fell over. He blew out the wine in his mouth, and dashed the glass to the floor. "It's drugged!" he said. "You damned black-leg! You doped it when you went to the sideboard!"

Jack was also on his feet. His face turned sharp and rat-like. "You lie!" he snarled. "You can't make a charge like that and get away with it! Apologize!"

The Colonel swelled up. "To you?" he said. "Don't make me laugh!" He started for the door.

Edda, sliding out of her chair, instinctively backed against the wall. Maud remained all hunched up in her chair, staring wildly. Jack, swift as a gliding snake, reached the door first, turned the key, put it in his pocket.

"Apologize!" he snarled.

The Colonel snapped his fingers under the other man's nose. "Open that door!" he command-ed, "or I'll kick it down!"

Jack, with his shoulders drawn up like a hunch-back's, whipped a black automatic out of his hip pocket and poked it against the Colonel's shirt-front, left side. Edda noticed that the crooked fin-ger exactly fitted the trigger. "Back up, old man!" he snarled.

It was a miscalculation. The Colonel proved to be the one man in a hundred or so who could not be stopped. His big hands closed around Jack's throat. Jack fired. The old man dropped like an ox when the axe descends, sprawling on the floor. His upper false teeth were jarred out. A showy crimson stain spread on the white shirt-front. His blue eyes remained open with a perplexed, questioning expression like a child's.

Edda stood, pressed against the wall, taking it in. She could feel nothing as yet. Maud was fetching her breath in a series of little gasps as if she was trying to save up enough to scream and could not. Jack put up his gun and dropped to his knees. His bony deformed fingers ran through the dead man's pockets.

"Out! . . . Window! . . . You know the way!" he snarled at Maud. ". . . Raymondo can hold the bag this time," he added with a spurt of laughter.

Maud ran staggering and gasping to the window, threw it up and climbed out on the fire escape. Edda snatched up her wrap and followed. It seemed the only thing to do. As she turned around to descend the ladder she saw Jack frisk a wallet from the dead man's breast pocket. People were pounding on the door now. Jack sprang for the window and came down the ladder so fast he stepped on Edda's fingers.

They dropped off the end of the ladder into a backyard. All quiet here. A door in the back of the fence let them into another yard with the back

of a house facing them, windows all dark. At the
side of the house was an arched passage ending in
an iron gate with a spring lock. Up four steps and
they were in Forty-seventh Street with a taxicab
waiting at the curb. It seemed providential until
it occurred to Edda that it had been planted there.

Maud scrambled into the cab, and Jack after
her. As Edda was following, he leaned out and
thrusting her back with a foul oath, slammed the
door. The taxi jerked into high and raced away,
leaving her.

Edda automatically started walking as fast as
she could away from there. To run would have
been fatal. She couldn't think. There was not a
soul in sight in the long street with its little pools
of light. With a groan of relief she got around the
corner into Lexington; a short block and around
another corner into Forty-sixth, Mildred's street.

The house was four doors from the corner. It was
a more modern walkup apartment. The entrance
door was always unlocked and you were supposed
to ring inside. Mildred lived on the ground floor
just inside the entrance. Edda knocked and rang
with a mad longing to get on the other side of a
friendly door.

There was no answer. At her feet stood an empty milk bottle with a note for the milkman stuffed
in its neck. Edda pulled it out. It read: "Leave

no milk until Monday. Gone out of town." Edda leaned against the door feeling sick.

Somehow or other she found herself alongside one of the side doors of the Conradi-Windermere, and turned in blindly. A corridor led her to the great central lobby which was quite empty, and had most of the lights turned off. She sank into an overstuffed chair, closed her eyes, and waited for whatever was going to happen.

A super-bell-hop approached and asked if she was waiting for anybody. Edda, who thought she was all in, discovered that she still had reserves. Her tongue of its own accord started lying quite naturally.

"Please ask at the desk if there is any message for Mrs. Manby of Montclair. There was some trouble in a speakeasy where I was having supper and I became separated from my friends. I came here because we dined here—we always dine here when in town, and I supposed that my friends would look for me here."

The bell-boy went away to repeat this to the night clerk at the desk. Out of the corner of her eyes Edda could see the two of them looking her over. She crossed her feet, and carelessly smoothed her skirt. At any rate my appearance is all right, she thought.

The boy came back. He said: There is no message, Mrs. Manby. But the night manager says he will be glad to accommodate you with a room until you get in touch with your friends."

"Oh, very well," said Edda. "Most kind I am sure."

When she awoke next morning the sun was streaming through the windows. She gazed at her surroundings in astonishment; the luxurious bed with its satin coverlet; the elegant furniture, the rare rugs. An ormolu wall clock informed her that it was ten-twenty. Had she been wafted to Hollywood or what? Then recollection rushed back and she shivered. She craved food to restore her courage. She put out her hand to the telephone, wondering if the fairytale would stand her for a breakfast.

It came, and with it a copy of the latest newspaper. The service was as deferential as if Edda had possessed a million-dollar roll. Why be insulted in a cheap boarding house when you can live for nothing at the Conradi-Windermere, she asked herself. She ate sitting up in bed with the newspaper spread beside her.

The unlucky Colonel had made the first page all right. Boiled down it ran:

"Shortly after three o'clock this morning the body of an elderly man in evening dress was discovered by a passing motorist in the Forty-second Street tunnel near the East River. He had been shot through the heart. Identification was established by means of a tailor's label sewed inside a pocket of his coat. The victim is Colonel Eversley Marconi, a wealthy and socially prominent resident of Batavia, N. Y., who is registered at the Conradi-Windermere.

"Inspector Scofield has taken personal charge of the case. Unfortunately the police have but little to go on. Hugh J. Marconi, son of the deceased, says that he and his father were supping with some men friends at the Club Splendide last night, when the elder Marcom was called to the telephone. This was about one-thirty. He never returned to his friends. As this had happened before they thought nothing of it until the tragedy was revealed some hours later. Colonel Marcom carried a large sum of money on his person.

"Hugh J. Marcom has offered a reward of five thousand dollars for the apprehension of his father's murderers."

Edda lit a cigarette and went into a study. Foolhardy to try to tell her story to the police without corroboration. Must dig up corroboration. Five thousand dollars! Oh, boy! it was worth fighting for. Five thousand dollars! It seemed to be emblazoned all around the walls; dollar sign, five and three naughts!

And she was closer to it than anybody else—except possibly Raymondo. The proprietor would be sore. Would he denounce Jack Scanlan for the sake of the reward? How could he after he had taken a hand in the disposal of the body? No, Raymondo would keep his mouth shut and seek a private revenge. She, Edda, had a clear field.

Her next requirement was clothes. From a bell-boy she learned that there was a dress shop in the hotel, and sent him to ask the manageress to come to her room. Guests of the Conradi-Windermere were expected to take a high hand with tradespeople. In due course the woman appeared; handsome, elegant, Broadway-wise. Edda had a hunch that frankness was the line to take with this one. She said:

"I couldn't come down to your shop because I have nothing to appear in but an evening dress. I have a chance of swinging a five thousand dollar deal today if I can get some clothes."

She paused with her nicest smile, but it was deflected by the woman's glassy front. The manageress simply waited.

"You must have had a lot of experience," Edda went on, "or you wouldn't be where you are. I need a smart costume suitable for a business woman calling on men. Look me over. Do you care to take a chance on me?"

The woman was startled into an almost human look. "How did you land here without any clothes?" she asked.

"I can't tell you the truth and I won't lie to you," said Edda. "I reckon you know that a lone woman is often up against it, though they have given us the vote."

The manageress rubbed her lip, and studied Edda lying in the bed. "I never had a proposition of this sort put up to me before," she said with a dry smile. She asked a number of questions. Finally she said: "You have the look of a winner to me. I'll take the chance."

Edda felt the color flooding her cheeks. "Here's where I ought to kiss your hand," she said, "but I'll let you off. You won't be sorry for giving me a leg up."

An hour later Edda was entering the old flat-house on East Forty-ninth Street. In the meantime she had visited a second-hand store where she had exchanged her evening outfit for a gun, a pair of handcuffs and a small sum in cash. Every time she opened her handbag the sight of the gun made her feel a little sickish. She hoped she would be able to use it if it came to such a point. She jollied herself along.

Edda the death-dealing sleuth! Edda eats-'em-alive. Am I afraid of man, woman or crook-fingered Jack? Not on your *passe-partout!*

This morning there was another woman sitting at the desk in the furnished flat-house. It made things easier. An old woman with a bunch of frizzes and a mouth that drew up like walrus hide.

"Have you any vacant flats?" Edda asked her.

"Nothing that would suit you," said the old woman morosely.

Edda realized that she was too well turned out for east of Lexington. "Well, anyway, show me what you've got," she said cajolingly.

"Who sent you to me?"

"I met some people the other night who mentioned that they lived here. Name of Scanlan."

The landlady's mouth relaxed some. "Oh, the Scanlans. Nice people."

They have paid up, thought Edda. Aloud she said casually: "Do they happen to be in now?"

"Left last night," said the landlady. "I didn't see them, but my sister told me. They got a joint engagement in Chicago. Left in a hurry because they had a chance to motor out with friends."

Sounds like one of Maud's artistic touches, thought Edda. "Then their flat is vacant," she said brightly. "Can I see that?"

"It's in a state," said the landlady. "Not fit to show."

"I'll overlook the state," said Edda. "They said it was a nice flat."

They climbed the stairs, and once more Edda found herself in the little sitting-room with the grimy, frilled pillows. It looked now as if a twister blown through. A big trunk had been brought in, and a sluttish maid was pitching the Scanlan's personal belongings into it.

"They could only take their satchels in the car," said the landlady; "so my sister said she'd pack their trunks and hold until sent for."

Edda would have given something pretty to search the trunk, but it seemed hopeless. The maid could have been bribed but there was no way of getting rid of the landlady. Suspicion runs in landladies' veins.

"Nice bright outlook," said Edda, stalling for time.

"Im-hym," said the landlady. She pointed out all the advantages.

The maid swept up a mess of letters and papers on the desk and threw them in the trunk. Edda saw her chance.

"Oh, don't do that!" she said. She gathered the papers out of the trunk and arranged them neatly on the desk. "Pardon me," she said, smiling at the two staring women, "but I'm just naturally a tidy person!"

Meanwhile she was looking at as many papers as she could. The billhead of a hotel caught her eye, and in snapping an elastic band around the bunch, she contrived to let that fall.

"You dropped one," said the landlady acidly.

Edda got a good look at it. "Just a hotel receipt," she said, slipping it under the band. "Hotel McArthur."

The landlady sniffed. "When they had money my house wasn't good enough for them! Maud Scanlan would never let you forget she had stopped at the McArthur. Her idea of heaven!" . . . She suddenly turned on the maid. "You pack that trunk tidy, girl, or out you go!"

She led Edda into the bedroom and enlarged on its virtues. A clean sweep had been made here. Edda, seeing that nothing more was to be got, said: "Well, I'll let you know." And smiled her way out.

She took a taxi to the McArthur. Jack Scanlan had let fall that he considered a big New York hotel the safest of all hiding places, and now she knew the name of the hotel they favored. It was a good deal. But her heart sank when she saw the size of the place. Until the Conradi-Windermere was built the McArthur had advertised itself as the biggest hotel in the world. Like looking for a flea in old Shep, thought Edda.

However she marched up to the desk and turned on the Manby smile for the gentlemanly clerk. "I represent the . . ." she said, naming the smartest of the society monthlies. "Do you mind if I look over your arrivals today? We like to keep tab."

The clerk didn't mind. He produced the cards for all the arrivals since midnight. There was a column for the hour of arrival filled in with certain hieroglyphic signs which Edda in her innocent way got the clerk to explain. Thus she learned that between the hours of three and five a.m. in addition to singles, three couples had registered at the McArthur. She made a note of the room numbers.

Cutting short the insinuating conversation of the clerk with an imbecile smile, Edda made her way out. Passing around by the street to another entrance, she reached the elevators without passing the desk.

The highest number on her list was 1927 and she commenced with that. On each floor of the McArthur there was a telephone switchboard

opposite the elevators, served by a girl who kept
an eye on all who came and went. Edda soon satisfied the girl on the nineteenth floor that they
belonged to the same lodge.

"There's a couple registered in 27 name of
Jackson," she said. "I'm wondering if they're the
Jacksons I know."

"He's a dark-complected guy with foxy eyes,"
was the answer. "Fresh. He give me half-a-dollar
tip and I noticed he had a finger bent in a funny
way. Like this, see?"

Edda's heart began to beat fast; then faster and
faster. She silently cursed it for failing her.

"As for the dame, she ain't showed herself since
I come on," the switchboard girl went on. . . .
"Look! Somebody coming out of 27 now," she
added, glancing down the hall. "Here she is."

Edda did not look. "Much obliged," she said,
and walked away slowly in the other direction.
She turned a corner of the corridor, waited, then
came back to the elevators. The coast was clear.

"It's them all right," she said to the switchboard girl, "but he's my friend, you understand."

"Sure," said the other girl. "These wives!"

Edda walked on toward the door of 1927. Within a space of about six feet she had to decide what
to do. Call the police? Jack might get out before
they came. And anyhow if the police took him

they would expect to horn in on the reward. Five thousand dollars on the other side of that door! She couldn't take any chances on losing it.

Her heart was beating like a bird in a net. Without giving herself any further time to think, she knocked on the door in a certain way; knock, pause, three knocks, pause, knock. Here's where I do a Sarah Bernhardt! she thought, gasping a little.

A key turned in the lock, and a surly voice said: "Come in."

As she entered, Jack was walking away toward the bathroom. He was in pajamas and dressing-gown, and her heart eased up a little; not armed! She softly closed the door. "What the hell!" he growled without looking around. "Can't you go out without you forget something?"

"Jack!" she said softly.

He turned, showing a face gone clownish with surprise. Half of it was covered with shaving lather. "Edda! For God's sake!" he said.

Quick! Don't give him time to think! she thought. She started blubbering realistically. "Oh, Jack, help me! Help me! I've got no money, no place to go! What am I going to do, Jack? You can't turn me off like this!"

"Where did you get those clothes?" he demanded suspiciously.

"Borrowed them from a friend. She can't do any more for me. You got to help me, Jack! I got nobody to go to! I got to have money!"

Gradually the suspicious look gave place to a wicked grin. He picked up a towel and wiped the soap off his face. He came toward her. In the morning sunlight he looked terrible. He put his arms around her. "There, little girl, that's all right," he purred. "Sure I'll take care of you! Leave everything to me."

Edda let him run on while she planned out what to do. All thoughts of using the gun had fled. Suppose she missed; suppose the gun wouldn't fire; suppose Jack managed to get it away from her? She couldn't even remember ever having held a gun before. Her glance was arrested by a painted steampipe which ran from floor to ceiling in the corner of the room. That was what she needed! She wriggled out of his embrace.

"Oh, don't!" she said, retreating toward the steampipe. "It isn't right, Jack!"

"A-ah! What the hell!" he snarled, turning ugly. "Crying, and begging for money one minute, and push me off the next! What do you think a man is?"

"What would Maud say?" she faltered.

"Maud won't be back for hours."

Edda made believe to relent. "Don't be cross with me, Jack."

Jack followed her up, and put his arms around her again. "Cheese! You're a lovely armful!" he murmured. "There's more to you than a man would think! I'm just crazy about you, Slant-eyes!"

Edda pressed back a little, bringing him immediately alongside the steampipe. Her arms were hanging straight down. She planned out every move in advance. Open the bag . . . take out handcuffs . . . let bag drop . . . kick it away . . . both sides of the handcuffs are open . . . bring up your right hand slowly . . . snap it around his wrist . . . then quick! shove his arm back and snap the other side around the pipe!

Click! It was done! She tore herself out of his arms. He plunged after her and was brought up with a jerk that almost tore his arm out at the shoulder. Edda backed out of his reach, and sat down on the nearest bed shaking like a top-heavy jelly mold. Am I going to faint? She asked herself. I will not! I will not!

The man's face was like a snarling jackal's that she had seen pictured somewhere. He jerked viciously at his fetter, cursing Edda in a manner that made the skin at the back of her neck prickle. However, the color came back into her face, and her back stiffened. She faced him out.

He can't pull the pipe down, she thought; and handcuffs are made to hold a man. He's no Samson anyhow. Let him curse!

She slung her feet over to the other side of the bed. The telephone was on a stand between the twin beds. She looked up her number in the book and gave it. "Why . . . why . . ." returned a frightened voice over the wire, "that's police headquarters!"

"Make it snappy, girl!" said Edda, "I want Inspector Scofield."

The Strange Affair at the Middlebrooks'

After waiting twenty minutes in the corridor of the Conradi-Windermere for Pete Fenner, the radio star, Edda Manby shrugged, and went on into the Colonna room for tea. "Pete's not so hot anyhow," she thought; "I'll have a better time on my own."

She chose a little table near the corner of the dancing floor that commanded a good view, ordered *bar-le-duc* and *gervaise,* and looked around to see what was amusing. The usual crowd; carelessly-dressed swells entirely unconscious of themselves, and would-be swells dressed up to the nines and more or less overpowered.

But there was something amusing to watch. Three tables pushed together at the edge of the dancing floor, surrounded by a rather noisy and frazzled party of sixteen or eighteen; both sexes. They were not at all in the key of the Conradi, and Edda wondered why they were not wafted out. She

saw the Captain watching them somewhat dubiously from a little distance, but he made no move
in their direction. Must be some special reason for
it.

All the members of the party were sufficiently well-dressed, but their excessive gratitude was
giving them away. There could be no question as
to who was paying; a young man seated in the
center of the group holding his blond head down.
His guests were trying to cover his dazed state
by pointedly addressing their remarks to him and
immediately answering for him. The whole story
was written in his hanging head—his all-day per-
egrination from one "speak" to another (speak-
louds nowadays instead of speak-easies, Edda re-
flected) rolling up this party as he went like a
mushy snowball with plenty of dirt.

Edda wished that he would look up. In the end
he did so. He was younger than she had expected;
the slightly backward college man who is about to
graduate at the age of twenty-four or so. A beautiful young man with a healthy red face and blue
eyes, now slightly glazed. She felt sorry for him.

His lost eyes met hers squarely. She smiled. He
did not smile back, but his mouth opened slightly.
Edda looked away. He was harpooned!

Out of the corners of her eyes she saw him
get up and start in her direction like a man in a

dream. He walked steadily enough. He was a fine big fellow, wearing the sort of smart-careless English clothes that she approved of. He neglected his appearance, but looked well anyhow. The eyes of most of the women in the room were following him. "He has everything," thought Edda—"but good sense."

"Hello!" he said abruptly.

Edda looked up with a good deal of surprise and a little resentment. "Well!"

"How come you're alone?" he asked.

He was smiling in the restaurant manner, but there was a kind of wretchedness in his eyes that caused Edda suddenly to feel maternal. She blamed herself for it. Turning soft! She said stiffly: "I am alone because my friend hasn't come."

"I can't imagine any man letting you down," he said.

"Can't you?"

"I've got a party over there. Will you join us?"

"So awkward to join a lot of people you don't know," objected Edda.

"I don't know them myself," he said dumbly. "Just sort of collected them." The orchestra started to play. "Will you dance?" he asked. "And let's you and I get acquainted anyhow."

Edda got up. There was no poetry in his dancing; he could only go through the motions. His haunted look suggested that his thoughts were far away from the Conradi. Edda made small talk to help him out. He paid little attention and broke in on what she was saying with:

"You looked like a girl a man could talk to, so I came over."

"What did you want to say?"

"Gee! I don't know. . . . Nothing! . . . The trouble with me is, I can't talk. Things just flop around in my mind and I can't deliver them. But I feel things. . . . I'm no good!"

"Oh, you're just at that stage," said Edda sympathetically. "Pretty soon you'll forget it all."

"I'm no good!" he repeated stubbornly. "I got all this money. . . . It's not right!"

"All right," said Edda. "You're no good. What then?"

"Ought to jump off a pierhead and leave it to charity," he mumbled.

"Very likely you're right. But I'm in no position to judge."

He held her away from him, searching her face with his wretched, dumb, boyish, sullen eyes. "What you trying to do? Razz me?"

"What else can I do?"

He enfolded her again. "I don't care. I can take it from you. I like you. You look as if you were square. So damn good looking, too. You don't expect it in a girl you can trust. Your skin is like angel food!"

"No samples given away!" warned Edda as his lips came close.

Just at this moment Edda saw Pete Fenner at the door of the room putting on a show of breathlessness. Handsome fellow, Pete, but a glass shot. Seeing Edda dancing with another man he walled his eyes peevishly, and looked about for a girl. Picking up the nearest approachable one, he started pursuing Edda and her partner around the floor.

When he succeeded in brushing against Edda he smiled in the manner of one conveying a benefit on womankind and said: "Was in a taxi smash on the way here. Had to stick around and testify for my driver. He wasn't to blame, poor devil."

Edda looked around as much as to say: "Speaking to me?" Then, as if discovering her mistake, smiled at her partner. "Do go on," she murmured. "I'm so interested!"

Pete suddenly discovered how charming his partner was. He faded.

Edda's lowering partner had not noticed him. "Know who I am?" he asked.

"No idea."

"Ray Middlebrook."

"Oh, that explains it."

"Explains what?"

"Many things."

"I see you have read about me in the papers."

"Who could avoid doing so?"

"Then you know that my old man died last week and left me shiploads of money. I don't know how much. The lawyers are still figuring. . . . Maybe you think it's pretty low to be seen here so soon."

"One mustn't be Victorian," said Edda.

"As a matter of fact we were practically strangers. My mother died when I was a kid and I've been in schools and camps all the time. My dad and I were embarrassed when we met. I believe he had great plans for my future, but he up and died before he started in on me."

"And here you are!"

"Here I am! . . . Besides I'm going to be married tonight. Got to get up courage for the ceremony."

Edda laughed. "Married! Just like that!"

"Oh, you can laugh. But I'm absolutely serious."

"Who's the girl."

"You wouldn't know her. Gloria Jackman. An actress."

"What's she been in?"

"Nothing, lately. You know what the managers are. In order to get a good part a girl has to—well you know. She was resting when I met her."

"Oh, yes?"

"Beautiful girl!" said Ray solemnly.

"She would be. Are you madly in love."

The question startled him. "Love?" he echoed with a flat, bitter laugh. "Oh, sure!"

"If that's the way you feel why get married?"

"I owe it to her, see? It's a promise. I got to make good."

"You could get out of it if you really wanted to."

"Who says I want to get out of it?" he demanded. "I'm proud of her!" And then with perfect irrelevance: "There isn't a mercenary bone in her body. She wouldn't take money. She loves me, see?"

"Oh, yes?"

They passed the table where Ray's party sat. "Is she here?" asked Edda searching among the faces.

"Lord! No. She wouldn't stand for that crummy bunch. She's getting fixed up for tonight."

They danced for a while in silence. Ray's downcast, sullen face was working confusedly. Finally he mumbled:

"Anyhow, I couldn't be worse off than I am at present. . . . I'm certainly at the end of my string . . . I can't stand it. . . . I can't stand it any longer."

"Can't stand what?"

His eyes trailed away. "I don't know . . . Just things. . . . Don't seem to be able to measure up to them. . . . All this fuss about my money. . . . I'm afraid of it. . . . Now Gloria, she's strong-minded. Maybe with her I can. . . . Well, you know . . ."

What could Edda say? "Just a lost lamb!" she thought. "And they call women the weaker sex!"

They danced on.

After a while the music stopped. "Aw, come on over to my table," he pleaded. "I'm fed up with those rummies. Want to talk to you!"

"No," she said. "Why should I stand for them? They're your collection. You can sit down with me for a minute if you want to."

"Thanks," he murmured humbly.

After some rambling talk he suddenly blurted out: "Say, will you come to my wedding tonight? I'll get rid of this crew before then. Gee! I'd like to have some nice people there."

Edda, chin on palm, regarded him with an indulgent smile. "Such a good-looking big lamb!" she was thinking. "With fleece of gold! And asking for a shepherdess! What woman could resist the call?"

"You have lovely eyes!" he murmured. "They crinkle!"

"Your figures are mixed!"

"Say, will you come tonight?"

"All right. I'll come."

"Swell! I'll go over and give my mob an exit cue and come back."

"No! That would be too conspicuous. I have to go home first to dress anyhow."

"Can't I come with you?"

"While I dress? Hardly the thing for a bridegroom, Lamb."

"Why do you call me Lamb?"

"No particular reason."

"Well, I like it anyhow."

"Where's the ceremony going to take place?" asked Edda.

"At my house, number — Fifth Avenue. Maybe you know the old mausoleum. It's near Seventy-ninth."

"It's been pointed out to me," said Edda dryly. "What time?"

"Eight o'clock. We dine first and have the ceremony afterwards. There's an alderman coming."

"All right. Frisk along, Lamb."

He got up very reluctantly. "Afraid of losing you," he mumbled. "Can I count on you tonight, no fooling?"

"Sure!" said Edda. "I'll be there with my ears pinned back and my hair in a braid."

Shortly after eight o'clock Edda was mounting the steps of the Middlebrook palace. Its grim plainness was suggestive of the "mausoleum." Grecian urns on all the pediments helped to carry out the idea.

The door was opened by a young man-servant in plain black livery. Behind him in the entrance corridor loomed the butler. Edda's attention was arrested by the latter. A striking, well-built man with rapacious black eyes and thin, blue-shaven jowls. Outwardly the correct and deferential house-servant, there was, nevertheless, a devil sitting half seen in his eyes, on the watch for devils in the eyes of others. "This looks like the wolf," thought Edda.

He looked Edda up and down covertly and sent the young servant away. "May I take your wrap, Miss?" he asked in a buttery voice. In lifting it from Edda's shoulders he allowed his fingers to touch her skin.

"This is no butler!" thought Edda. She stepped forward, clinging to her wrap, and turned around. "I beg your pardon," she said sweetly running up her eyebrows.

The butler looked down. "Sorry, Miss," he said. "It was an accident." There was still an ugly smirk about the corners of his mouth.

"Naturally," said Edda. "I think, however, I'll leave my wrap in the dressing-room."

The butler bowed and opened a door off the corridor.

When Edda came out there was a hateful look half hidden under his lowered lids. He was the sort of man who prides himself on never mistaking his women and his self-love had been wounded. "What name please, Miss?" he asked with offensive obsequiousness.

"Miss Edda Manby."

"Friend of Miss Jackman or Mr. Middlebrook?"

"Of Mr. Middlebrook."

He took a small book from his pocket and made believe to consult it, but his eyes never moved from the same spot. "Sorry, Miss, but I don't appear to have your name on my list."

"Are you inviting me to leave?"

"So sorry, Miss. But you understand with newspaper reporters and mere curiosity seekers trying to get in we have to be extra careful."

Edda took a cigarette from her evening bag, tapped it on the back of her hand, stuck it between her lips and lighted it. All very deliberately while the butler watched her from under his lowered lids. She sat down in a fauteuil and crossed her legs.

"You may go and tell Mr. Middlebrook that Miss Manby is waiting."

He hesitated, studying her warily, then apparently made up his mind that she would be less dangerous to him inside the house than out. He wreathed his face in a false smile. "Oh, in that case, Miss, please step upstairs. I see now that it's all right. Pardon my hesitancy. One has to be so careful on an occasion like this."

He led the way into the house and Edda followed, sucking at her cheek until it dimpled.

The corridor opened into an immense central hall soaring up to an illuminated dome in the roof. Edda whistled to herself. Even the multiest of millionaires cannot permit himself such magnificence in these thin times. At one side a wide shallow stairway swept up to the main rooms of the house, and on up from floor to floor.

There were several of the black-clad servants about, who exchanged wary glances with the butler. They had more the look of confederates than fellow-servants and an internal shiver passed through Edda. "I was a fool to trust myself in this house alone," she thought. "I haven't a friend here but Ray Middlebrook and he's no knight in armor."

She was handed over to the conduct of an under-servant who led her upstairs and announced her name at the door of the grand salon in the front of the house. A confusion of noisy talk assaulted her ears. The huge room had evidently been patterned upon the hall of mirrors at Versailles; gorgeous, gilded and glittering. She saw at once that Ray had not got rid of his rowdy friends but had added to them. There were about forty

people present. The room would have accommo-
dated four hundred.

The guests had instinctively divided into two
groups; on the left the dressed-up ones, stiff and
ill at ease; on the right the crowd that Ray had
been carrying around with him all day, still in
their street clothes, a little more frazzled than before. The chief interest of this crowd lay in the
free drinks that were being passed.

In the formal group sat a dark beauty in a black
evening gown enframed in a big golden chair. Obviously Gloria Jackman. Edda went to her smiling.
Her hair was drawn smoothly back, and her long
black eyes further elongated by mascara. She was
not at all put about by the noise at the other side
of the room. Her face was a pale mask express-
ing no feeling whatsoever. "Isn't sure what line to
take," thought Edda, "and so plays the Sphinx."

Gloria without rising extended a slender hand.
"How do you do," she drawled. "I suppose you are
Ray's friend. I sent him away to dress. He'll be
here directly."

Tough accent, thought Edda; is working hard
to overcome it.

"Dinner will be a little late," Gloria went on,
"because Ray brought home more guests than the
servants expected. They are rearranging the table."

She turned languidly away to signify that she had
no further time to give Edda.

"All right my lady!" thought the latter. "You are
not through with me yet." She engaged a young
man with a fluty voice in conversation. A servant
passed cocktails.

The butler entered bowing his head and veiling
his bold eyes. He made his way by a circuitous
route toward his mistress. The latter was immediately conscious of his entrance. As soon as Gloria
looked at the man Edda was aware that these two
were lovers. The man whispered in Gloria's ear her
eyes flew to Edda's face. Edda was making believe
to be looking elsewhere. "Warning her against
me," she thought.

Ray Middlebrook entered, blond and comely
in his evening clothes but still showing the slack
mouth and the glazed eye. He came to Edda like
a needle to the magnet and the fluty young man
faded. "Swell of you to come!" murmured Ray.

"I don't like this set-up," whispered Edda bluntly.

He looked at her dazedly without answering.

"Are these your old family servants?" Edda
asked.

He shook his head. "They were discharged and
the house shut up after the funeral. Gloria got
them."

"What's the butler's name?"

"Smithers."

"Do you know what I would do if I were you?"

"What?"

"Walk out on the show. Hop on a train for Montreal and telegraph back to your lawyer to get these people out of the house. My God! you'd be getting off cheap with the loss of a few household belongings."

"Will you come with me?" asked Ray brightening.

"Thanks, Lamb," answered Edda dryly, "but I'm dated far ahead."

He relapsed. "Couldn't do it now," he muttered. "Things have gone too far."

Edda said no more. She thought: "Can't expect any help from him if I want to snatch him from the wolves. Anyhow I've got to have evidence." Out of the tail of her eye she saw Smithers had left her. "Run and play," she said to Ray.

Edda herself turned "to take the Sphinx by the horns," as she put it. Sizing up her sister woman as she approached her, she thought; "She's not so bright; she can take flattery like mineral oil." Arriving in front of Gloria's chair she said with a disarming laugh:

"Ray is completely washed up! Can't talk about anything but you!"

Gloria smirked self-consciously.

"Gosh! but you're a lucky girl!" Edda went on, "the fellow is so darned good-looking! It's too much to expect in a millionaire. I'm frantic with jealousy!"

Gloria held a scrap of a lace handkerchief between thumb and forefinger and swung it. "Ray is a darling!" she simpered.

"You fool!" thought Edda. "Do you think that's getting over?" Out loud she said: "I suppose you've been buying stacks and stacks of beautiful clothes."

"Oh, a few things."

"Where have you been for them?"

"Here; there; everywhere," said Gloria with waves of the hand.

Edda groaned in envy. "Oh! and I think myself lucky if I get four new dresses a year!"

"Ray gave me *carte blanche!*" said Gloria, bringing out the French phrase like a child with a new toy.

Edda shook her head enviously. She remained significantly silent in order to force Gloria to say it. And out it came.

"Would you like to see my trousseau?"

"No!" said Edda. "It would make me sick."

This was like music in Gloria's ears. She smiled and hoisted herself out of the golden chair. "Come on," she said. "I expect it will be quarter of an hour before dinner is served."

Out in the hall Edda saw Ray and Smithers standing apart with their heads close together. Smithers was telling his master something with a friendly man-to-man air false as hell. Ray was too much bemused to realize that this was rank insolence from a servant. Edda had one of her hunches. "Ray will turn against me now. Why did I ever come to the damn house?"

Smithers looked sour when he Gloria and Edda ascending the stairs together. Evidently this inspection of the trousseau was not included in his plans. But he couldn't stop it now.

Gloria's suite was spread across the front of the house over the salon; boudoir, dressing-room, bedroom. Activity centered in the dressing-room which was done in primrose. Four wardrobe trunks stood against the wall and articles of apparel were scattered all over the room. Two maids were packing.

Gloria sank into an easy chair and motioned to Edda to another alongside. "Show Miss Manby my new dresses," she said to the elder maid.

The woman paled slightly. "But, Madame! Everything is packed!"

"Unpack it," said Gloria with a cold stare. "You have plenty of time to pack it again." She turned to Edda with a resumption of her languid smile. "Ray and I are sailing on the *Baratoria* at midnight. We have the Imperial suite."

"Not if I know it!" thought Edda.

The dresses were duly unpacked and displayed; dresses for sport, for afternoon, for evening; with scarves, bags, furs, wraps to match. There was a whole separate trunkful of hats and another of shoes. The room began to look like Eve's paradise, modern version. Edda laid it on with a trowel, but privately she was not too envious. The things had come from the most expensive shops in New York, and they were beautiful, but they lacked the least touch of individuality that Edda got into her clothes at one-tenth the cost.

Gloria and Edda got up and moved about looking at this and that. Edda spied a little gray cock-eyed hat on a shelf in one of the wardrobes. "There's a duck!" she cried.

"Oh, that!" said Gloria. "Had it for ages. Almost a year. But I wouldn't give it away, because it does suit me."

"It would," said Edda. "With your eyes. Try it on."

Gloria took the hat down and stood in front of a mirror, Edda at her shoulder. As Gloria gave the hat a downward shake to settle the lining into shape Edda looked into it and read the maker's name: Fleurette, Atlanta, Ga. Gloria put on the hat and perked her head at different angles.

"Wickedest thing I ever saw!" cried Edda, clasping her hands.

"If you think so I'll have it copied," said Gloria, pitching it back on the shelf.

Smithers appeared at the door of the room; looked from one to another sharply. "Dinner is served, Madame.

Edda thought: "Bet it goes hard with you to crook your neck to her." Aloud she said; "Goody! I'm starved!"

Down on the ground floor there was a good deal of confusion in the dining-room because some of the guests were completely unknown. Gloria referred them to Ray and Ray shrugged at them. Finally Gloria said impatiently: "Oh, sit down wherever you find yourselves!" Then half a dozen of them picked on the same chair.

Ray was standing by the table with a lost air like a stranger at his own board. An ugly, pained look had come into his face. Edda guessed that somebody had been plying him with liquor—or a drug. Out in the hall she could see Smithers watching him, and rubbing his blue lip.

When Ray saw Edda standing alone he approached her swaying slightly. A painful sneer lifted his lip. "I've got your number now," he mumbled. "Thought you were getting at me nicely, didn't you?"

"My mistake," said Edda running up her eyebrows. "Good-night!" She turned from him. "Poor silly lamb!" she thought.

The confusion in the room enabled her to slip out without attracting notice. She was bent on leaving the house now—for awhile. She passed Smithers as if he wasn't there. He followed her to the entrance corridor and contrived to slip between her and the door into the ladies' dressing-room.

"Beg pardon, Miss." His voice was still respectful, but there was now an open leer in his bold eyes.

"I want my wrap," said Edda.

"What for, Miss?"

"What business is it of yours? I'm going home."

"Sorry, it's against orders."

Edda felt her face reddening. "Keep cool!" she warned herself. "Whose orders?" she asked, lifting her chin.

"Mr. Middlebrook's. He said nobody could leave until after the ceremony."

"I doubt that," said Edda. "Nobody can stop me."

The man took a step nearer her. "I can," he said with an evil smile. "And I will."

Edda, glancing down, saw a blackjack half protruding from his right sleeve. A chill struck through her veins. "What a fool I was to let myself in for this!" She could not appeal to the dining-room for help without showing her hand. Besides, what help was to be obtained there?

Smithers was looking her up and down with a grin that made her flesh crawl. "I'll let you go out if you'll submit to a search in the dressing-room."

Edda, stalling for time, opened her little bag and took out a cigarette.

"The house is full of valuables," said Smithers truculently. "And Mr. Middlebrook don't know you very well."

Edda looked at him thoughtfully. "I have changed my mind," she said. "I'll stay for the ceremony." Turning, she slowly retraced her steps across the central hall and up the stairway. She believed that the women on the second floor were genuine ladies' maids. Smithers followed her up the stairs. On the first floor she glimpsed a telephone through the open door of the library and changed her plan. She went into the library and shut the door behind her. There was a key in the lock and she turned it thankfully. The room had no other door. She heard Smithers laugh outside.

She ran to the phone, but her voice rang dead in the transmitter. Wires cut! She opened one of the casement windows. A stone ledge ran along outside with a heavy metal ladder descending to the ground at one end. About fifteen feet below was the terrace outside the dining-room windows. All the houses in this block had thrown their back-yards together to make a common garden.

"It can be done," thought Edda, "but I must have some kind of a wrap before I can go out in the street." Glancing around the room, her eye fixed on a Buddhist cape of rare antique brocade spread over the back of a carved bench. Snatching it up, she climbed out on the window ledge.

She gained the terrace in safety. Somebody had drawn back one of the dining-room curtains, and a bacchanalian scene was revealed to her through a haze of tobacco smoke. More noise than fun. At one end of the long table Gloria Jackman with every hair in place, surveying the rabble with a sneer; at the other end Ray Middlebrook slumped down, lost and dazed. In the doorway Smithers rubbing his lip to hide a grin.

Edda explored the garden for a way out. The houses were built solidly all around. Looking down into the rear area-way of one of the houses facing on Seventy-Ninth Street, she saw a lighted kitchen window with two women servants moving about inside. Running down the steps, she knocked at the door. How astonished the two women were to discover a young lady in evening dress and a bro-cade wrap on their kitchen threshold.

"So sorry to trouble you," said Edda. "I was at a party in the Middlebrook house and I didn't like the set-up. Wanted to get away quick."

The women glanced at each other. Humph! Middlebrook house! their eyes said. Nice goings-on in an exclusive neighborhood. They approved of Edda's desire to escape.

Edda continued: "Will you take me through your house and let me into the street where I can get a taxi."

"Certainly, Miss. Happy to oblige."

The open street looked good to Edda. She hailed a cab and had herself driven to the Portman, the nearest first-class hotel. Seeking out the telephone alcove, she addressed herself to the young woman in charge with the smile that never failed.

"I want to call a party in Atlanta, Georgia. She may be difficult to find. Ask the telephone company to get busy and show us what they can do in an emergency. Tell them we want to see if they can live up to their full-page advertisements in the quality mediums."

"Madame Fleurette, milliner, Atlanta. That's all I have. She won't be at her place of business now, of course, but she will have a telephone in her home. And the Atlanta exchange must know her private name."

The operator set to work while Edda sat down and tried not to let her limbs twitch or her foot tap the floor. To pass the time she counted the number of different magazines displayed on the newsstand.

In just a little time the operator looked around her switchboard with a smile. "Here she is, Miss. Booth number three, please."

"Stout old telephone company!" said Edda.

"Hello!" she said into the transmitter. A woman's voice answered her having a suggestion of the brogue. Fleurette was a flower of Erin. "My name is Edda Manby," Edda went on. "You don't know me. I'm . . . er . . ." A grin creased the corners of her mouth. "I'm a private investigator working on a case here. I have to establish the identity of a woman who is wearing a hat made by you."

"But good God, Madam, I make hundreds of hats," answered the voice.

"I know," said Edda, "but this is an original creation. As a woman I can appreciate its distinction. It's a masterpiece. I'm sure you will remember it."

"What sort of hat?"

"It's a kind of cross between toque and beret. Made of a fine quality of gray suede cloth. Has a hard crown with collapsible sides, and is worn with the crown pulled a little to the right. It looks to me as if you had got the inspiration from the French military kepi—without the visor, of course."

"Yes! Yes! I remember," cried the voice. "You have an eye, Madame!"

"Have you made many from that design?" asked Edda anxiously.

"No, Madame, only one. It was too extreme for Atlanta."

"Who did you make it for?"

The answer came instantly. "Jennie Howe."

"Please describe her to me so that I ran be sure it's the right one."

"Jennie Howe was a local girl here. She was only the daughter of a teamster, but a remarkably beautiful girl. Bound to get on."

"She has got on," put in Edda dryly.

"She was tall with a beautiful figure and hair like a raven's wing. Regular classical features except her eyes which were elongated and oriental."

"That's the one," said Edda. "Is she anything to you?"

"Nothing whatever. I made her the hat gratis because she was a walking advertisement. Mentally she registers about ten above zero."

"If it should be necessary would you come to New York to identify her? All expenses advanced, of course."

"Ask a milliner if she'll come to New York! Oh, girl!"

"In the meantime tell me what you know about her."

The conversation continued.

Afterwards Edda called up police headquarters. She was known to Inspector Scofield by reason of her part in the capture of Jack Scanlan. In fact the Inspector had offered her a job on that occasion, but she had turned it down. As she put it to herself: Irregularity is the spice of life. She was too fond of lying abed in the mornings.

The Inspector had left a number at his office, and she presently succeeded in getting him on the wire. When he had heard her story he said at once that he would send two men in plainclothes to accompany her back to the Middlebrook house.

"Won't one be enough?" said Edda. "I don't want to make melodrama."

"It is the rule of the department to send two on an important case."

"All right. Please pick men who can pass for guests at a smart wedding."

"Sure. Where are you now."

"Telephoning from the Portman."

"Wait there for them."

Officers McArdle and Rohrty turned up in about half an hour. Edda sucked in her cheek at the sight of what the Inspector considered suitable timber for wedding guests. True, they both wore well-fitting dress suits, but the effect was marred by their 10-Ds with half-inch soles. However they were both broths of boys, and they all fell for each other at sight.

"What's this has happened to Ray Middlebrook?" asked Rohrty—or perhaps it was McArdle; Edda had difficulty in distinguishing between them.

"Tell you on the way there," she said.

Edda rang the bell at the Middlebrook house and the door was opened by one of the black-clad servants. When he saw who stood outside he attempted to close it again, but McArdle's 10-D was already inserted in the opening, and McArdle and Rohrty's shoulders soon widened it. He attempted to run then, but McArdle collared him.

"Lock him in one of the closets, said Edda. "We don't want to start a panic here."

This done, the three of them went on.

"We appear to be too late," said Edda. "But it hardly matters."

The noise above grew louder and suddenly the whole boisterous company appeared around the turn of the stairs coming down. Ray and Gloria headed the procession arm in arm.

Ray seemed not to recognize Edda now. His eyes were not focusing. Gloria cried out in the dulcet tone that a woman uses towards the woman she most hates:

"Oh, there you are, darling! I missed you at the ceremony! Congratulate us!"

Edda answered. "You're not married, darling. At least, not to him."

"What do you mean?" demanded Gloria.

"You're married to a man called Mortimer Beale—anyhow that's the name you married him under. And here he is!"

A service door alongside the stairway had opened, and Smithers appeared carrying smart suit-cases. When he saw the husky young man standing beside Edda, he quietly dropped the suit-cases and went back through the door. Rohrty sprang forward and fetched him in again.

Edda ignored the interruption. "You were married in Atlanta, Georgia, on January seventeenth last," she went on. "Beale, or whatever his real name may be, was a touring actor—not a very good one. He picked you up in a local dance hall. I suppose he saw in you an easier way of making a living. Anyhow he married you and brought you to New York to make both your fortunes. It was a mistake for him to marry you. There were witnesses to the wedding, and I can produce them."

"Do you mean I am not married at all?" Ray said incredulously, later.

"No more than I am."

"Thank God for that! You were the one I wanted to marry all the time!"

"You don't want a wife, Lamb, but a keeper."

His face fell absurdly. "Aw, Edda!"

"I don't want to marry anybody but you," he mumbled.

"Forget it, child! You owe me five-fifteen, telephone call to Atlanta and taxis."

Death by Appointment

Edda Manby had an idea for a feature story: Girl Reporter on a Murder Case. So she put on her best bib and tucker, and went to see the Sunday editor of the *Sphere*. He approved the idea—and the bib and tucker, and sent her down to the city room to get a suitable murder for a background.

The city editor's name was Blanchard; quite a wit in his own estimation. He grinned and said: "Sorry we have no murders today." But while Edda was there, the telephone rang, and after hanging up he said, "Here's one now. Woman found dead in a hairdresser's shop."

"Sounds promising," said Edda.

Blanchard shouted down the room: "Barnhill!" and filled in a card that would pass Edda through the police lines. "Don't let the boys know you're new to the job, or they'll give you a runaround."

"Thanks for the tip," said Edda dryly.

He glanced at her. Not such a downy chick as she appeared!

A long-legged young man with a humorous nose came striding to the desk. Blanchard said: "Barnhill, this is Miss Manby. I'm trying her out on an assignment. Let her go with you. The address is, Paul's Hairdressing Parlor in the Peerless-Grober Building. Customer getting a permanent just found dead in the chair."

"Well," said Barnhill, glancing sideways at Edda to make sure she was getting it, "she'll be all fixed up for her funeral!"

Edda thought: Thinks a little too well of himself. She looked blank, and Barnhill was dashed.

He said no more until they were on their way in a taxi. "This your first assignment, kid?"

Edda fished a little mirror out of her handbag and looked in it. "Must be my school-girl complexion," she murmured.

"What rag do you work for then?"

"Schenectady *Register*."

"Never heard of it."

"We are crushed!"

"You have a kind of New York look to me," he said.

"Oh, yes?"

"Yes! Sort of Pierre's, Central Park Casino, Conradi-Windermere look."

"A girl can buy that."

"I doubt it . . . I got to see more of you, Edda. Will you lunch?"

"I generally do."

"I'll hold you to that. Mind, if any other newspaper guy tries to date you up, I saw you first. I'm the best-looking fellow in the bunch anyhow."

"Average must be low."

The Peerless-Grober Building was at the center of things. There was a subway station in the basement and an all-night drug-store on the Forty-Second Street side. Many out-of-town newspapers had their New York offices upstairs; consequently streams of people passed through the lobbies at all hours of the day and night.

Paul's establishment was on the second floor at the head of the stairs. A uniformed officer was located at the door; knots of the curious stood about in the corridor, whispering. Entering a gray and old-rose reception room with French furniture and mirrors Edda found the elegant apartment profaned by a number of large, coarse detectives and newspapermen. There was a feeling of ugly excitement in the air.

The proprietor was addressing the press with tears in his voice. He had a continental accent.

"Men, I beg you not to mention my name in your stories! It will ruin me! If it is published that there has been a death in my atelier nobody will come! I pay an enormous rental here and you wouldn't want to see all my refined young ladies thrown out of employment!"

One of the reporters answered gruffly: "It can't be left out, Paul. The public's entitled to know the particulars."

"If anything to my credit had happened here you wouldn't mention my name," wailed Paul. "You'd be afraid of giving me a free advertisement. But you will tell about this and ruin me!"

The reporter interrupted him bluntly. "What do you know about this woman?"

"Nothing, I tell you. I never saw her before."

"Who sent her to you?"

"I don't know. She landed from the *Europa* this morning. Yesterday afternoon I got this wireless. Read it! Read it!"

The message was handed around. Edda moved up. Barnhill drew her arm through his with a pro-prietary air. She quietly removed it.

"Keep your mind on your job," she whispered. She read over somebody's shoulder.

"Paul
Peerless-Grober Building
"Want appointment for permanent nine
A.M. Tuesday

Detmold."

"My establishment does not open until ten," the hairdresser continued, "So I asked my assistant, Miss Polly, to keep this appointment. I told her she could order her breakfast sent up from the restaurant below."

"Did she do that?"

"She did. The lady was prompt to her appointment. She came direct from the pier bringing her hand baggage. Miss Polly put her in the chair in alcove two, wrapped her hair and affixed the curlers. The lady said she wanted a tight permanent, which takes twenty minutes, so Miss Polly gave her a magazine to read, and went back to the assistants' room to eat her breakfast."

"Leaving the customer alone?"

"Yes. But there was a push button on the arm of the chair so she could summon the assistant if she wanted anything."

"During this time was the outer door of the suite locked?"

"I don't know. Presumably not. Miss Polly would unlock it so the customer could enter, and naturally she would leave it that way."

"Go on."

Paul squeezed his manicured hands together. "At the end of twenty minutes Miss Polly returned to the alcove and found . . . and found . . . Oh God! . . . the woman sitting in the chair with her hair in the curlers just as she had left her . . . dead!"

"What did the girl do?"

"Ran out in the corridor screaming for help."

"Where were you at this time?"

"On my way here. I arrived ten or fifteen minutes later. The police were in charge then."

"Where is Miss Polly now?"

"In the assistants' room in the rear. A detective in questioning her."

Edda turned to look the scene over. Barnhill was still at her elbow. "You stick to me," he murmured. "I'm a dab at murder cases, you know!"

"Oh, yes?"

Across the front of the suite ran the three little rooms which Paul had referred to as "alcoves." The door of the middle one stood open, and inside, Edda caught a glimpse of something that caused her flesh to creep as if clammy fingers had been drawn over it. She clenched her teeth, and followed Barnhill in.

In the elaborate porcelain and nickel chair sat Paul's last customer bolt upright with a bunch of curlers clipped in her hair, all the cords running straight up. Like Medusa with her snakes standing on end. The curling apparatus was holding her head up as straight as in life. Her sightless eyes looked straight ahead; the make-up stood out crudely on her livid skin. A woman of about thirty-two, a natural blonde, who obviously had been beautiful in life.

Beside the chair a detective was kneeling on the floor going through the dead woman's hand luggage. It was the red-headed Sergeant Crehan, whom Edda knew.

"'Lo, Edda!"

She spoke up briskly: "'Lo, Pink." The only way to get by, was to make believe the thing was not there.

Barnhill looked at her reproachfully. "From Schenectady!" he murmured.

"Ugly work for you," said Crehan with a jerk of his head toward the chair.

"You have to take it as it comes," said Edda.

"No wound on her," said Crehan. "Not a mark anywhere."

"Could she have got an electric shock?"

"Impossible. The voltage carried by these wires couldn't hurt her."

"Natural causes then?"

"So it would seem. However, there'll be a stomach analysis, or an examination of some kind."

"She would scarcely take poison while having her hair done," murmured Edda.

"Carried a German passport," Crehan went on, rummaging through the bag. "Name of Ida Detmold. Visaed by the U. S. consulate in Berlin. Couple of hundred dollars in her pocketbook. Railway ticket to Washington, D. C. . . ."

"Let's see it," said Edda. The ticket was handed up. "Stamped yesterday," she said casually.

Crehan snatched it back. "That's so! And she wasn't supposed to have landed until this morning. You have stumbled on something, girl."

Edda smiled dryly. "Stumbled? What would it have been if you had found it, Pink?"

He made believe not to hear, "No papers on her. Except a slip, with two names written down. The first was Robert Bassett, Assistant Secretary of State, Washington D. C. . . . Looks like she might have been an international spy."

Edda thought: Dicks are always hypnotized by names written down! Why couldn't the woman remember two names that were important to her? More likely the slip was planted in her bag.

"The second name was Carl Buller. . . ."

"I know that name!" cried Barnhill. "The papers were full of him a while ago. Supposed to be at the head of the Nazi propaganda in America. Then he disappeared . . . By God! I have it! A spy! Sure she was! A Nazi spy! Came to this country to sell their secrets to our government!'

Edda stole a glance at the strangely still figure in the chair, and shivered slightly. How queer to be discussing her in her presence!

"The Nazis followed her here, see?" Barnhill went on, "and rubbed her out before she could betray them!"

"How, rubbed her out?" asked Crehan sarcastically.

"I leave that to the medical examiner."

"If they followed her across the ocean, why wouldn't they throw her overboard?" asked Edda mildly. "Easier and safer."

"Maybe she knew her danger and stayed inside the whole way."

"How would she know about Paul's place?"

"Some American passenger on the ship recommended him to her."

"Well, if you ask me, I think she just had a stroke," said Crehan.

"A stroke! Rats!" said Barnhill. "Young and healthy people like that don't die from strokes! . . . I'll go down to the *Europa* to interview officers and stewards. I'll telephone Bassett in Washington. I'll cable our Consulate in Berlin. I'll have this case solved for you before twelve o'clock, Sergeant!"

"That's real kind!"

"Come on, Edda!"

"Think I'll stick around a while," she drawled. "You get the facts and I'll soak up human interest."

"Don't forget lunch. I'll keep in touch with you by phone." He ran out.

Crehan shut up the second bag. "Nothing in this but clothes."

The medical examiner entered the alcove with his assistant and his bag of tools. He called back into the reception room:

"Hey, Paul! Come and unfasten these gadgets!"

The hairdresser ran in and set to work with tremulous fingers on the curlers. The strong light from the front window was cruel to the pretty manikin. Forty if he's a day, thought Edda. He was breathing light and fast like a fever patient. . . . Deprived of its supports one by one, the head began to loll to one side.

"Hold her!" cried Paul in fright, "or she'll fall on me!"

When he had removed the curlers, Paul of old habit, began brushing the released hair around his fingers. Edda seeing the soft, natural curls, thought: The heat was not turned on for twenty minutes or anything like it. Her eyes told her other things. The woman was wearing a perpendicular corsage of three orchids of which the middle one was badly crushed. Why only the middle one?

While the medical examiner was doing his job, Edda looked into the two other alcoves. That on the right was precisely the same in every particular, that on the left was a larger room and more luxuriously furnished. This, clearly, was where the master practiced his art upon select clients. In addition to the hairdresser's chair, it contained a chintz-covered chaise-longue, a dainty dressing table with every requisite for the toilet, a locked cabinet that Edda suspected was for liquid refreshments. It had a cord plugged into a wall outlet. Refrigerating compartment?

Edda sniffed at the cut-glass perfume bottle on the dressing-table. The extract was *Adieu Sagesse*. She knew it well. Seductive odor.

She sat down on the chaise-longue while her eyes travelled around from object to object. A little powder had been spilled on the floor in front of the dressing table. It had been brushed up but not expertly. She noted the key on the inside of the door. Feeling a little roughness under her hand on the chaise-longue, she looked and discovered some microscopic bread crumbs there. Also a crumb or two on the floor in front. Strange! Because the suite had undoubtedly been cleaned before business hours. It suggested that this little room had been locked up when the cleaners were making their rounds. Who had lunched there?—*or breakfasted?*

Edda was drawn out of the alcove by the sounds of a slight commotion at the entrance door of the suite. A woman's voice was demanding admission. "Paul! Paul!" she cried.

Edda looked at Paul. A queer change came over his face. It remained waxy smooth, but a little lump stood out on either side of his jaw. He hastened to the door. "It's all right," he said to the officer stationed outside.

She entered. Edda had an impression of beauty, but quickly corrected it. Only the woman's clothes were beautiful. She was dressed for thirty years old and was double that. As soon as she spoke, all the aids to beauty failed her. The effect was ghastly. She had preserved some remains of a figure, that was all. Nobody was deceived but herself.

She clung to Paul's arm. "Oh, darling, what has happened?" she cried tragically. Her unnaturally bright eyes darted from face to face around the room. Edda thought: Feeds on excitement like a drug!

Paul's face wore the stormy look of a man who is holding himself in, and Edda saw for the first, that there was force in the pretty fellow. The reporters scenting something good, hastened up to the pair—including Edda. One asked with the bluntness of his trade:

"Who are you, Madame?"

She was visibly savoring the situation. "I'm Mrs. Paxton. The widow of J. Eddiloe Paxton, President of the Erie Central. I'm Paul's best friend. In fact we're engaged to be married, aren't we, Paul?"

He patted her hand. "Of course!" he said stonily.

Edda studied him through her lashes, but was unable to penetrate the mask. She thought: Why need he have been so cut up about the ruin of his business if he's going to marry the rich Mrs. Paxton?

"Tell me what has happened?" cried Mrs. Paxton.

The blunt reporter informed her in a sentence. She appeared to be fainting, but was able to check the weakness. Paul led her to a chair. She favored the press with further particulars about herself:

"I live at—Fifth Avenue. I built the apartment house on the site of my former mansion. I never go into society—such a bore!—but I entertain extensively in Bohemian circles. Joe Figueroa, Pete Fenner, Ronald Mannering and Ethel La Claire are my intimate friends. Among my friends, that is the people who do things, it is nothing that Paul is a hairdresser. We honor him as one of the greatest artists in his line!"

They bombarded her with questions. She had taken off her gloves and held up her wrinkled hands

covered with expensive rings. "Please, please; one
at a time!"

Edda thought: She loves it!

"How did you know there was trouble here,
Mrs. Paxton?"

"One of the girls telephoned me. She was so
overcome, I could not understand her."

Edda made a mental note: Ask the girls about
this.

"How long have you known Paul, Mrs. Paxton?"

"Oh, a very long time. Ever since he came to
this country four years ago."

"That was before your husband died, wasn't it?"

Mrs. Paxton affected not to hear.

"Would you mind telling us the circumstances
of your first meeting?"

"Certainly not!" she said, bridling like a girl.
"Nothing is sacred to you boys!"

There was a general laugh.

One asked: "Can you throw any light on this
matter, Mrs. Paxton?"

"No indeed! How should I?"

"Would you mind taking a look at the body,
just to make sure you've

never seen the woman before?"

"No!" said Paul sharply.

"Why not?" she said. "I'm no bread and butter
Miss."

She crossed the room without any sign of weakness, the reporters huddling around her. Edda took up a place where she could watch her face. She looked in through the door of the alcove. The medical examiner had tipped the hairdresser's chair back, and the body was now lying in a recumbent position, partly unclothed. Crehan was beside the doctor taking notes.

"Still in the chair!" said Mrs. Paxton shrilly.

"I can handle her best this way," said the doctor."

"What killed her?"

"I can't tell you, Madame."

"A strange case!"

"Very!'"

For some moments Mrs. Paxton gazed at the body. As if slightly drunk on morbid excitement. "No, I never saw her before," she said, turning away. "Ugh! how ugly she is!"

At that moment a detective came through the door leading to the rear of Paul's suite, bringing Miss Polly and another of the assistants. Both girls wore their graceful tan and green linen working uniforms. The detective signed to them to sit on a sofa, while he went in to consult Crehan. Polly was in the wide-eyed stage of hysteria. The other girl had an arm around her.

It was the first chance the reporters had had at the star witness, and they gathered around Polly, leaving Mrs. Paxton. Edda went with the bunch, but continued to watch the old woman covertly. Paul was speaking to her swiftly. His face was still masklike, but his words had a powerful effect. Mrs. Paxton went flat; gazed at him imploringly. They got up and passed through the door to the rear.

Edda had a hunch that Paul was getting the woman out. She quietly left by the main door. "Got to telephone my story in," she said with a smile to the officer on guard.

Sure enough, Mrs. Paxton presently appeared through a door further along the corridor. This would be the employees' entrance to Paul's suite. Edda waited for her to come up, and followed her into the elevator. She looked her age.

"Isn't it terrible?" said Edda ingratiatingly.

Mrs. Paxton bridled in her usual manner, but the pressure was low. "Oh, you were one of the reporters in there." She primmed her lips. "I'm not talking!"

"I quite understand how you feel," said Edda. "It's awful the questions those men ask. I'm not a reporter. I'm a feature writer."

"It's all the same to me," said Mrs. Paxton. When the elevator door opened, she started for the Seven Avenue entrance.

Edda stuck to her elbow. "I feel sorry for Monsieur Paul," she said sympathetically. "He's such a wonderful man! To think that this thing should happen to him!"

This was a direct appeal to Mrs. Paxton's complex, and the old woman's eyes burned with the light of infatuation. "Wonderful?" she breathed. "Nobody knows!" She held herself in with an effort. "Nothing to say," she snapped.

"I'd like to write an article about him," Edda persisted. "Not about this ugly affair. This has nothing to do with him. But about his art, and his great success. I'm sure you have had a lot to do with it."

Mrs. Paxton was sorely tempted. She drew in breath enough to say plenty, but feebly let it out again, and shook her head. "He does not wish me to talk."

"Of course I should submit my article to you and to him before publishing it."

"No!"

By this time they had reached the pavement. Mrs. Paxton looked for a taxi but there was none at hand.

"Such an article would counteract the unfavorable publicity that this will bring him," said Edda seductively.

"He doesn't have to work," said Mrs. Paxton.

"Oh, is he giving it up?" said Edda. "What a loss that would be to his clients."

"I didn't say he was," said Mrs. Paxton sharply.

"Well, I'm glad of that. . . ." Then very casually: "Wasn't it strange about that wireless message?"

"Nothing strange about it," said Mrs. Paxton. "Americans travelling in Europe have spread Paul's reputation all over the continent." Immediately afterwards she added: "Paul showed me that message last night."

Eda thought: Saved herself by a hair!

A taxi came across Forty-second Street and Mrs. Paxton hailed it. Edda made one last attempt.

"I would like to get Paul in an article! Such a fascinating character! Couldn't we go some place and talk about him?"

But Mrs. Paxton opened the door of the taxi without answering.

"Where to, ma'am?" asked the driver.

"Go on. I'll tell you later."

When the door slammed, a whiff of *Adieu Sagesse* puffed out in Edda's face.

She looked for another taxi. As luck would have it, northbound traffic was stopped at that moment, and she had the mortification of seeing Mrs. Paxton's cab turn the corner and disappear. The woman's address had not registered on her mind, and she ran into the drug-store to get it from the telephone book. When she came out the lights had changed. Hailing a taxi, she gave the driver the Fifth Avenue number.

Mrs. Paxton's door was opened by a maid who looked as if she had stepped out of an English parlor comedy. Mrs. Paxton was not at home, she said.

"Are you expecting her soon?" asked Edda.

"I can't say, Miss. She left no word."

"But she's in town, isn't she?"

"I can't say, Miss."

"But you must know whether she slept at home last night or not."

"I don't know you, Miss. And my instructions are not to give out any information to strangers."

"Naturally," said Edda. "I am Miss Manby. Mrs. Paxton and I are well acquainted."

"I don't doubt it, Miss, but you see . . ."

"I see that you know your job," said Edda with her best smile. "Might I come in and write a little note to Mrs. Paxton?"

The maid looked her over. The best bib and tucker did Edda good service then. Deciding that she was neither crook nor canvasser, the maid stood aside. "Certainly, Miss."

From the spacious foyer Edda looked through a vista of gracious rooms. Whatever Mrs. Paxton's personal taste might be, she could afford the best. The maid brought paper and envelope and Edda sat down at a table in the foyer with her own fountain pen. While she scribbled a meaningless note she interrupted herself to ask careless, friendly questions. "You're English, aren't you, . . . How do you like our country? . . . This ought to be a pleasant place . . ." And so on. The maid relaxed and began to chatter. In the end she fell into Edda's little trap.

"I hope she'll get this before lunch time."

"When she went away last night she said she'd she back for lunch today

The maid caught herself up, and looked at Edda anxiously. Edda was writing away.

A key turned in the entrance door and Edda stiffened. Mrs. Paxton appeared on the threshold. She was carrying a black satchel. Her overnight bag! "You!" she exclaimed seeing Edda.

Edda arose smiling. "Hello, Mrs. Paxton." She tore up the note.

The maid meekly offered to take the bag. Mrs. Paxton held it from her. Edda thought: Too precious!

"What do you mean by letting this person in?" Mrs. Paxton demanded of the servant. "How many times have I told you. . . ." She scolded the girl roundly.

All Edda's desires centered on the black bag.
. . . Picked it up somewhere on the way home! If
I could only see what was in it! . . .

Edda said smiling: "It's not her fault, Mrs. Paxton. I beguiled her."

The older woman turned on her then. "I never
heard of such persistence! I have already answered
you."

Edda saw that there was fear mixed with her
anger. She said: "In my profession we are not allowed to take no for an answer."

"Well, it's all you'll get from me! Please leave!"

"But Mrs. Paxton. . . ." Edda remonstrated
good-humoredly.

"Go!" she cried with a stamp of the foot. "Or
I'll have you put out. I have men servants here,
too!"

"A newspaper woman is not accustomed to
this," said Edda quietly, with a certain meaning.

Mrs. Paxton got it. She considered the consequences, and paled. She swallowed her anger. "I'm
sorry, she muttered. "Just a momentary irritation.
But I won't give any interview."

"That's all right," said Edda soothingly. "I was
just hoping that I might be allowed to see your
beautiful apartment. You are bound to be written
up you know, and the public loves such details."

Mrs. Paxton hesitated, biting her lip. She adored publicity; she couldn't see any particular danger in showing Edda through. "Very well," she said. "Excuse me a moment, and I'll be with you."

Turning into a side corridor, she opened a door. Edda had a glimpse of a luxurious bedroom. She was of a mind to follow Mrs. Paxton to make sure of the contents of the bag. But that lady without closing the door, put it on a chair and came back again.

"Now," she said, turning on a badly-worn smile. She was ugliest when she smiled.

Edda was led through the beautiful rooms: library, living-room, dining-room, boudoir. She made suitable noises of appreciation, but her mind was ever with the black bag. How can I get into it? How can I get into it? She thought of a dozen wild schemes and discarded them all.

Mrs. Paxton showed no disposition to take her into the room where it lay. "What's in here?" asked Edda as they passed the door.

"Oh, just my bedroom."

"I must see that!" said Edda opening the door and entering.

There lay the bag on its chair. Edda decided that the boldest method was the best. She picked it up. "I'm going to take this," she said. "It's useless for you to protest."

Like a flash Mrs. Paxton was out of the room. Edda tried the catch of the bag. Perhaps a glimpse of the contents would be sufficient. It was locked. Before she could get to the door, Mrs. Paxton ran back through the little hall, presenting a gun. She looked like a crazy witch then.

"Drop it, you thief!" she cried hoarsely. "And get out! I'll give you that chance before I call the police!" With her free hand she was changing the key from the inside of the door to the outside.

"Nice of you," drawled Edda.

She had to do some quick thinking. There were two other doors; bathroom, clothes closet. No way out except through the door that Mrs. Paxton held. The woman would certainly shoot before letting her get away with the bag. But if the bag was disposed of, it would do her no good to shoot. Edda turned and threw it out of the window. Somebody would get it.

There was a silence. Then the smack of the bag on the pavement below. A choked cry broke from Mrs. Paxton. She slammed the door and turned the key. Edda heard her running away. She ran to the window. The bag had burst open on the sidewalk. A man was in the act of picking it up.

"Hold it until I get there!" Edda screamed to him. "There's a reward." He looked up and nodded.

A ledge ran along outside the window, and it was a small matter for Edda to climb out and in again through the window of the adjoining bedroom. But she lost precious time. Mrs. Paxton had a good start on her out of the apartment. Edda dared not wait for the elevator to come back. She had the layout of the rooms in her mind. She rushed to the kitchen, thrust the amazed servants out of the way, and ran down the service stairs.

When she got out on the sidewalk, a small crowd had gathered. In the center of it the man who had picked up the bag and Mrs. Paxton each had hold of it. Edda smiled grimly when she saw part of a tan and green linen dress protruding from the burst side. A long needle dropped to the sidewalk. Edda picked it up unnoticed, and stuck it in her dress. The hall servants were backing up Mrs. Paxton.

"It's all right," they answered the man, "This lady lives here. It's her bag."

"I want the reward," he grumbled.

"I'll give it to you!" gasped Mrs. Paxton. "Come upstairs!" Anything you want!"

But her frantic terror gave her away. Everybody was conscious of it. She trembled so that she could scarcely articulate. Her dyed hair was flying. The man hung on to the bag.

"You ain't the one who hollered to me out of the window!"

A policeman pushed up. Everybody started explaining at once. Edda bided her time.

"Hollered out of the window and told me to hold it until she came," said the man. He pointed to Edda. "That's her! She offered a reward."

"Right," said Edda. "I only have five dollars in my pocketbook, but I'll double it if you come to my hotel. It's the Marston, and the name is Edda Manby."

"But it's my bag! It's my bag!" screamed Mrs. Paxton.

"Officer," said Edda, "I suggest that you take me and this lady and the bag to the station-house and let the lieutenant decide. And keep your eye on the bag!"

About half an hour later, after two speedy rides in a taxi, Edda and Mrs. Paxton got back to Paul's suite. Mrs. Paxton was now escorted by two officers from the West —th Street police station. Edda had the bag. She had been gone little more than an hour, and the situation was scarcely changed. Some reporters had left; others had come. Paul and his two assistants were sitting on a sofa in the reception room with strained faces.

When Paul saw Mrs. Paxton coming in under guard, he quietly keeled over in a faint. One of the girls held him up, the other ran for water. Before Crehan and the medical examiner were attracted by this slight commotion, Edda entered the alcove where they were still working.

"I have found the cause of death," said the doctor. "Some tiny object, possibly a needle, was thrust between eyeball and socket into the woman's brain. There is a spot of blood bigger than a pinhead on her eyeball.

"Something in Barnhill's theory" said Crehan. "Two followed her in here. The first one threw an arm around her holding her in the chair. That's how the orchid got crushed. He clapped his other hand over her mouth—you can see where it's bruised. The second man come up in front of her and did the trick with the needle. So far it's clear. But it seems funny she would let them come up so close without raising a rumpus."

"Not at all funny," said Edda. "One of them was her husband, and the second, a woman, was dressed like one of the assistants here."

"Her husband?" said Crehan staring.

"Paul," said Edda. "He and Mrs. Paxton wanted to marry. She was mad about him. So they brought over Paul's lawful wife from Germany and put her out. . . . If Mrs. Paxton had married Paul," she added reflectively, "I reckon she wouldn't have lived long either."

"My God!" murmured Crehan and the doctor together.

"Here's the needle," said Edda. "The linen dress and other evidence are in the satchel. Paul and Mrs. Paxton spent the night, or part of it in the adjoining alcove. They were right on hand when the assistant went back to the rear of the suite. After the murder was done, they had only to go out through the door, run downstairs and mix with the crowd in the lobby. Paul walked around for a quarter of an hour and came back. Mrs. Paxton drove to Grand Central—you can hire dressing-rooms there, you know; changed into her own clothes, and checked the bag."

"How do you know that?" demanded Crehan.

"The end of the check is still hanging to the bag. . . . She made a fatal error in coming back here. Paul had told her to keep away, but the woman had such a craving for morbid excitement she couldn't resist it. Do you remember when she saw the body, how she screeched out: 'Still in the chair!' That gave me my lead."

"My God!" murmured the doctor again.

"How did you find out about Paul being her husband and all?" asked Crehan.

"That's in the bag, too. The woman had a little writing case in one of her valises. They took it when they went through her luggage. There were a lot of letters in it. They didn't have a chance to destroy them. One of them was from Paul. It's in German. I took German in High School, and I can translate it roughly. Listen:

"'My Darling Wife:

"'At last I am able to send for you to join me. I can scarcely wait for the day when we shall be together again! Business has been fine lately. I want you to sail on the *Europa* first-class, and give yourself every comfort. I am enclosing a draft for — marks.

"'The only obstacle in the way of our complete happiness is the silly old woman who set me up in this business. She imagines that she is in love with me as I have told you, and she watches me like a cat. Of course I have never told her I am married, or she wouldn't have done what she has for me. So we'll have to keep our marriage a secret. I'm sure you won't mind that if we are happy. We'll have many a good laugh together at the silly old fool. And as soon as I pay off what she has advanced me, I'll tell her to go to Hell.

"'Under the circumstances I can't meet the ship. I suggest that you send a wireless to my business address the day before you land, asking for an appointment to have your hair done at nine A.M. One of my girls will receive you, and afterwards I will slip in. What fun, eh? . . .'

"There's a lot more," said Edda grimly. "But that's all that matters. He tells her to destroy the letter when she has digested the contents, but she had nothing on her conscience, and she neglected to do so."

Crehan gravely shook Edda's hand. "I was on the way, kid, but you beat me to it."

"Sure, Pink. What does it matter? You take the case; all I want is the feature story."

When Edda left the building she met young Barnhill striding up to the door. His tail was down.

"Couldn't get anything on the *Europa*," he grumbled. "They said Detwold was just an ordinary quiet passenger. Bassett in Washington, said he never heard of the woman. Undoubtedly lying. No answer from Berlin."

He eyed her hungrily. He was a good-looking fellow, and Edda's heart softened. My fatal good nature! she thought. Slipping her arm through Barnhill's, she told him the story as they walked along. He could scarcely take it in for staring.

"Telephone it in," said Edda, "and then come and buy me that lunch you promised me."

"But . . . but," he stammered. "You got the story. Don't you want credit for it?"

"Oh no," said Edda airily. "I've decided not to be a reporter."

Barnhill was a little dazed.

Life in the Raw

"Well, I hope you're satisfied," said Fred Maier sorely. He was in one of his most difficult moods. Complexes working overtime.

Edda Manby looked around her. It was a little gin clinic on East Houston Street with tables against the walls and a small square of linoleum in the middle for dancing. Three-man orchestra; piano, saxophone and drums playing torch songs in dead-march time. There was a furtive look about the customers that made Edda shiver slightly—but she wasn't going to let Fred see that.

"More than satisfied," she answered calmly. "What did you bring me here for?"

"You're always wanting to see life," said Fred. "Well, here it is. In the raw."

"I like it better cooked," said Edda. "Let's go back to the Conradi-Windermere."

"Oh, let's make the most of it now we're here. This is the real thing. Not like those joints uptown where they provide alleged gunmen as dancing partners to give the Park Avenue dames a thrill. This is a place where a real tough guy can bring his doll. Nice to see them off duty."

"Swell!" said Edda dryly. When Fred got off on this line, it only made him worse to argue.

"They say that this is the secret hang-out of Monk Eyster. King of the post-repeal liquor ring. New York's public enemy number one. These gangsters look up to him as a kind of god. I suppose he has a room upstairs where he holds his court every night."

"Rather unhealthy here for people like us," Edda suggested.

"Oh, you're perfectly safe when you're with me."

She said nothing.

"You like to make out that I'm a kind of tame man," said Fred bitterly. "Well, here you have the wild variety. Look 'em over."

She did so.

"Parasites!" Fred went on. Never did an honest day's work in their lives. They like to make out that it's the dangerous life which attracts them. All stuff! My brother's on a big construction job in the West Virginia mountains. He needs men to drive his trucks. Plenty of danger in that job. Could you get one of these brave boys to take it? Not on your life!"

"You can't prove it by me," said Edda mildly.

"Take that lad across the floor," said Fred; "there's the real flashy type of gunman. I swear his clothes fit him better than mine do. What is he?— Jewish? Italian? Irish?—or a combination of all three? I suppose you would probably call him a handsome lad."

In his way," said Edda, "like a bear."

"Exactly! And I'm a sheep."

"If you insist on it," she murmured.

"Wouldn't you like to meet him?" he demanded.

"No. I prefer my bears behind the bars . . . Besides, he's fully engaged."

"She hardly measures up to him," said Fred.

Opposite them the young man with the bold, cruel glance was addressing a girl across the table with blasting contempt. She was a thin, pretty little dummy all dressed up like Pain's Fireworks. Her eyes were fixed on her companion's face with a crushed and adoring look.

"I suppose that's the way a girl likes to have a man treat her," said Fred with extreme bitterness.

"Not my type," said Edda.

When the dark, heavy young man finished what he was saying to the girl, he coolly jerked his head toward the door of the room. She got up without a word, and hanging her head to hide the springing tears, crossed the dancing floor and left the room.

"Brute!" muttered Fred.

"Well," said Edda, "sex is a battle."

For some reason the remark infuriated Fred. As the bear looked gloweringly around the room and fixed his glance on Edda, Fred got up muttering something about "showing her" and went over to him. Presently they returned together. The insolent dark eyes were fixed on Edda.

"Mr. Sanner, Miss Manby," said Fred.

"Dance?" asked Sanner with an air of indifference.

Edda could not take a dare like that from Fred. She got up with an equal air of indifference and let Sanner swing her away. They left Fred sitting at the table with a painful sneer fixed on his face. Funny how a man could insist on punishing himself!

Sanner held her close. He danced marvelously, like an Argentinian, dragging his feet a little. He was a big man; and his arms and back under the smart double-breasted jacket were banded with steel.

"They call me Torpedo Sanner," he said casually.

"Oh yes?"

"Did you send him over to fetch me?"

"No. It was his own notion."

"What's the idea? I'm not the sort of a guy that a fellow introduces his doll to."

"Well, he was sore."

Against her breast, Edda was aware of an ominous hard lump. Drawing away a little and slipping her hand down, she felt the outline of a stubby automatic under his coat. He grinned infernally.

"My pal, my sweetheart, my meal ticket," he murmured. "She goes wherever I go."

"Over your heart?"

"Sure. That's where I draw quickest."

Edda said nothing.

"Like the idea?" he asked.

"Sure!" she said coolly. "Every woman adores danger. But I don't know if you're the real thing, or just a fake."

He laughed briefly.

Nothing more was said while the music lasted. When they stopped he said coolly:

"You got to stay with me now."

"Nothing doing," said Edda. "I leave a place with the man who brings me."

"I'll fix him," said Sanner grinning. "I got three or four friends here. Hahvahd will never know what struck him."

"Five against one!" said Edda. "Is that your notion of fair play?"

"Hooey!" he said contemptuously. "What's fair play to me? I get what I want in the easiest way. I'd be a fool not to, wouldn't I?"

"All right," she said, "but I'm not going to stand for it."

"What you going to do about it? You're the doll I been looking for. You're mine now. Anyhow, for the evening."

Edda felt a chill as if a trickle of ice water had run down her spine. What had Fred's folly got her into? The orchestra started to play an encore, and they went on dancing.

"So I come up to specifications," she said, stalling for time. "I'd like to know what they are."

"I got to go to a swell party uptown, and I want a doll to take with me who can measure up to the place, see? The real thing; Fifth Avenue mansion and all. That floozy I asked to meet me here, Cheese! she looked crummy. So I gave her the gate. I'll take you now."

"Not unless you take Fred, too."

"Don't make me laugh, girl. It brings on the hiccups. Me and my friends will use Fred for an oily mop to freshen up the floor!"

Edda looked into his stony, grinning face and saw that he was capable of it. But she kept her flag up. "Even here I guess a girl has got some say as to the man she is going with," she answered coolly.

"What I say goes in this joint," retorted Sanner. "I'm known here. There ain't ten men together here would stand up to me."

Edda set her jaw. "All right. If there's going to be a fight I fight on Fred's side, and you can beat us up together!"

He held her away from him for a moment, laughing devilishly in her face. "By God! I believe you would, too!"

Edda let it rest there. They danced for a while in silence.

"Look," he said finally, "I don't take dictation from a woman, but I'm willing to compromise."

"How?"

"If you'll do a sneak out of here with me while the music's playing, nobody will touch Freddy. He can sit here waiting for you to come back until he grows whiskers."

"And if I refuse?"

Sanner grinned. "Me and my friends will play football with Hahvahd. I hate the slick Johnny anyhow, just because he's here with you. It would be a pleasure to me to maul him."

Edda hesitated. She thought: Fred got me into this, but I've got to get myself out of it, and him too! She said: "All right. I'll go. I have no choice."

"Okay!" said Sanner, holding her close.

The music stopped. At a curt nod from Sanner the leader started to play a second encore. Fred Maier sat at his table scowling at them sorely.

What a fool to give himself away like that! thought Edda. Some men never learn.

Down at the rear of the dancing floor there was a door opening on a stairway that led up to the street floor. As they came opposite it, Sanner steered Edda through.

There were so many dancing couples between they could not see Fred, hence Fred could not see them. Sanner urged her swiftly through. Four of his friends made a screen around them; all of a type; young, well-dressed, wary, trained to a finish. They handed Sanner his hat and coat, and Edda her green velvet evening wrap, on the run.

"What name you want to give at this party?"

"My own name," Edda said, surprised.

He shrugged. "Suits me!" To one of his friends he said: "Dap, phone and tell them Miss Edda Manby is bringing Mr. Skinner. I gave you the number."

"Okay, Tim."

The four young men were looking her up and down admiringly. Sanner took hold of her elbow, and shoved her out through the door.

"Why shouldn't I give my own name?" she demanded.

"You never know," he said.

Edda thought: Oh, well, I'll give him the slip first chance I see.

Sanner hailed a taxi. It was a bona fide taxi, and Edda entered it without hesitation. He gave a number on Fifth Avenue in the Eighties. So far so good.

As soon as they got under way, he attempted to embrace her. Edda put her arms up between them. "Nothing doing," she said.

"How you going to stop me?" he asked, grinning.

"I'll put up a fight. If I get all mussed up you can't take me to a swell party."

He released her, grinning still. "You're a smart Bertha, all right. However, there's plenty time."

"Give me a cigarette," said Edda. "Why all the mystery? You've got to give me the set-up, or I won't go into the house."

"Perfectly simple," said Sanner coolly. "Ever hear of Miss Mildred Bevans?"

"The actress? Surely!"

"Well, it's her house. She's giving the party. She's a friend of mine, she's fallen for me, see? But for certain reasons she can't ask her boy friends to the party."

"Is she married?"

"Yes . . . no . . . I don't know. What difference does it make?"

"Who pays the rent of the Fifth Avenue mansion?"

Sanner grinned. "I don't know."

"She isn't prominent enough in her profession to rate it."

"Sure. Somebody pays the rent. So she just asks her girl friends. And the girls bring the boys. That's why I phoned your name up. You're bringing me, see? Naturally she doesn't want any crashers."

All this was a little too glib, but Edda let it pass. Her curiosity was aroused.

They really entered a Fifth Avenue mansion, a tall, narrow marble-fronted house, a little old-fashioned now, but still grand. There was a red carpet across the sidewalk and a peppermint striped awning. And it really was Miss Mildred Bevans who greeted them at the head of the stairway. Edda had seen her on the stage. Beautiful woman but no great shakes as an actress; red hair skillfully brightened with peroxide.

She was a little surprised by Edda's style; surprised and resentful. Her jealous eyes flew from Edda's face to Sanner's. What was there between these two, they asked. Her voice dripped sugar syrup.

"So glad to see you, darling! How sweet of you to come. Introduce me to your friend."

"Mr. Skinner, Miss Bevans," murmured Edda, suppressing the desire to grin.

Other guests were behind them, and they moved on. Edda saw, in the way Mildred Bevans' eyes followed Sanner, that she was hard hit. It was an intriguing situation. She gave up the idea of slipping away. Fred would have to take it.

The whole second floor of the house had been cleared for dancing except a small room at the side where a bar had been set up. Sanner paused in front of it and ordered Alexanders. Edda looking over the company, saw that it included a number of well-known men; Sam Siebert the theatrical manager; Lou Deane the big real estate operator, Frederic Coulson the screen star, and so on. The women were mostly beautiful unknowns.

When the drinks came, Sanner toasted her with his infernal grin: "To crime!"

Edda said, to draw him: "I won't drink it with you."

"What the heck!"

"With anybody else it's a joke. You're a fool for crime."

"Cheese! I never thought you'd start preaching at me. Pretty as you are!"

"I'm not religious," she said. "I'm a beauty-lover. You're so darn handsome I can't bear to think of it being locked in a cell!"

"Aah!" he drawled. "See any fuzz on my chin?"

Just the same she marked the smirk of gratified vanity.

"Ever taken the rap?" she asked.

"Twice. Been convicted three times."

"You'll soon land there again, little one. Nobody can beat it."

"Not me!" he swaggered. "On a fourth conviction it's life. They'll never take me alive."

"What's the good of being dead?"

"A short life and a merry one!"

"Old stuff, boy! I'm for a long life and a merry one!"

Sanner tossed off his drink. "Well, now you're here," he said with his damnable insolence, "fluff along and enjoy yourself, kid."

"Just like that?" asked Edda, running up her eyebrows.

"Aah!" he drawled. "I got obligations here."

She had no notion of allowing herself to be shipped so easily. Not until she could see the bottom of this situation. "Do you like that red-headed woman better than me?"

"She's business and you're pleasure, kid. I'll see you later."

Edda staged a feminine pout, and slipped her arm through Sanner's. "You brought me here and you got to stand by me. I don't know a soul."

"Aah, ain't no trouble for you to get yourself a fellow."

"Well, dance with me just once."

Sanner with a bad grace allowed himself to be led out on the dancing floor. It was a big party but the long suite of rooms gave the dancers plenty of space. The famous Dan Dixon's orchestra was stationed near the rear windows. Somebody with a jam roll was paying for this. Sanner had turned sullen and wouldn't talk. Clearly, his plans were being interfered with. But he had rhythm in his bones. If Fred could only dance like this, thought Edda.

In the middle of the rooms Mildred Bevans was standing in an arched opening leading into the hall. Several men surrounded her. She was twitching a big green feather fan exactly like an angry cat with its tail. Her jealous eyes were following Sanner. Edda thought: She's got it bad. He's using her somehow.

At the front of the room Sanner stopped. "Too damn hot," he muttered.

They dropped on a little sofa. The window beside them was open. Edda saw from Sanner's sulky scowl that an explosion was coming. She turned on the chatter-tap in order to divert it as long as possible. He ignored what she was saying. He kept glancing down into the street. Edda looked too—without appearing to. Presently she saw an old touring car with the top down buzzing up the avenue. In it were the four quiet little gunmen; Dap and the others. They looked up at the windows.

Sanner glanced at her to see if she was looking. She wasn't. Out of the corner of her eye she saw him make a little signal to his friends, meaning: Not yet! Edda's skin prickled all over. Murder afoot! A moment later the thought came to her: And whatever happens I will be an accessory to it. She felt a little sick. The touring car passed again, going the other way.

Sanner turned on her: "For God's sake, are you going to hang onto me

all night?"

That revived her. Edda's first maxim dealing with a man was: Always go him one better! "How dare you speak to me like that?" she cried running up the old eyebrows. "You cub! Does your limited vocabulary include the word cub? That's what you are. A mass of conceit with a schoolboy mentality; showing off and talking big to impress the little kids! Go get a drink and see if that will put you in a better humor!"

Clearly no woman had ever spoken to Sanner like that. His eyes goggled at her; his mouth opened. He was so astonished that he got up without another word and went away to the bar.

When she had thus got him out of sight for the moment, she rose and crossed the room to where Mildred Bevans was standing. Edda's smile was honeyed. "Darling!" she murmured as she came within earshot.

"Darling!" said Mildred, looking daggers.

Pressing past the men who rounded her, Edda kissed her and murmured in her ear: "I must speak to you alone!"

Mildred glanced at her sharply, hesitated, made up her mind. "Downstairs," she murmured, turning on the smile. And to the men: "Please excuse us for a moment."

On the street floor she led Edda into a little reception room alongside the front door. She turned off the smile. "What do you want?" she asked brutally.

Edda could be brutal too. "What do you know about the young fellow who brought me here tonight?"

Mildred tried the woman-of-the-world smile, but it was labored. "A handsome boy," she said airily. "What more need one know?" Under Edda's steady gaze her voice suddenly scaled up. "What do you know about him?" she demanded.

"Nothing. He picked me up in a dive on East Houston Street an hour ago."

"A dive!"

"He's a professional crook," Edda went on undisturbed. "He is carrying a gun in the breast pocket of his coat and another on his hip. He has come here tonight 'on business' which means robbery or worse."

"Has he quarreled with you?" sneered Mildred, turning her diamond bracelet.

"That's neither here nor there," said Edda. "He has four confederates running up and down the street in front in a touring car. He just signaled to them. You can probably see the car if you look out of the window."

Mildred weakened. "I can't believe it!" she murmured.

"Well, that's up to you. If you don't take action, I reckon there'll be blood to wipe up on your beautifully polished floors."

Mildred rapidly went to pieces. "Oh my God! What can I do!" she murmured, squeezing her hands together.

"Draw his teeth," said Edda. "You have plenty of men servants about. If you can't trust them, I'll undertake to find men among the guests to disarm him.”

“No! No! No!” wailed Mildred. “I can’t have any trouble! Leave it to me! I’ll get him out of the house.”

“You’ll find him in the bar,” said Edda.

Mildred ran up the stairs. Edda waited, so as not to be seen returning with her. She peeped through the window curtains. The touring car buzzed up the avenue again.

When she returned upstairs a nice-looking young man was standing in the archway. “Swell party,” he said for an opening.

“Swell,” said Edda. “Look here, put me wise like a sport. I don’t want to drop any bricks. Who pays the rent for this shebang?”

“I thought everybody knew that,” said the young man. “It’s Armand the restaurateur.”

“Thanks,” said Edda, moving on.

“I say, will you dance?”

“Sorry, I’m engaged for this one.”

Armand! Like everybody in the know, Edda was acquainted with this famous figure around town. Proprietor of several of the smartest speakeasies during the drought, he now owned the restaurant of the moment. His earnings were said to be princely. So this was his private life!

She moved through the rooms looking for Mildred and Sanner. Not to be seen anywhere. She wondered if they had gone upstairs. There was a cord stretched across the stairs at the bottom to signify that the bedrooms were not included in the party. Necessary nowadays. Before going up, she tried the conservatory in the rear of the dancing rooms. The orchestra blocked the French windows that opened into it and not many guests took the trouble to get through.

Under a screen of palms in the corner of the conservatory she saw a man's patent leather shoes and the hem of a woman's dress. She maneuvered until she was able to see to whom they belonged. It was Sanner and Mildred seated on a bench. Mildred had fallen back lost to the world in the young man's arms. Their lips were pressed together. They didn't see Edda.

Edda went back into the dancing rooms. So that's how she gets him out of the house! She longed to be out of the whole ugly business now. Get out, and let it ride, she said to herself. It's not your affair. But she couldn't. That ugly phrase "accessory before the fact" nagged her. The thing to do was to phone somebody she knew on the police force.

When she looked around for a servant to lead her to a phone, she saw one coming toward her; a young fellow with an embarrassed look. "Is this Miss Manby?" he asked.

"Yes."

"Would you mind stepping out into the hall with me, Miss?"

"What for?"

"I have something to say to you."

"Why not say it here?"

"Please step outside, Miss."

Edda got a little hot. "Say it here!"

"If you please, Miss, if you please . . ." he stammered. "I have been instructed to ask you to leave the house."

"Well!" said Edda smiling broadly, "By whom?"

"Miss Bevans, Miss."

So this was the outcome! "And if I should refuse to obey this polite request?" asked Edda.

"Oh, don't do that, Miss! Don't do that!" the man murmured in distress. "I should be obliged to . . . obliged to . . ." He stuck.

"Obliged to put me out?" said Edda. "Calm yourself, I'm going peaceably."

She went slowly down the stairs, the servant following. She would have to telephone from outside. The victim evidently was a guest who had

not yet arrived. Suppose he comes while I'm telephoning, she thought, and her horrid anxiety
was redoubled. Damn! It would still be my fault!
Somehow, I've got to stall for a while.

When she entered the ladies' dressing-room, the
man servant waited in the hall. Inside, there was
an attentive maid making play for a tip. "Leaving
so early, Miss?" she asked.

"Well, I've seen everybody," said Edda. "And I
must go on to another party."

"Monsieur Armand hasn't come yet."

A light broke on Edda. She thought fast. "I'm
sorry to miss Armand," she said. "If I thought he
was on his way here, I could wait a few minutes."

"I could telephone to the restaurant and find
out, Miss." There was a phone in the room.

"Please do," said Edda. "If he hasn't left yet ask
him to come to the phone and I'll speak to him."

While the maid phoned, Edda picked up somebody's long white gloves, and very slowly drew
them on and smoothed them. The maid hung up,
saying:

"He's just left."

"Well, it isn't far," said Edda. "I'll wait."

She engaged the maid in friendly conversation.
The latter was charmed by her affability.

There was a knock on the door, and the man
servant stuck his head in. "Shall I call a taxi for
you, Miss?" he asked suggestively.

Edda was still smoothing the gloves.

"Don't bother, thanks," she drawled. "I'll pick one up."

In a minute or two there was a ring at the door bell. Edda went out into the hall. Armand entered the house, a large, handsome man with a manner both suave and wary. He was attended by two well-dressed, hard-looking men friends.

"Monsieur Armand, I must speak to you!" said Edda a little breathlessly.

He backed away, startled. Instantly the two "friends" blocked Edda off. One of them patted her expertly all over. He said quietly: "Unarmed, Boss."

"What do you want?" demanded Armand.

Edda said softly: "There's danger upstairs."

The three men exchanged glances. Armand said, opening the door into the reception room: "Come in here."

Edda had kept an eye on the gaping man servant in the background. "Better bring him, too," she said. "He might spread an alarm."

One of the men jerked his head toward the open door, and the servant slunk through it. They followed him in.

"Who are you?" asked Armand of Edda.

She gave her name. "Of course, I'm only one of hundreds who patronize your restaurant. Mr. Fred Maier took me."

"I know him. Go on."

"There is a plot to get somebody in this house tonight."

Armand laughed grimly. "Ha! it might be me! . . . What do you know?"

Edda told her story swiftly. Some feeling of loyalty to her sex prompted her to soft-pedal Mildred's part in it. She did not mention the kiss. Mildred was bound to lose her rent-payer, anyhow.

Armand swore savagely in French. "*Me faire cocu avec l'apache!*" But he was a self-controlled man. He cut it short. "Ever hear of this Sanner, Butch?" he demanded of one of his men.

"No, Boss. But Monk has dozens in his pay. This must be a new chump. His first murder job."

"Well, go up and get him."

The two went out. The man servant remained standing in the corner, scared half out of his wits.

Armand patted Edda's hand. "Good girl!" he said. "I shan't forget you. I been looking for this. Hence the bodyguard. But the skunk would have got me in spite of them, because I felt safe in this house. . . . It's the big Gee of the bootleg ring who is back of this. I keep a restaurant. I sell a lot of liquor, and like everybody else I've been buying it from the ring. But I can afford to go along with the government now. I'm organizing an association of all the restaurant keepers, and we are pledging ourselves to buy nothing but stamped goods. That's why this d . . . . b . . . . —excuse my language—is out to get me."

They had left the door open. The music was playing languorously; a pleasant murmur of voices floated down the stairway. Edda listened with nerves stretched like banjo strings. But there was very little disturbance. A slight scuffle followed by the noise of Sanner being hustled down the stairs. They were twisting his arms until it brought the sweat out on his face. They thrust him into the little room. He caught sight of Edda and cursed her.

"So it was you ratted on me!"

"Ratted?" said Edda. "I like that! I made no deal with you to do a murder!"

The guests were pressing down the stairs all agog with curiosity. Edda had a glimpse of the sick white face of Mildred, just showing at the top. She was leaning back against the wall, half fainting. The music was still playing. Edda thought: A heavy price to pay for gangster love!

From the doorway of the little room Armand addressed the crowd on the stairs with good-humored contempt. "Go back to your dancing, folks. This is nothing. Just a little sniper who was sent here to smoke me because I am determined to conduct my business according to law!"

The crowd broke into loud applause. Only Mildred did not applaud. Armand's contempt overcame his good humor. "Go back and have your fun while you can," he cried. "I'm paying for it, aint I? But understand—whoever hears me—after tonight not a damned cent!" He slammed the door.

The two men released their hold of Sanner. He stood with his back against the wall panting, his eyes darting this way and that. All the swagger had gone out of him. Just a desperate boy, faced by a life sentence. But he had not whined.

Edda's heart softened dreadfully. As Armand started for the door, she said sharply: "What are you going to do?"

"Send for the police," he said.

"Don't do that!"

"Why not?"

"There are three convictions standing against him. It will mean life."

"So much the better," said Armand turning the handle.

"He's not your real enemy. He's only a hired gunman."

"I know that. I know who hired him, too. But I have no legal proof. The police have ways of forcing him to talk."

"The police will get nothing out of him. Look at him. It's his code."

"Well, it will be a satisfaction to put him behind the bars anyhow." Armand opened the door—then closed it again. "Wait a minute!"

"Have you changed your mind?" asked Edda, staring.

"Yes," he said with a grim smile. "I've got a better idea. . . . If he was sent up for life it would make a martyr of him, and every member of his gang would be out to get me in revenge.—That's part of their code, too. Well, I'm obliged to lead a public life. Whatever I do, I can't insure myself against a chance shot. One of them would probably get me in the end."

Armand came back thoughtfully chewing his cigar. "But if I let him go," he went on, debating the matter with himself, "that would be something they couldn't understand. A gesture of contempt. And my God! what publicity for me if I handle it right. 'Armand, attacked by a gunman, coolly sets him free!' It would bring the restaurateurs on the run to sign up with the association. And if the association is a success Monk Eyster is sunk!"

Going to the window, he peeped between the curtains. "His friends are waiting for him by the curb," he said with a chuckle "Take him into the hall, boys, and let him go!"

They opened the room door. Sanner hung back. "Don't send me out empty-handed," he muttered hoarsely. "Give me one of my guns. If I go out there licked . . . they'll think I sold them out!"

Armand and his men laughed in his face. "That's up to you, fellow!"

Edda saw that he was saved from one danger only to be plunged into a worse. "Wait!" she said quickly. I'll get rid of them." To Butch who was nearest her, she said with her best smile: "Be a sport. When I run out, give me five seconds, then come to the door and holler after me. Don't come out on the pavement or you may get shot."

"Okay, lady," he answered grinning. "If you will have it!"

To Sanner she said: "When I'm gone, take a taxi to the Hotel Marston and wait for me."

She ran out of the house as if in wild agitation, slamming the door after her. As she came out from under the awning, Butch pulled the door open again, and stood there bawling: "Stop that woman!"

A man on the back seat of the touring car rose up with a submachine gun in his hand. Passersby ran wildly for cover. Butch retreated inside the door, slamming it. There was no shooting. Edda sprang on the running-board and was hauled inside the car.

"Quick! Quick! Get away from here!" she gasped.

Automatically the driver let in his clutch, and they leaped into motion. "Where's Tim?" they all asked at once.

Edda covered her face with her hands. "They got him! They got him!" she sobbed.

"Aah! The — fell down on his job!" one snarled.

"No!" cried Edda. "Somebody had tipped Armand off. They were laying for him. He had no chance to draw! They are telephoning the police!"

"Cheese! There'll be a general alarm out in a couple of minutes!" growled the driver. "This doll is dangerous to us!"

"Oh, let me down anywhere! Anywhere!" gasped Edda. "I'll find cover!"

They turned the first corner, sped across Park, Madison and Lexington against the lights, and roared through a quiet block to Third Avenue. Turning North, they barely stopped beside the curb, unceremoniously thrust Edda out, and went on. They disappeared under the elevated railway.

Edda, still gasping with excitement, began to grin. She could scarcely believe that she was there, safe, sound, free to go home to bed. A taxi appeared. Hailing it, she gave the driver the name of her hotel. She settled back in the cushions, grinning still.

As she approached the Marston her driver slowed up. There was a taxi ahead of him. Tim Sanner got out, paid the man, and hustled inside. She presently followed him. She had to borrow her cab fare from the night clerk. Sanner stood by, biting his fingers. The relief with which he greeted her appearance was in sharp contrast to his contemptuous manner at the beginning of the evening.

Edda led him into a little parlor off the lobby. Sanner made haste to pull down the blind over the front window.

"Well, what's to be done with you now?" said Edda.

He merely scowled, and shifted his weight from one foot to the other. The bear was tamed.

"Reckon you've had enough of murder as a profession," she said dryly.

"Aah," he growled, "I never had no chance to go straight. Thrown out on the streets when I was a kid."

"Every man is entitled to one chance. Can you drive a car?"

"Sure!"

"Then I'll get you a job. After that it's up to you."

"Got to get out of town," he muttered.

"This is a West Virginia job."

"Got no money for the fare. You got any money?"

"Bless you, I never have any money. But I can borrow."

Picking up the telephone, she called Fred Maier's apartment. When he answered she said sweetly: "This is Edda."

A snort of indignation over the wire. "Where are you?"

"Safe at home, honey."

Fred exploded then. So like a man! Useless to argue with him. But he should pay for the damage he had caused. All she said was: "You introduced him to me."

"I didn't expect you to go out with him!"

"Well, it's a long story. I'll tell you when I see you. . . . Got any money on you?"

"Money. What the deuce! . . . Well, about seventy-five dollars."

"Come right over, honey, and bring it with you. Better bring your checkbook too. They'll cash a check for you here on my say-so. I've got a good man to drive a truck for your brother. . . . And Fred, throw a suit, a shirt and a tie in a suit-case and bring it with you. He's bigger than you, but it will have to do. . . . And Fred, have you got my pocketbook?"

Very sullenly. "Yes."

"Oh, thank you so much!"

"Now look here, Edda! What does all this mean? You have a cheek if you ask me! After treating me like this. . . ."

She let him run on. When he had relieved his mind somewhat, she said pleasantly: "Yes, I know, honey, but the point is, you must let me know if you're not coming over, so I can call somebody else."

A note of alarm crept into his voice. "Sure, I'll be over with the money and the pocketbook."

Edda smiled and hung up.

COACHWHIP PUBLICATIONS
CoachwhipBooks.com

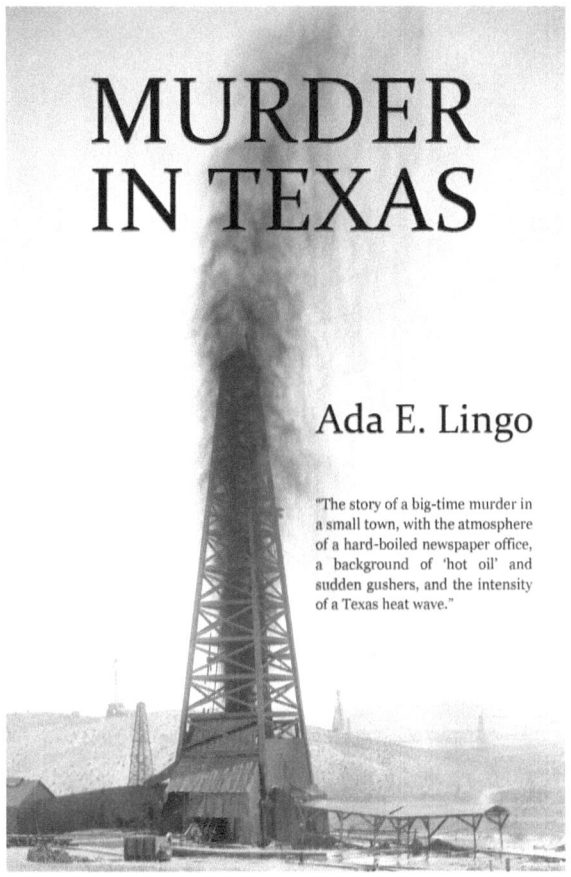

MURDER
IN TEXAS

Ada E. Lingo

"The story of a big-time murder in
a small town, with the atmosphere
of a hard-boiled newspaper office,
a background of 'hot oil' and
sudden gushers, and the intensity
of a Texas heat wave."

COACHWHIP PUBLICATIONS

CoachwhipBooks.com

NOW I LAY ME
DOWN TO DIE

ELIZABETH TEBBETTS-TAYLOR

COACHWHIP PUBLICATIONS
CoachwhipBooks.com

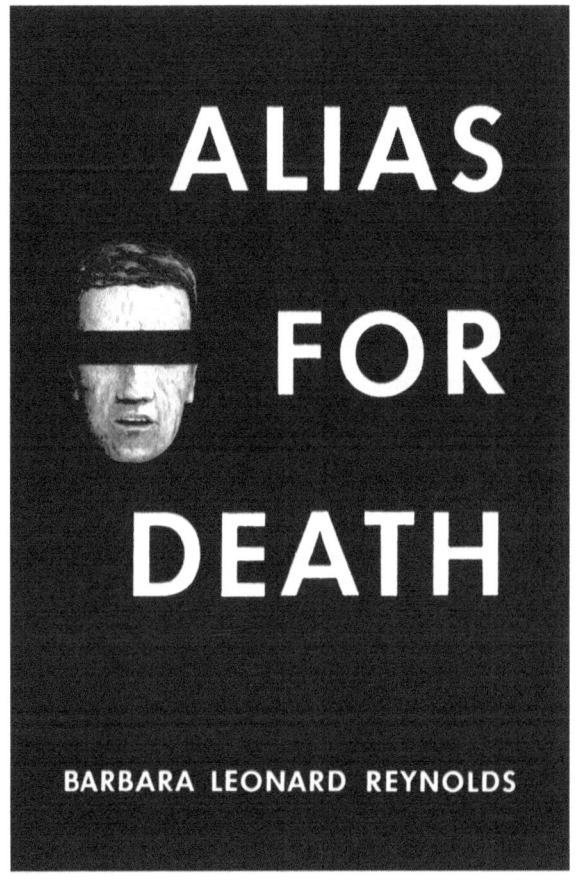

COACHWHIP PUBLICATIONS
CoachwhipBooks.com

SAMUEL ROGERS

YOU'LL BE
SORRY!

YOU LEAVE
ME COLD!

COACHWHIP PUBLICATIONS
CoachwhipBooks.com

THE
SARA ELIZABETH
MASON
MYSTERIES

MURDER RENTS A ROOM

>>> <<<

THE CRIMSON FEATHER

COACHWHIP PUBLICATIONS
CoachwhipBooks.com

DRESSED
TO KILL

Emma Lou Fetta

COACHWHIP PUBLICATIONS
CoachwhipBooks.com

DETECTIVES

2

Miss Cayley's Adventures
Grant Allen

Hilda Wade
Grant Allen

COACHWHIP PUBLICATIONS
COACHWHIPBOOKS.COM

DETECTIVES

MISS MADELYN MACK
HUGH C. WEIR

VIOLET STRANGE
ANNA KATHARINE GREEN

MISS VAN SNOOP
CLARENCE ROOK

FLORENCE CUSACK
MEADE & EUSTACE

www.ingramcontent.com/pod-product-compliance
Lightning Source LLC
Chambersburg PA
CBHW020917020726
47495CB00002B/222